DESPERATE VICTORY

BAY RIDGE ROYALS
BOOK SIX

HEATHER LONG

Honestly, I had no idea how this was all gonna work either.
Thankfully, the characters did.

SERIES SO FAR

FOREWORD

Dear Reader,

Welcome to Desperate Victory, the sixth and final novel in the Bay Ridge Royals saga. If you have not read any of the books in this series, please set this aside and go grab them. This series is best read in order.

All of that said, what do you *need* to know? Let's talk, previously, for the Bay Ridge Royals...

So much happened in Violent Chaos...

So, so much.

Let's start with the TL:DR: Dude. Harper kidnapped Lainey planning to marry her to get her inheritance whether she liked it or not. Adam, Milo, and Bodhi rescue Ezra, first from a marriage he didn't want, then a poisoning. In turn, they are swift to go after Lainey. They begin to take account of all their enemies and inflict harm on them. The rest of the book details their hunt for information even as they grow their personal relationship and connections. The guys aren't fighting over Lainey anymore, they are working together.

That's a little simplified, but here's the longer look:

FOREWORD

Lainey was kidnapped at the end of the previous book (*Wicked Surrender*) so we open *Violent Chaos* with her waking up in a strange place, nude, with no idea where she is. While she sorts that out, Milo, Adam, and Bodhi go after Ezra who is trying to fall on his sword to save Lainey and Adam. The boys prevent the wedding, marching out with Ezra only to have him collapse.

Poisoned by Oksana (who didn't want to marry him either), Ezra is stuck in the hospital while the others hunt for Lainey. At the Reed estate, Adam, Bodhi and Milo find Lainey climbing out the window to "rescue" herself. They then go and seek retribution on Harper Reed, Adam and Andrea's father. They also discover that Andrea is more than missing, Harper has sold her.

Milo and Bodhi torture the information out of Harper, also extracting their pound of flesh for his "plans" for Lainey. He wants access to her inheritance. To that end, he sold her sister (his daughter) and arranged to kill his wife (Lainey's mother).

Once Harper is dead, they return to the hospital for Ezra. When Adam was there before, he discovered Melissa Benedict Reed had also been admitted, gravely ill. Lainey spends time checking on her mother, but they are desperate to find Andrea.

Margareta Waldemar meets with them, the enigmatic woman tells them about her son. Her hatred for King is because she blames him for her son's death. She is also trying to build alliances with Lainey and the guys, but Lainey isn't sure about her.

They reach out to Em, because she knows people in Eastern Europe. Also, Lainey is investigating everyone around them. She is suspicious of her best friend Tally's secret lover and by book's end, Bodhi has identified him: It's King.

Lainey, Adam, and Ezra share an intimate moment that involves Ezra sucking off Adam while Ezra is also sinking into Lainey. It's Adam's attempt to build the bridges and understand the emotion and attraction.

In the meanwhile, Bodhi also gives Lainey a present in the form of an emerald gemmed butt plug that vibrates. He experiments with her varying levels of pleasure and then invites Milo to join in as the men are growing more and more to accept each other.

As the Vandals come to town to help, the group is digging more and more into King and his ties to the various families. A DNA test among them reveals that Milo and Ezra are cousins. That makes Julius King aka Jeff Hardigan, Wallace Graham's brother from another mother (literally).

Lainey and Adam also confront Jason Reed, Adam's uncle about what he may know regarding Lainey's parentage and the rumor that Jason was her father. (Spoiler: he's not). He does know who is and gives them a name: Yuri Leistung.

Finally, Lainey is there when her mother passes though Melissa warns her with her last breath to not look for her biological father, he is too dangerous.

Lainey and Adam have a heart to heart as he admits he isn't sure about being bisexual or not. He's never been interested in guys, but he is interested in Ezra. She points out he might be pansexual, he's attracted to individuals, not gender. In this case, he wants her and he wants Ezra.

The book ends with Lainey more determined than ever to find her sister, right the wrongs done to her men, and find *all* of their missing siblings.

This brings us to Desperate Victory. Whew... right, here we are. From the day Lainey first appeared on the page in Vandals, I loved and admired her. She was so damn loyal and there was nothing she wouldn't do for Em. Over the course of the Vandals series we got to know Adam, Ezra, Milo, and Bodhi.

These four men are at once absolutely nothing alike and don't even seem like they would get along (in fact for huge portions they don't), but they are all in love with the same woman. For her? They'll do what they have to not only to protect her but to stay in her life.

I had no idea when I first started this how *any* of it would be possible. I didn't know if Ezra's chaotic bi energy would result in a relationship with Adam or heartbreak. I didn't know if Milo would be able to accept other guys in her life. Frankly, I was almost positive I'd have to bind and gag Adam to get him to accept it. Then Bodhi walked in and let me know he was here too and... they figured it out.

The characters sorted it out themselves. This journey has been an amazing one and I can't wait to share this final chapter. Be sure to check the afterword when you're done.

As stated previously, *this* series contains some spoilers for 82nd Street Vandals, there's no way to get around that. If you do decide to check out 82nd Street Vandals, be sure to start with *Savage Vandal*.

For a little housekeeping. Bay Ridge Royals is a why choose romance with characters exploring and coming to terms with their evolving sexuality including a possible bi-awakening, identities, and relationships.

TWs: Mentions of SA. Kidnapping. Intimidation. Car accidents. Threats of violence. Discussion of trafficking. Smuggling. Be kind to yourself, this is a dark romance series.

Thanks for reading the Bay Ridge Royals!

Happy reading.

xoxo

Heather

P.S. Human voices only. All the work involved in this and all my novels from the stories themselves to the covers, to editing, to the audio are human-produced materials and voices only.

BAY RIDGE ROYALS

Main Characters

Elaine "Lainey" Benedict
Milo Hardigan
Adam Reed
Ezra Graham
Bohdi Cavendish

The Families

Benedict
Reed
Graham
Adley
Clifton
Marlowe
Cavendish

PROLOGUE

LAINEY

We're dying from the moment we're born, Grandfather told me not long after my fourteenth birthday. I can't even remember what prompted the comment. It could have been anything really. That had been a difficult year for us. Grandmother had been getting sicker, she'd been forgetting more. Watching the light go out in her eyes haunted me.

Worse, watching the light in Grandfather's eyes as hers dimmed. "We're dying from the moment we're born, sweet girl. You have to remember that. You have to remember that we only get pieces of the people we love. A sliver of their life, a partial print of their soul, the gift of their time. Never mistake time for anything but a gift."

My heart broke for him. He loved her so fiercely and the feeling had been deeply mutual. Some days, she acted like they were young again, even teased him about being her boyfriend. Other days, she stared through him as if she couldn't quite imagine who he was.

"Those pieces," Grandfather told me. "They kindle the fire in us. We keep each other warm. Over the years, your grand-mother has been there for me when my temper was too much or my judgment too harsh. She kept me stable, she helped me find a better way. I've never been an easy man."

The wistfulness and pragmatism were so much a part of him that I couldn't imagine Grandfather being any other way.

"Your grandmother told me over and over, she never asked for easy. She never wanted it. She only wanted me. So yes, this is difficult. But I'm not asking for easy, I'm asking for her and every moment we can have. Some candles... they go out slowly, guttering bit by bit until they extinguish."

I heard what he wasn't saying. The unspoken truths sliding under his words. The ferocious love he had for her.

"Your grandmother loved me in spite of my flaws," Grandfather said. "She made me more human. She kept me honest. She gave me something to fight for... and I wouldn't be your grandfather without her."

He loved her so much. I couldn't imagine loving someone that much. Not at fourteen. Probably not at sixteen either. I'd loved Adam and Ezra for a long time by then, but was I in love with them?

I had no idea. Their light always seemed to smother mine. Their darkness shrouded me and isolated me as much as it protected me. Did they care? Yes. But Adam had been right.

I'd been too young to fully grasp it all. I still needed to grow and to learn and to become myself.

Now? I understood my grandparents on a level I never thought possible. My grandfather would tear the world apart for her, and he'd build it back up again. All she ever had to do was ask.

He had one woman. I have four men.

There's nothing I won't do for them. If we have to destroy everything in our path to make our future happen... it will be a pleasure to burn.

CHAPTER
ONE

LAINEY

The clip of my heels as I crossed the tiled lobby offered a staccato beat to the morning's agenda. Karagiani followed in my wake. Bringing him with me had been a choice. The guys needed the peace of mind that I had backup, while I also preferred to know that each of them were not out there running alone.

The list of tasks we needed to accomplish had grown longer, while the window in order to complete them had narrowed even further. I'd chosen today's outfit with care. Word of my mother's death was practically front page news for the gossips among us.

The black pantsuit and blazer set the right tone for "mourning," even if I could barely register grief for Melissa Benedict Reed's death when almost all of my focus was on Andrea. Where was she? Who was she with? What was happening to her?

Appearances, however, had to be kept. The fact Tally was

at a woman's power breakfast meant this was an ideal location to corner her. King wouldn't be with her, nor most of her family.

"Miss Benedict," a familiar voice said, equal parts solicitation and sympathy. It took a moment for me to register the woman approaching with her hand outstretched. It was the salt-and-pepper hair pulled fiercely back from her face and secured into a tight chignon that gave her away.

All hard angles and high cheekbones, Mrs. Johanna Thorpe had been born an Adler, however, I didn't hold that against her. She'd been a very good friend to my grandmother. I was well-aware that she sent her thoughtful gifts of her favorite flowers and the occasional treat basket though more and more, Grandmother didn't recognize any of us.

I accepted her offered hand and summoned a wan smile. The part I needed to play as a grieving daughter had some specific requirements. The gloves covered my hands and added to the atmospheric black I wore as did the equally opaque sunglasses. Grief, as with all things, needed to be fashionable.

"Mrs. Thorpe," I greeted her and tilted my head easily as she leaned in to press air kisses to each of my cheeks.

"Darling girl, what are you doing here? I assure you, everyone would have understood if you skipped the event."

I lifted my shoulders in the most careless of shrugs. "Mother had many interests, as you know."

None of which was the power of women entrepreneurs or the development of future leaders. Then again, a large number of the donors in attendance didn't do more than pay lip service and arrive promptly for the breakfast and the mimosas.

"She would be so very proud of you," Mrs. Thorpe said, her sympathetic smile turning a bit maudlin. "I wish—"

"So do I," I said, cutting her off before she brought Grandmother into it. "But if you'll allow me, I'm just going to make an appearance, listen to the introductory speaker and then slip out quietly so I don't distract from the rest of the event."

"You won't be a distraction at all." Despite her firm words, some of the worry around her eyes eased. "But if you need anything, anything at all. Let me know? I'm sure you will release the funeral and memorial service plans soon."

Well, this was as good a time as any to begin spreading the word. "Perhaps. Though with the crash and all..." I just let it trail off and Mrs. Thorpe nodded swiftly.

"Of course, of course. That makes so much sense. That poor family and your sister..." Genuine sorrow inhabited her voice and my heart wrenched at the open display. "Is she home...?"

"Not yet," I told her. "I'm going to her soon. We thought it best we keep her out of the immediate fray." I hated this lie more than any other. While we would absolutely have kept her out of the "fray", committing to the lie was a soul deep bruise that throbbed more with every passing moment. "If you'll forgive me, Mrs. Thorpe..."

I needed to escape this conversation before her pity drowned me. She squeezed my hand once more but nodded, murmuring, "of course, of course. Do let me know if I can do anything..."

Not lingering, I withdrew my hand and continued down the hall to where the marble tile gave way to carpeted floors. The lush hotel was an ideal location for the gathering of this size. The conference center meeting rooms easily accommodated more than twice the number I expected to see inside. The tables were spread out, with the more prominent members up front.

As always, wealth and power dictated precedence. Inside,

the lights were lower and I had to remove my sunglasses. Wearing them through the hotel allowed my eyes to adjust to the gloomier room far more easily.

Serving staff weaved among the tables, delivering coffees and orange juices. The Benedict table was at the front. I didn't bother going to it. Every seat was filled with executives from different charities, as well as two vice-presidents from the company. Prior to the dimming of the lights, those executives would have given everyone a good look at my "absence" and fed the hungrier gossips.

For the moment.

The executives and the vice-presidents were better off attending than I was anyway. They didn't need to be wealthy to benefit from the networking and speeches. I scanned the room even as I moved more to the side. Karagiani actually settled next to me, his bulk offering me something resembling cover while I searched for my second oldest friend.

My *other* best friend. The bruise on my heart grew claws and dug in deeper. That sorrow couldn't be allowed purchase. I had a task to accomplish today and finding Tally was just the start of it.

As expected, she wasn't at the Marlowe table. Her family's wealth and position afforded her many of the same privileges as mine did. More so, at times, she wasn't the designated heir. Once upon a time, I'd envied her freedom but I was second-guessing everything now.

Everything.

As the director of the foundation crossed the stage to the podium, Tally murmured something to the woman she'd been speaking to and rose. I tracked her as she made her way through the room, skirting the center with the kind of skill we'd both developed over the years. Some presentations were deadly dull. If the only purpose for being there was to *show* our support and be seen, then our work was generally done when the presenters began.

The attention would be on the stage, and the much-lauded guests they'd spent a large amount of money to see while eating a generally tasteless meal of chicken and vegetables. The luxury wasn't even found in the seating arrangements. No, it was all about making sure the foundation got the bulk of the money and we got to pat ourselves on the back for our devotion to charity.

Mission accomplished as it were.

Tally paused. A hand to a shoulder here, another to the back of a chair, or a quick handshake as she made her graceful exit.

"You may follow," I reminded Karagiani. "Remember, I want to talk to her alone."

Another consideration, as we'd discussed this earlier. What Tally and I had to say was for us and no one else.

"I'll make sure no one interrupts. Don't leave my line of sight." Compromise offered.

"I can do that." Compromise accepted.

"Lead the way," he murmured. As Tally finally left the orbit of the tables, I moved. She was already diverting to an exit on the far side. If I recalled correctly, it was a hallway between other meeting rooms. She was either escaping to "powder" her nose and head to the bar or she was just leaving entirely.

Karagiani matched his pace to mine. I kept to the edges of the room, going wide. The only people in my path were wait staff who were placed at intervals in order to refill water or clear away finished plates. Not thirty seconds after Tally pushed out of the door, I was right behind her.

The light was brighter out here. A wide array of doors at the end of the hall opened out of the hotel, but I didn't let those distract me as I followed. There were no signs posted about other events taking place. I hadn't noticed any when we came in.

This was good.

Tally had her phone out and her focus was on it as she walked. Her fingers flew as she answered some text messages. My stomach sank as I tried to focus on everything I needed to know and everything I needed to say.

None were words I ever imagined saying. I picked up speed, gripped her arm and cut left through an open door into an empty meeting room. The low lights were more than enough to make out the stacks of chairs and folded up tables.

"What the he—Lainey!" Tally said abruptly as she spun to face me. "Oh my god. I've been so worried about you." She wrapped her arms around me in the kind of hug we often exchanged. So familiar and normally so welcomed. She even smelled like Tally with the faint touch of something floral underscoring her perfume.

In heels, we were practically the same height. Some of my unease must have communicated because she pulled back, her phone still fisted in her hand.

"I didn't know you were going to be here," she said, the faintest of tremors in her voice. It wasn't quite baby doll, but it betrayed a hurt she didn't want to advertise. My eyes narrowed at the first notes and I pursed my lips as I took a step away from her.

"Clearly," I said, hating every moment of this. Tally was my *friend*. One of my very best. If you'd asked me who were my most trusted, I would have said Em and Tally. This betrayal...it cut so deep and what was worse, I didn't think Tally even realized it. "But we needed to talk and I needed you to be unprepared."

Her eyes were troubled and her expression deeply

concerned. She glanced from me to the doorway where Kara-giani stood guard then back again. I didn't take my gaze off of her. "Alright. What's wrong?"

"Are you seeing Julius King?" So many questions I'd wanted to ask. Too many more I wanted to say. But it all came down to this one question. Tally adored older men. She always had. She loved them older, wealthy, and just this side of scandalous.

Julius King more than fit that criteria.

Even with the proof that Bodhi had brought me, a sliver of me held on with both hands to the numb hope that we were wrong. That it was just a coincidence or a rumor. Maybe it was something else entirely.

The moment I asked her, her expression shuttered and that fragile hope died a swift death. "Why are you asking?" Her eyes narrowed. "You know I don't always talk about my paramours."

"Usually because they are married," I reminded her of a string of regrettable decisions during our twelfth year at school. "Or engaged. Or friends of your father." The words fired out of me like bullets. "I don't care about any of them. I care about whether you are seeing Julius King. Is he your man of mystery from the past year?"

"Lainey..." Pleading joined the surprise in her voice. "I—"

"It's a simple yes or no, Tally. Is Julius King your lover?" It made me want to vomit even saying it.

Her gaze darted everywhere but me. The crash of my illu-sions and our history seemed to be fracturing like so many panes of glass. "I hate that you're asking me this."

"You hate it?" I raised my eyebrows. "I loathe that I have to think of that man putting his hands on you or you rushing into his bed."

"You've never cared before." Her nostrils flared. I'd insulted her. "Julius is quite the handsome man and extremely discreet. So I would very much prefer to *not* answer the question."

Which, of course, was an answer.

"Tally..." She really was seeing him. "Do you talk to him about me?"

"Of course I—" She hesitated when I raised my hand. "Lainey what is this about?"

"Tell me, do you bring up me? Or Pretty Boy? Or anything that you've seen or heard around me?"

"I assure you, that the men I'm seeing and I have far more to talk about than my best friend." But her discomfiture grew more intense. "You know, maybe we should go somewhere more private..."

"Do you know who Julius King is?" I said, ignoring that overture. "Who he *really* is?"

"Very well, I suppose we're doing this here. Have I mentioned you? In passing, yes. I love you and I worry about you. Sometimes, when he asks me what is troubling me, I tell him. You'd be amazed at what a wonderful listener he is. I promise, I've never been too indiscreet nor betrayed you. Though—I have brought up all the men who seem to be interested in you. It's rather sweet you know..."

Tears burned behind my eyes.

"Honestly, he wasn't all that interested. He just gave me an ear when I wanted to confess how worried I've been and how worried I still am. You have so much on your plate right now. Almost too much. I know with your grandmother and your mother... Then of course there's Hardigan. I'm glad he makes you so happy, but you've always had a thing for Adam and Ezra definitely has eyes for you. Even my brother can see it. When he sees something you know how real it is." Her smile turned almost coy. "I heard rumors about you and

Phillip Cavendish though, and if that is true you've been holding out on me."

"Tally, Julius King had another name before he came to the city, before he took over the Royals and before he began twisting our families around his finger and sending them out to do his bidding." When she would have opened her mouth, I raised my hand. "That name was Jeff Hardigan. He lived in Braxton Harbor."

"Hardigan..." She almost stuttered. "What are you talking about?"

"Well, it would seem that your lover is so discreet he *is* keeping secrets from you. How unfortunate... But I need to make something exceptionally clear. Jeff Hardigan is the man who abandoned Milo and Emersyn when Emersyn was a baby. He is the reason Em was adopted by the Sharpes because he left them in the care of their drug-addicted mother."

Tally paled.

"He abandoned them. Then he came here and manipulated his way into controlling the Royals and using those connections to control others through blackmail, coercion, and lies to do his bidding, whether it was killing people or stealing from them. He is in every way a loathsome man who makes the emptiest of promises, because all he wants is to win and he doesn't care who he uses to get there."

Head dipping, Tally stared down at her phone and then up at me.

"A few months ago, he came to tell me that Andrea was being tapped because Adam had walked away..."

Horror drifted into Tally's face.

That horror offered me the smallest measure of comfort.

"She's twelve—thirteen. She's still a kid."

"He doesn't care. How old do you think Adam and Ezra were? How old do you think your brother was?"

I knew who they all were now. Adam and Ezra had given me every name. Not all of them were influential, but he had his hands into every family.

"So maybe you should ask yourself who you think you are sleeping with and what he wants from you..."

"Lainey, I promise you. I didn't know."

"I believe you," I said. "But I can't trust you right now, Tally. I don't know that I can again. King made moves against Milo, against Andrea... against so many." He was involved in that damn arranged marriage too. "Whether you realized what you were telling him or not, you are in bed with the enemy."

That was what I'd come to say as much to get the last bit of proof and to give her that warning. I owed her that much.

"What can I do?" She grasped at my arm, the horror in her eyes a real misery. "Please tell me what I can do. I didn't know. I'm so sorry..."

"Get away from him. Get out of that relationship. Walk away and protect yourself." I didn't have the resources to protect her right now. "I mean that, protect yourself. You can't stay with him. If you decide you are going to... then understand when I come for him, I will burn down everything standing between me and that goal."

If she betrayed this, then my warning to King would be delivered. If she didn't, if she escaped... then at least she might be safe. Either way, it was a calculated gamble. I really hoped she left him.

Tugging my hand from her grasp, I slid my sunglasses back on and pivoted. I had nothing else to say. No other words to push past the crushing weight in my chest. I was walking away from one of my oldest friends because her choices endangered everyone else I loved.

Karagiani swept aside as I approached and I didn't look back as I strode down the hallway. I hated leaving Tally behind, but I couldn't save her from this. I'd warned her. It was on her to save herself.

I had to save my sister and protect my lovers.

CHAPTER
TWO

MILO

Ivy opened the hotel room door before I could even lift a hand to knock. "Before you yell at me," she said, pulling the door wide as she held up her phone. "Rome and Liam told me you were on the way up to get me."

I frowned. "You're here alone?"

"Yes," she said, waving me in. "Mickey had to go back to Braxton Harbor for the week. He'll be with us before we need to leave. Jasper and Kel are holding down the fort there, though depending on our plans, that may change."

"Freddie and Vaughn went to get supplies, and Bodhi is downstairs waiting for you."

"You really are a brat," I muttered because her grin had just gotten wider and wider.

"I know, but you love me." She gave me a hug. "And I promised the guys I would go with you back to Bodhi's place since we can't go to Lainey's."

Hugging her tight, I closed my eyes. I loved the warmth and happiness that radiated off of her. Each and every time I thought about the absolute tragedy of her life, I wanted to beat the shit out of every single person who should have protected her.

Two of them were dead. The third—well, she had her own issues and if Ivy could find a way to forgive her, then I would leave it alone. As for the fourth and final one? Well, we would be dealing with him sooner rather than later.

All accounts were due.

"Where are the terrible twins off to?"

"I don't know," she said as she retreated a step to grab her jacket and tug it on. I should have recognized the setup for what it was. She was dressed in jeans, a loose tunic kind of shirt and boots. She was ready to head out and the guys weren't here.

No way in hell would I leave her here on her own, period. Particularly not now when everything was in flux. I was going to throttle them. Then again, the twins had been downstairs waiting for me to get here. Yeah, this was definitely a setup.

She picked up her huge bag and slung it over her shoulder. I didn't even pretend like that was okay. I lifted it by the strap and transferred it from her shoulder to mine.

"I am capable of carrying my own things," she told me in that tart little tone that made me grin, even if she was giving me lip.

"Yet, you don't have to and I know the boys wouldn't make you carry a damn thing if they're around." The amused gleam in her eyes betrayed her.

"Of course not," she said, threading her arm through mine when I offered it. "It wouldn't be polite."

A real laugh escaped me and I shook my head. It would absolutely be impolite and Jasper had cracked heads for far less. I pressed a kiss to her temple.

"What was that for?" Like she didn't know, but still, I

adored that easy smile on her face. The fact that everything that had been done so wrong to her was healing and she was... Fuck me, she was happy.

"Because you're adorable when you're smug," I teased her then led her out of the suite and toward the elevators.

The last few months on the road had done her a lot of good. There was warmth in her eyes, color in her cheeks, and their time in Florida netted her a bit of a tan. Not that I could imagine her out in the sun that much. I'd heard about her training sessions. They were grueling, but...

No, no buts. Ivy was *thriving* and I loved it for her.

In the elevator, she pressed the button for the lobby before dropping back to lean against the wall in the corner. The guys really had taught her well. It was a defensible spot and out of direct line of sight when the elevator doors opened.

"Stop brooding," she said, poking me.

"Doing my best," I told her, not even bothering to try and dismiss the charge. "Just a lot on our plates right now, Ivy."

"That's why I'm here. Why we're all here."

It was. They were coming to help. All of them. Ivy. The Vandals. Adam's cousin—how he got plugged into the Network I didn't know and I didn't ask. I appreciated the Network, and respected it. I also knew to keep a healthy distance.

As much as I wanted to ask her for everything immediately, I waited. We were limiting delicate discussions to spaces we controlled. The hotel was one of Adam's, I thought. But I could be wrong. Still, it was too public. Bodhi's penthouse was far more secure and the man took threats to his privacy seriously.

I liked that about him.

When the doors opened, Bodhi rose from where he'd been

reading a paper and having a cup of coffee like he did this everyday.

Maybe he did.

"PPG," he greeted Ivy as he fell into step with us. Bodhi hadn't parked. The SUV idled out in the valet area in perfect view of the lobby.

"You remember I'm right here, right?" I rolled my eyes at the nickname. I knew exactly where that started and I could appreciate the fact he shortened it, but seriously...

"Was I not supposed to?" Bodhi deadpanned as we stepped out into the cold. Ivy laughed and gave Bodhi a kiss on the cheek. There was an ease to him around Ivy that I'd only seen when he was with Mayhem.

Where it was a possessive protectiveness with Mayhem, Bodhi's watchfulness with Ivy was far more brotherly. I could respect that.

Once she was in the car though, I glanced at him. "Does Mayhem know you call her PPG?"

He smirked. "Yes. She doesn't have a problem with it." Then he clapped me on the shoulder and I chuckled.

My phone buzzed as I slid into the passenger seat. Adam planned to go out when we were back and he was asking for an ETA. So far, we'd stuck to the plan of no one moved alone.

Mayhem consented to the bodyguard when we couldn't be there or she wanted to handle something solo. Ezra was never left alone. He refused bodyguards so he was stuck with us or Mayhem. Preferably, one of us as well as Mayhem.

Granted, his choices had been about protecting Adam and Lainey. I could respect that. But it was going to take a while for Adam or Lainey to not worry if he was out of their sight. Time they needed to heal and until we dealt with everything, they weren't getting that time.

So, Ezra dealt with the overprotectiveness the same way

Lainey did. Adam, Bodhi, and I were afforded a little more freedom, but we were still trying to make sure we weren't flying solo. Too many players on the board.

Now we had unknowns.

Easier to defend if one of us was there and not chasing after the fact. We'd gotten lucky when that corrupt son of a bitch took Lainey. Damn lucky.

On our way back now. You have backup?

He didn't make me wait too long.

Meeting with friends. May ask B to go with if he's available.

That worked.

"Adam has a meeting," I told Bodhi. "I'll have Ivy and Ezra, you free to go with him?"

"Yep," Bodhi said, then glanced at the time. "Lainey will be another hour at least. Let me know when she gets back?"

"Done."

A soft laugh came from the backseat and I glanced to where Ivy grinned widely at us, hands clasped together, and just looking altogether too delighted.

"What?"

"Nothing," she said, her smile growing. "Just enjoying the vibe in here."

The vibe...

I rolled my eyes but that just made her laugh more. "Behave brat, or I'll tell the boyfriends on you."

"Tell them what?" She dared me, not sounding even a bit chastised.

"I don't know, I'm sure I can think of something." Despite my protests, I was chuckling right along with her.

"Hate to break this to you, Milo, but if this is your idea of intimidation, it needs work." The observation from Bodhi cracked Ivy up further and I caught the hint of a smile on his face.

Shaking my head, I went back to scanning the streets as Bodhi drove. I recognized the route he was taking and the changes in roads as he checked for tails. Just because we were paranoid didn't mean people weren't out to get us.

At his place, Bodhi parked in the garage and rode up with us. Ivy gave us both a patient look even if she did shake her head. She got it, even if we were entertaining her. Fuck knew she was used to being watched over. The Vandals weren't letting her run alone, not yet and maybe not for a long while.

They all needed to heal.

"Oh, thank fuck, they're home," Ezra said in the most aggrieved of tones. "Now you can leave and not sit there glaring at me like I'm going to poof and disappear."

Adam rose as we entered and he was already collecting his coat. "Emersyn," he greeted my sister and offered her a one-armed hug. She returned it easily and pressed a kiss to his cheek. "Don't mind, Ezra. He's in a mood."

"Yes, I'm in a goddamn mood. I'm not five. I can look after myself for a few minutes."

"Clearly," I said as I tugged off my own coat and then took Ivy's. "You sound very mature at the moment."

"Bite me, Hardigan." He only trotted out my last name when he wanted distance these days. I could respect it.

Ivy laughed. "We'll look after him. Go to your meeting."

"Stay inside," Bodhi said. "Doors locked." Then he pointed to the coat closet. "Gun's in a small cupboard in the back. Milo can show you the safe room." Those instructions were all for Ivy's benefit. Then Bodhi lifted his gaze to mine and I nodded once. I had them both. No one would touch them on my watch.

"Thanks," Adam said. "I'll talk to you more later," he added for Ivy. "Ezra, don't be a dick to your cousins." Then he was out the door with Bodhi right behind him.

Cousins.

"Assholes," Ezra muttered and Ivy bumped me with her hip as she passed me.

"Be nice," she scolded Ezra and he gave her a dark look as she stared down at him, hands on her hips. Ezra wasn't a bad guy most of the time, but if he took that attitude out on her, I was gonna feed him my fist.

"I'm not in the mood to be nice," Ezra muttered. "I'm fucking tired of everyone hovering."

"Well, then stand up and give me a hug, *cousin*," she said. "Because outside of Milo, you're the only other good thing that's happened to me *because* of King."

I blinked and I wasn't the only one caught off guard by the comment. Ivy despised King. Not for what he'd done to her, but for his choices where *I* was concerned.

"Em," Ezra said and he rose as she backed up a couple of steps. "It's—It's just a bad day."

"Bad days happen," she told him in a tone that was light enough to offer hope that they would also end, but sober enough to accept that they were very much a fact of her life. "We don't have to let them be in charge."

He shook his head and then when she wrapped her arms around him, he hesitated. The resistance was just a flash, one he fought to cover almost as soon as it appeared. The moment I saw it though, I couldn't unsee it.

Ezra didn't expect anyone to give a damn about him. It was why he was always acting out or pushing at Lainey and Adam. He wanted to push them away because it would be easier if he was the one who did the rejecting.

Fuck his family. Jasper had the same goddamn problem at one point. An abusive father destroyed, and Ezra was the walking wounded.

When he wrapped Ivy up tight, I nodded. That was better. She would be good for him. Like Mayhem was, because she wouldn't let Ezra just get away with it.

"Better?" she asked, still hugging him.

"Weirdly," he admitted with a brief glance at me. "Yes." Then he pulled back and looked at her. "How did you do that?"

"I've had practice," she said, then patted his arm. "Practice and a big brother who foisted all of his protective bossiness on me." She flashed a grin at me. "But it's cool, cause now I can give him all the shit and be a brat while he lets me."

"Huh," Ezra said, then cut a look toward me.

I just shrugged. "She's not wrong. Besides, you are family. That means you just have to accept it."

"So, who do I have to bribe to get a coffee?" Ivy asked. "I can make it myself."

"I got it," Ezra said. "And... sorry about being pissy when you got here."

"You weren't pissy at me," she told him.

"Good. Right. You want coffee, Milo?"

"That'd be great. Should we order food or make something?" I looked at Ivy. "Cause you're probably not filling us in until Mayhem gets back."

She rolled her eyes. "Maybe... Depends." Then she cast a look toward a retreating Ezra who vanished into the kitchen. "He's not okay."

I adopted her soft tone. "No, he's not, but he's working on it."

When she bit down on her lower lip and folded her arms, I could practically read the indecision on her face.

"Trust me, kiddo. We have him. Me, Mayhem, Adam, even Bodhi. None of us are going to let him fall."

"You can't smother him though." She blew out a breath. "It's hard when you've been hurt—I know you know that. You don't want to feel vulnerable and you really don't want to feel like it's all out of your control. Don't hold on so tight you're taking that control from him."

"I hear you," I promised her then rubbed her biceps so she'd relax a little. "I'll talk to the others."

She nodded, then glanced back toward the kitchen. "I can talk to him... It might help if it comes from someone he's not so close to."

I hated to burst her bubble... "He was protective of you before he knew," I reminded her.

"That was because of Lainey." She couldn't just hand wave this off but it wasn't time for this fight right now.

"Uh huh." I nudged her over to take a seat as the sound of the coffee grinder and the milk steamer drifted out from the kitchen. When she curled up in the corner of the sofa, I studied her. "Did you find out what we needed to know?"

"Some."

"Define some?"

"I know people we can talk to, people who are familiar with the business in that part of the world. I can also get you in to talk to them. We might get a lot more there. They may not be as amenable to talking as others, but I trust you can persuade them."

I frowned. "How?"

"Every single time I toured in Eastern Europe, it was always very popular. We only ever played in two cities, so the audience came to me."

"Why only two?" I swore she was talking around the point, making light of something that was far more serious.

"Because," she said, then glanced back as Ezra reappeared with our coffees. "Yay! Coffee time."

I let her have the distraction as Ezra handed over our coffees before he took a seat on the other sofa. "What are we discussing?"

"Europe," she said. "And why did I only ever perform in two cities when we went there—well in Eastern Europe." At least she didn't try to downplay it.

"The reason was...?"

"The company always had to hire me bodyguards when I was there." She blew out a breath. "Uncle Fuckbucket would pay for it, particularly after the first time there was a kidnapping attempt."

The first time?

Ezra snapped forward. "The first time? That means there was a second."

"The first one was the only real close call, after that I had bodyguards. But my performances brought in all types and I was very popular in some circles." She made a face. "I didn't really think about the audience that much, we just went, I performed, and we left..."

"Em—are you telling us that traffickers actually *came* to your shows and tried to acquire you?" The fact Ezra could deliver the line so coolly earned him points.

I pinched the bridge of my nose.

"I can't say they were definitively traffickers," she said before taking a sip of her coffee. "Some were just rich, fat men who wanted a young girl."

Anger lit a tempest in me.

"I recognized it, and I did everything I could to avoid it. So, yes, when I went, I had big burly bodyguards, often two at a time, to keep my 'fans' at bay and so no one had to worry about me going missing."

Because her uncle was already a pedophile who wanted to claim ownership of her. I wish we could resurrect that piece of shit just so we could kill him. Again.

"Anyway, I'm not worried about that this time. Because I'm never alone and the guys would never let anything happen to me. Nor would you." She motioned to the two of us. "I also know a lot more about fighting, using a knife, and shooting a gun. I'm not an easy target anymore."

Anymore.

"Ivy..."

"I love you too," she murmured. No, she wasn't making light of her history or her experiences. "Lainey needs this. She needs help to find Andrea. If she's in Eastern Europe, and 'sold,' then we need these people. People who can point us in the right directions. Of all of us, I can do this. I can bring them to the table..."

I fucking hated that she was right.

"How the hell are you convincing Liam and the others to even consider this?" Ezra demanded.

"Well, I'm going to let Milo talk to them first."

Right...

The door locks tumbled and I rose, half-aware of Ezra standing too. A moment later, the door opened to reveal Lainey and I was able to take a deeper breath. She was here and she was safe.

Trusting her to look after herself was one thing. Setting my own eyes on her was another. Her troubled gaze lightened as she met mine then she smiled at me before glancing at Ezra and then Ivy.

All at once, Mayhem's smile vanished. "Em... what's wrong?"

I shot a look over my shoulder. Ivy had gone painfully pale and her hand shook, but she wasn't looking at any of us.

She was staring at Karagiani and he was staring at her.

"Ivy?"

"He worked for my uncle…" The paper-thin rasp of her whisper ripped through me. I didn't miss a single thing crossing Karagiani's face.

Or the fact that Lainey was between us.

CHAPTER
THREE

LAINEY

E m went deathly pale and her gaze wasn't on me or Pretty Boy or even Ezra. It was on my bodyguard.

"Em... What's wrong?"

She said nothing, her eyes seemed almost unnaturally large. My stomach dropped at the clear horror reflected in them.

"Ivy?" Pretty Boy prompted. He and Ezra were both on their feet. Ezra cut his gaze back and forth between Em and me. He seemed nearly as mystified as I was by her response.

I'd never seen her look like this...

"He worked for my uncle..."

The words seemed to rip out of her like we were tearing off a sheet of paper. Ice threaded through my veins at the mention of that vile man twined with Em staring at Karagiani.

He worked for her uncle.

He *worked* for her *uncle*.

It was like a dozen scenarios cascaded through my mind,

each one going from terrible to worse. Dead almost a year and Bradley Sharpe still inflicted wounds.

Hell. No.

A flash of movement warned me as Karagiani shifted his stance. I had no idea what I intended to do before, but he didn't give me time to consider any of them. I twisted, caught his forearm as he went to seize me and pushed him past me.

Using his momentum, I pivoted on my heel. There was a stutter of disbelief on his face as he went past me. I didn't have to do another damn thing because Ezra was just *on* him. He pummeled Karagiani with a series of blows. His fists struck with meaty force and blood spattered me from a cut that opened on Karagiani's face.

Ezra charged him in the middle and half-picked him up as he slammed him into a table. Something shattered and there was a crack in the wall. Fists clasped together Karagiani drove both down to hit Ezra in the back.

My baton was already out but I needn't have bothered. Milo caught the next swing of Karagiani's fists and he wrenched his left arm down and back. Ezra took advantage of the distraction and slammed his fist into the man's stomach until he doubled over.

Then the bastard staggered Ezra with a blow from his foot right to the center of his chest. I half-caught him as he fell backwards and then slid around him and used the space to strike the baton against Karagiani's knee as he pulled it back for another blow.

The head butt he gave Milo had no effect, he kept twisting Karagiani's arm until the man actually let out a scream. Then he pushed it further. The sickening crack of bone echoed into the silence and Milo used the force and the pain to put Karagiani on his knees.

Ezra started forward again, blood in his eyes. Milo shook

his head once, I put up an arm to block him. My purse was somewhere on the floor and I had the baton in my right hand.

"I want answers," I said before Ezra could begin beating the man again. "We *need* them."

"We need to secure him," Milo said, not that he seemed to have any struggle keeping Karagiani on his knees. Pretty Boy's expression arrested me, however, his glower at the man he held couldn't shake the worry and the pain in his eyes whenever he glanced at Em...

Fuck. Em.

I pivoted to where she now stood. There was no hiding the violent trembling as she fumbled with what to do with her arms. I collapsed the baton and slid it into the inner pocket of my jacket.

"Em... come on, we're gonna go get the Zip-ties."

When I held out my hand, she gave me a shaky look. Her pupils were enormous. "I don't want to run away..."

"You aren't," I promised her. "We're going to do this together." Right now, she needed to be the fuck away from Karagiani. She needed to catch her breath. We needed to secure the bastard.

I needed to send messages to the guys.

Em hesitated for only a second longer, then her hand was in mine.

"We'll be right back. Ezra, close the door. Pretty Boy, you have him?"

"Yes." He still lifted his chin to me, with a flick of a look at his sister. I ushered her along with me. Bodhi's office was back this way and I knew exactly where he kept the restraints there.

I had my phone in my pocket, rather than my purse, and I pulled it out as I tugged Em into the office. Two quick texts, one to Bodhi and the other to Adam.

Karagiani worked for B. Sharpe. Em at the apt. Pretty Boy restraining him. Questioning imminent.

They both read the message almost immediately and Adam's response was as colorful as I would have expected. Bodhi's was far more succinct.

On my way!

Lowering the phone, I turned to Em. "You don't have to spend another moment with him."

"I love you," she whispered. "But I can do this."

Away from him, some of the color had come back to her face and her pupils weren't quite so huge. The trembling was still right there. She was also still panting. My dislike for Karagiani had magnified a thousand times over.

"I need to do this, Lainey." That I understood so much.

"Okay." I squeezed her hand once then let her go. "Give me a sec."

It didn't even take me that long to find the zip-ties. They were stored in a credenza of all things. The drawers were neatly organized to include handcuffs, zip ties, and some kind of other flex tie. There were also a variety of gags. Then the drawer next to it had several lengths of rope.

Em let out a little laugh as I turned with the zip ties in hand. "You know, I'm just going to accept that Bodhi has those like I do the guys."

I grinned. "We get all the toys and the fun."

Real laughter escaped her and more color came back to her face. That was better. She didn't hesitate to follow me back out to the living room where Karagiani was sweating and glaring.

He wasn't begging or complaining either. Ezra and Milo seemed to be in the same positions as they had been before, but Karagiani seemed to be bleeding more. His jacket was open and his gun was no longer apparent in the shoulder holster.

Em followed in my wake and she stayed near me while Milo got Karagiani secured. I didn't know if we were going to move him from here for the interrogation, but we would need to do something.

It irked me that this happened in Bodhi's space. His home that he'd opened to all of us. I shifted my attention to Ezra. He leaned against a chair, his posture betraying more than his pained expression.

Karagiani had kicked him in the chest.

"I'm alright, Kotyonok," he murmured as he caught my gaze. He flattened his hand as if to tell me to stay where I was. "Really. It hurt, knocked the air out of me, that's all."

I glared at Karagiani. So many questions burned on my tongue.

So. Many. Questions.

Pretty Boy swept me from head to toe with a look then he glanced past me to Em. He wanted to go to his sister. Wanted to comfort her. But he wouldn't leave Karagiani unattended.

All we had to do now was wait. First Tally. Now this. As aggravating as this discovery was, I was glad to know it before Karagiani learned anything else about us. He *worked* for her uncle. No one decent could work for that man.

No one.

That wasn't just guilt by association, that was evil by choice. I rather doubted we would have long to wait, but I was going to have a coffee and maybe something a little stronger.

Interestingly, Karagiani still said nothing at all as I collected my purse. "Did he have a phone?"

Pretty Boy nodded to where the weapons had been laid out on the coffee table. Yes, there was a phone. I picked it up and studied it then waited for it to ask for facial ID. It didn't. Just wanted a passcode.

Disappointing.

We'd figure it out later.

"Em, you want another coffee?"

She was staring at Karagiani again, but Ezra actually moved into her line of sight and broke it. I threw him a smile. There was more stiffness to his motion than I cared for, but I would get a good look at his chest later.

Blowing out a breath, Emersyn glanced at me, then shook her head. "Not really sure I could drink it."

"Come with me while I make mine?"

She gave me just a small reproachful look but I didn't back off on the offer. In my opinion, Em was one of the strongest people I'd ever known. She'd had to be, to survive everything her family had put her through.

Thankfully, she offered no argument and followed me into the kitchen. The silence from the other room was more telling than anything. Karagiani had a broken arm and he wasn't making a sound. Pretty Boy was ready to gut him, but he wanted answers for Em.

Ezra? I'd never seen him so angry. He could barely take his gaze off Karagiani. Then again, he'd been the one to hire him to look after me.

I tilted my head back and closed my eyes.

"Hey," Em said as she slipped an arm around my waist. I leaned into her, accepting the offer of support. "We're okay."

Yes. We were. We stood like that for a long moment. "We are okay," I repeated. "We're going to *keep* being okay."

"Of course we are," she said. "Because who would dare argue with us?"

It was my turn to chuckle. "Every single man we're involved with and we wouldn't have it any other way."

"You have a point." Still, we didn't pull away from each other. I needed the comfort as much as I needed to offer it.

"I talked to Tally today," I told her. She knew what Tally had done, and *who* she was involved with. It had been Em who said she didn't believe Tally could know who King really was or how it would affect us.

She was right, but I just couldn't find it in me to forgive it. Gross oversight or no, Tally's choices had hurt people I loved. I wasn't sure I could ever forgive them or her.

"I'm sorry," Em murmured. "That had to be hard."

I nodded. Tally and Emersyn were my oldest friends. Emersyn had been my secret best friend and Tally had been my public one. Neither ever begrudged the other. Even now, I suspected I could call Tally for help and she would drop everything.

It didn't change anything and that was the part that left regret souring in my stomach. I was still turning that over in my head when Em started making the coffee.

"I was going to do that," I told her and she gave me a small smile.

"I know. But we take care of each other. It's what we do."

Yes, it was. "I'm sorry you found him here." This piece of her past that brought her uncle to mind.

"I'm sorry he's anywhere near you." The fierce declaration made me smile.

"You know," I told her. "It occurs to me that he's made a grave mistake." She didn't ask me what it was and I didn't have to explain. After the coffee was ready, I took a sip and we stayed in the kitchen long enough for Em to pull herself together again.

The scars were there. The places where the knitted together tissue of her life pulled taut. She'd survived so much brutality and betrayal. More, she'd begun to thrive and I hated that anything threw a wrench at her, much less something like this.

At the same time, I marveled at the way she gathered her composure. When we walked back out to the living room, she seemed far more like her. Karagiani, however, was bleeding from more wounds.

Ezra's knuckles were bruised and bloody. Funnily enough, Pretty Boy looked neither annoyed nor moved. Karagiani listed hard to the right, but defiance was still etched into his face.

Thankfully, we didn't have to wait for answers much longer. The door opened to let Bodhi and Adam in, along with Liam and Rome. I was surprised the others weren't here yet, but I didn't doubt if they were on their way.

Rome paused to stare at the man on his knees, as did Bodhi. Adam swept me from head to toe, then Ezra. His eyes narrowed at the bloodied knuckles, but Ezra's stare was so bland, I almost laughed.

Liam though, he came straight to Em and I loved that for her. "Hellspawn?" Then he wrapped her into a hug and I drifted closer to Ezra and Adam, rubbing a hand down Ezra's arm to offer him comfort. He snaked that arm around me and pulled me to him.

Letting them take care of me was how I took care of them. Like Emersyn, Ezra shook a little. His trembling wasn't fear.

It was rage.

Rage that he pointed wholly at the man on his knees.

"How do we want to do this?" I asked because I really didn't want any more blood in Bodhi's place. I rather doubted he would mind, but...

"Soundproof room." Bodhi seized Karagiani by one arm and Pretty Boy took the other. They hauled him through the apartment with all of us following. Instead of the research room he'd opened from his office, the soundproof room was located on the other side of the downstairs guest room.

It was small, plain and utterly unremarkable save for the plastic sheeting on the floor, and the large eyelet screwed into the ceiling. Well, those and the entire shelf full of sharp and rather menacing looking devices.

"You know," Ezra said. "I'm really starting to like you, Bodhi."

"I grow on people," Bodhi answered as they secured Karagiani to the eyelet. It meant loosening his restraints, but he wasn't going anywhere. A grunt of pain escaped the man as they pulled his arms higher.

No sympathy existed within me.

"PPG?" Bodhi said and I shook my head. That nickname was amusing, if it bothered Em, Trouble would never have used it. But the tense air around her lightened and the source of the nickname gave her room to breathe.

I would never find fault with that.

"He worked for my uncle," Em explained and she had the attention of everyone in the room. "The day I was taken back... he was there. He stopped the one guard who sliced my wrists, but he wasn't my friend. He made that very clear."

Every word came out stronger than the last.

"Did he hurt you, Ivy?" Pretty Boy's question belied the intensity in his glare.

"Not directly."

Well, that was one point in his favor.

Not that it was going to sway much.

"So, you didn't hurt her directly," I said, meeting Karagiani's gaze and holding it. "But you were ready to assault me the minute she recognized you." The temperature in the room plummeted. "I want to know why."

CHAPTER
FOUR

EZRA

Dolion Karagiani worked for Bradley *fucking* Sharpe. The bastard uncle who tortured Emersyn for most of her life. Karagiani was there when the guy tried to kill her by cutting up her arms. He was there when Sharpe held her prisoner at his home.

Frankly, I didn't give a fuck if he'd actually struck her or not. Complicit with the torture made him guilty in my book. My knuckles burned where I'd punched him and the bones in my hand ached. My chest took the worst of it though. I was pretty sure I was gonna bruise, where he'd slammed his foot into my breastbone.

As much as I wanted to rub at the spot, I didn't. Awareness of Adam's observation swarmed over me and he wasn't the only one watching me. Lainey hadn't moved far from me since she'd wrapped her arms around me in the living room.

With Karagiani strung up to the ceiling, she leaned against my side. The weight of her a comfort I barely understood that I needed. The rage inside me seethed like a stormy tide crashing against the rocks.

I wanted to gut the man with fish hooks and spread out his entrails so he could stare at them while he died. The bloody image was so visceral, I curled my hand into a fist.

Milo and Bodhi were the two closest to him, along with Liam's twin. I was surprised Liam wasn't up there but he'd planted himself at Em's side. Or rather, at her back. He wrapped around her, a dark and dangerous cloak of violence ready to strike with prejudice.

Honestly, I'd never understood Liam more. Karagiani had done literal harm to his wife. Had I known he was guilty of that, I'd have sent his head to her as a present instead of hiring the dick to shadow Lainey.

Fuck...

Fresh anger poured through me like a gushing wound, the gash too deep to stitch.

"Just kill me," Karagiani said, finally. His dead-eyed gaze fixed on Lainey. Blood dripped from a cut on his lip. There was another that had sliced across his right eyebrow.

I wasn't sure which of us did it, but the blood on my hands suggested it was me. I was more than okay with that.

"The lady told you what she wanted to know," Bodhi answered. "If you want to die, I suggest you cooperate."

"Why?" Karagiani dragged his gaze off her and that settled me some. A hand came to rest on my shoulder. The grip was a lot stronger than Lainey's and the weight a lot steadier.

Adam had my left while Lainey leaned into my right. They were holding me up when I should be cloaking her. The anger spread like a fire through me, eating away at everything in its path.

I'd put this man in her life.

More than once.

Fuck, in the months right after he'd stood witness to the depravity of Emersyn's uncle, I put him right into Lainey's orbit.

So many goddamn mistakes.

"Because dying is inevitable," Bodhi told him, so comfortable with what was to come it should actually terrify me. Cavendish had always seemed more than a little unhinged.

Right now, I liked unhinged.

I was beginning to feel more than a little unhinged myself.

"It's only *how* you die that's on the table," Milo said. "Fast. Slow. Easy or hard. Death comes for everyone but if you don't cooperate—we can make it take forever."

"Then let you heal up and do it again," Bodhi offered up almost cheerfully, like the idea actually delighted him. "Tell the lady what she wants to know."

"No."

One word.

All defiance.

"PPG," Bodhi said over his shoulder. "This is going to get messy."

"I'm okay," she answered in a voice that didn't quiver. "But thank you for the warning."

Bodhi twisted to look over his shoulder and he grinned. "You're welcome."

I saw the move even as Milo and Rome did, Karagiani tried to lash out with a foot to kick Bodhi. He took no one by surprise. All he got was his leg trapped in Bodhi's grip followed by a distinctive *pop*.

A vein throbbed in Karagiani's forehead but he didn't give in to a yell. Not this time. The man was still hanging by a broken arm. What was a dislocated knee?

Head canted, Bodhi seemed to be studying Lainey, not that I could tell what the hell was going on behind his eyes. Then again, maybe I could. Karagiani had tried to hurt her.

He was also choosing a bloody and brutal death.

"How badly do you want to know?" Bodhi asked and Lainey let out a slow sigh.

"Badly," I answered for her. "But she'll give it up and move on if we let her."

That earned me a stink eye as she twisted to glare up at me. "I am not that obvious."

"No, Kotyonok, you are not remotely obvious to anyone. But I have watched you sacrifice time and again. It's why I wanted you to have a bodyguard—I just wish I'd never hired *him*."

"You didn't know," she said in a tone that brooked no arguments. "You would have killed him yourself if you had." No doubt seemed to exist within her. As much as I'd let her down, she still had faith in me.

"Yes," I promised. "I would have."

"Then we get the answers you want. It might take a while, but we get to be creative." Bodhi let go of his leg and glanced at Milo. "You want the first crack or should we give it to the twins?" He didn't wait for an answer. "No, the twins can have him after. We need answers first. Acceptable, O'Connell?"

"Acceptable," Liam said in an easy tone. "Rome..."

His twin didn't move. "I'm just watching until after."

Despite the pain twisting his expression, Karagiani actually cut a look toward the silent twin who was just "watching" him. He actually paled the longer he stared.

So, pain didn't bother him, but Rome did?

I kind of wondered what he saw in his eyes. Then I decided maybe I didn't want to know. I snapped back to the conversation in the room. Milo was moving, he had a knife

40

and slashed it along the achilles tendon of the man's unin-jured leg.

His teeth clamped together, the clack of them audible. But he didn't scream. His pain tolerance would be impressive if it weren't annoying.

"You good?" Adam asked, his voice low and close to my ear. A warmth seemed to spread out, a wall against the fire still burning inside of me. Lainey still leaned into me, her arm around me and I recognized what she was doing.

She was comforting me. It was why Adam was still here.

"Get a pound of flesh for me, too?" It was a simple request but when I met Adam's gaze, there was no mistaking the retribution shining in his damn near purple eyes.

The violet in them always seemed subtle until he was really angry. The violence brought out the darkness in them or maybe it was the darkness in him that brought out the violence.

It was really fucking attractive. If we were anywhere else, I'd kiss that sensuous mouth of his. Raincheck, I promised myself.

"Just a pound?" Adam asked, flicking a look to Lainey for a moment. Long enough that I could admire the possessive heat in his stare and marvel at the fact he was including me in his display.

"Trying not to be greedy," I told him and the weight of his stare landed on me again.

"Be greedy," he said. "I'll let you know when it's too much."

Fuck.

Me.

Desire geysered upwards, splashing lava on all the burnt embers left by my temper. That raincheck was more than guaranteed.

I'd never been so damn hungry for him.

Did he have any idea of what he did to me?

I was about to make myself *stop* staring at him so heatedly before I just threw all caution to the wind. Karagiani absolutely needed to die and we could make out over his corpse—or not.

Then Adam winked at me before he strode forward.

He *winked.*

A huff of laughter escaped me...

"Your father knows," Karagiani said through gritted teeth, blood flecking each syllable he spoke. "You know that, right?"

I stared at him. "Not what the lady wanted to know." Yes, I was aware of my father's knowledge.

The next blow Karagiani took was to his kidney. Fists were effective. So were knives. I had no doubt that he was going to suffer a thousand cuts.

A dark laugh escaped him that turned to a grunt as Adam struck Karagiani again. The blows were calculated, didn't follow a natural rhythm. It just happened when he felt like it.

Not letting the betrayer brace for any of the strikes.

The man hissed as Milo sliced down his side. The shirt was going to be shredded. The shallow cuts were probably the worst. They would sting and bleed. Each injury chipping away at him.

"He hates that you can't even be a real ma—," Karagiani spit as Adam landed an even harder blow. "Ha... he *hates* you."

I waved a hand, almost bored with this attempt to incite me. "Not telling me anything I didn't know." Right now? I found it hard to care. The two most important people in the world *loved* me. Graham Wallace could go fuck himself.

Bodhi dislocated the other knee as something in Karagiani's shoulder popped and this time, he did scream.

"Everyone breaks," Bodhi said into tense silence. "Everyone."

"I killed them," Karagiani admitted, but he wasn't looking at them. He was still staring at me. My gut soured. "Killed them and made sure it hurt. His instructions were specific. He wanted you to know exactly what would happen."

The men my father had killed. Genevieve. The warnings of what he would do to Lainey and to Adam...

"That's why you were going to attack me?" Lainey said into the tension brewing around all of us. "Because Graham Wallace is a cowardly prick who gets off on terrorizing his son?"

She sounded...*offended*.

Karagiani spat out blood. His pallor was growing more ashen. He was losing blood. But we didn't want him to die too quickly.

"Did you work for my father the whole time?" It wasn't what Lainey asked but it was close enough.

The bodyguard started laughing, and it turned to coughing as more blood spilled out of his mouth. Where the hell was all the blood—

"He took something," Bodhi said sharply and Milo swore. Then everyone was in motion, but the blood spreading in a pool on the floor just kept getting wider.

As much as I wanted to see him dead, I didn't want a single piece of him touching Lainey. When I drew her back from the bloody pool, she retreated with me.

Emersyn stared in horror as Rome also joined us. They got the man down, but it was no ruse. He seemed to be bleeding from his eyes, his nose...

Hell, there was even foam bubbling out of his mouth. What the actual fuck...

Not that we'd get any answers to that. His eyes glazed

over and emptied of anything resembling life. The ashen complexion just went pale and waxy. Dolion Karagiani was dead.

Just.

Like.

That.

"Well, that was anticlimactic," Bodhi said, with a note of disgust.

"And messy," Rome added but the dry comment just made Bodhi chuckle.

"Sorry Buttercup, PPG, we wanted to make it hurt more..."

"It's fine," Lainey said, rubbing a hand up and down my arm. The fact she'd been stroking me in gentle, slow comforting motions penetrated and I glanced at her. "Would I have liked more details? Clearly."

The little shrug she offered at the end of the question wasn't an act or affectation. She wasn't particularly bothered by the loss.

"He needed to die," Liam said. "He's dead. The only thing we don't know..."

"...is how much he compromised us." That was on me.

"It won't matter," Lainey said, then she twisted to look up at me as I frowned. "It won't." The two words were so firm they demanded I believe her. "We'll take care of it."

"She's right," Milo said. "Whatever it is, we will take care of it."

"If he set us up in some way, we'll deal with it," Adam added. "He worked for your father and Graham is already on the list."

"This just moves him to the top," Bodhi stated and I blinked slowly.

"You're going to kill my father?" All these years, I'd wanted to. It had been there, in the back of my mind, and I couldn't say I hadn't imagined it. He'd had me beaten, more than once. Done the beating himself until I got too tall. Then he had men for the job.

"Yes." The answer came from Lainey, succinct and simple. "You don't have to do anything."

"You don't," Bodhi agreed and Milo nodded.

"We will take care of it," Adam said at the end.

Casual, direct, and accepted. We were even discussing it in front of Emersyn, Liam and his twin. Then again, Liam knew us and Emersyn...

The horror radiating off of her when she'd seen Karagiani had pissed me off instantly. The horror was gone, replaced by a kind of rough sympathy.

"That's what family does," she told me. "They help us face our demons and when we need it, they take those demons out."

Take the demons out.

I tugged Lainey a little closer and she went pliant against me as I wrapped her up in my arms. "I like having you for a cousin, Em."

Her grin was wide and accepting. "You're not so bad, but cousins doesn't mean you get to be bossy."

"He's already bossy," Lainey muttered and a weird feeling broke in my chest, it crackled and popped. It was as though I'd been drowning from pneumonia, the pressure unbearable, yet now I could breathe again.

"You like us bossy," I murmured and Lainey pinched me even as she held me tight. I was still shaking, and I wasn't a fan of it. But every breath seemed to fill me more, bolstering me.

"That leaves really only one question," Milo said.

"Not it," Rome and Liam said in a single breath and Milo just snorted.

"Not it, for what...?"

"For cleanup," Bodhi said in a droll tone, then rolled his head from side to side.

"I can help," Lainey offered. "Body disposal is not something I've really done before."

I pulled back and stared at her.

"What?" She swung a glance around the room. "I haven't."

Fuck, was it any wonder I loved her?

LAINEY

B ody disposal was *not* fun. Then again, I hadn't expected it to be. The boys didn't object to my helping. Though Bodhi offered up the best descriptions of each step of the process.

Em made a face when he got a little graphic and the twins took her back to the hotel. For all that she'd held up, this had to be bringing up some really bad memories for her. We could go over her plans after this was done. The whole Karagiani reveal had derailed all of us.

Step one in the process involved getting rid of the clothes we were wearing, as well as washing up. Everyone had to scrub off any blood spatter that had gotten on their skin. I was a little sad about my outfit and shoes. But clothing could be replaced.

After, we put on some really terrible plastic outfits over our fresh clothes that reminded me of hazmat suits you see in the movies.

Step two, bag up the body. Despite the fact he'd been on plastic sheeting, the blood was everywhere.

"Keep the gloves on," Bodhi instructed. "The blood will clean up but it's going to be messy at first."

Milo returned with sand then. They used sand to help soak up the blood.

"Do I want to know where you learned to do that?" I kind of did want to know, but it was more curiosity than anything else.

"CSI," Bodhi deadpanned and a laugh escaped Ezra. A real one.

"I almost believe you," he quipped with a slow head shake at Bodhi.

The laugh was a good thing. Ezra had been a mess and he was blaming himself for everything. Wrapping the body took time and effort. Karagiani was also heavy. The guys didn't let me help with that part.

Once he was completely sealed up, we had to get him out of the apartment building. Bodhi and Milo *debated* whether to put him in a deep freeze for now, then we could dismember the body and it would be easier for transport.

What amazed me even more was how clear their understanding of the process was. Adam and Ezra added their own thoughts on what would work better. The biggest time constraint was getting the body into something *before* rigor set in. Eventually, the freezer was decided on. Bodhi had one here, but it was actually packed with food and supplies.

It meant offloading a big portion of it and trashing more. Couldn't be helped, but we got it down. They managed to get him into the freezer. It wasn't pretty and I was pretty sure bodies weren't supposed to fold the way they bent him.

Then again, he was dead, so it could hardly hurt the

corpse. An hour after we packed him away and dealt with the debris, we finished cleaning up the little torture room and the contents, along with the plastic coveralls were ready for an incinerator.

"Food," Bodhi said and I frowned at him. "You're pale and this has been a long day. We also need to plan." Then he flicked a brief look at Ezra.

I would have argued about my so-called pallor, but one glance at the dejection and weariness on Ezra's face decided me. "I'm starving," I admitted. "Though, I don't know that I'll be able to eat without smelling all of this."

Ezra's throat convulsed once as he swallowed, then he lifted his eyes and locked his gaze on me. He gave me a small smile. "We'll find something, Kotyonok. But I know one thing that will work pretty fast."

"What's that?" I could play my part. Adam brushed his fingers down my arm and Milo touched my shoulder as I accepted Ezra's outstretched hand.

"Follow me." The flatness in his voice betrayed his continued discomfort. Still, he guided me downstairs with Bodhi, Adam, and Pretty Boy following. They were giving me the lead on this.

Ezra guided me all the way into the kitchen, he popped open the freezer then pulled out a bag of coffee beans. It was the rather delicious blend that Bodhi favored. I'd never heard of it before and I would bet he had a coffee plantation somewhere that grew these heavenly beans.

Opening the bag, Ezra held it up to me like an offering of flowers. "Take a deep breath." Light chased some of the shadows from his green eyes. Leaning forward, I filled my nostrils with the rich, heady scent of the dark roasted blend. "And again..."

I blinked my eyes open at the hint of laughter under-scoring the words. The combination of scent coupled with the lightness in his voice soothed the battered edges of my soul.

It had been a long day before it even started.

Another deep breath and the lingering scents of blood and death faded beneath the earthier, bold flavor of the dark roast. Coffee was the perfect antidote, the smokier chocolate and caramel erasing the metallic taste of copper coating my throat.

When my stomach actually rumbled, it was the first time in the days since I found out Harper sold Andrea and my mother died. My appetite had all but died in the same time frame.

"Good," Bodhi said. "Sit, we'll get coffee and food. Then plan."

Ezra pressed the bag into my hands and I cradled it as I let them nudge me over to the table. Like my penthouse, the kitchen at Bodhi's had a table and chairs in the corner. It was a lot cozier and we actually used it more.

Adam pulled out a chair and then I was seated. I wasn't the only one, Adam hustled Ezra over right next to me. "Park it, both of you. What do you want to drink? Besides the coffee?"

"Maybe a couple of shots of whiskey straight," Ezra said, scrubbing a hand over his face.

"We're out," Pretty Boy said as he crossed to the fridge. "So it's coffee, milk, juice, or soda."

"Out?" Ezra gaped. "How the fuck are we out?"

"Because I dumped it." Bodhi punctuated the sentence with the coffee grinder and Ezra glared until I put my hand over his.

"You don't need it," Adam told him, the command snapping beneath each syllable he spoke. I stole another sniff of the coffee beans as Ezra's expression darkened.

It had been a really long several days. "I get it," I said, smoothing my hand down Ezra's arm and pulling all the fire in his eyes toward me.

His temper had never frightened me. Nor would it begin to bother me now. The scowl on his face grew fiercer.

"Adam has a gift for making everything an imperious order, even when it's just him trying to show you he cares." Surprise rippled across Adam's face, but I ignored him for the moment. Ezra needed to hear this. "How many times has he bossed me around? Thrown me in a car? Or just picked me up and hauled me out of a place?"

"I don't know," Bodhi said slowly, his voice dropping. "How many, Reed?"

"Not the point she's trying to make," Pretty Boy interceded and it took everything I had to not smile. Because he was not defending Adam. "But I've seen that overprotectiveness up close. Sometimes it was necessary."

Now I did stick my tongue out at him and Pretty Boy winked as Adam scrubbed a hand over his face. Impatience? Irritation? Regret? Maybe some odd combination of all three?

As much as I'd like to poke at him, I refocused on Ezra. His scowl shifted to a more troubled expression. "You had no idea," he murmured. "I'm not a child."

"Nor am I..." I raised my hand to Ezra's cheek and he leaned into the contact. That was a good sign. "But Adam only knows one way to protect who and what he cares about."

"Still kind of sucks," Ezra muttered and I grinned. The anger was fleeting and there was more speculation in his eyes now.

"Maybe, but you're also still recovering and while I won't tell you that you can't drink, I will say you shouldn't. Not while we're getting this cardiac issue under control and not while we have so much else on our plates."

Guilt flared to life in his eyes and I shook my head.

"We need your brain, Ezra. We need you to be sharp and focused. I get it if you need the drink because it's a lot right now." Now I sighed. "I really do get that. But can you try, for just a little while, without? We'll see what we can do to distract you and blunt the edges?"

Ezra leaned forward and kissed me. It wasn't particularly passionate at all, but a fierce connection. His lips held mine as he cupped the back of my head. The move was all aggressive demand coupled with feverish declarations.

"I love you too," I whispered against his lips as he eased back. The long sigh of his tension releasing echoed through me.

"Thank you, Kotyonok."

"Always," I promised him. Bodhi told me to see the flaws, and I did. But it didn't make me love them any less.

"I'm still waiting for an answer, Reed," Bodhi said and I glanced up to find Adam wearing a thoughtful expression as he studied Ezra and I both. I got it, I really did. He was scared to death Ezra was going to get himself killed.

So was I.

But there were ways to do this that weren't quite so damn domineering. Even if he was hot as fuck when he got pushy.

"Tell you what," Adam said, dragging his gaze off of us to look at Bodhi. "Raincheck, you can kick my ass for stupid decisions later."

"It's a date." Bodhi nodded once, then looked to me eyebrows raised. Did I need him to do anything else right now?

I shook my head. "I *am* hungry and we still have a lot to talk about."

The words galvanized everyone. They made breakfast for dinner and it was fine by me. Instead of trying to help or retreating, Ezra stuck close to me. When the coffees were ready Adam delivered them. Pretty Boy claimed the chair on my other side while Adam took the one on the other side of Ezra.

Bodhi brought the plates of food over and honestly, it was probably the kindest meal I'd ever eaten. Between the coffee, eggs, and bacon, I was able to push all the cloying scent of death away.

Gradually, through the meal, Ezra relaxed. "Kotyonok," he said. "I am sorry..."

"Nope, nothing for you to be sorry about," I told him but the mutiny in his eyes told me this was going to be an uphill battle.

"Ezra, Mayhem is right. This isn't your fault. You hired him to do a job. The fact he was also working for your father is just another strike against *him*. Not you." Pretty Boy laid it out like it was fact. "Betrayal sucks. We've all faced it on some level. The problem is solved, for the moment. If you really need to beat yourself up for it, we can do that, but it won't help you or Mayhem right now."

"You can take a raincheck with Reed," Bodhi offered and if I hadn't been watching him, I might have missed that hint of a smile. "I agree with Milo and Lainey. The betrayal was not yours."

The troubled frown he'd worn through the whole meal eased, but it didn't go away. "I hate... I hate that my father took advantage of me protecting you to put you in more danger."

Not shying away from it, I nodded. "I hate that your

father does anything to you at all." I didn't have to focus on Adam to see his hand clench or the muscle ticking in his cheek. Wallace Graham needed to go.

Sooner rather than later.

As long as he was out there, Ezra was in danger. As for his mother, Dinah, I would make that decision when we got there.

"Right... " Ezra sighed again. "I'll stop. What did Em have for us?"

He wasn't ready to let this go. He may not ever be ready to but he was making an effort. I wouldn't ask for more. Not yet.

"She has a plan..." Pretty Boy began and I could already tell, he wasn't a fan. Two sentences in and I got it exactly.

Em knew a lot of people. Sometimes, it was easy to forget that she had traveled the world with her performances. That some of those places included sleazy types that dealt with human trafficking shouldn't have surprised me.

"We won't let anything happen to her. Though I don't doubt the Vandals will be right there if anything *tries* to happen to her." It wouldn't be happenstance. It would be deliberate. But Milo nodded, he did understand, though he would never like it.

"Then we need to make our plans. The memorial service has to be observed." Despite what I'd said on my way in to see Tally... "We need to deal with Graham and King before we go too."

I didn't want to leave a single dagger behind to knife us in the back.

"Do you want to talk about Tally?" Adam asked, and I would give him points for the rough sympathy there. Of everyone here, he and Em were probably the only two who really understood how much that friendship had meant to me...

"She didn't know," I said. "While I don't agree with her willful blindness or letting her sexual obsession..." I grimaced because thinking of King in any sexual situation, much less with Tally, was not an image I wanted in my mind. "I believe her when she says she didn't know about the connections. She believes everything about who Julius King is supposed to be."

"Which means she could be in for a world of hurt if Jeff Hardigan has to deal with her." Milo shook his head. "Will she warn him?"

I'd been asking myself that question since I left her. "I don't think so, but we'll handle it if she does. She doesn't know enough of our current plans to sabotage us and what she betrayed already..." I shrugged. "That's done."

Milo pressed a kiss to my shoulder and then wrapped an arm around me. "I'm sorry, Mayhem."

The silence ballooned around us, because what else was there to say. Bodhi had already offered to deal with her for me, but I'd declined the offer. I didn't want to kill her. I might never trust her again and I would mourn the loss of that friendship...

But I didn't want to see her dead.

"We could always make arrangements to relocate her for the next few months so that she's safe while we deal with things," Bodhi said and I summoned a smile for him.

"No," I said with another slow shake of my head. "She's an adult. I wouldn't thank you for removing me from a situation, I won't do it to her. I gave her enough information to remove herself."

One by one they nodded.

"Do we really think Andrea is still okay?" Every moment we delayed leaving made me sick. I wanted to be there

55

already. But we were still going in blind and we weren't doing *nothing*.

"We're going to find her," Adam said. "No matter what else happens, we will find her and we will make this right."

That didn't mean she was okay *now*.

It meant she would be.

She had to be.

CHAPTER
SIX

ADAM

It was early morning and I hadn't slept yet. It should have surprised me more when Milo invited himself along when I came down the stairs. The man even had coffee ready. Probably should have asked him what gave me away, but I doubted he'd gotten any more sleep than I had.

Lainey had gone up with Ezra after dinner and I spent most of the night sitting in the chair in the corner of the room watching them both sleep. She'd tried to coax me into the bed with them but I wasn't ready to relax yet. I didn't think I would be ready to relax for a really long time.

I already had my phone and my keys out. "Do I need to send a message to Bodhi?" I wouldn't wake up Lainey or Ezra. There was a note in the room for them.

"He knows," Milo said as he opened the front door. "He was the one who reminded me we pulled you back early."

Nodding, I led the way and called the elevator. It was kind of funny how much Hardigan had changed since moving to the city. Then again, it was for Lainey so clearly worth it.

The custom suits were cut more for comfort and versatility than flash. Better for his personality and allowed him to carry concealed. The elevator dinged open and he followed me inside. I'd been planning to talk to Liam the day before but the revelation about Karagiani had definitely taken precedence.

Taking Milo with me wasn't the irritation it probably would have been even a few months ago. Hell, even a few weeks ago I'd have been more inclined to just drop him at Grand Central and leaving him there.

Silence accompanied us to the garage and my car. He dropped into the passenger seat, and didn't even ask where we were going. Probably wanted to see his sister or maybe he had shit to talk to Liam about too.

Or maybe...

"I need to have a private convo with Liam," I said, rather than assume. "That going to be a problem?"

Milo cut a look in my direction. "Long as you're with Liam, he'll watch your back. I can visit Ivy or talk to Rome and Freddie."

"You want to talk her out of Eastern Europe." It wasn't a question. Knowing Emersyn? It wouldn't happen. She and Lainey were cut from the same bolt of stubborn cloth.

Yet, I couldn't fault him for the effort. Emersyn had suffered more than enough at the hand of her bastard uncle. Dangling her like chum for the sharks was not on my list of good ideas. Ever.

"Yes, but I won't. She's already made up her mind. She still has to sell it to the boyfriends..." But his long sigh suggested that wouldn't be difficult enough for his liking.

"Sisters are hard," I said, pulling out of the garage and accelerating. Another hour and traffic would fill these roads, but we had time to get to the high-end hotel where Liam had parked them. "But worth it."

"Kind of my feeling on the subject," Milo admitted. "As much as I want to keep her far away from this dark shit... I know she knows more about it than I do. I also know, she has the right to say what she can and can't handle."

"Long as you get the same right," I told him. "What you can handle, what I can... it's a far cry from what I'm prepared to see Lainey have to fight. Or Ezra for that matter." Honestly, now that I'd finally started paying attention, I couldn't not see it. I'd tried to protect Ezra the same as I had Lainey.

It was why I cut him out when Liam and I faked my death. It was why I didn't want him following me to Waldemar or any of the other tasks ahead of us... The little shit kept trying to throw himself on the fire for us and that needed to stop too.

All of it did.

We had to be a team. They had to be involved. It was why I left them a note about where I was going. Why I didn't argue about Milo going with me *and* why I needed to have this damn conversation in the first place.

"Yeah," Milo said, then scrubbed a hand over his face. "I'd take every single blow she's ever had to endure. Every damn one."

"For what it's worth... so would I." I sighed. "I always knew it was bad. I loathed Bradley Sharpe. My father admired him, that was enough to make me dislike him. But there was always... something about him. If I'd realized just how bad it was..."

"You offered to marry her to get her out," Milo said, the corner of his mouth kicking up. "Could have sunk yourself with Lainey forever."

"Maybe, but it protected her to protect Em too. Emersyn

doesn't have a bad bone in her body. Lainey... she was never going to stop going to her and trying to protect her." Bradley Sharpe would have tried to kill her or worse... No, getting Emersyn out and securing her with my name was the only option I had at the time.

"Look," Milo said as we pulled up to the hotel. It was one of mine. Pretty sure Liam hadn't realized that when he checked in, but I liked it cause it meant I could keep an eye on their security too. "We agree on more things than we ever fought over in the past. I can't disagree with a single choice you made where Ivy or Mayhem are concerned."

"Does that chafe to admit?" I could give him shit. I really could, but this wasn't about that. Not in the slightest. It was about... finding that common ground. Fuck knew we were finding it with Cavendish of all people. Hardigan was a lot easier to like.

"Nope," he said, then pushed his door open as the valet opened my door. I handed him my keys.

"Keep it close," I ordered, then added, "please." Staff was here to help, treating them with anything less than respect encouraged them to betray you.

"Yes, sir."

Milo was a half-step behind me as I headed toward the interior. It was still early and a wall of warmth struck as we stepped inside. Liam rose as we entered and folded up the newspaper he'd been reading.

"Coffee," Liam said, nodding to the gourmet shop that occupied one corner. There was already a line. The three of us stood there, waiting our turn. Then Liam sent Milo up to the room with a tray of coffees for them while he and I took our coffees. "Where?"

I glanced back at the lobby. There was plenty of seating, but I wanted some privacy for this. "Follow me."

One upside of owning the hotel, I knew it inside and out. We took the escalator up to the next floor. There was a steakhouse here that didn't open until the afternoon. Like the rest of the hotel, I owned it.

The security guard who kept an eye on the level unlocked the door for me and then absented himself. We carried our coffee in and claimed one of the more luxurious booths in the back. One call and I shut off the cameras to this part of the restaurant.

"The cloak and dagger is getting impressive," Liam commented in the drollest of tones.

"I'm not quite the exhibitionist you are." I hadn't forgotten his particular affinity for cameras everywhere.

"Better to keep an eye on my space when I'm not there." Liam wasn't going to apologize for it. Not that I expected one.

We'd been honed by the world, well worlds for him, we'd grown up in.

"I prefer my privacy as well as freedom from potential extortion."

"You say potato..." He grinned and I rolled my eyes. "Anyway... what's up?" Raising his coffee cup, he saluted me once before he took a drink.

The day before, I'd sauntered around the point. We'd actually had some business to discuss, but that wasn't why I'd scheduled the meeting. We didn't need to talk in person for most things.

"How did you know you could do it?" I cut to the chase. "You, Emersyn, your brother, and all the other guys?" There were seven of them in total. They were all with Em. She was with them. That relationship saw her thrive in a way I couldn't define nor would I question.

She was good for Liam too. There had always been a darkness in him. A darkness I understood, and respected. He was also...*happier*. So however they were making it work, it worked.

"I wanted her happy more than I wanted her to myself," Liam said as if it were the easiest thing in the world. "Almost didn't happen though... Not because of the guys, but Rome."

I frowned.

"Rome has never wanted anyone for himself. She was the first person I've ever seen him actively seek out. I wasn't going to fight my brother and I wasn't going to step on what they could have." He shrugged. "Eventually, they both smacked me around, but the thing is... I want her to be happy. Her happiness is all I want. Hers and Rome's. The other guys 'cause they are family. What we have works. If it weren't them though..."

Liam shook his head.

"You wouldn't have ever shared her with me." It wasn't a question. The flat look he gave me promised this was not a road we needed to spend much time on. "I never wanted her that way, but even if I had..."

"No," Liam said, succinctly. "Probably not. But if Hellspawn had needed you in some way..." His grimace spoke volumes and I raised a hand to stave off any other response.

"Intellectual exercise only. You made it clear you would shoot me if I continued to press the proposal." Probably not the best idea to tweak him, but the flat look he gave me was enough to make me chuckle.

"Jackass," Liam commented.

"Sometimes," I agreed. "Non-intellectual exercise of a question. I also need you to be my friend for a few minutes."

"I've been your friend for a lot longer than you deserved it," Liam reminded me. "Ask. If I can answer it, I will. Leave Hellspawn out of whatever it is."

"Done." Not a hard promise to make. "Lainey..." This was

a challenge to even discuss. I never brought her up to Liam. Keeping her compartmentalized had been about protecting her from all of us. "Lainey has decided the multiple partner relationship is for her."

Liam nodded once, not commenting. I had all of his attention.

"Ezra... I can handle. But that's another issue. Cavendish was an unexpected wrinkle and Milo..."

"...is well and truly already established and you don't mind him or you'd still be calling him Hardigan."

I shrugged. "I don't actually mind either Bodhi or Milo, as shocking as that feels to admit. I loathed the idea of *anyone* touching her that wasn't me, but now? No, they'd gut anyone who touched her and they can take care of her in ways I didn't. They can also protect her when I'm not there."

"They make her happy." Again, not a question.

"Yes." I could keep it succinct too. That was it in a nutshell. It made *Lainey* happy. The four of us were there for her. I'd already gotten used to them and had started to rely on them too.

Milo and Bodhi had both been there for when my father took her and when Ezra went down.

"I think there's something a little different for us though."

"Such as?" Liam prompted when I didn't keep speaking. Instead, I took a long drink of the coffee.

"It feels almost stupid to say this, now that I'm trying to verbalize it."

"Discussing feelings in general pretty much sucks," he told me and he really wasn't wrong.

"Agreed," I said. "So, I'm going to rip the Band-Aid off and just get through this. My best friend is in love with me...and I am pretty damn sure I love him too. Love him enough to attempt a relationship with him as well as with

Lainey. Yes, before you ask, she knows and she is encouraging us."

"Cool."

I blinked.

"That's it?"

Liam raised his eyebrows. "Were you expecting something else?"

Falling back in the seat, I scrubbed a hand over my face. "I just told you that Ezra and I are...probably, no, not probably. We're definitely starting a relationship. I'm going to be with him and Lainey both and you say—*cool*?"

"Adam, you two have been a couple for as long as I've known you. You even fight like a couple." The blunt delivery —and frank acceptance—shocked me even more than his casual *"cool."*

"Really?"

"Yeah," Liam said, then shrugged. "Look, I don't judge. You're not an asshole most of the time. Ezra can be, but his heart is generally in the right place even if his mouth is constantly writing checks the rest of him has to pay."

A more accurate description I'd never heard.

"But if he makes *you* happy and the two of you are also making *her* happy, who gives a fuck what I have to say on it? The only people who are important are you three. I assume Milo and Bodhi are fine with it."

They hadn't said a damn word. They'd just—accepted it. Bodhi parked me and Ezra in the same room even, which I appreciated more and more. Beyond that, they were helping us look after Ezra.

"Just..."

"Just?" Liam nudged verbally as he sat forward. His coffee was gone and he focused on me. "Just what? You thought your girlfriend was your sister for years. You sacrificed to keep her safe. Then you find out she's not, but now, you and your best friend are ass deep in trouble with King, with the Royals —with your father."

My father. Ezra's father.

Bastards, all of them.

"Now, we have more problems, but we're also eliminating enemies. Life doesn't always give us that many opportunities to be happy. You gotta make the choice to take what you can, to embrace it, and to make the most of it."

"When did you get so damn wise?" It should irk me more, but I really needed to hear him say all of that.

"I've always been the smartest one of us. Don't let the good looks fool you." He grinned easily.

"You're an ass," I said, shaking my head and chuckling for real.

"Smartass," Liam confirmed. "But you feel better, right?"

I did. "Thanks," I said, meaning it.

"Anytime." The moment lasted about three seconds before Liam said, "Though, if you ever really need me to knock some sense into you—I got you covered."

Hell, I couldn't even deny him that, so I just toasted him with my coffee. I was on the right track. This... this was going to be my life, so we needed to get some shit done.

"You feel like knocking some heads in with me?"

The other man just grinned. "Whose car are we taking?"

CHAPTER
SEVEN

LAINEY

You can only wake up once from a dream. Mine hadn't been particularly comforting of late. The shift of weight in the bed and the hot hand sliding down my torso snapped me awake. Deep green eyes seared into mine as the morning sun edged the curtains and left the bedroom cast in a gray twilight.

"Kotyonok," Ezra half-groaned the endearment before nuzzling a kiss along the corner of my lips. With only scant seconds to appreciate the heavy weight of his cock on my thigh, I parted my lips and he claimed my mouth.

The kiss stole every ounce of my breath. Teasing hands pushed up the t-shirt I'd gone to bed in before tugging and then my panties were a memory.

I stopped trying to track how he was tormenting me, the pinch of his fingers against my nipples. The caress of his hands as he cupped and kneaded my breasts. The way he kissed me like he needed me more than oxygen.

His boxers were gone and the silken steel of his cock was

right there, filling my palm and gliding against my skin as he pumped his hips. The pre-cum soaked cock was right there for me to wrap a hand around.

With a scrape of his teeth, Ezra shifted gears from soul-stealing kisses to love bites. The first to my lower lip, then to my jaw as he nibbled his way to my throat. I closed my hand around the base of his cock and gave him a squeeze.

The low moan he released had my thighs clenching, but Ezra was already in the cradle of them. He blanketed me everywhere.

"I need you, Kotyonok," he groaned against my throat, his hips rolling even as he slid a hand down to drag my knee up. I still had his cock in my grip and I stroked him from base to tip, teasing his piercings. The pair of bars he'd had inserted one for me and the other for Adam.

My pussy clenched in anticipation, I loved the way those stroked me inside. There was just something so damn erotic that had me panting while I wanted to drive him as mad as he made me.

Ezra fisted my hair and tugged once. My scalp lit up and tingles raced through me. Shivers danced up my spine and seemed to cascade over my nipples. I dug my fingers into his shoulder and flexed my hand around his cock.

At this angle, I could drag him back and forth along my slit. It was torture for both of us. But what delicious torture. Ezra stared down at me with hungry eyes full of questions and heat.

"Kotyonok," he whispered, the endearment was a revelation. So much emotion punched through each syllable. That nickname. He'd stuck me with it years ago and yet it had remained a treasured secret, a name just for us. Now, I heard all the things in that single word that he'd never been able to say.

The longing.

The need.

The love.

It had all been there, tangled up and hidden away. From me, from himself, from the rest of the world. Loving was dangerous for Ezra...

Hatred for his father bubbled through me. That Ezra *could* love was a testament to *Ezra*. Not the family that raised him and tried to fill him with their poison.

"La—"

"I love you," I told him, because I didn't have a nickname or an endearment, I just had the words themselves. "You know that, right? That I love you? I would die for you, fuck knows, I'll kill for you too—"

Wonder punched through the desire in his eyes even as I nudged his cock toward my entrance. "Kotyonok... I would never ask you to."

"You never have to," I promised him. None of them did. "You're mine. I will protect what is mine. I will protect all of you." Arching my hips, I enjoyed his swift inhale as he nudged inside of me with a kind of torturous care. Just the tip, nothing more and yet I'd never been more aware of him.

He circled one of my nipples with his finger and the skin puckered tighter. It was the perfect amount of teasing, not quite giving me everything yet at the same time making me want it.

"My kotyonok," Ezra said, his whisper almost hoarse. "Mine." The word stamped so far below the surface that no one would ever erase it.

I was his.

I was Adam's.

I was Milo's.

And I was Bodhi's.

They were also mine.

"Me and Adam." I cupped his face, staring up at him. Adam didn't have to be here to be with us.

Ezra's expression crumpled for a moment, the raw vulnerability peeking out from behind the darkness, leaving him open and unguarded. "You are perfect."

I chuckled. "No one is perfect—" I arched to nip his lower lip. He chased my mouth with his own, sliding in to the hilt. The moment he sank home, we were both gasping. "Ezra," I whispered his name against his lips. "I love you."

He groaned and deepened the kiss. Each time he lifted his head to allow us to breathe, I exhaled his name again. The soft huff of his laughter as his chest rubbed against my breasts and the full weight of him settled on me was a miracle.

Nothing else mattered. We were together. I loved him. All of him. All the broken and scarred bits he hid beneath brashness and sarcasm, dipped in alcohol.

He hid nothing from me. Not his needs or his wants. Not his fears or his nightmares. You only got to wake from a dream once, but we could dream of each other again and again.

We could wake up like this, together. He ran his tongue over his lips. I drank in the sight of him from the wet lips to the sleepy-eyes to the rumpled hair. Loving them consumed every part of me and it seemed to grow the more time I spent with them.

Honestly, obsessed was not a strong enough description for what Ezra aroused in me. The hunger in his kiss fired my own and I rocked with him. I couldn't get enough, I didn't think I would ever have enough.

When he rolled onto his back, I moved with him. He wrapped me up tight like I was his favorite blanket. Feet flat

HEATHER LONG

against the bed, he controlled the rhythm and I didn't fight him for it.

Every strike of his cock deep inside lit me up. My inner muscles clenched around him. Hands on his shoulders, I rolled my hips. Every thrust matched our rhythm together and he clamped his hands down on my ass.

"You're so goddamn beautiful," he told me in a hoarse voice. I kept my gaze on his, no matter how hard we pushed each other. Then I fell into him as our mouths collided. There were no more words, just skin on skin, fingers digging in and the pure liquid heat spiraling out from within me.

He stroked my ass, my back, and then cupped at my breasts. With every teasing brush of his thumb or light squeeze of his fingers, he dragged more pleasure out of me. Light pressure, firm pinches, the teasing rolls and caresses, every single one did something different.

When he abandoned my lips and locked his mouth around my nipple, I couldn't stem the tide. It was like my orgasm just broke out. The force of it shattered me and he just slammed into me, the internal pressure so perfect it threatened to undo me.

It was my turn to drag his head upward once more and when our lips touched this time, he came in a hot spurt that added fresh fuel to my fire. We lingered there, savoring the kiss. Little nips and licks that reminded me we were together while I blanketed him.

Satisfaction and need twined together. The musk of sex perfumed the air and I found myself wanting to wrap my mouth around him. Give him a blowjob that would blow his mind. At the same time, I didn't want to let go or move away.

Later, I promised myself. Right now I needed this as much as Ezra did. I lost track of time as we lay there. He stroked his fingers up and down my spine. A soft knock on the door brought an end to the interlude.

"Yes?" I called lifting my head. The door opened and Bodhi glanced in. His gaze found mine and there was warmth in there as well as a bit of an apology.

"Adam called," he said. "You haven't looked at your messages. But he and Milo are on their way back to get us."

Us.

Then he'd spoken with Liam. The others would back us and I glanced down at Ezra. "You don't have to go."

Adam hadn't been able to kill his father, and I would never have asked it of him. I wouldn't do it to Ezra either.

We'd discussed this. If Ezra stayed, Milo or Bodhi would stay with him, because I *was* going. Wallace Graham had a lot to answer for, not the least of which were the scars on Ezra's body but also the ones we couldn't see.

"I'll go," he said and I pressed a soft kiss to the corner of his mouth. "You should probably shower in Bodhi's room, because I'm more likely to fuck you against the wall in the shower."

I chuckled. "Tempting."

"Raincheck?" The offer was sweet and I gave him another kiss.

"It's a date."

"Downstairs in fifteen," Bodhi said as I rose. He gave me a delicious once over that sent a very pleasant tingle through my aching cunt and definitely made me wish we had more time. "I'll have coffee ready."

"You love me," I murmured, pausing to give him a kiss as he held the door open for me.

"I do."

"Does that mean he loves me too?" The snark was all Ezra, his masks slotting firmly back into place.

71

"Sure," Bodhi said. "But I'm not kissing you."

I caught the look of shock that rippled over Ezra's face before Bodhi closed the door. He followed me to his bedroom and the en suite.

"What's up, Trouble?" I still had Ezra's cum on my thighs, not that it seemed to trouble Bodhi in the slightest.

"You sure about taking him, Buttercup?"

Was I? I gave the answer a lot of thought as I got the shower started. "Yes. I wish he wasn't going. It's going to be hard for him. It would be hard for anyone. But it has to be his choice."

Absolutely, one thousand percent his. Arms folded, Bodhi leaned against the door frame as I slid into the shower. If he needed a moment, he could take it.

It wasn't until I'd soaked my hair down that Bodhi finally responded. "We'll keep an eye on him. But if one of us pulls the plug and says to get him out—I need you to be the one to do it."

Because Ezra would do it for me. He would protect me. I really wanted to gut Wallace Graham with a spork. It sounded hideous and appropriate at the same time. Yet, I could see Bodhi's point.

"Okay," I said slowly. "If I need to leave..."

"You just tell me what part of him you want, Buttercup. I'll deliver it on a silver platter."

That really should not be hot or romantic, but it was both. "Thank you."

"Always," he said, then left me to finish showering. Ten minutes later, I put my hair back in a braid that would keep it out of the way and neat. The clothes I wore were all black—as much for the mourning as to hide evidence of blood.

The boots were also black, but not my favorite pair. They would also be more likely to clean up and not need disposal.

72

Cosmetics were light enough to not take long, but also efficient enough to hide the smudge of worry from beneath my eyes.

When I descended the stairs, I found all four of my guys waiting for me, along with a couple of extra Vandals. Adam lifted his chin, the darkness cloaking him, one I wanted to embrace.

Because we were going to get our pound of flesh for Ezra and close that particular door permanently. Wallace Graham would never lay a finger on him again.

Harper could never hurt Adam or Andrea again. We were getting our sister back. And Wallace Graham?

He was a dead man.

Just another name on a list we were going to check off.

No more enemies left to come at us from behind.

None.

CHAPTER
EIGHT

BODHI

Adam and Milo returned with a pair of Vandals to join us on the family excursion. Liam O'Connell and Vaughn Westbrook were excellent choices as backup. O'Connell because he knew all the players. Westbrook, on the other hand, was nearly six and a half feet of heavy, layered muscle decorated with tattoos.

He also had red hair which was utterly at odds with his genial nature. I didn't have a problem with it, I'd never met a red-headed man that wasn't an absolute barbarian when it came to fighting or madder than a goddamn hatter.

I approved of both. Since this ginger was relatively polite and easy-going the rest of the time? Fine by me. Always needed to watch out for the quiet ones.

Ezra came down before Lainey. The wet hair betrayed his shower. He'd gone for casual, and dark colored clothing. Solid plan. There would definitely be blood spilled.

"Liam," Ezra said by way of greeting and the other man

nodded. When Ezra glanced at me, I pointed to the coffee on the table. I'd made it for both him and Lainey...

There she was, and I enjoyed the time it took her to descend the stairs to just savor her appearance. From the neat braid of her hair to the careful tucking of her pants into her boots. Nothing in her appearance or her wardrobe betrayed our plans.

Except...

I canted my head to the side as she took the coffee.

"I know," she murmured. "I need to get my gun. I wanted coffee first."

That was part of it. "You need knives for your boots. We're going to update your wardrobe before we leave."

"You want the tags done now or after?" Vaughn asked. It was his first question since he arrived. That explained the case he'd brought with him. James, the doctor who ran with them, and Vaughn were both skilled at under the skin geo-tags.

"After," Lainey said after taking a drink. "I don't want any more delays. If one of us has a reaction, I'd rather not split us up."

"Good points." Adam agreed with her and Milo just gave her a long look before he nodded.

"Are you sure we all need to get chipped?" Ezra grimaced.

"Yes," Lainey said firmly. "We're all allowed our privacy, and I will never use the tracker unless we think you're in danger. But too much has happened and we're all going to feel better if we can find each other when it matters."

No argument would survive against that reasoning. To give Ezra his due, he gave up the fight without even waging it. If we'd had to pin him down to tag him, we would have. Cooperation, however, was appreciated.

"Plan," I said, taking over. "We're splitting into two vehicles. Lainey B, you're with me and Adam. Ezra, you're with Milo and Liam. Vaughn, I'll give you the option of choosing which team you go in with, but I want you to take the front door *after* we deal with external security."

Ezra frowned. Yes, I was separating him from Lainey and Adam. With them, he was a distraction. Milo and Liam were more than capable of watching his back and he was less likely to engage in theatrical heroics for them.

It was a win for everyone.

For his part, Vaughn merely nodded. "Fine by me. How many are we expecting?"

The plan was relatively straightforward. Ezra had the security codes and he wrote it down for everyone. Adam knew the layout of most of the guard positions as well as where the main security office was.

"We'll start there," Milo said. It was where I'd wanted his team anyway. As much as I enjoyed removing security issues, it kept Ezra out of the direct line of fire with his most dangerous opponent.

Wallace Graham.

Lainey took a long drink of her coffee then studied the screen on the laptop. Wrapping an arm around her middle, I tugged her back to sit in my lap. It would let her study the layout for Harrows Park that I'd pulled up. She relaxed against me, though there was a tight little frown where her brows drew together.

The house was a monster and it was parked on a very large tract of land. Strategically, it could be a fortress. The Grahams, however, had embraced entertaining and socializing instead of more intense security measures.

Still, they had a staff of more than forty for security and another twenty or so for the household itself, not counting groundskeepers and gardeners. Sixty some odd people who could get in the way…

"What if they have guests?" Lainey didn't look at the screen anymore, she glanced at Ezra. "I know your mother begins preparing for the Daughters League this time of year."

"She isn't hosting," Ezra said. "That honor went to the Mansfields of Bridgeport, so the ballroom will remain closed."

That was good.

"There are too many variables to account for every single one. So we're going in quiet. You three will hit the security office, close it down and make sure no one can signal law enforcement. Locking down the garages and the gates should be next." We went over every aspect of the plan until it was time to move.

Plans always had to be fluid. It made life interesting and coordination like this survivable. Coffee finished, Lainey strapped on her shoulder holster and covered it with a jacket.

"Be safe, Mayhem." Milo ordered her before dropping a kiss on her lips.

"You do the same, Pretty Boy." She winked then glanced to where Ezra still wore a frown. He hated this. I couldn't blame him. His father was a problem.

We were fixing the problem.

"I'll be good," Ezra promised. "Mostly. Liam will probably kick my ass if I'm not."

"Accurate," Liam said, then waved him to the car.

Lainey blew Ezra a kiss then Adam gave him a long measuring look. When Ezra grinned and saluted, Adam rolled his eyes.

Better.

They were finding balance.

"Let's go," I said, opening the passenger door for Lainey.

All the smiles faded. It was time to get to work.

Once on the road, Lainey and Adam were both on their phones. She made calls to track down Dinah Graham while Adam handled getting his security in place to replace the Graham security.

A few had already been bought and paid for, but that wouldn't be all of them. I already had a cleanup crew on standby. When we finished with Graham, we had one more target to eliminate before we left—if time allowed. If not, we'd deal with him when we came home.

The drive to Harrows Park was over an hour and it flew past as Lainey and Adam made plans. Some calls they didn't want to put Ezra through. The rest? Well, we couldn't make the calls until it was time.

"She's definitely out," Lainey said as we arrived at the gates to Harrows Park. No one was in the guardhouse and the main gates were closed. "She's checked in for a full spa day to get ready for the memorial service."

I nodded then used the remote from Ezra to open the gates. Both cars had one. They were entering from the back, while we came from the front. I wanted all the attention on us.

Honestly, I wanted all the resistance on us too. It would be great fun to see them try to keep us from doing what we came here to do.

I parked in the porte cochere and took my keys before sliding around the car. Adam was already out and he had Lainey's door open. I gave them both a nod as I ascended the steps to the entrance.

Unsurprisingly, these doors weren't locked. They opened right into the foyer. The doors on the far side of the foyer might be locked, but I wasn't concerned. Security cameras, patrolling security, and an estate of land offered the feeling of protection.

Arrogance. The downfall of so many and a lesson that the wealthy and the powerful should have learned. Influence was only valuable to the people that needed it or wanted it. The rest? Well, it only provided a shield against those not willing to take what was owed to them.

Pushing open the doors to the main house, I wasn't surprised to find a footman hurrying to greet us. "I'm sorry, Mr. Graham is not receiving visitors today."

"Henderson," Adam said as he swept past me. "We need to talk."

If we didn't have to kill the staff, we wouldn't. Some of them would have to go. Unfortunately, some would have blind loyalty, either bought and paid for or earned over the years.

They could no more sacrifice it than they could their own families because they built their whole lives and identities around the families they served. It was a throwback to a different age, and a different place. I never wanted staff like that.

Frankly, I didn't want staff. I preferred people with principles that would turn on you if you turned out to be a raging psychopath who locked up your wife. Or beat your son. Or plotted the sexual slavery of your stepdaughter.

I didn't think that was unreasonable.

Lainey walked at my side as we trailed behind Adam. He collected another footman, then a butler on our way to the kitchen.

The housekeeper rose as Adam and his entourage swept in ahead of us. The cook turned around, his expression fierce. Yeah, we were intruding on *their* territory.

"Gentlemen, ladies," Adam began, summoning their attention to him. "I have an offer for you and it's only available for thirty seconds."

Outside the windows, I could see one of Adam's security teams moving. Excellent. Touching Lainey's shoulder to remind her I had another task, I left her guarding Adam's back as I took the door down to the wine cellar.

The Grahams had quite the collection stored in temperature controlled vaults, along with a few other artifacts and items they didn't share with the public. Vaults within vaults.

I liked digging through secrets. However, I wasn't down here for the secrets. We'd have time to sort all that out for Ezra later. Right now, I wanted the primary security room.

As much as I disliked applauding the man, I had to give the Grahams credit for this. Stored within the wine vault, in a room of its own and on a separate feed, was the primary servers and control room for the whole house.

Security had access to *some* feeds and *some* cameras. This room recorded everything. It was how Wallace Graham manipulated and extorted his way to the top. He had dirt on a lot of people, all safely stored where no one could get to it.

Ezra knew two of the codes.

Adam actually had a third.

But Lainey B surprised us all when she handed over the last one. Her amusement at how stunned Ezra and Adam were had shown.

"You boys are so cute that you think I don't pay attention to everything going on around me."

I would never make that mistake.

The codes got me into the first wine vault. Then into the second, and finally the last two opened the door behind the wine rack that took me into the security room. Quite paranoid in the placement.

I approved.

Inside, the room had several dark monitors but one touch of the mouse and they populated. Camera angles for every single room, several on the ballroom, the courtyard—the bedrooms.

Sick fucker watched his own son?

Another confirmation that he needed to go. I found Adam and Lainey in the kitchen. All but two of the staff had gone. Unfortunately, those two would be leaving the same way as their employer.

Now, where was Graham senior?

Of course, he didn't have the cameras in his office on an auto feed. Probably didn't want the wife spying on him. Though that might require Dinah Graham to think beyond the next major event.

There he was...

The camera was dormant until I activated it. He sat behind his desk, tie and jacket free, the collar of his shirt unbuttoned and a large glass of bourbon or maybe it was brandy.

He wasn't on the phone or with anyone, he was studying something on his computer with a scowl on his face. Straightening, I swept the room around me.

No cameras in here. That was a blindspot. Returning to the screens, I spotted Milo's team heading toward the main building from the security cottage. Another sweep of the grounds and I identified eight more.

Raising my phone, I texted everyone to give them the locations of the targets, as well as the primary. That done, I began shutting off the recordings one at a time. If Ezra wanted to turn the system back on later, we'd overhaul it.

For now, what happened next was for no one's consumption. Once I cut the feeds, I cut the hardline. Then I paused to stare into the room next to the server boxes.

A wall of tapes. Discs. Other hard recording media.

They were labeled.

I took Benedict as soon as I spotted it. Cavendish was a shelf below. Nothing on Reed. Harper probably scared him. I recognized nearly all of the names on these shelves. If he had this much physical media...

We had another task for Fletcher Reed when this was done. For now, I stored the discs in the inner pocket of my jacket and sealed it up.

Upstairs, I found Liam and Ezra in the kitchen with Lainey and Adam. Our two members of staff were no longer visible. I trusted them to have handled it.

"Milo on the way?" I asked.

"He's meeting us," Adam said, then flicked a look at Ezra. "You can stay. You don't have to watch what comes next."

For all that this had troubled him, Ezra straightened and his jaw set. "No, I do. Because he's used the two of you as leverage for a long time. I want to see him learn his lesson." He took another deep breath. "I need this."

"Then you'll have it," I told him. "Shall we...?"

CHAPTER
NINE

LAINEY

"Stay sharp," Pretty Boy commented. "We have four unaccounted for."

"They're probably with Dad or in his outer office," Ezra said with a sigh. "If he's brought the guards in that close, he's worried about something."

Adam shot him a look but Ezra shook his head once.

"It might be Oksana's family. We didn't bring him into those negotiations and he made them promises."

True. They could extract his failure out on him and leave Ezra alone. We'd paid to make sure that Ezra was free and in the clear. Still...

"It doesn't matter where they are, other than we'll need to deal with them first. Are we ready with a cell jammer?"

"Right here," Liam said in a droll voice. "If you five want to give me and Vaughn a minute, we'll clear the guards out for you."

"You just want to have all the fun," was Bodhi's only comment, but he held up a hand and the rest of us halted.

"Cavendish... you get to have plenty of 'fun,' and I made Hellspawn a promise that I intend to keep."

I had to bite back a smile. Every single one of the Vandals had a name for Em. The funny thing was, every one of those nicknames fit her. I had to admit though, I was rather fond of "Hellspawn," because it went well with Pretty Boy's nickname for me.

Mayhem and Hellspawn.

"True," Bodhi said, then flicked a look to Adam as though deferring, however briefly. "You fine with it?"

"I want the target. Liam can have everything else he wants." All playfulness fled the moment. The murderous sobriety in Adam's eyes darkened them to near purple.

"I like it when you agree with me," Liam said, rolling with it though Pretty Boy frowned. "Let's not make it too much of a habit, Adam. You and I are far better at the snarking."

The attempt at humor didn't land. As much as I wanted to comfort Adam, it wasn't going to happen. We needed this retribution, for Ezra, for us, for our family. The fact Wallace Graham had survived this long was an affront, period.

"Go," Pretty Boy said, confirming his agreement. Vaughn and Liam didn't make any of us wait. They were already on the move. Ezra's father's office was located in the west wing of the home, on the far side from the family's suites and the downstairs entertaining rooms.

It made sense. A lot of men preferred their offices to be a bastion of quiet and very private. So whether they were fucking a mistress on their desks or making a call to have someone killed, no one would interrupt them.

My grandfather's office had always been right in the middle of Der Sonne. He was never apart from my grandmother or me. I would follow his lead. If I had to hide who I was from my family?

No. I refused.

A gentle stroke down the side of my hand pulled me to the present and grounded me. I took a deeper breath. Anger thrummed through my veins, throbbing like an old bruise.

Pretty Boy and Bodhi were both watching me. The corner of my mouth twitched upward. Just enough of a smile to let them know I heard them. I was here. I could see and feel them.

It seemed to satisfy them both and I glanced over to find Adam staring at me. He had his hand on Ezra's shoulder, bracing him. Ezra's head was down, his frown fierce. This was going to be hard on him. When I raised my eyebrows, Adam nodded to Ezra.

He wanted Ezra away from this. So did I, but this wasn't our decision. Ezra *needed* to see this through every bit as much as we did. I swore Adam and I argued for a thousand years in that one stare, then he relented.

No, he didn't have to like it. Just as he never *wanted* me in this fight, but he couldn't keep me from it. The sound of a thump from around the corner made me curious to look, but I waited

In the scant few seconds since Liam and Vaughn moved out, there had been no sounds rushing out to detail their actions. A positive sign, because the guards had no reason to be quiet.

Didn't make the waiting any less of a strain.

Another thud, then a softest drag of a shoe against the rug alerted us to Liam's return a moment before he poked his head around the corner.

"Tag, lady and gentlemen, you're it."

Adam surged ahead and I followed right behind him. Ezra was behind us with Bodhi and Pretty Boy falling in around him. They were very much letting us have this one, only acting to protect us as needed.

The smaller library waiting area outside Wallace's office was quiet. I swept it with a look as I stayed with Adam.

There were four men, somewhat stacked together like cordwood. They'd also been stripped of their weapons. At a glance, I couldn't really tell if they were even still breathing.

Frankly, I didn't care. At the doors to Wallace's office, Adam waved us all to the sides. He didn't bother with subtlety when he pulled out the Desert Eagle and shot the lock. It damn near blew off the handle. The gun's report was loud in the close quarters.

Then he hit the door with his foot, kicking it open. Pretty Boy was right there, shoving the second door wide and they were both pointing guns at Wallace Graham, sitting behind his desk, an open bottle of Scotch on his desk and a half-full rocks glass in his hand.

The disheveled look didn't suit him. His eyes were harder, colder, and his skin far more ashen than I was used to seeing it. There were also deep shadows beneath his eyes.

"What's the problem, Wallace?" I asked as I walked in with Bodhi and Ezra. "You look a little troubled."

Rather than answer me, Wallace focused on Ezra and his smile turned cruel. Before I could say a word, Adam knocked the drink out of Wallace's hand and sent the glass tumbler flying. It shattered and when he would have protested, Adam put the Desert Eagle right up to his forehead.

There would be no head if he fired at this distance.

I struggled to think of why I cared beyond the fact it would be too swift of an end for him.

"Still hiding behind Reed," Wallace said, his tone dismissive. "Pathetic, Ezra. As always." There was no shock in his eyes, no fear. In fact, there was very little reaction at all. Then he focused on Adam. "Maybe you wouldn't be so eager to protect my weak son if you knew how he felt about you."

"Save it," Adam said. "I've known everything I ever needed to know about Ezra from the day he lied to my father's face and said he'd broken into the bar instead of me."

Wallace snorted. The corners of his mouth turned down. "How unfortunate that you're as damaged as your mother—"

He didn't get to finish the thought. Instead, Adam used the broad side of the gun to pistol whip him right out of the chair. It sent the older man sprawling. Rather than follow with his gun, Adam stripped off his jacket, holstered the Desert Eagle, then stripped the gun holster as well.

Pretty Boy accepted the weapon like they did this every day. Taking his time to roll up his sleeves, Adam circled the desk. Wallace was still on the floor, blood staining his lip and cheek crimson. More dripping from his nose.

"You can't treat me like this," he said around his rapidly swelling lip. "Do you not remember—"

Adam helped him to his feet, dragging Wallace upward before he slammed his fist into his face and sent him staggering.

"I know exactly who you are, Wallace Graham. I know how you abuse your son. Collude with your brother. Kill innocents to make a point. Make deals with the devil to sell your own child..."

Adam dragged Wallace up again, then delivered three rapid blows—two to his stomach and the third to a kidney before the man went down again.

"Maybe you need to remember who the fuck *I* am. My name is Adam Reed and Ezra is my best fucking friend and you have hurt him repeatedly for the emptiest of reasons..."

"Bullshit," Wallace snapped back, pushing himself up this time. Blood flecked his spittle as he shot Adam a venomous look. "Power is never an empty reason. I was trying to make him stronger. Losing cause that it was... if he'd been a man, he never would have bent over for those boys."

"Fuck you, Dad," Ezra said. "You don't know shit."

"I know you'll get on your knees," Wallace wavered on his feet and he swayed toward Ezra, but I stepped between them. It brought those hate-filled eyes in my direction. "Oh look, it's the bastard of Reed's little slut. How does it feel to be the prime piece of ass that everyone wants for her money? I bet my son would bend over for you too."

I lifted my brows. "You seem to be badly misinformed," I said and he put a hand out like he was going to shove me away. He never touched me, I struck with the open palm of my hand right to his nose and he reeled backwards, yowling.

"You little bitch."

Rather than say another word, Adam was just on him in a hail of vicious jabs and punches. Yet with every blow he rained down, he wasn't delivering the full force. He was making it hurt.

It wasn't long before Graham's whole face was a mess of bloody contusions, snot, tears, and swelling. One of his eyes was closed fully, but Adam let up when Graham was on his knees.

The harshness of the man's breathing betrayed the cracked ribs. Those hurt like a bitch. He tilted his head back, trying to glare at all of us. Not that he seemed to manage much.

"You want the little freak," Graham said. "Have him. Good riddance."

"I can't believe I was ever afraid of you," Ezra said slowly and Adam backed off another step from Graham. The blood spattering his shirt had darkened his gray-black shirt to something closer to midnight. "You terrified me. With your threats and your blows... all the times you whipped me. You weren't doing that to make me a man."

"Stop whining at me," Wallace said, spit flying from his lips. "You were weak as a boy and your mother coddled you. I tried to fix that and you would rather bend over and serve others. Running around after a child, pining for another man..."

"So the fuck what?" Ezra demanded. "I did every nasty job you ever asked of me. I got dirt on people. I went to work for your *brother*, a man you didn't even acknowledge and you have to know what he asked of me."

That was when Graham started laughing. It was a sick, wet sound with a bit of a wheeze on the end. "You really don't get it, if you were a real man, you would have dealt with Julius before he became an issue. As it was, you couldn't even figure out *who* he was until he revealed himself. Nothing you did moved you up, but you backed every play Reed made. His climb wasn't yours and then that mutt O'Connell over there came along and he climbed right alongside them. Stupid... weak... useless..."

Ezra shook his head. "That's all it is to you... a power play."

"That's *life*."

"No," I said, shaking my head. "That's not life. That's cruelty. You didn't deserve Ezra and we don't need you anymore, Mr. Graham. But there is something you should know..."

"What's that?" He sneered at me and I smiled.

"Ezra doesn't want your company or your legacy. So I'm going to take it apart, piece by piece, deconstructing everything you ever did and destroying it down to the last nut, bolt, and screw. Then we'll keep the pieces we want and sell off the rest."

"You wouldn't *dare*..."

"Of course, I would. There isn't anything I won't do for Ezra. Because he deserves so much more than the yoke of your so-called miserable legacy. You're going to be in the dirt while we celebrate life."

I really wanted him to try to strike me. Honestly, I would have settled for him to spit. But at this point, I was just done.

"Is there anything else you need from him, Ezra?"

"No," he answered without hesitation. "I haven't needed anything from him ever. I just didn't know it until now..."

I flicked my wrist and slid the hidden knife into my hand. Graham opened his mouth to spew more hate and I slit his throat. I stepped to the side so the severing of the carotid and jugular didn't spray me with blood.

It would make a mess though. The rug was definitely ruined.

Frankly, the place needed to be redecorated as it was.

"Holy shit," Liam said into the silence and I glanced over my shoulder to find all of them watching me with a bit of shock, though Bodhi wore the proudest smile.

Ignoring the rest for a moment, I waited for Ezra to look at me. "We meant it when we said no one is allowed to hurt you anymore."

"I didn't think you'd be the one who..." Ezra blinked slowly, then shook his head. "Kotyonok..."

"I know, but Adam got to beat him up. I just got to shut his hateful mouth forever." I rather liked that.

"That was pretty hot, Mayhem." Pretty Boy's compliment made me glow.

"It was impressive, too. You managed to avoid most of the blood." Adam grinned.

"That just leaves us deciding what we want to do with the rest of this place," Bodhi said. "That and body disposal..."

"Did you mean it," Ezra asked, still focusing on me. "You'll destroy it all?"

"Everything," I promised him. "But only if that's what you want. We can claim it and clean it up and make it yours. He'll never know."

I wanted him to die thinking it was all going to be gone.

Forever.

Ezra scrubbed a hand over his face as he looked from me to Adam and then back. Finally, he pivoted to Bodhi. "Do you know how to burn this place to the ground?"

CHAPTER
TEN

MILO

Arson took a while to make sure it didn't look like arson. I knew enough about setting fires to know I didn't know enough about making this work. Fortunately, Bodhi—a man of many talents—was not so similarly limited in scope.

"We don't have to make it look like it wasn't arson," he said. "In fact, we should *make* it look like someone set it deliberately."

"To distract," Mayhem said after a moment. "Focus everyone's attention on Wallace's enemies."

"Well they won't be lacking in that department," Adam said, raking a hand through his hair. His fists were bruised. They weren't broken open and bloody, but we'd need to make sure nothing of Wallace was left to match damage to his hands. "We need to be careful of one thing, however..."

"The coincidence of Harper dying in a plane crash and Dad dying in a blaze of glory at home?" Ezra's tone held the bitterest edge. Then who could blame him? While he may not have cornered the market on terrible fathers, he'd definitely suffered thanks to his.

For all that King had attempted to destroy me, I'd at least been spared his company most of the time. The fact that I'd *had* to endure seeing him day in and day out recently only reinforced my opinion that I didn't *need* or *want* Julius King or Jeff Hardigan or whatever he wanted to call himself in my life.

"So we make sure we make it look like what it is... an execution and cleaning up the mess." Sometimes, the best lies were the truth. "I don't care if they link it to Harper. Maybe they take a second look at the crash, but we keep everything else separate. Graham has enough enemies and the fact he just failed to honor an agreement with the Russians will only add to the suspect pool."

Expression taut, Ezra stared into the middle distance. "We need to make sure that while the authorities might get suspicious nothing links them back to Oksana's family."

"Agreed," Mayhem said. "We've already snipped off that thread, let's keep it that way."

"Electrical overload," I suggested and Bodhi nodded.

"It won't take out the temperature-controlled rooms downstairs, but that makes it look all the more authentic. They are on a separate system. Good thing we didn't kill all the guards yet. Smoke inhalation will also sell it."

Mayhem's expression shifted briefly at the mention of the guards that had survived so far. Only a handful would be allowed, the ones that could be absolutely trusted. None of the rest.

As much as straight up murder wasn't my favorite activity, if left alive they would be a threat to Mayhem. Not *could* but would. Men who were willing to work for someone like Wallace Graham and get dirty with him, would no doubt try to capitalize on their survival.

No, I didn't have to like murder, or in this case, preemptive defense, to agree to it immediately, I would not allow anything to come back at Mayhem. Not from the past.

We were over the past striking at her. My past. Adam's. Ezra's. Bodhi's—though I wasn't sure if anything from Bodhi's past survived long enough to even attempt a hit at her.

It didn't matter. We would take care of this.

"It'll take a minute to set up." Though I planned to defer to Bodhi, I considered everything we would need to pull this off. This wasn't my area of expertise. We would be better off if Kel were here. If I needed to get him on the phone so I could pick his mechanic's brain, I would.

"Agreed," Bodhi said and then he focused on Mayhem. I didn't even have to ask what he was thinking.

"I'll be fine," she said, eyeing both him and then me. "Tell me what I can do."

Go somewhere safe was at the top of my list. That said, I might not want her involved, but I liked the idea of her being out of reach a lot less.

Bodhi didn't appear to disagree, because he merely nodded before he glanced at Ezra and Adam. "Ezra, if there are any items you want specifically, go get them now. Milo, back him, Adam, you're with me and Lainey."

Once again splitting those three up. I got it. Ezra's expression tightened, but Ezra was a huge blindspot for Mayhem and Adam both. Bodhi would protect them, I would look after Ezra. When we got this shit wrapped up, they could work out the rest of their issues.

"Meet you in the main hall in ten." I was already giving Ezra a nudge toward the stairs. He frowned, but Mayhem just winked.

"The faster you go, the faster we get out of here. Besides, I'm learning all kinds of new things today."

A faint laugh with an underlining note of hysteria bubbled out of Ezra. "Kotyonok, I love you."

She grinned, her eyes lighting up. "Excellent. It means you are not remotely put off by my crazy."

I snorted even as Ezra shook his head, still chuckling.

"Let's go, Romeo," I said, giving Ezra another nudge. Mayhem caught my gaze and I shooed her away with a wink. "I got him, Mayhem. You keep those two in line."

"Done," she agreed almost too easily, but the relief in her voice said it was more for Ezra than anything else. They were so damn worried about him.

Time to work on the new cousin.

Cousin. That was still a strange thought.

Ezra picked up speed once we were away from Mayhem and I jogged up the steps behind him. The house was enormous. From the interior courtyard to the long marbled halls with their colonnade lined mezzanine that looked down into the courtyard and other areas of the downstairs.

It was strange, frankly, everything about the place felt foreign and old world. Yet, it was also gaudy in their choice of gold fixtures and the artwork. An obscene temple to wealth.

"You know," Ezra said as he pushed open a pair of doors into a suite that looked as clinically sterile as a place with overly dramatic decorations could look. It definitely didn't offer up anything of his personality. "I should have asked you about what you wanted to do."

"What I wanted to do about what?" I scanned the room as I moved from door to door. I had a gun in hand automatically, clearing the room just made sense. We had swept the place, but we'd also just been distracted with Graham senior.

"The house... Harrows Park," Ezra said as he pulled a bag

out of the closet and then headed into his bedroom. Like the sitting room portion of his suite, there weren't a lot of personal items in here... at least not displayed.

He nudged something with his foot at the base of the bed and a panel slid open and a drawer came out. There were photos in there, a small bundle of notes, and a few other items.

Keepsakes. Mementos with emotional ties. Secreted away and not displayed.

"Better to not leave them where Dad or one of his spies could find them. I have a handful of spots. I moved it periodically, just safer for everyone that way." The last sentence ended on a sigh. "Not that it did much good in the end, I suppose."

I shrugged. "I get it. Growing up in the group home, we were careful about who we shared what precious few items we had and we guarded each other's with prejudice."

Ezra frowned as he lifted out the small packet of letters. No, not letters at least not all of them. Some were postcards. "I keep forgetting you grew up like that. I guess all of you did, except for Em."

"She would have," I admitted. "But when the Sharpes came looking, I thought their money and their affluence meant she wouldn't want for anything."

"I can't..." He frowned, the confusion evident in the way his brow tightened. "I can't picture them as offering any kind of comfort."

Shrugging, I holstered the gun and moved to stand guard at the door that looked out into the sitting room. "When you have nothing, you don't see the problem with having so much. You only see the benefits. I knew what it was like to go to bed hungry. I never wanted that for Ivy. Wealth—it seemed to offer a lot of those benefits with very little downside. Clearly, if you had money, you knew how to keep it."

"You don't really associate pretty perfumed people with the darkness all that glitz and glamor can hide." Not a question.

"Nope. My world was pretty basic. Good people. Bad people. Haves. Have nots. I've been on the far side of nothing for a long time. I value people. I value their time. I value their commitments and their loyalty. Those are worth a hell of a lot more than money." Like Mayhem. She was phenomenal all by herself. Her inheritance didn't interest me in the slightest beyond making sure no one bothered her.

"You're a poet, Milo," Ezra said as he stared down at some rock he'd pulled out of the drawer. "You look like a thug with all your tats, and like you belong with the rest of us thanks to that angelic face... but you're a poet. We would not have liked each other when we were younger."

"We didn't," I pointed out. "You and Adam were very intent on kicking my ass that first time we met."

His frown passed with a hint of fresh laughter. "Yeah, that didn't work out so well for us."

"Live and learn. Live and learn. I don't think you're such an ass now. I think you can be. I think you're a lot more than your money and your position in society—because neither of those things makes you happy."

The dark look on his face redoubled. "I don't know who I am without those things. I've spent my whole life disappointing my father and worrying my mother. Nothing I did ever seemed to be enough." He shook his head, closing his fingers around the stone before looking at me.

"Fuck 'em," I said without missing a beat. "Shitty parents don't get the right to judge us. They had their opportunity. They failed. Not you." I shrugged. "Julius King is a walking, talking, piece of shit that thinks he hung the damn moon when all I will ever see is the man who walked out on my mother and baby sister. A man who wanted to punish me because I chose them over him. I don't give a rat's ass what he thinks about me."

"I wish it was that easy," Ezra admitted. "I wish...fuck, I don't know what I wish any more."

"Yeah you do, you're just afraid to look at the good stuff and see that it is good. You're braced for it to go bad. You're waiting for Mayhem and Adam to cut you loose. Or for me and Bodhi to kick you to the curb because you screw up. You're convinced you're going to—and I don't disagree. You'll fuck up."

Shock stamped its way across his face.

"But here's the thing, *cousin*," I said, emphasizing that last word and punching it up. "Real family? They don't walk away because you fuck up. They don't let you chase them away. They might kick your ass, and they will definitely slap you upside the head if you take too long to get your head out of your own ass, but they don't abandon you."

I checked the time. It seemed a century and yet it hadn't been more than seven minutes since we came upstairs.

"You mean that," Ezra said, almost bewildered.

"I do. I told you once, I'll never let you hurt Mayhem. You've treated her badly, but you've also made up for it. You chose to suffer rather than let her get hurt. That matters. But you've also been hurt and it scared her. Scared Adam. That means you get to live with everyone being a little overprotective for a while."

"How long's a while?" He pocketed the rock then emptied the last few items from that drawer into his bag before he went to the dresser and popped out another secret hidey hole.

"Ten or fifteen years, I would imagine." The droll delivery

pulled a real laugh from him. "Anyway, what were you saying earlier about asking me?" I hadn't forgotten.

"The house—Harrows Park. Technically, it should be part yours and Em's too. I mean, if my grandfather had ever claimed King beyond the private fund he gave him."

Wait... "Private fund?"

"Fuck, I knew I'd forgotten to tell you. I found out about it in some of Dad's old papers. Grandfather paid off King's mother, she was his mistress for years but he refused to acknowledge him. Just paid for everything." He zipped up the bag and slung it over his shoulder. "After he died, he left a codicil in his will that said if King were ever to sue for his name, he would lose everything. Every dime. Pretty ruthless. But King and Dad met at some point and became... friends I guess.

"At least until some other guy in the old Bay Ridge Royals chased King off. He was pretty vicious about it. So then King disappeared for a few years...and I guess he came back at the right time, Dad needed the help. King could do things he couldn't and well... you know how it goes."

Yeah, I did.

"Anyway, the house, the land—all of it. It should right-fully be half yours, half Em's..." He looked around the room. "There's actually some nice stuff, I suppose. The best art pieces are down in the vaults below, so not too worried about losing them and Dad's taste was pretty shitty."

"I really don't care about the house. I don't need some giant ass palace or pseudo mausoleum." Not that I'd tell Adam that, but the Reed place felt more like a crypt than a mansion. Lainey's grandfather's place had lots of personality but I was pretty sure that was Lainey and Leopold.

"You really don't care," Ezra said, amazement creeping into his voice.

"Nope," I said. "I'll earn my keep and do my work. This place? It's more a house of horrors for you. So burn it down, sell it, demolish it—and build something new in its place. But do what you need to do to heal."

"You do cousin real well," Ezra said after a minute. "Nicky says I suck at it, but I'm gonna get better."

"You're fine," I said. "Now let's go, we're going to be late and make Mayhem worry."

"She wants to know how to burn a house down and get rid of a corpse," Ezra actually chuckled at the end of that sentence. "Is that as attractive to you as it is to me? Or am I just warped?"

"Oh, you're warped," I assured him. "But it's really fucking attractive too."

Some of the weight seemed to leave him as we walked out of the bedroom and then the suite. He was abandoning a childhood that had abandoned him a long time before.

Frankly, it was a damn good thing. Burning this shit down felt right.

CHAPTER
ELEVEN

LAINEY

The fire they set at Harrows Park had been *incredible*. The smoke was visible for miles around. The storm of flames swept through the marbled halls consuming everything in its path...

The unfortunate fate of some of the staff as well as the "master" of the house would take a few hours to be discovered. We didn't hide from the fire department and the police when they arrived—though it took them far more time than I expected to get there.

Maybe they weren't fans of Wallace either. Everything stank of smoke. It was in my hair and my clothes. It coated everything. The heat from the fire damaged the glass, scorched the stone, and there was a collapse from farther inside.

The crews stopped trying to save the house and focused on containment. Bodhi had wrapped his coat around me and I leaned into Milo as we all stood there, watching it burn.

I suppose we could have left earlier, yet none of us had

made the move to leave. Ezra stared at the mansion as it burned. Harrows Park, even if any of the structure was left, would need to be demolished afterwards.

There was no saving the main building from the flames consuming it. The greed with which the fire acted, mirrored the home's former master. It had become a funerary pyre of sorts. For Ezra, we could stand here and be witnesses.

Eventually, Ezra turned away and Adam slung an arm over his shoulders. It was time. Liam and Vaughn had left earlier after the body disposal conversation. If we really needed assistance with the cleanup, we could call Fletcher and Vienna. Adam's cousin knew a lot of skilled people.

As it was, Bodhi spoke to the authorities. I had no idea what he said, but they accepted his answers and let us leave. The drive back to the city would have been a long one, only we weren't going to the city.

We went to Der Sonne where Grandfather was already striding out of the front door before the car even stopped moving. Milo exited first, then helped me out of the backseat. I barely got to my feet and Grandfather hugged me so tightly I wanted to cry.

"I saw the smoke," he said, his gruff tone a balm and a chastisement in one. He smelled of familiar cologne, and a pipe tobacco he favored when he thought no one paid attention. "Now I smell it all over you and you didn't answer your phone."

He pulled back, his grip on my biceps firm but hardly painful. The searching look in his eyes was far more of a rebuke than him yelling. I'd scared him.

"I'm sorry, Grandfather. There was a lot going on and I didn't realize my phone was buzzing." I wouldn't make excuses. "I shouldn't have worried you that way."

One by one, Adam, Ezra, and Bodhi exited the car. We

were a sight, I was sure. Smudged from the smoke, and more than a little disheveled. Grandfather gave us all a once over.

"Inside," he said firmly. "We'll have coffee and something to eat. You need to get cleaned up." When he touched my cheek with a weathered hand, I leaned into the contact.

He was mourning my mother in addition to the grief he felt about my grandmother every day. Then I scared him. "I am sorry... I promise you, I was safe. The guys would never let anything happen to me."

Without a word, Grandfather pressed his lips to my forehead and held the kiss there. "Forgiven, darling girl. Absolutely forgiven. I am just relieved to see you. Go on up, I'll sort your gentlemen out with the guest rooms."

I bit my lip, but rather than argue, I surrendered without even a battle. "Of course," I murmured, then kissed his cheek. "I'll meet everyone back downstairs?" It was as much a question for the guys as it was for Grandfather.

The faintly bemused look on Bodhi's face suggested he was more than fine with the plan. Though, I doubted any of them would agree or disagree aloud right now.

"Behave," I said gently, including Grandfather in the admonishment.

"Go on, Mayhem," Milo told me with a gentle smile. "We'll be fine."

It was cold out here and the sunny skies were just utterly at odds with the bleakness of everything around us. I went upstairs directly, the stink of smoke seemed to grow stronger the farther away from the others I traveled.

The nice thing about my room here was I had everything I needed, including fresh clothing, toiletries—everything. It took me very little time to strip out of the clothes I'd worn, the unrelieved black appropriate for mourning and blood.

Still, I scanned each piece before I stuffed them into a

laundry bag. I doubted I would be laundering any of this, but I also stowed my boots in as well. Once I closed the bag, I hung it on the back of the bathroom door then climbed into the shower.

The hot water hit every muscle with a solid pounding of heat and force. My back and neck were a dark mess of knots. Even turning my face upward, into the spray itself only seemed to magnify the tension headache crawling over my scalp.

When the door to the shower opened, it was hardly unexpected. Nor were the heavy male hands settling on my hips or the thick cock pressed against my ass as my companion pulled me to him.

"Adam," I said on a sigh and he pressed a kiss to my shoulder before pulling me around to face him. With his hand in my wet hair, he tugged my head back and then his mouth was on mine.

Hints of soot, smoke, and sulfur added fire to the taste of him on my tongue. I wrapped my arms around his neck even as he cupped my ass and lifted me. When I glided a hand down to grip his cock, he groaned against my lips.

Not once did he let me up for air. No, he savaged my mouth with swift, parrying strokes of his tongue. He demanded all of my attention and the moment I lined him up, he thrust inside of me.

His thickness threatened to split me apart as I struggled to accommodate the stretch. I had enough slickness that the ache he created hurt in the best way.

My scalp lit up at his pull. The pleasure collided with the shock of cold as he pressed me against the tiles of the wall. The shower splashed against our shoulders and cheeks. It added slickness everywhere as he powered into me.

There was no room for thought or even breath between

us. The scrape of his teeth, the pinch of his fingers on my ass, the grind of his hips to mine and the first wave of an orgasm detonated not because of his touch but the low growl of sound vibrating out of him.

Adam was all fierce touches, from where he dug his fingers into my flesh to pulling my hair. There was no gentleness in the fierce strokes as he thrust into me like he was determined to bury himself as deep as he could get. The wall kept me up as I fought to take him deeper, touch him more.

Need collided with desire and desperation—I came as he ground his pelvis hard against mine. The tease on my clit was almost unbearable. That and the fact that he lifted me higher and every stroke of his cock struck the right spot to make me see stars.

No scream left me though because his kisses swallowed every potential sound I could have made. Instead, I clung to him, desperate to ride the feeling as he thrust over and over.

"I'm not going to last," he whispered against my lips, punctuating every thrust. "But we're taking a night and I'm going to make you scream every way I can..."

The fluttering of my inner muscles gave away to a fierce clamp as I locked down on him. His groan teased me, sending a caress all the way to my soul. Then he came, his hips stuttering and filling me with his hot release.

I mouthed kisses against his shoulder as he braced one arm on the wall. We clung there, breath coming in short, fierce pants. I should slide down, but I didn't want to let him go. He didn't seem to be in any great hurry to leave either.

Eventually, I leaned back against the wall. Boneless didn't begin to cover it at the moment. He was softening, but still hard enough to stay inside me. I liked that feeling. The connection, the weight of him leaning into me.

The fact Adam *would* lean on me at all.

He raised one bruised hand to cup my cheek. "Thank you," he whispered.

"You're welcome." I almost laughed because I wasn't entirely certain what he was thanking me for. "Though I should probably be thanking you. That was definitely a pick me up."

"Same," he whispered, then brushed his lips to mine. "I was thanking you for killing Wallace."

Head canted, I studied him. The darkness that inhabited his eyes had faded though they were more purple than ever. "Ezra needed him gone." That was the truth. "I needed to know he could *never* hurt him again. I didn't touch Harper..." Nor had Adam. "Because you were the important one to me then. You needed me more than I needed that."

"Elaine Benedict..." I almost didn't mind the use of my full name. "You are—the best woman I've ever known. One of the best people. I really am not good enough to polish your shoes, but understand, I'm never letting you go. I tried for years to cut you loose..."

"I never wanted that," I whispered and his expression gentled. "Never. I've only ever wanted to love you and be loved by you." It was my turn to cradle his face. "Now we know Wallace can't hurt Ezra, and you aren't the one who killed him."

His frown was swift...

"Shh," I murmured, stifling his argument. "You and Ezra are discovering so much right now, having death on your hands would only complicate it."

"But not you?" The challenge made me grin.

"Of course not, I'm his kotyonok, he adores me."

The fact his eyes flashed with jealousy briefly before they turned full of affection amused me. "You are very lovable."

I didn't snort, but I did trace my fingers against his cheek.

"It took us time to find that trust, Adam. It took a lot of pain —we've all hurt each other. The big ones, the rejections, we understand. They were done in the name of protecting each other."

It didn't mean they didn't leave their own scars. Those marks had been gouged deep in some cases. Adam had done his own share of rejection and control. Eventually, I'd lashed out at both of them. We were all guilty of it to some degree or other.

"But it's the little wounds, the little cuts, and lies that we tell each other that have been allowed to get infected. Until we clear all of them out, until we stop trying to shield ourselves from what *might* happen, we're never going to have what *can* happen."

"What can happen—you with all four of us, building a life?" He frowned for a moment. "Me and Ezra figuring out our part. Can we have that, Lainey? All five of us? Milo's probably got the easiest of it. He doesn't have a dynasty or inheritance to worry about."

I shrugged. "I want it enough to make it happen. If that means we sacrifice, then I'm willing. If it means we fight, then I will take on the rest of the damn world. I love you. I love *all* of you."

No one was taking that from us.

"To hell with the inheritance and the legacies. This is *our* time. *We* are going to be the ones who make the rules and set the tones. If that means I have all four of you and you and Ezra have each other, then that's what it means. No one is going to stop us. Besides...the five of us together are stronger than any other family. What chance do they have?"

"Not a damn one," Adam murmured. "Not against you."

"Us," I reminded him.

"Oh, don't you worry. I know just how to be an enforcer, so do the others. Knights and Bishops for our queen."

Heat scorched my face at the endearment. "Not yet..."

"Queen takes King, that's the match."

"No," I said, shaking my head. "That's a move on the board to get rid of him. The match is getting our sister back and bringing her home."

His lashes dipped as he closed his eyes and then he held me closer. A long moment of just being, then he eased me to my own feet.

"Stay," I told him when he would have slipped out. "You need to shower as much as I do...and I like having you here."

"Your grandfather is going to have words."

I chuckled. "Probably. Is that going to scare you off?"

"Not even a little," he promised. "I'll stand there and take it on the chin from Leopold because at the end of the day, we both love you far more than any old feud that may have existed between him and my father."

"He'll come around," I said. "I can be quite persuasive when I really want something."

"No," Adam mocked me gently. "Really? I would never have guessed."

I elbowed him lightly before I reached for the shampoo. Showering with Adam relaxed another jagged little part of me that had been disconnected. This was natural and normal now.

Being together was *how* it should be and after so many years of being pushed away, I craved these little moments.

"Adam?"

"Hmm."

"I love you."

He paused to glance down at me, the shower spray leaving droplets on his face. The tenderness in his eyes would have made his feelings clear even if he'd never admitted them before.

"I'm damn lucky you do," he said, one corner of his mouth kicking up before he dropped a kiss on my lips.

"Yes you are," I teased, bumping his hip with mine. "Don't you forget it."

"Oh," he promised in between nibbling kisses. "I won't."

CHAPTER
TWELVE

EZRA

D ad was dead. Not playing dead. Actually dead. All the times I'd ever imagined it, I'd *relished* the idea. Sometimes, I even prayed for it. The fact it was the only thing I prayed for probably wasn't okay with God, but like whatever.

Wallace Graham, my tormentor, the man who hated me more than he ever loved me, and spent most of my life making me endure pain, was dead.

Good. Fucking. Riddance.

The pleasure I thought I would take in his demise, however, was curiously absent. Relief, sure, that was present, but no real joy. The only thing filling me at the moment was an emptiness that stretched out into the void.

While I might never miss him, I wasn't entirely sure I'd be able to dismiss him mentally the way I needed.

"Gentlemen," Leopold said in that firm voice of his after Lainey disappeared upstairs. "There are showers out in the pool house that you can use. Young Mr. Graham there is well aware of the location." Clearly, we were *not* invited to follow Lainey up.

Adam didn't say a word, just pivoted on a heel and strode out. Leopold's glare followed him. The dislike the old man had for him needed to go.

"Of course," I said, then nodded to Milo and Bodhi. "You guys can take the first showers. I'll go last." Hopefully, Adam was already getting cleaned up. The stench of smoke seemed infused into my skin.

"Go ahead," Milo said to Bodhi. "I'll wait for Ezra."

Wait for...

"I'm good right here," Bodhi responded before he faced Leopold as well. "You wanted to have a discussion, sir?"

Sir.

Holy shit. Bodhi deferred to almost *no one*. I said almost because I'd seen him with his step-great-grandmother once. Her, he treated with utter consideration and courtesy. Lainey and Em were the only other two I'd seen him offer the same kind of gentle respect.

Now Leopold Benedict fell into that category.

Funnily enough, the old man just gave Bodhi a firm look. "Don't try to charm your way out of this one, Phillip. I'm well aware of your interest in my grand-daughter as I am of this reprobate—" Oh look, I had a place in the list. "And *Reed*." Reprobate actually ranked higher than Reed.

"Leopold," Milo began, but the old man cut him off with a slice of his hand through the air.

"Milo, my boy, recognizing the competition means identi-fying their weaknesses, flaws, and points of leverage. I don't doubt for a second they wouldn't take her away from you given the first opportunity."

I frowned.

"I'm telling you all right now, you will not fight over her like some choice cut of prime beef."

Every single word in that sentence was an insult.

"She's chosen Milo here and I've given my approval. The rest of you boys need to accept that." Leopold nodded firmly. "That goes for Reed as well. His family has done enough to mine. I will not let him hurt her."

"Mr. Benedict," I said, inserting myself into the quiet hanging off that last sentence. "Adam loves Lainey without reservation. He's not his father. He's a thousand times better than him."

Leopold fixed me with a look. One I refused to shrink from.

"As much as I hate to admit it, Bodhi is a damn good man. Odd at times. More than a little intimidating. He's also handed me my ass more times than I care to confess, but—he would kill for Lainey. If anyone stands a chance of cutting off a threat before it even darkens her doorstep, it would be him."

Fuck that was so weird offering up the defense for Bodhi, almost like a damn endorsement.

"Is that so?" Leopold glared at me. "I take it you don't approve of my choice in Hardigan then?"

"I don't care about your choice," I admitted, not shying away from that heated look. Fuck, I'd stared my own father down. Leopold was intimidating as hell, but this was bullshit. Hate Harper Reed all you wanted but leave Adam out of it. He was a far better man than I would ever be. "Milo's fine. In fact, he's better than fine. But you don't care about my opinion, so why should I care that you approve of him over everyone else?"

Eyes narrowing, Leopold studied me. "No defense for yourself?"

"You don't like me because I'm Adam's friend." Before, I

wouldn't have cared to figure out why he didn't like me. The old man was really important to my kotyonok though, so it was better for me to win him over now rather than put her through the need to defend me. "You also didn't care for my drinking or carousing over the years. That's on me. If I need to earn your respect, then I'll work on it."

Rather than respond to me, he shifted his gaze to Bodhi and Milo. "Nothing to say?"

"I think he's doing fine, sir. He's also correct. None of us are our parents. Not me. Not Milo. Not Adam. Not Ezra. The same can be said for Lainey... wouldn't you agree?"

Goddamn, I envied Bodhi's directness.

Rather than being put off by it, Leopold met him stare for stare. "One could argue that Melissa was never her parent."

"One could," Bodhi agreed with him. "Yet, you raised both Melissa and Lainey, sir. So, I think at least fifty percent of the problem *and* the accolades could be attributed to you."

While Milo didn't wince outwardly, his expression took on a firm neutrality. It was a mask. One he did really well. It kept his opinions and thoughts to himself.

"Do you think couching insults in speculation will gain you something?" Leopold countered with an attack of his own.

"An insult, sir?" Bodhi made the inquiry sound deeply puzzling to him. "I didn't think we were insulting at all. No more than you were in your observations. Is this not talking as men do? Putting all our cards on the table?"

"All your cards are not on the table," Leopold pounced on that fact.

"Are yours?" Bodhi dared him.

The silence stretched out almost painfully. Adam's absence had also grown a little more noticeable. I had to wonder if *Leopold* guessed what I suspected. Adam needed

Lainey at the moment. We all needed her, but sometimes we needed her more than the others at different moments.

"I've made my feelings clear," the old man said decisively. "No one will be using my granddaughter for her inheritance or her reach."

"No sir," I said, in absolute agreement. "No one will. We would never allow it."

"While I appreciate your confidence in me, sir," Milo added, his respect clear despite the hardness of his tone. "My father is Julius King. If you disapprove of Adam because of his father or Ezra for his, you can't possibly like me because mine is one of the worst people I've ever met. He's despicable on every level. He doesn't deserve to breathe the same air as Mayhem or anyone else for that matter. He's a bottom feeder in a ten thousand dollar suit."

"They aren't that expensive," Bodhi said. "He uses cheap tailors and moderately priced cloth to make himself look more important than he is."

"Five thousand dollars then?" Milo checked with him.

"Give or take." Bodhi nodded. "Doesn't matter, the clothing can't disguise the man inside."

"Precisely my point." The two shared a long look of understanding. Bodhi and Milo seemed to get each other.

Resentment reared its head as they nodded to each other then faced Leopold Benedict with the exact same expression. They barely knew each other, but they were already tight. Or as tight as two guarded people could be.

A part of me protested. Milo was *my* cousin. The two of us should be on this same page. Yet he was tight with so many people who weren't me.

And whose fault is that? The nasty little voice crept out to taunt me. *You've been an asshole to him from day one.*

Only I hadn't known he was my cousin then. Em was a

cousin too, but I'd never been a raging dick to her. Fuck, I was such a jackass.

"You can't judge them by their parents rather than the content of their character if you won't judge me on mine. Besides, Ezra and I are cousins, so you could say we were cut from the same bolt of cloth. Doesn't mean we're as bad as the layers that came before."

Surprise jolted me. *We're cousins*. Milo made it sound so simple. Maybe it was, but at the same time...

"Since when are you cousins?" Lainey's grandfather pinned me with a look like it was my fault and I shrugged.

"My grandfather apparently had a woman on the side. Her son turned out to be Julius King. Definitely not my fault. You wanna blame something, blame your own contemporary." Okay, maybe that came out snottier than I meant it to, but goddammit, I was trying to keep my assholish side under control.

It didn't help that disapproval radiated off of Leopold Benedict.

Wait...

It didn't matter.

"Actually, you know what, I'm going to let you three talk and go shower." I needed the break, but I met Leopold's gaze this time without flinching. "With all due respect, *sir*, whether you approve or not is moot. Lainey has always had teeth and claws, she will do as she damn well pleases and I'm not going anywhere until the day she tells me to get the hell out."

Even then, I wouldn't go far.

"I'll see you guys in a bit." I made it exactly two steps before Leopold cleared his throat.

Not turning, I stopped and spared him a glance over my shoulder. As volatile as my emotions were at the moment,

Leopold was still Lainey's grandfather. For her, I could tolerate his ferociousness.

"Yes, sir?"

For a long moment, the old man said nothing. Finally, he looked from Bodhi to Milo then finally to me again. When he focused on me so firmly, I pivoted to face him. Probably rude not to at this point.

"When the time comes for her to decide between you, will you respect her decision even if you're not the one she chose?"

I opened my mouth, then snapped it closed without commenting. Biting my tongue wasn't so painful after all if I gave it any thought.

"Absolutely," Bodhi informed him.

"Will you?" Milo asked.

Holy shit. Better him than me, but at the same time, I kept my attention on Leopold. What would he think of that challenge?

The older man let out a long sigh and his age seemed to just suddenly be there. Hard to not notice what a force of nature the man was. My father had always done his best to never cross him.

Frankly, I'd never met a person who was eager to draw Leopold Benedict's attention or ire. Except maybe us...

But Lainey was worth it.

So, if the old man hated me. I'd accept it. It was the least I could do.

"I don't have to like Lainey's choices to respect them," Leopold admitted finally. "I want her to be happy. She deserves it. Her mother was not good to her. We did every-thing we could. But I won't allow anyone to treat her badly."

"Then I think all of us are on the same page," I said, not letting the surprise rippling over the older man's face faze me. "Because we won't allow anyone to do that either."

When Leopold's gaze locked with mine, I didn't hide my meaning. Her grandfather wielded tremendous influence with Lainey. I didn't doubt my kotyonok's will. She would do as she damn well pleased, she always had even when it put her in danger.

But any kind of fight or falling out with Leopold would hurt her. That I didn't want.

Ever.

"Very well," Leopold said with a slow nod. "Shower, I'll have clothes sent out for you and you can get those laundered. Then we'll eat. Tonight, we'll sort out plans. Tomorrow, we have a memorial service to attend."

That hit harder than I expected. Not just the inclusion but the fact Adam, Lainey and I had all lost parents this week. To be fair, Adam and I got rid of ours, but Lainey's mother had also died.

None of us argued, I rather doubted we would. Instead, I pivoted and headed out to the pool house. I'd stayed here plenty of times before. There were two fully outfitted bathrooms. I let Milo and Bodhi figure out who was getting the other one first.

I'd barely stripped off my clothes when the door opened behind me and a freshly showered Adam stood there, dressed in clean clothes and sporting a smooth face.

He'd shaved.

He also smelled like Lainey's preferred shampoo.

"Lucky bastard," I muttered.

"Yes, I am."

Adam stalked forward and pinned me to the wall. His hands were hot against my chest, hotter still when he gripped my neck. It wasn't until we were practically nose to nose that I realized the acrid taste of smoke burned my nostrils.

"How are you?" The soft words lulled me and I dragged

my attention up from the way his mouth shaped the syllables to find him staring at me.

"I'm—" I searched for the right words because I wasn't *fine* or even *okay* but I was... "I'm content."

His eyebrows rose at that description.

"Don't ask me why." It was a plea. "Not because I don't want to tell you but I don't think I know myself."

A slow nod was his only answer. Then he worked his fingers against my neck, the slow massage melting away some of the tension holding me rigid. My dick saluted instantly. I was painfully naked and he was standing right there looking absolutely delicious in his button down with the collar open and giving me a good look at the solid chest beneath.

"I won't," Adam whispered and his breath feathered over my lips. "I didn't mean to abandon you with Leopold."

"You didn't." I licked my lips. "I mean you did, but I got it. You needed Lainey. I've been there. She probably needed you. Bodhi and Milo backed me." That still had me marveling.

"Good." Adam teased his nose along my jaw and then tilted his head until our lips were just millimeters apart. "I'm going to work on learning how to suck your cock, but how do you feel about me jerking you off right now?"

Fuck.

I would die.

All I said was, "Really?" It came out the most embarrassing of squeaks. When he wrapped his hand more thoroughly around my throat and gave the lightest of squeezes, I swore my dick stiffened even harder.

"Yes, really. I told you I was serious about you being mine and you need a release. I want to be the one who does it."

I'd died. I'd gone up in flames in that house and this was my heavenly reward. Adam wanted me and he...

The warmth of his free hand wrapping around my cock stuttered my thoughts and scattered them. A moan so low and needy it should have embarrassed me, escaped my throat.

Rather than being disgusted or amused, Adam stared at me with a fiery intensity and I didn't dare look away. I could drown in the blue-violet of his eyes. This close, they were almost pure purple. His hands were bigger than mine, at least that was how it felt. He could easily grip over half my cock without trying. When he glided his hand up and down again, my hips thrust forward.

"Fuck," I whispered and then bit my lip. Maybe I should shut up... He was pushing himself for me. I'd seen him jerk off before. It had happened a couple of times while we were together, but I'd always made myself not stare while also pretending that he stared at me.

Him touching me was so fucking different. So fucking...

"You're a noisy boy in bed, Ezra," Adam said, before he licked my lower lip and pulled another moan out of me. "Tell me what you like. Harder? Tighter? Smoother? Slower? Tell me how to make you feel good."

"You're already doing it."

"Yeah?" His breath was hot and his words more scorching. "What am I doing?"

"You're touching me." Admitting that took everything, yet I was violently eager for me. "Fuck, Adam... Getting to touch you is fan-fucking-tastic. Having you touch me? I could die a happy man."

He bit down on my lower lip, the nip more painful than erotic. The sting ripped apart the hazy curtain of pleasure. "You don't get to die," Adam said, the order curling around me like the stiffest pair of shackles and chains. The locks clicked into place. "Do you understand me?"

"Yes, sir," I whispered. The flare in his eyes had me thrusting against his hand. "Can I come please?"

"Since you said please..." He stayed close. His mouth teased mine like he was on a precipice of a kiss, but he didn't quite fall over.

Every stroke of his hand took me from balls to tip. He toyed with my piercings, the tugs gentle, but they lit me up more. When he didn't reject my thrusts, I met his strokes with my own and I gripped his shoulders as much to stay on my feet as to keep him close.

My balls were dragging upward as my spine went liquid. "I'm gonna come..."

"Good boy," Adam whispered as he kissed me hard once then went to his knees. His mouth closed over my tip and everything exploded out of me at once as my brain went white-hot.

I wasn't fucking his mouth but he was swallowing me... my cum...

The world shattered and then came back together again. If not for his grip on my hips, I might have collapsed. I fought to open my eyes as Adam moved his whole head, carefully taking my length past his teeth. I could feel the suction of his swallows and I swore it pulled another load right out of me.

The elation I'd wondered about earlier flooded me. Sure it was endorphins and hormones, but it was also Adam, on his knees—sucking me off after he made me come.

When he finally let up, I was shaking. My cock ached for more and at the same time, even the teasing whispers of his breath against the damp flesh of my tip was too much.

He licked his lips. "Almost as tasty as Lainey..."

My eyes widened as a speculative gleam filled his eyes. I ran my tongue over my lower lip as a shudder went up my spine. "Tastes even better when I eat you out of her," I told him. "You should try it."

"I plan to." Then he stood slowly, the bathroom had shrunk to just him and his shirt clung to him, like he was sweating. Oh, it was steamy in here. "Now shower like a good boy."

Oh, I could be a good boy. "For you, I can do anything," I told him and then pressed my lips to his. He didn't make me fight for it. His mouth opened. The salty taste of my own cum added to the earthy connection that seemed to have opened between us. He had his hand around my throat and his mouth dominated mine.

I was fine with that. Adam could have everything. No more secrets. No more running away. No more life without him and Lainey.

My cock twitched. I wanted to be between them again. I wanted to fuck Adam between me and Lainey and for them to fuck me. I wanted to explore all the ways we could have each other.

He dragged out my lower lip, licking gently over the small bite cut he'd left earlier. Finally, he leaned back and he made sure I was steady before he took his hands off me.

"Shower." The order wrapped around me. "I'll be out there until you're ready."

"Okay... and Adam?"

He was at the door. "Hmm?"

"Thank you."

His grin turned wicked. "It was my pleasure and I am looking forward to learning more about what you like."

Then he was gone and I swore my legs went rubbery. I nearly fell down. Had that really just happened? Had Milo and Bodhi defended me to Leopold? Had the old man accepted my presence? And more... Had Adam just sucked my cock?

Eyes closed, I embraced the startling amount of emotion all of the above provoked in me. The death of my father had nothing on this new life with my *real* family.

The earlier elation surged through me again and when I climbed in the shower, it was with a smile on my face. Oh yeah, I was all in for this new life.

LAINEY

The funeral was a very quiet and private affair. The service took place at the graveside, the plot a family one. Grandfather was letting Mother back into the family. Adam's father would be interred with the Reeds and my mother here with the Benedicts.

Frankly, I didn't think either would have cared, other than Leopold won in finally separating them. But death had succeeded before he could. Now wasn't the time to worry about those things we couldn't change.

With all the distance between us, Mother and I had never really built any kind of stable relationship. Harper had been her whole world. Right or wrong, she'd committed herself to him before my birth. She'd remained committed to him long before they married.

I was the transgression of their relationship. Andrea the one who finally united them. Mother gave up everything for Harper Reed. Disgust coiled through me. Turned out that the bastard gave less than a damn about her in the end.

He killed her, and sold their daughter, all so he could marry me. If that weren't gross and disgusting enough, he'd done it in a calculated move to seize my inheritance, the one Grandfather denied him access to when he'd disinherited Melissa.

I wish we could kill Harper twice. Letting Mother die without knowing what he'd done, to her, to me, and to Andrea had been the only kindness I could offer her. What would she really have done if I'd tried to bring it up?

As it was, the last conversation I'd had with her haunted me. A hand settled gently on my spine, a reminder that they were there and it pulled me back to the present. I glanced up to find Pretty Boy watching me, his eyes intent and focused.

I leaned into his side, accepting his offer of strength. Adam stood as a silent sentinel on my other side while Ezra and Bodhi stood on either side of Adam and Milo respectively.

Grandfather stared at the plot they'd arranged. Rather than a coffin, we were interring an urn. She'd been cremated. Her wishes apparently. It made the graveside service easier, I supposed. Though we hadn't opened the invites up, Margareta Waldemar had arrived just moments before the minister began speaking.

She stood on the opposite side from the rest of us. Dressed in formal black with a wide-brimmed hat and dark sunglasses, she seemed almost chic while also being utterly unreadable.

We were all dressed in unrelieved black. Somehow, Grandfather and the guys coordinated right down to the black dress shirts, black handkerchiefs, and black suits. My dress was a little more understated, though the cold wind against my legs left me chilled.

The dark coat I wore helped. I'd also chosen black, knee-high boots, both for warmth and practicality. It was still winter and the weather hadn't been particularly kind to anyone.

"While Melissa's beloved mother could not be here with her father or her daughter, we know that like Melissa, she is with us in spirit."

Wistfulness curved through me. I missed my grandmother so much. I missed her sly wit, and her easy smile. I missed the joy she brought out in Grandfather. I just missed *her*.

"Melissa was blessed with two daughters, beautiful souls in their own rights. It is to them that the family will look. To them that will uphold the future. They are the legacy..."

Grandfather's jaw tightened, albeit briefly. I was the one who insisted on Andrea's mention. While his reluctance had been plain, he didn't fight me on it. His only question was would she be coming to the funeral.

I couldn't tell him what Harper had done. Not... not yet. Maybe not ever. Lying to him was not something I enjoyed, nor preferred. The words literally died on my tongue before I could give voice to them.

It was Milo who stepped in and said, "We discussed it and she wasn't ready for anything public, particularly after her father's death as well. It's better she stays out of sight until everything calms down."

Grandfather accepted the explanation easily. Almost too easily. Maybe I was being unfair. He and Andrea just didn't know each other. He'd been coming around to making an attempt and now she was missing, his daughter was dead and his nemesis also deceased.

It was a lot to take in.

I understood, maybe more than he realized. My soul ached for Andrea. Every single day that passed while we were here and she was—out there—I died a little more on the inside. Every moment was another opportunity for her to be hurt or worse.

We weren't doing *nothing* even if it felt like we weren't moving fast at all. We had people looking for us on the ground in four different Eastern European countries. Fletcher was hacking into CCTVs, and searching for any sign of her.

Em had been reaching out to event coordinators and venues all over Europe. She was booking dates that would give us cover just in case. Maybe it was anathema to others, but someone might understand that Adam and I would gut everyone in our path to get Andrea back.

Yet, here we stood, on a cold, gray, dismal morning as they placed Mother's ashes into the opening in the land they'd made.

"Ashes to ashes and dust to dust," the minister droned on. I kept tuning him out. Probably not the most polite, but I wasn't all that keen on the service in the first place. Eventually, he finished and offered to let Grandfather and I drop dirt into the plot before the cemetery keepers filled it back in for permanent interment.

Did I want to drop the dirt in? Not particularly, but Grandfather hesitated and I understood. That distance with my mother had cost him dearly. For all that he cut her off and hadn't looked back, he wasn't a heartless man. The cold facade was just that, it was a facade. He wore the disdain for her like armor to keep his disappointment at bay.

Straightening, I moved away from Milo and crossed to where Grandfather stood. I took a scoop of the dirt into a gloved hand and then glanced down at the urn inside the hole. It was such a small, ignominious end for a woman who had once burned so bright.

"Goodbye, Mother," I murmured and let the dirt fall from my fingers.

Grandfather echoed my farewell by taking a handful and letting it fall from his fingers, rather than throwing it in. "Goodbye, Melissa. May you find the peace in the next life you never found in this one."

He took my gloved hand in his and we stood there as they filled in the grave spot. The minister murmured some platitude and Grandfather nodded, but said nothing to answer him. It wasn't long before he withdrew, leaving only our small party and Margareta Waldemar present.

She said nothing as we waited for the hole to be filled in, only when it was finished did she step forward and place a single, blood-red rose on the grave stone. Not the grave itself, but the stone.

That finished, she turned her attention to Grandfather and me. "Mrs. Waldemar," I said, keeping my tone polite and even. "Thank you for coming."

"Even if you weren't invited." Grandfather's tone turned gruff as he moved a couple of steps away from the grave and she followed. The guys moved too, forming a semi-circle. Mrs. Waldemar's bodyguard was present, but several feet away next to another tree.

I could admonish my grandfather about manners, but I didn't disagree with him. "This was a private service for family only."

"I understand," Mrs. Waldemar said, her tone conciliatory. "I truly do. Burying one's child is... an experience no parent should ever have to face."

The words brought me right back to her charge that King had killed her son. I hadn't forgotten about any of that, but Andrea's disappearance on top of everything else just took precedence.

"I lost Melissa a long time ago." The dismissive note might fool others, but I recognized the distraction for what it was. Grandfather felt vulnerable, no one enjoyed that sensation. "This just put a period on the end of a somewhat bleaker chapter in my life."

"I can see that," Mrs. Waldemar said as she tucked her small handbag under arm before clasping her hands together. While I couldn't see her eyes beneath the sunglasses, I felt the weight of her gaze. "I can't imagine closing the book feels any better no matter how much acrimony existed."

"Perhaps," Grandfather declined to finish the thought. "What can we do for you, Mrs. Waldemar?"

"I thought I would come to pay my respects and perhaps talk to you, Mr. Benedict as well as with Miss Lainey here."

Really? I couldn't quite fathom the subtext of her statement. Cryptic didn't quite cover it. Frankly, I wasn't sure I wanted her to include my grandfather in anything. The veneer of absolute civility that she wore like a lady's crown was just that... a veneer. A position she occupied thanks to her wealth and privilege.

She was just as cold-blooded as the rest of us when it came to defending what was hers. Perhaps nearly as ruthless.

"Odd timing for a tête-à-tête," Grandfather said as he offered me his arm and motioned for Mrs. Waldemar to walk. "And I believe I invited you to call me Leopold previously."

"As I invited you to call me, Margareta, but since you went formal, I thought I should be as well." The ease in her manner made me want to smile. As it was, she made grandfather chuckle. Very little else was breaking through his stern visage. He kept his grief very close and tucked away where he could worry at it in private.

"Very well, Margareta," he said as though conceding the point. "We have a short walk back to the cars, and at the risk of becoming rude, I would prefer to finish any business here and not take it home."

"Agreed," she said and she fell into step putting me between them.

Bodhi and Ezra walked behind us but Adam and Milo ranged ahead. They were forming a perimeter guard. I supposed if I checked over my shoulder, Mrs. Waldemar's bodyguard would also be on the move.

"I could play coy, but I would much prefer to address the issues directly without the softness of conversation."

"Hence, bringing business to a funeral," I interjected. My mother dying had only put an end to the idea of ever truly reconciling with her. The distance had been there for so long, the only thing her death did was relieve me of an obligation.

That felt a very cold amount of pragmatism to experience at a funeral. Then again, maybe I would be able to mourn her properly later.

"It is not my first choice of venues for such conversations, but there are a great many changes happening in our circles. Melissa's death as well as Harper's and that terrible fire at Harrow's Park." She glanced over her shoulder, presumably at Ezra. "My condolences young man."

I supposed he'd only nodded at her because he hadn't said anything aloud, nor did she linger.

"These are the kinds of changes that threaten companies, control, and interests. I wanted to discuss with you the idea of uniting our assets to create a—more defensive position as the other families try to scavenge from the losses."

"That presumes any of our families will experience losses," Adam said, and the absolute chill licking each syllable reminded me of death. Eerily appropriate I guessed.

"This is also true, but I've learned that there are always losses of some kind during power shifts. Nature and business abhor a vacuum and there are many who would willingly step in to fill those shoes. Men like King, for example. I imagine he is already making moves."

We were almost to the parking lot and Grandfather stopped to face her. To my surprise, she slid her sunglasses off.

"You're an honorable man, Leopold. I trust your word, over and above a contract. Only a fool wouldn't seek to take advantage of the situation as it is and I'm not a fool. That said, I believe working together we can achieve far more than working independently."

"And you don't want me for an enemy." It was delivered in such an unironically flat tone as he stated the fact as though it were absolutely undisputed.

"You have grandchildren in the mix," she told him. "So do I. You will fight for yours as I will fight for mine. However, if we work together, we can win for both."

"Very pleasant fairy tale, Margareta. I appreciate your directness. I hope you won't mind a little candor on my part." Grandfather shifted his posture. Though my arm was still threaded through his, he positioned me a half-step back, as though he intended to step in front of me to keep Margareta away.

"I look forward to your candidness, it's such a rare attitude in our world."

"Maybe, or maybe too many of you enjoy verbal sparring along with keeping secrets like they should be worn as precious jewels. I have no time for fools, as you stated already. I have even less time for those who want to use subterfuge. Your interest in my granddaughter has not gone unnoticed."

I didn't dare breathe. For a moment, Margareta's eyelids twitched. It was the faintest of tells from a woman who rarely displayed any in my experience. Grandfather had surprised her.

"Leopold, I am very fond of Lainey."

"You can be fond from a distance. You can also stay away from these young men in her life. I'm not sure whether your interest in them is over their assets or hers, but understand... I will counter any move you make toward them."

Lips pursing, Margareta studied him. "You are genuinely concerned about my interest."

"Ma'am, you haven't made a single uncalculated move since you arrived. I may not comment, or even involve myself, but don't mistake that for complacency. Lainey is my granddaughter. I will defend her and hers with everything at my disposal. If you wish to take on King, then enjoy yourself. I have no objections. You will not involve my family in your drama or anyone else's. Are we clear?"

The older woman said nothing for far too long, then she nodded slowly before she slid her sunglasses back into place. "Well-played, Leopold. Well-played. I knew you were the one to watch for."

Grandfather neither accepted the compliment or responded to it. "Good afternoon, Margareta."

"Good afternoon, Leopold..." Then the weight of her gaze was on me again. "Lainey." It was almost a relief when she ceased staring at me. "Gentlemen." Then she turned, giving us all her back as though she had nothing to be concerned about.

That wasn't a show of trust, but one of power. As moves went, it was interesting.

"Be careful of her, sweet girl."

"I planned on it," I promised.

Grandfather nodded, then glanced at Adam. "When is Harper's funeral?"

"In a couple of hours. You don't have to attend," Adam answered. "Frankly, if I could get away with it, I would just flush what remains they gathered from the crash site and call it good. But I'll put in an appearance, briefly, then leave. The will reading is still a few weeks out. The attorneys are already working on the dispensations."

"Yes, there are investigations as well," Leopold said. "And I'll go with you to the funeral. Appearances should be kept. Margareta was right about one thing...the jackals will be circling. United front, my boy. United front."

Surprise stamped across Adam's face and I had to bite the inside of my lip as Grandfather started toward the parking lot. We'd all ridden together, and we were all dressed for a funeral.

The protectiveness in his manner toward Adam and the others was new.

But I liked it.

I liked it a lot.

We had one more thing to deal with after this next funeral, then we could go. We could join the hunt for Andrea.

CHAPTER
FOURTEEN

ADAM

I wish I had been kidding about the services for my father. Though we didn't have a body, Hamilton had insisted on a casket for the funeral. Something over the top, luxurious and expensive. Since I'd wanted little to nothing to do with the planning, it had gone ahead.

The service had been a brief one before we moved to host the memorial itself at the country club, because where *else* would Hamilton plan an event? It was beyond gaudy, and more than a little tacky. Then again, that was my uncle to a tee.

Leopold's snort of derision when we arrived was well-deserved. For now, they were keeping their distance while I made a few strategic stops. Unlike Hamilton, I didn't need to court the board or their cronies. I'd been gathering stock in Reed for a long time.

I also had a few of my own allies. One of which, surprisingly, turned out to be Leopold who apparently owned more than ten percent of the company all by himself. When Lainey

133

had stared at him, her own shock evident, I'd felt a bit better. The old man had seriously been intent on doing some damage to my father, possibly taking the whole company down.

Now?

He said he'd back whatever play I made as long as Lainey approved. I wasn't sure what happened in that conversation with him when I'd gone to find Lainey, but something had clearly changed. The dark suspicion that edged all of his words and actions seemed to have faded.

The fact he included all four of us in his scope of protection when he spoke to Margareta Waldemar promised as much. This wasn't a new ploy or plot. He was supporting Lainey and that wasn't something I would argue with.

Jason, like me, didn't bother with moving to the front of the dining room where Hamilton held court. He was talking to investors, board members, and more.

"He's shoring up support," Jason warned before he took a sip of the vodka on the rocks he'd ordered. It sounded good to me, but I wanted a clear head. I didn't doubt that Hamilton would make a move before they even took the empty casket away for interment in the family mausoleum.

Depressing place. Mother hadn't actually been put there. She had her own gravesite, near trees and a stream. It was a lovely spot. I could visit her without having to deal with the rest of my family.

I rather doubt my father intended to do me any favors with that choice, but I accepted it in full. I didn't need to see him again and I was glad there was no body to put in there. If this were a horror movie, we'd need to salt and burn the corpse just to make sure the demon was gone for good.

"Do I want to know what you're going to do?" Jason asked. Like Hamilton, he was also my uncle. Unlike Hamilton,

134

he wasn't a raging shithead. He was also the father of my favorite cousin.

Our detente had definitely grown after Fletcher called him as part of an agreement to get more answers out of Jason, particularly about what he knew regarding Lainey and her biological father.

"I don't know," I said, taking a sip from the tumbler I had in my hand. The watery iced tea looked enough like a bourbon, that no one commented. If they did? I really didn't give a damn. "Do you?"

Jason paused, lowering his drink. The reproachful look he shot me might intimidate some. Unfortunately, my father had made a habit of baleful looks and dismissive stares. I was immune.

"I thought I made my support quite clear a few days ago," he said before taking another sip. "What do you need? A contract in blood?"

"No," I told him. "We already have one in blood. Blood doesn't make for trust though. You back the strongest player in the room. It was why you backed my father."

Why he would back me.

Instead of dismissing the charge, Jason nodded once. "I also kept my distance unless he pushed the issue of wanting me involved. There's a difference between support and apathy."

The logic was sound. "Agreed."

"I'm offering you support."

Offering.

"For Fletcher?" It was more curiosity than anything else.

"Yes. For Lainey and Andrea as well." The mention of Andrea was a fresh dagger. For all that Jason had been helpful, I didn't trust him enough to ask him about Andrea.

Frankly, if I found out he knew the people my father used for trafficking...

Well, it would be Fletcher burying his father next. I didn't hate Jason and I needed to know he wasn't involved. Something Fletcher was also investigating.

"That said," Jason continued, his gaze firmly on his surviving brother. Hamilton schmoozed so well as he glad-handed his way through the circle of sycophants trying to figure out if he was the "newly-minted" head of the family or not. "I'm also doing it for you. Because *you* deserve more than Harper ever did for you."

I wanted to say thank you and mean it. I wanted to believe him. We weren't there yet. Trust had to be earned.

"I get it, Adam," Jason said. "Guard your secrets, and keep your own counsel. But if there's something you need me to do, just tell me. No questions asked."

"Someday, I'm going to tell you that you should always ask questions. Blind obedience was Harper's way." King's way. Wallace Graham's way. Those ways needed to die with the men. "It won't be mine. However, if you're serious. I need Hamilton dealt with and distracted. I have more pressing matters to deal with before I take care of him. Can you handle that?"

"Am I free to throw money at the issue?" The bland tone surfacing behind the question almost made me laugh.

Almost.

"Depends. We're not paying him off to go away."

"Oh, that wouldn't work anyway," Jason said, then nudged me with a nod to move to another location in the room. More curious than anything, I followed him while keeping Hamilton in my periphery.

Bodhi wasn't far behind me. He wasn't invading the conversations, but he stayed in range. Milo and Ezra were with Lainey and her grandfather. They would keep Hamilton well away from her too.

As odd as trusting Cavendish used to be, it seemed far more natural now. I also didn't have to worry about a knife in the back. Very little distracted him and he didn't have to engage in pleasantries. He had a reputation for rudeness and I kind of wish I'd cultivated something similar.

"I assume you wanted a more private discussion?" I prompted Jason after he tossed back the last of his vodka. He set it on a waiter's tray as the man passed us and then Jason faced me.

"Yes, I'm saying we can't pay him off. We can distract him by making him think he'll get one over on you..." He smirked faintly.

"A wild goose chase?"

"Something like that," Jason said. "He's been trying to gather a power base together for more than a decade. He's never gotten close. Harper allowed it because it kept him busy and out of his hair. Sometimes, he would throw a bone out there... a comment, a company... a *problem* that he was having. Hamilton isn't deep in the slightest."

"He went for it every time?"

"Pretty much. He's gotten close to becoming more than a nuisance, but his greed always ends up bankrupting him. Then after Harper made sure he took everything, he would 'bail' him out and bring him back to heel."

Then the pattern repeated itself. "Well, at least my father was predictable."

"Precisely," Jason said. "Tell me something that you 'need' and I'll let it slip at some point after another drink. Hamilton will think he has the inside track and he won't be able to help himself."

"Have you used the same technique on him previously?" I

drained the rest of my tea before setting the glass on another waiter's tray.

Jason chuckled. "Once or twice. Usually when Harper made me deal with him. If you can't tell, I'm not really fond of my brothers. I'm happier when we have whole continents between us."

"I can't say I disagree." Though now I was curious. "If you know how to push his buttons, did you know my father's?"

"Yes, point out someone had beaten him. His ego would never have stood for it and he would become obsessed with doing everything he could... it was why he was insane about Melissa for a while."

I frowned. "Someone beat him..."

Then it hit me.

"Lainey."

Jason nodded. "She was punishing him, had that affair, then she got pregnant and she refused to bow to anyone. Not him. Not her father. No one. Lainey is the living breathing proof of Harper's failure. He didn't knock her up first, and he didn't get the inheritance."

Jason sounded almost joyful about that. He didn't know about the kidnapping or I doubted he'd take that tone. As it was, I could understand enjoying my father's pain.

I had... With every single finger they'd removed from him. The sobs and screams of agony were going to be a balm for my nightmares for a long time.

"If you wanted to get me?" It was an idle question, but I was still curious.

"Depends on what I wanted to get from you. Your obedience? Threaten your girl. Your murderous rage? Harm her. Your enmity for all time? Kill her."

I swung my head around and glared.

"My point," Jason said, not remotely deterred. "She is

both leverage, and a cataclysmic error if you don't understand how dangerous threatening her is. You will burn the world down for her and you've been this way for years. That kind of volatility, however, is far more dangerous than it is useful."

"Threatening her in any way..." I warned and Jason nodded once.

"...is a terrible idea. We agree. However, you asked me what would work on you. That would be the fastest way. It could also backfire tremendously because she has her own allies as well."

"Did my father know?"

"I doubt it. Though he might have. Leopold kept him from moving on it though. Leopold's far cannier than most people give him credit for..." He paused as a man came up to us and offered his condolences. A pair of handshakes later, he was gone, leaving Jason and I alone once again. "So, yes, using Lainey against you would be effective, but only if you knew the precise pressure point and how far you could go without igniting reprisal that far outweighed any gain you might achieve."

I had no problems with that. No one would touch Lainey.

"Your best friend was another source of leverage, but he was too volatile on his own. That wild temper of his and that drinking problem." Jason gave me a considering look. "Either one could get him killed, both are a bad combination."

I was aware. "He'll be fine." If I had to drag him up a sober hill every damn day, he would be. We'd eliminated a good portion of the problem already. The rest would take time.

"I suppose the house burning down would be a wake up call." Jason checked his watch. "You have anything you want to share or should I just make something up? I'm fine with making something up, but it might not distract him as long as the real thing."

He had a point. I turned it over in my head and then glanced at where Bodhi stood. He'd been close enough to listen. At my raised eyebrows, he closed the distance and murmured in a low voice that wouldn't carry.

"Mention your interest in Standish and bringing them back into the fold."

Standish was a large conglomerate, but they were in no way on the market for a merger or a partnership. In fact, their current CEO had a history with all of our parents. Despite his return to the area, he hadn't gotten involved with any of his former friends and associates.

"Pointless exercise," Jason said with a grin when I offered up that morsel. "But Hamilton will think he just needs the right leverage."

"Don't let him hurt anyone. Distracted is fine, I don't want him killing people or worse..." Standish had a kid. Leverage came in all shapes and sizes.

"I won't," Jason told me, then clasped me on the shoulder. "Go ahead and get out of here if you want. I'll deal with Hamilton. He's already salivating over what you and I are discussing. If I play dumb for a day or two, he's gonna be like a dog with a bone."

The description was amusing. "Thanks..." I hesitated pausing in mid-step to pivot around to face him. "Can you put together a briefing for me on Julius King, everything you know—no research, just what you know. And about Isla Cavendish. Maybe more on that guy Yuri Leistung."

I caught Bodhi's hard stare drilling into my head, but I didn't change my mind. Jason wanted to be useful? We could use the help.

"How soon do you need it?" My uncle looked intrigued, but he didn't ask me why I wanted to know. It was a gamble, but one I was willing to risk. Right now, we really did need all the information we could get our hands on.

"Last week," I told him.

"I'll take care of it." Then he grinned as he held out his hand. I gripped it. The smile was utterly at odds with the reason for us being here. "Hamilton is gonna be over here in seconds after you leave. So don't mind me, I'm going to wander off and make him craz—ier. Yes. Make him crazier."

With that, Jason turned and strode away like he didn't have a care in the world and a huff of laughter escaped me. Who knew? The man had a bit of a twisted sense of humor. Kind of wished I'd known this about him all along.

"Can we trust him?" Bodhi asked.

"Not sure," I admitted. "But I'm willing to find out. Whether he can find out anything for us, it's no harm if he can't."

"True." Bodhi said. A moment later, Hamilton was stalking across the room in the direction that Jason had disappeared. "He does know his brother."

That he did.

"Let's find our girl and her grandfather and get out of here. I've had enough of this ass kissing contest. No one here really liked Harper." I didn't want them kissing my ass. Everyone would be figuring out things had changed soon enough.

FIFTEEN

LAINEY

We'd barely returned to the city after Harper's "memorial service" when the Vandals arrived at Bodhi's place. Em was with them and it was time to put our heads together for the plan. We were going to be using private jets to get to Europe and not one of ours directly—we were *borrowing* from friends.

As much as I wanted to stay and catch up with Em, Bodhi murmured in my ear that Hans had called. It was an offer for me to go with him and since it had everything to do with his potential sibling as well as Em and Pretty Boy's, I agreed.

"We'll be back soon," I promised Pretty Boy with a light kiss. He gave me a steady look then glanced at Bodhi before he nodded.

"Go armed, Mayhem. Watch Bodhi's back."

"Good thing he has a nice ass." The light comment had Em whipping around to stare at me as Pretty Boy grinned.

While Ezra and Adam both looked like they wanted to go,

they refrained from insisting. I left them each with a kiss. They'd work out the finer points while we went to get information.

I was still dressed in unrelieved black, but it was slacks, a tucked in turtleneck, and a jacket that hid my gun holster neatly. The boots had room for knife sheaths in them. Apparently, Bodhi hadn't been kidding about wardrobe additions. My baton was in my purse, which made it readily accessible.

Bodhi studied me in the elevator on the way down and when I raised my brows, he shook his head. "Just planning, Buttercup."

"Should I be intrigued or worried?"

He merely grinned. "Yes."

Fortunately, our meeting with Hans was not in a sex club. As titillating as our adventure to The Underground had been, I didn't want to spend time on the distractions. There was too much happening, and we were too close to leaving to find Andrea.

Instead, Bodhi drove us to an elegant, Romanesque Revival-style home located in a quiet Sugar Hill neighborhood. The architecture heralded to a more elegant time. It even still had a carriage house, and a receiving door.

Now, it was used by valets who took vehicles to park. Bodhi circled the car to open my door before he handed over the keys. We were not the only arrivals. The couple arriving behind us were dressed a little more formally, his suit and her dress more than acceptable for a business dinner, but maybe not a night out at the opera.

"Are we underdressed?" I asked as Bodhi guided me toward the doors.

"Not at all," he murmured with just a hint of a smile. A doorman admitted us and offered to take our coats. Since I just had the light jacket, I declined and Bodhi hadn't bothered with one at all.

Once we were passed the foyer though, I understood that we were far from underdressed. If anything, we were a tad overdressed in a very clothing optional atmosphere.

"It's a museum," I murmured, more to myself. One I hadn't heard of before.

Erotic art decorated the walls, with statues and other objects placed around the room. In the corners, there was *living* art. A woman on her knees, performing fellatio quite eagerly to a man who seemed on the edge of orgasm.

In another corner, it was a woman who sat in an old style chair, legs spread with a man's head poking up through the hole. It gave him the perfect access to her cunt, which he was devouring with a singular intent. Very well, based on the noises she was making.

I was almost sorry the guys hadn't come with us. Though, we might be too distracted and forget why we were here. Honestly, the volume of stimuli was a bit overwhelming.

"What do you think?" Bodhi murmured as he waved off the waiter who came around to offer us glasses of champagne.

"It's definitely different," I said. "Private collection?"

"Something like that," Bodhi said. "You've been to the Museum of Sex on Fifth Avenue?"

Amusement bubbled through me only to pop and evaporate before I finished forming the answer. "Yes, Tally and I went." I sighed, the ache of Tally's betrayal fresh again. "Right after our eighteenth birthdays. We took an afternoon and went to be scandalized."

"This is—far different." The living art was one example. The sensuality in the art was another. Still, that had been a fun afternoon.

Bodhi trailed his fingers down my back, it was a light caress. A reminder that I wasn't alone. Another sigh escaped before I could corral the sorrow and put it away.

"Don't let her current actions spoil a fond memory," Bodhi said as he guided me into another room. There were monitors in each room, or maybe they were called curators here, that seemed to be keeping an eye on everything and everyone.

This room had its share of art objects and paintings, as well as living art. It seemed more devoted to pain as pleasure and the different takes on it was fascinating.

Maybe a little on point. I was curious, but I'd never considered pain something I enjoyed. Definitely not heart pain.

"I'll try," I said, then forced myself to shake it off and focus on the room. I hadn't seen Hans yet, but that didn't mean he wasn't here. Our last meeting at the Underground had involved a pseudo tour through the pleasures and depravities available there as well.

Sex must be Hans' hobby. Or maybe he took advantage of the privacy enforced in these locations to conduct business. Maybe both?

We didn't find Hans until after we'd made our way through the bondage room—this time the art actually did capture me. Some of the paintings had a Renaissance feel to them but they were definitely modern depictions.

It wasn't just women artistically strung up by ropes in the paintings. I'd heard about Shibari but hadn't spent a lot of time studying it. What fascinated me were the men who were also being bound. Men. Women. Couples.

The poses on display with the living art was even more breathtaking. Near each corner was a statue that showed two fantasy creatures making love. A pair of mermaids—well a

HEATHER LONG

mermaid and a merman— interlocked, tails twining together.

Above the statue the man and woman were wrapped around each other with the ropes making up the tails for them. I couldn't actually tell if there was penetration happening but that didn't seem to really matter.

In the next corner, there was a statue of two dragon—people for lack of a better term, interlocked in a sixty-nine. Her mouth was open in ecstasy, his cock against her lips, and his face was buried against her cunt.

The pair behind the statue had been tied up in a similarly erotic pose and they were absolutely acting out the pleasure. The man was definitely a noisy eater and his partner was very much engaged.

I fanned myself a little as my face heated. The mixture of fantasy and bondage was not one I would have thought to be that erotic and yet... I really wanted to spend more time here.

"You like?" The soft question from Bodhi tickled my ear.

"Far more than I expected." To be fair, I wasn't even certain about my level of intrigue. Did I want to be one of the ones in the ropes or just savoring the view?

Maybe?

"We'll make time for another viewing later." The sensuous promise teased through me.

"You said that about the Underground." He'd told me that we could go again, explore, and enjoy—whatever we wanted.

"We will," he said, pressing a kiss just behind my ear. The light touch stroked flames through me. Desire, I wanted to act on, but we had a lot to do *before* we indulged. In this instance, we needed to find Hans.

Thankfully, our quarry was in a drawing room on the second floor. The door was open, but a velvet rope restricted access. Though it was the guard at the door that kept the guests moving.

"Cavendish," Hans said as he rose. "There you are and the lovely, lovely companion. I am very pleased to see you again."

The guard removed the velvet rope so we could enter. Hans greeted Bodhi with a firm handshake, then he offered me a similar welcome. Or at least similar in that he took my hand. When he gripped my hand between both of his, I raised my brows.

"You are an enchanting creature. I very much wish to know all your secrets, particularly how you've successfully captivated our mutual friend." The German flavor to his accent was a reminder of his "heritage."

"*Mit dem Feuer sollte man nicht spielen.*" At my light warning to not play with fire, he gripped my hand just a bit tighter as delight lit up his dark eyes.

"If you were with any other gentleman..."

"You still wouldn't have a chance," Bodhi said easily. "Now, let her go before she takes offense."

I almost laughed at Hans' expression. "Very well, should you ever decide against this one, do look me up, liebchen, I beg you."

Shaking my head, I withdrew my hand and Hans motioned to the guard who closed the door.

"Sit, both of you... Would you care for a drink?"

"No," Bodhi said as he waited for me to sit on the love seat opposite the sofa Hans occupied. Neither man sat until I did. Bodhi joined me and Hans reclaimed his own. "You said you had news."

"I do," Hans said. "I definitely do." Leaning forward, his elbows resting lightly against his expensively tailored pant legs, he smiled. "I have names."

Nothing about Bodhi's posture changed. He didn't seem

to react. Yet the energy around him shifted. This was the kind of news he'd been waiting on getting. "What type of names?"

"First, the name of the woman who gave birth to the third King child. She was a challenge to track down, and a bit of a hellion herself. I would advise being prepared to lock her down should you need to speak to her. She was quite vexed that I located her." He reached into his jacket pocket and pulled out an envelope.

Bodhi took it and passed it to me. "That she's alive is impressive. I take it she isn't local?"

"Yes and no, she married into one of the Bridgeport families, the newer money. But a rather acrimonious divorce, as well as a hefty payout from her prenuptial, keeps her in comfort. She has no interest in returning to New York however. She not only changed her name, she changed it again after she married. She is very much not Tracy Dunlop from Brooklyn who had an affair with Julius King and served as his mistress for four years."

I opened the envelope and pulled out the sheet of paper. It was older, the texture of the paper a little softer and finer as it had aged. It was a birth certificate.

Baby boy.

Theodore Julian Dunlop.

Mother Tracy Dunlop.

There was no name filled in for the father, just the mother.

A boy.

Milo and Em had a baby brother. My heart filled and crashed in the same breath.

"Does she have the boy?" Bodhi asked but Hans was already shaking his head.

"This was the part I found most difficult. She didn't want to part with any information. In fact, she became downright hostile until I made it clear that her life could become much more unpleasant. Finally, she admitted that she made arrangements for the boy to disappear. She wouldn't share the details but that she'd made it clear to the father that he would never see the child again."

"King could simply kidnap and torture her." It wasn't like he was above that.

"Perhaps, liebchen..." The faint smile touching his lips as he glanced to Bodhi while saying the endearment almost made me roll my eyes. "However, she has buried her identity very well. She took from him what he wanted most and made sure he couldn't have him. She mentioned using his own contacts against him. I can get more details, but it will take time."

Used his own contacts. "King is into human trafficking."

We'd known. Of course, we'd known. But we'd never had concrete proof.

Was King the one Harper used to get rid of Andrea?

The sulfurous scratch of anger lit inside me. Hans had names.

"I also have another birth certificate."

Another...

"For King?" The energy around Bodhi shifted once more. It grew almost deadly in its stillness.

"No," Hans said, withdrawing another envelope from his inner pocket. "This one would have been impossible without Ms. Dunlop's assistance. It would seem, one of the reasons she knew how to hide the boy was because she'd seen it happen to another woman's child."

Ice shivered over me.

"My mother." The two words escaped Bodhi like bullets being fired.

"I believe so. The certificate of live birth was buried, and the name isn't correct on it. However, the times, the place, and the dates all line up with everything else you've learned."

When he held out the envelope this time, Bodhi didn't move. He stared at the sealed rectangle like it would communicate the secrets of the universe.

"Shall I?" I asked gently and Bodhi gave the slowest of nods.

I put away Theodore's birth certificate and then took the new one. I slit it open.

"I wish I had more to offer you, my friend. These challenges have truly been a pleasure to dig into. I can, of course, continue to find more—should you require it."

Bodhi didn't even seem to be breathing as I opened the envelope and extracted another birth certificate. Like Theodore's it was slightly older, softer and worn. The timing seemed almost beyond coincidental. It couldn't have been more than a year before Andrea had been born.

Pain fisted around my heart. We would find her dammit.

Forcing my mind to the present, I scanned the certificate.

Another baby boy.

Levente Cassidine Noble.

I frowned at the name. The name of the mother was listed as Ayla Winters.

"If you're wondering, I did check—there was no Ayla Winters at that hospital nor any hospital in that region during that time. The name is very conspicuous as it's close to Isla." The absolute sobriety in Hans' manner was a distinct contrast to his earlier playfulness. "Without DNA, I cannot confirm one hundred percent..."

"But he was sold and moved into this pipeline that removed the King child?"

"Indeed," Hans said. "She gave me a couple of names that she used then but they were dead ends. Most likely aliases."

"But we can still talk to her," I said. "Find out if she has any other ideas?"

Two boys, relatively close in age—what? Seven months give or take between their births. If the birth dates were accurate. Even if they weren't, it was most likely within a year.

Why did it seem like everything bad that happened tied back to King?

"You can," Hans said. "I will provide you with all the information. But I'm telling you, she is skittish and a wholly despicable woman only interested in two things...money and punishing King."

I really didn't have a problem with the latter.

"Thank you, Hans," Bodhi said as he rose. The men shook hands and this time, it was Bodhi's hand that Hans held for a longer moment.

"My friend, it was my pleasure. I only wish I could bring you more concrete information. I am flying to Berlin tomorrow, to do a little more—looking into this Yuri Leistung. Be wary, what little I have already turned up says he was quite connected. I'll get more if I am there than through calls."

I didn't react. It made sense that Bodhi would have reached out to Hans, I just hadn't given it that much thought.

"Be careful," Bodhi told him. "We will be in Europe soon enough. If something feels dangerous, wait for us to be there."

Hans sniffed. "You worry too much and I haven't had this much excitement in a while." With that he clapped Bodhi on the shoulder and then gave me a polite tilt of his head. "Liebchen, it is always a pleasure to see you."

Bodhi held out a hand to me and since I'd already secured the birth certificates in my purse, I rose and took his hand. "*Danke schön.*"

Touching a hand to his chest over his heart, Hans said, "*Gern geschehen.*"

We left, Bodhi was no longer interested in taking our time as we weaved through the other visitors to the private museum of the erotic. I stayed with him, my hand clasped firmly in his.

The energy around Bodhi surged hot and then cold to hot again. A brother.

He and Pretty Boy each had brothers. It was an answer to a question Bodhi had held for so long, that I couldn't imagine what he was thinking right now.

Only, I knew what our next step was going to be.

And *who* it would have to be.

"Buttercup," Bodhi said in a low voice as we reached the exit.

"I'm here," I promised him. "Take all the time you need. I'm not going anywhere."

He lifted our clasped hands and kissed my knuckles. "I'm going to need your help."

"You have it," I said. "Anything."

CHAPTER
SIXTEEN

BODHI

The feeling of the wheel beneath my fingers as we pulled away from the private museum grounded me. When Lainey settled her hand on my thigh though, that helped even more. She'd been the reason I walked out of that house without inflicting bodily harm on every person between me and the door.

An unfamiliar rage had begun to pool in my gut as Hans revealed the names of the two children he'd identified. His flirting with Lainey had been mildly amusing. I found even his less than sly effort to get under my skin to be entertaining, particularly when she shut him down with a careless kind of grace that just made her all that more attractive to me.

Then Hans mentioned the name Ayla...

Ayla.

My bastard of a father not only took my mother's child from her, he even robbed that child of her name. Anger like I hadn't experienced in years flooded me. It wouldn't take that long to drive to the family compound, to let myself in, dismiss the staff and then paint the walls red with his blood.

The provocative nature of that image shouldn't be so damn tempting. Because killing him would only satisfy me for a very brief moment, on an extremely primitive level.

It wasn't enough. Nothing would ever be enough for what he did to my mother. That said, I wanted to *destroy* him. I wanted to do to him what he'd done to her. I wanted him to *suffer* and to understand that nothing he did, ever, would save him. I wanted him to wish for death, but be trapped in a miserable existence.

A few decades like that might actually begin to repay some of the debt he'd incurred in locking my mother up.

Instead of driving out to Long Island, I headed uptown. The penthouse where I'd invited everyone to live was not my only place in the city. Like my step great-grandmother, Sophia, I had my own loft, secured under a holding company and unlinked to me directly.

It was a haven for me when I needed to disappear for a while. I wasn't Phillip Cavendish there. I wasn't anyone there, for that matter. With that destination in mind, I kept the speed of the vehicle controlled.

Three blocks from the museum, the volcanic chaos boiling over inside of me slowed even if it didn't come near cooling. I pressed a single button on the steering wheel and Milo's phone began to ring, the heads up display showing his contact info.

"One second." Milo didn't wait for a reply, but the hum of conversation carried over the open line. The Vandals were still there. So much planning that still needed to be done.

Too many people in my space. Even if they were people I liked for the most part.

"Okay, I'm alone. Everything all right?" The question

shouldn't have surprised me. Milo and I didn't converse via phone often and I'd brought Lainey with me. He would also be correct in assuming if everything wasn't all right, I would call him for assistance.

This was not a matter he could help on. I liked him. Respected him. Trusted him with Lainey. But our friendship —it didn't matter. I needed one person right now and I had her with me.

I was also in no mood to share or be gentle with the others in her life.

Most days, fine. Not today.

"No," I told him. There was no point in lying. Secrets from others was fine. But we had to be able to be direct with each other. "It's not. Hans had information. Information. Answers. More questions. But I need a few hours to process it and I need Lainey."

"Not coming back here tonight?" It wasn't really a question, but I appreciated the confirmation.

"No." Then because directness was required, I asked, "Unless there is a pressing need for us to be there?"

If they had a location on Andrea, that would take precedence...

"Still in a holding pattern on that one. Fletcher called an hour ago. He said he's close, but he needed more time. There's someone trying to cover the trail and from what Adam said, he sounded more annoyed than anything."

Not finding Andrea yet wasn't a relief, but not having to go back definitely was. I glanced at Lainey. If she had her own questions...

"Thank you, Pretty Boy. You can message if anything changes. But we'll be back in the morning."

"Will do... stay safe you two."

"She will." My safety was not as important as hers. "She's also right, call us if anything changes."

"Done."

"Love you, Pretty Boy."

He chuckled. "Love you too, Mayhem."

I couldn't blame him for the laughter. There was something about being loved by a woman like Lainey. She didn't need any of us. Even when she was hurting, she didn't need us. She chose us. Chose me. That was worth more than most would understand.

"Thank you," I said after we'd gone another few blocks. Every breath I took helped to still the beast clawing inside my skin. The need to inflict damage and pain to the one that hurt my mother—it was still there. It burned in vibrant hues of red and orange.

"You're welcome," she said, not dismissing my gratitude or making light of it. "Just tell me what you need."

"You." It was that simple. She was what I needed. For her, I could cage up every violent response and shackle it until I could think again. There were so many better ways to take revenge. Bloody retribution had its place, but I would not let my temper control me.

I had far too much to lose now. I pulled into the private parking garage near my loft and followed the route upward to the reserved slot. The rattle of the rolling door sliding up and letting me tuck the car away before it rolled down soothed on a very basic level. The last bit of clatter was the lock turning, sealing me inside the cage I very much needed to be in.

Sealing me inside with Lainey.

The weight of her hand on my thigh helped me take a deep breath and then release it. Then another. By the third, I was ready to get out of the car. I glanced over at her. "There's still time for me to take you back—"

"Don't," she said. One word. Her decision had been made. "You said you needed me. This is where I'm going to be."

A stone pressing down on my heart rolled away. It wasn't the first time the rubble had dislodged. But the debris had been thick enough to entomb my emotions and keep them contained.

Raising my hand, I cradled her face and she leaned into the contact. The trust shoved aside another broken rock, smashing it to the side. Every one loosened another breath.

Pain speared into my chest. My singular focus on answering my mother's quest had been my personal obsession, my circles of hell as if I were trapped in Dante's nightmare.

Breaking out from under the cairn of the past hurt. On some level, it was a betrayal. A betrayal of being only the man obsessed with finding his sibling, obsessed with finding the answer, and destroying everyone who had brought harm into my mother's life—who had made her cry and broken her heart.

Broken mine.

Lainey? She needed more than the broken me. She needed me whole and present. If we found my *brother*—brother. I had a brother. If we found him, he would need more than the demon who had hunted for him all these years.

"I'm here," Lainey whispered, the lifeline wrapping around me and giving me somewhere to go that wasn't a river of ice or fire.

I would die for her. I would kill for her. Most of all, I would *live* for her.

Leaning forward, I captured her lips. The kiss could probably have waited until we were inside, but I needed to taste her now. I needed the way she opened her mouth to me. Craved how her tongue swept forward to duel with mine.

When she retreated, it beckoned me to follow. Then she sucked against my tongue. Her hunger matching my own. Every wet lick, every biting nip, and every soft gasp in between as I drank in her taste even as I inhaled her breath.

This was what I needed.

It took everything I had to pull away. Then only because I needed to take her inside. Doing this here would be uncomfortable for her and I wanted hours...

At some point, I would take days.

For now, hours would do.

Sliding my tongue over my lower lip and savoring the taste of her, I wrenched open the door and climbed out. She waited for me to come around to get her. For all her independence, letting me take charge was a gift.

I would never abuse it.

"Do you want me to leave these in the car?" She motioned to the envelopes in the purse.

"You can leave the whole thing in here. Bring your phone. You won't need anything else."

She put her purse on the floor, tugged out her phone and then took my hand. I kept the contact light. Once we were inside...

I counted down the moments. Unlocking the door, I turned to the keypad next to the entrance and entered in a code. "I'll give you your own for here. I only ask that you bring no one else."

"Done."

I paused as I closed the door, then reset the alarm before I glanced at her. In the dim light cast by the runners along the ceiling, her eyes took on the softest shape. Open, no guile or cunning to keep me out. Emotion filled those hazel eyes of hers. Like the chips of gold amongst the dark forest, she offered me something beyond precious.

"I will never willingly hurt you," I promised. "But I am... raw and I need so much."

"Then take it," she said, flattening her hand against my chest and the contact burned even through the fabric of the shirt.

"If it's too much," I told her, and when she would have opened her mouth, I pressed a finger to her lips. "If you are uncomfortable or frightened or even just overwhelmed, you will tell me to stop. One word. One syllable, Lainey. Then it stops. Tell me you understand."

This close, her pupils seemed to swell and drown out the color. Her nostrils flared, and her breath got a bit of a hitch to it. But not once did she pull away or look disturbed.

She pressed a kiss to my finger then whispered, "I understand. Take what you need."

Closing my eyes, I sucked in a deep breath. I wanted to smell nothing that wasn't her, feel nothing that wasn't her... "I love you," I whispered before I slid an arm around her waist and lifted her.

She hooked her thighs to my hips like she'd known what I was going to do. I stalked through the loft, ignoring the space as I carried her toward the riser where the bed was.

Every inch of this loft was mapped out in my mind. I knew where the chairs sat. How many steps to climb to bring me to the level where the bed sprawled. I knew where the silks and the ropes were stored.

More, I had the one woman who might be willing to indulge this side of me without question or reservation. A woman I trusted that I cared about more than I craved the release of losing myself in utterly.

At the bed, I dipped to lay her down. When she would have sat up, I pressed a hand to her chest. "Stay," I ordered. I needed to be in control. She said she could give me that, so I allowed her a moment to decide.

When she went slack and settled against the black bed covers again, I nodded. I didn't bother with lights, I didn't need them. The low ones along the ceiling were enough. They came on automatically at dark and shut off a few hours later. Another security feature. The windows overlooking the city also added another layer of twinkling lights. The mirrored exterior kept anyone from looking in.

Her boots came off with a gentle tug. I was careful of the knives she had stored there. Then I peeled off her socks, her pants and panties came next.

I paused for a moment to check the scrap of silk. It was soaking wet and smelled only of her. I lifted it to take a cleansing breath. Then another.

The beast raging inside my skin settled, the clawing sensation relaxing. We had what we wanted right now. We had Lainey.

I had her.

It would soothe that primal side until we could extract the punishment owed in blood, pain, sweat, and tears. For now, I pushed all that away. None of that belonged here.

Setting aside her clothing, I stroked my hands up her legs to her bare pussy and pressed a kiss to the mound. Her arousal perfumed the air. As tempted as I was to lick, nibble, and taste, I would get distracted. There was so much more I wanted to do first.

"Sit up," I commanded, taking her hands and helping her sit now. With care, I pushed off her jacket and she unbuckled the gun holster. I could have done that but I didn't argue. Getting her naked was the goal.

At least, it was the first goal. I set the gun to the side, away from us and then helped her shed the shirt and finally her bra. When she wore nothing but her skin, I leaned in close to take another deep breath of her.

A shiver raced over her and her nipples went hard and peaked. How lovely they were and I had barely gotten started. Taking her stack of clothes I moved them to a chair, then I pulled out a mask from the nightstand drawer.

I had all the tools here, all the equipment. None of it was used. Everything I'd stocked here had been for her specifically. Before when I allowed myself to play, I'd always done it somewhere controlled where others could intervene if necessary.

Moving back to her, I dangled the mask before I teased it against her cheek. She tilted her head back, letting me see her throat.

"On your knees on the bed."

She swung her legs up and moved gracefully to her knees. It brought her head level with my chest and I let out another sigh. The obedience sanded off the jagged and broken bits that threatened to stab and cut me.

When I covered her eyes, I kept my attention on her face as I secured the mask behind her hair. It would block out everything in her vision. I'd tried several until I found the perfect one.

This was cut from the softest silk, it wouldn't chafe or leave marks. It would sit like a kiss over her eyes.

"Good?" I asked once it was in place.

She swallowed once then she took a deep breath, the sharpness of her inhale audible.

"Excited," she admitted and I almost wondered if she'd flushed. She did that sometimes. For all her pragmatic spirit and daring nature, she was still new to many different things. I hadn't forgotten her reactions at the club or the museum.

I'd never been more grateful for her openness than I was right now.

"Good," I whispered, stroking her cheek with one finger then trailing it down her throat to her breasts. I didn't quite connect with the nipples and when she swayed toward my finger, I gave that breast a little slap.

Nothing damaging, but the sharpness of the sting caught her off guard and she let out a hiss.

"Stay still," I told her. "I get to touch. I get to decide. All you do is get to feel."

Another small test. I had faith in her. She could do this. She said I could have whatever I wanted.

She was what I wanted.

Wetting her lips with a swipe of her tongue, she nodded once. "I'll stay still..."

I closed my eyes, soaking in the moment. "Remember," I whispered. "If you are ever uncomfortable, uncertain, or frightened... just say stop."

"I'll just say stop," she promised and I returned to gliding my hand down her body. I stroked and petted her, soothing myself as I made plans. The hooks were sturdy and I had everything I needed.

"Good," I whispered. "Because I'm going to make one of my fantasies come true."

CHAPTER
SEVENTEEN

LAINEY

"Stay still," Bodhi told me. "I get to touch. I get to decide. All you do is get to feel."

The heat in that order sank into my bones. There was a fragile intensity to Bodhi in this moment. An intensity I wouldn't shy away from for anything in the world. He rarely asked *me* for anything. I found I would deny him nothing.

At the same time, the liquid desire in his voice held dark promise. One I wanted to embrace and ride until we were both spent. I licked my lips, even if my mouth had suddenly gone dry. "I'll stay still..."

"Remember," he whispered. "If you are ever uncomfortable, uncertain, or frightened... just say stop." The words looped around me like an embrace, fastening me securely to him in a way I didn't pretend to understand. The only thing important here was that he needed me.

"I'll just say stop," I repeated the earlier promise as he stroked his hand down my arm to my side, then over my hip. Softness marked his touch, the gliding contact familiar, and it offered *comfort*. Whether it was for him or for me, I wasn't sure and honestly, I didn't care. If he needed this then it was his.

"Good," he whispered finally and goosebumps erupted over my skin. My nipples went taut. "Because I'm going to make one of my fantasies come true."

One of his...

Heat flooded me at that declaration. His fantasy. He wanted *his* fantasy to come true. Tears filled my eyes as emotion clogged my throat. At the same time, liquid need unfurled within me as he continued to stroke his hands over my skin.

Everywhere he touched me turned electric. Bodhi never failed to delight me. With each and every interaction, he opened the door into himself wider. Nothing hidden. No place forbidden.

"I love you," I whispered, the emotion demanding to be let out. His soft chuckle was like a feather dusting over my senses. Then he pressed a kiss to my bare shoulder.

"I didn't even bring you shoes this time." The lightness in his statement was so at odds with the emotion drenching his tone that I was torn between laughter and tears.

"You brought me you—" I never finished the full thought because he swooped in to capture my mouth with his. The slow massage of his lips to mine sent a frisson of delight to splinter my thoughts.

He framed my face with his fingertips, the stroke of his thumb beneath my chin nudging my head back. The silkiness of the mask struck me as my eyes closed. Yet, the stroke of his tongue dipping in to tease mine deepened the sensuous nature of the kiss.

The fragile intensity in the kiss wasn't usually Bodhi's style. He'd always been so bold in our interactions. Normally, he seemed to take a near savage delight with how he could tease me right up to the edge before plunging us both over.

Keeping the contact light, he glided his hand down to my throat. The firmness of the way he collared me triggered me on such an erotic level, I had to gasp for a breath.

Dampness coated my thighs, but Bodhi didn't release my mouth. Every breath he allowed me to take came from him and the world fell away until all that remained was the two of us. He was my anchor in the darkness, his touch keeping me from drowning utterly even as he stroked his thumb over my pulse.

"Sweet Lainey B," he whispered against my mouth, every syllable punctuated with another hot caress of his tongue. "My sweet Lainey B..."

The possession in those words looped around me even more firmly than his hand on my throat. "Bodhi," I whispered back. "My Phillip."

A laugh bubbled out of me at the nip of his teeth to my lower lip. He really didn't like his given name and on some level, I understood. Yet, it was *his* name and he should be allowed to claim it for him and no one else.

"For you," he promised. "But only you."

I smiled, then bit him back and his groan rolled along my spine like the tide coming in. "The perfect Trouble for me."

That earned me both, another searing kiss, as well as a stinging slap against my hip. The dichotomy between the dueling connections lit me up. Particularly when he flexed his hand around my throat and massaged the heat into my skin.

Pain had never been a kink of mine, or at least one I had been aware of, but these men... They brought out all the dark desires within me, both imagined and not.

I drifted as he devoured my mouth, content to meet his demanding kisses with the ferocity of my own hunger. Yet, even as he seemed to sate my need, he struck a match to a fresh fire within me.

I wanted *everything*.

I wanted to give him *everything*.

One by one, these men of mine had awoken a side of me that I never could have imagined. Now, I refused to live without them. They sharpened my protective instincts yet also provoked my need to surrender. Not because I had to, but because I *could*.

They didn't want to control me. They complemented me. They didn't want to own me, yet I would give myself to them body and soul. They did the same.

Bodhi was perfect for me and in this moment, suspended in this darkly sensual world, he was *my* everything.

Gradually, he pulled away and took my breath with him. A low sound escaped me. I couldn't really tell if it was a moan or a whimper. It was needy though.

"Shhh," he hummed the sound as he released my throat to trace a finger across my chest, drawing a line from one shoulder to the other. He didn't quite touch my breasts and yet my neck seemed almost painfully naked and too cold.

A shiver raced over my skin, pulling my nipples taut. He didn't dip his hand lower, just drawing lazy patterns down toward my breasts and up again until the tension locking up my shoulders released.

"That's my beautiful, sweet Lainey B," he murmured, the drift of his words adding another layer of fire to the path he drew particularly when he teased a new design around one of my nipples.

It puckered tighter and my cunt clenched. The lightness of his touch, coupled with the absence of his hand on my throat, left me vibrating with awareness of him.

When he extended to the torture to my other nipple, I

pressed my shoulders back and leaned into the contact. All it succeeded in doing was making him chuckle and he lightened his touch to that of a ghost.

So. Frustrating.

Another sound escaped me, but his laughter was infectious. Because he was enjoying my reactions. Truth be told, as much as I ached for more, I savored every nuance of this—his fantasy.

Just when I'd grown accustomed to the feather light soft touches, he suddenly traced his tongue over one turgid tip. The unexpected contact sent a jolt through that only magnified when he blew a breath over the damp nipple. Heat flushed my chest and my face.

With my eyes hidden, I could almost imagine that I lit up like a blazing neon sign. Then he bit that nipple. The scrape of his teeth an erotic promise that had me swaying. Another nuzzling kiss, this one to the neglected nipple and he pulled it taut to his teeth.

A hiss of air escaped me as he sucked harder, tracing his tongue against the tip. His wandering hand dipped between my legs and I bucked at the single brush of his finger to my clit.

Need throbbed through me. The embarrassing sound I released disguised nothing of my reactions. I soaked his hand and I swore I could feel my pulse in my clit.

"I like you like this," he whispered against my breast. "Panting, needy, and so wet for me, it perfumes the air."

His hand left my slit even as he pulled back from my breast. The sound of light sucking followed by an hmmmm, sent another shudder through me. He was lapping me up from his fingers.

I could hear him, but not see him. The pleasure of

witnessing his reactions a new torture in this assault on my senses.

"Are you still willing to let me play, Lainey B?"

"You can have me whatever way you want me." The stutter in my words only served to illustrate my point. I wanted him. I was fine with *everything* he needed.

Whatever everything was.

"I love you," he whispered, the simplicity of those words at odds with the dark emotion in his voice. Then, he added in a far more commanding tone, "What do you say if you need me to stop?"

I couldn't deny that tone even if I wanted to and I really didn't want to. "Stop."

"Good."

Then he was gone, his touch, his whispered words, even his breathing. I knelt there on the bed, chillier in his absence with my breasts aching and my body cold and yet flushed in the same moment.

Whispers of sound reached me. In the absolute quiet of the room, it was so loud. A part of my mind tried to track his movements. What was he doing? Why was he doing it? But only a part of my mind, the rest of me waited, anticipation curling in my belly.

Something exquisitely soft rubbed along my arm. A fresh wave of goosebumps spread out over my skin. It seemed even softer than the mask, if that was possible. Or maybe it was the fur lining that added to the sensation.

Either way, I sighed. A soft rip of velcro and then the softness wrapped around one wrist and sealed shut. Then the other. Head tilted, I tried to follow his movements.

He nudged me onto my side, then stroked a hand over my hip and along my flank until he wrapped another cuff around my right ankle. Then my left. Everywhere he touched me, he left a little trail of arousal that just seemed to build.

With careful hands, he pulled me back up to my knees then there was something soft and silken wrapping around my throat. This didn't come with the rip of velcro, but instead the faintest of little clicks.

"An emerald?" The tease fell from my lips so easily and he chuckled.

"Emeralds do look beautiful on you, Buttercup. Even better when decorating something inside of you. This is different." He smoothed his hand over the collar—and it was very much a collar for how it hugged my throat like his hand did. There was something at the center, an oval-like object that was harder than the rest.

A cameo?

"Something special, for you." A whisper of a kiss over my lips. "But later... now, can I gag you?"

"With your cock?" The brief moment of silence before he let out a sharp, warm, and wonderful laugh made me grin.

"Tempting," he whispered, teasing his knuckles along my cheek. "So very tempting. But no, I want to gag you so that you can't speak. You will still be able to make sound, but no words. Is that alright with you?"

Head tilted, I didn't need long to consider my answer. It was right there. "Yes. Whatever you want."

"You will spoil me," he whispered against my ear and I shivered, not opposed to that idea at all.

The gag, as it turned out, proved a more challenging choice for him. He tried three before he settled on the last, it had a small ball in it that would let me bite down, but it didn't cut into the corners of my mouth and it actually fit comfortably. The fact it tasted a bit like strawberries and nothing like rubber also helped.

"Now, I know I said you had to say stop," he continued as something soft began to rub against my arm. "The gag will prevent you from speaking, so I need you to choose a sound that tells me to stop."

I considered that for a moment as he threaded what I presumed was rope around my chest, until he criss-crossed my breasts. It lifted and separated them. The snug fit was comfortable, even more so when he began drawing it down to my legs and in between them.

For a moment, I worried he was going to have me strad-dling it, but instead of sliding it along my slit, it wrapped against the inside of my thighs. There was something elegant and soothing about the way he wrapped me. I went from being on my knees, to on my feet, to my side, to my hands and knees.

There was something relaxing in the motion and letting him position me wherever he wanted. He hummed as he worked, checking with me periodically until he finally threaded his rope through loops on the wrists bands and the ankle ones then along my back.

I was well and truly tied up. I don't think I'd ever been this turned on before and he wasn't teasing or touching me more than necessary. Yet my cunt was soaking and I hadn't missed his happy little sound when he'd had his hands between my legs.

The scent was also unmistakable. If my nose wasn't wrong, he was no less turned on than I was. "You... look exquisite like this, Lainey B." The sheer pleasure in his voice sent hot tears to my eyes. "Perfection. Lovely. Powerful. Sweet. Utterly mine in every way... mine to love, mine to serve, and mine to enjoy."

My throat convulsed as he nuzzled kisses to my breasts. I was the perfect captive audience, upon which he lavished praise and adoration. He punctuated his kisses with nips, scrapes of his teeth, and long drawn out suction that sent pulses of pure need to my cunt.

A groan escaped him as he traced kisses against my shoulders, as he moved around behind me. The beauty of this was I had no control, none, and yet I wasn't worried. Bodhi had me. He would let *nothing* happen to me.

Well, nothing we both didn't want to have happen.

"Do you know the sound you will make for stop?" He asked, wrapping himself around me. The weight of his cock was right there against my ass. Oh, someone was as naked as I was and I'd missed it.

That was all right. This was what he needed.

I had thought about the sound I would make, but now, all the thoughts fled at the contact of his kisses along my shoulder. Then he rubbed his cheek and the hint of stubble there sent electric pulses through me. The prickles of contact skating over my skin and through my blood.

The ball gag made me drool more, but frankly I didn't care. I trilled a sound, it was lower, and vibrated from my throat. It wasn't a sound of a cry or a scream. It wasn't even a moan. It was a far more deliberate noise.

"Oh," he said, exhaling the syllable like it was everything he needed. "I like that... excellent. If you want me to stop, make that sound..."

I didn't even get to acknowledge it when there was a sudden hoisting and I wasn't on the bed anymore. Suddenly, all his loops and ties made sense. He was suspending me, like the exhibits in the museum tonight.

Suspended for his pleasure.

For mine.

The trembling came from my core, and the first brush of his cock had me moaning.

"Yes," he whispered. "Just like that... Mine to wreck, and to use, until we're both spent."

Then he thrust inside of me and the wracking orgasm took over. Thoughts scattered, obliterated in a wave of pure white bliss.

Everything honed down to the place where his body filled mine and to where he anchored me to the earth with his hands on my hips.

Flying... this was what it was like.

I was flying.

And Bodhi was soaring with me.

CHAPTER
EIGHTEEN

EZRA

The planning session with the Vandals went late into the night, continuing well after Bodhi notified us that he and Lainey weren't returning to the penthouse. My reaction? Lucky bastard.

Adam's response surprised me more, honestly. He just lifted his chin in acknowledgement when Milo shared the info with us quietly. While I might be the more impulsive of us, Adam definitely had the worst temper. When it came to Lainey, he'd never been reasonable.

Never.

The fact neither of us experienced immediate jealousy or irritation stunned me when it sank in. Maybe he did get a twinge and was better at hiding it than I was, or maybe he didn't.

The thing was... my kotyonok was with Bodhi. No, she wasn't where I could see or touch her, but she was with someone who would not hesitate to kill in her defense. He would protect her. She was *safe*.

Surety in that knowledge relaxed the tension in my lower spine. Dismissing the urge to get a drink, I settled for coffee and followed it with water. Eventually, the Vandals were wrapping it up and preparing to go.

"I'm going back with them tonight," Milo said as the others left and he dragged on his jacket. "I'll be back in the morning." He glanced toward the door, and said, "I'll be out in a sec."

Liam lifted his chin then shut the door, leaving the three of us alone.

"I'd protest about heading out alone, but you're hardly going without backup. They are more than capable of keeping an eye on you." The dry comment pulled a faint smile from Milo.

"Yeah and I need to talk to Doc. With everything we're juggling, I don't want to lose sight of anything. Particularly King and his ties, this—new sibling Ivy and I apparently have, and everything else." He raked a hand through his hair. "You two good? No plans to raise hell or burn anything down tonight?"

"Not at the moment," I said, shrugging. Anything was possible. "Night's still young."

"No," Adam grunted out the word and gave me a fierce look. Oh, there went the vein in his forehead. My grin widened. "We're not going anywhere."

Oh, that was definitely an order. I almost chortled, but managed to contain it before I glanced at Milo. "Go check on your friend. I solemnly swear, I'll send you a text if we plan any riots."

"Uh huh."

Milo and Adam grunted those two syllables in the exact same tone. Try as I might, I couldn't not laugh. It was funny as fuck.

"I won't be far," Milo said to Adam. "Good luck."

Good luck? Some of my amusement drained away. The fact Milo clapped Adam on the shoulder didn't help.

I scowled as Milo strode out, closing the door behind him and leaving us in Bodhi's penthouse. Bodhi's place... I got why we were here. He wanted us in a more secure location. For Lainey...

Suddenly, it seemed too silent, too large, and far too empty. Pivoting, I glared at Adam. The desire for whiskey burned in my throat. I could practically taste it.

"Why did he wish you good luck?" The demand escaped with all the grace of an angry toddler. Irritation raced through me, slamming headlong into embarrassment and shame.

The idea that Milo knew something about Adam that I didn't? It... it grated.

"You know what," I snapped, surging to my feet. "I don't care. Keep all your secrets. I'm going to bed."

What I really wanted was a drink. Bed wasn't quite a substitute but it would have to do. The alcohol in the penthouse—what I'd seen of it—was under lock and key. The rest had been thrown out. No one trusted me.

The anger revved inside of me as my thoughts continued to collide. Pivoting on my heel, I stalked out of the living room and headed for the stairs.

"Ezra..." Adam called, aggrieved didn't begin to cover his tone. No. He didn't get to fucking do that. I was the injured party here. Him keeping secrets.

Again.

It wasn't until I hit the top step that I realized he wasn't even bothering to follow me. Pain stabbed right through the fury in my system to impale my heart. The emotional wound only made it pound more furiously.

Fuck, I would kill for a drink. I slammed the door on the

175

bedroom that Adam and I had been sharing for the past few weeks. The fact Bodhi had given it to "us" hadn't really registered at first.

But Adam hadn't skipped out of the room or told me to sleep in here by myself. Didn't stop him from keeping secrets. I slammed the door behind me again, then turned the lock.

It was petty as fuck.

At the same time, it was ridiculously satisfying. I leaned back against it and dragged in a couple of deep breaths. My eyes burned with the tears I refused to shed.

I shoved away from the door, stripping off my clothes on the way to the shower. As much as I hated cold ones, I needed to clear the cobwebs. I needed to—

The crash of the door opening behind me jerked me around. I forgot how to breathe as Adam glared at me. His blue-violet eyes were so dark, I swallowed convulsively.

Adam was pissed.

He stalked across the room after me.

Apprehension shivered up my spine. I opened my mouth, but he raised a finger and silenced me in one motion.

My teeth clacked together when I snapped my jaw shut. Then Adam was just there, invading my space. He half-ripped the shirt from my hand and flung it away before he pinned me to a wall.

The weight of his hand on my chest burned me. Nose to nose, he locked his gaze on mine and it didn't matter how angry I was, I couldn't look away from him if I tried.

"You piss me off so fucking much," Adam snarled, the coffee on his breath teased my nostrils. It added to the rich earthy scent of him. Oak and amber, all underscored with sage.

Filling my lungs with the smell of him was a cleansing experience. It didn't even matter that he was glaring at me right now. The vein in his forehead throbbed, and a muscle in Adam's cheek jumped.

He was livid.

My dick began to pulse in time with that angry vein. I wanted to lick it.

Lick him.

More—

"You're not even listening to me." It was like I'd unlocked some new level of rage intimacy with my best friend.

"You're pissed," I said, belatedly trying to fill in the blanks. "I piss you off so much." Wonder filled me and I grinned.

His eyes narrowed. "What the hell are you smiling at?"

"I make you crazy," I said, suddenly delighted. "I do, don't I?"

Seemingly speechless, Adam just gawked at me. It was a heady sensation. *I* made *Adam* crazy.

"It's good," I whispered, then surged forward to kiss him. Shock seemed to hold Adam captive, his mouth hard and unyielding. Like the rest of him.

Where Lainey was soft and had curves I couldn't wait to fondle, Adam was a brick wall. Dense muscle, physically fit to an extreme I doubted most ever saw. But then I'd worked out with him, grappled with him, and I knew his body.

Fuck, I'd gotten to suck his cock. My dick went rock hard and the zipper of my jeans threatened to leave an imprint. I licked at Adam's lips and he went from frozen to motion.

His hand fisted in my hair as he wrapped his free hand around my throat. All those fucking control issues. We were so goddamn damaged.

It was sexy as fuck.

The pressure of his erection ground against mine as he opened his mouth. Then his tongue was staging an invasion as he took over the kiss. Every stroke of his lips to mine was a hot demand. Our tongues dueled as he thrust his hips against me.

An errant image of him going to his knees for me when I'd been in the bathroom, him sucking me off after that handjob damn near finished me had me groaning.

"I want you," I managed to get the words out in between his hot, demanding kisses. He growled when I would have pushed him back. There was just something incredibly appealing about Adam pushed to his limits.

I'd always thought he was sexy as fuck when Lainey drove him to distraction. Now I got to do it...

That lit a sparkler in me like it was the Fourth of July.

"Shut the fuck up," Adam groaned as he kissed me again. The force took all of my breath and then he jerked back before giving me a once over.

Fresh apprehension hit me. Had I gone too far? I did that. I knew I did...

I almost fucked it up with Lainey so many times.

I opened my mouth to apologize, but Adam's hands were on my jeans. He flicked the button out and then peeled down the zipper. The relief lasted only until his hand wrapped around my cock. Then I was thrusting against his fingers.

Fuck, I was ready to come right now.

"You're going to do exactly what I tell you," Adam said and when I opened my mouth, he gave me a narrow-eyed look that had me snapping it closed again. Giving me a nod of grim satisfaction, he almost smiled. "Better. Now get naked and get on that bed. You and I are going to settle something right here, and right now."

We were?

We were going to settle—

Adam squeezed my dick.

Right. Naked.

My hands were shaking as I pushed down my jeans. The fact he had to release my dick was frustrating. Licking my lips, I glanced at him. Naked wasn't hard to achieve when I was halfway there.

"Bed, Ezra."

Right. I forgot.

When I would have sat down, he said, "Hands and knees."

I almost fell at that comment. My legs went weak and I cut a look back at him.

"Did I stutter?" The whip crack of command in his voice had my stomach dropping and fluttering all at once. He was so damn hot like this.

While I continued to stare at him, he unbuttoned his own shirt. Each new opening to reveal more of his beautifully sculpted chest.

It wasn't until he undid his belt that I managed to drag my gaze upward. "No," I said slowly. "But..."

"But?" He raised his eyebrows, practically daring me to continue.

Did I want to discuss this?

That thought paralyzed me for all of three seconds. Why the hell was I fighting him? "Hands and knees."

It came out jerky and uncertain.

"Hands and knees." His confirmation was all the boost I needed. I turned to the bed and climbed on it. My cock stretched up toward my belly, tapping me with every motion.

There was something utterly vulnerable about being on my knees like this, facing away from him. It was also erotic as all hell because Adam lowering his zipper suddenly drowned out the sound of my racing heart.

"You're getting naked too."

"Obviously." There was just a hint of dry humor there. Like he was indulging me.

"But I don't get to watch?" Yes, I was never not gonna push him. It was who I was.

"I would have let you earlier, but then you stomped off in a tantrum." A hand landed on my ass and it was large, callused, and I almost forgot how to think with him rubbing over my hip and then back again.

He wasn't anywhere near my crack...

"I was—"

"Having a tantrum," Adam said, cutting me off and then he was gripping my cheeks and all the air backed up in my lungs cause he was parting them. "Acting like a spoiled brat who didn't get his way because instead of asking or listening, you just assumed something nefarious."

Spit struck my anus and I shuddered. Oh fuck. Oh fuck. Adam followed the spit with a thumb that traced my rim.

"Always betting you will be last. Always choosing to fight and rage at the world, rather than just ask for what you want..."

The words didn't make much sense because Adam tested his thumb against the ring of muscle and my cock jerked at the first push. I was in no way lubed up enough for this.

He spit again.

"That won—"

"I'm talking," Adam snapped, thumb tracing that spit over my asshole even as he delivered a slap to my ass. The heat of it blazed through me.

The fuck did he think he was... I tried to choke out my inner asshole. It needed to shut the fuck up right now.

"Good boy," Adam almost crooned the words and the precum leaked out of my cock. It smeared against my belly and I dropped my chin, as my breath went ragged cause he'd pushed his thumb in. It was a little stretch. It didn't really hurt, but it wasn't exactly comfortable either.

No way to not be aware of him. Adam was fondling my ass. I thought I'd died when he let me suck him off while I fucked Lainey. I reached heaven when he finally stroked me and teased my cock.

This?

This was purgatory. Heaven. Hell. All of it rolled up into one violently sexy bastard I couldn't get enough of.

"You make me crazy, Ezra. You are such an asshole. You suck cock like it's your job, you can make our girl come with a scream, and you literally try to kill me with your mood swings."

No, I really didn't, but he was thrusting his thumb a little deeper with each word and a little more spit. If we were going bigger than the thumb...

"You were pissed at me because Milo said good luck."

Oh, it all crashed back in and the haze of pleasure drowning me, jerked back like a yanked curtain. "Secrets..." I choked that one word out. "I hate the secrets."

"I'm not keeping secrets from you, asshole." His lips were at my ear and he was bending over me. The tease of his cock against my ass was a whole new level of torment. "He said good luck because you and I were going to be alone. He was giving us the night so we wouldn't feel self-conscious."

Wait...

Adam bit me. The scrape of his teeth on my shoulder grounded me and had my cock jerking.

"You stupid asshole," he muttered as he pulled away. "Milo may be a lot of things, but a blind asshole is not one. Apparently, you got all of that in the family."

The insult could have hurt if it wasn't so accurate. Milo

left to give me and Adam privacy. I didn't know how to respond.

"But no, you can't just accept that he might say something you don't understand the reference to immediately without blowing up. So, my fucked up friend," Adam continued, his voice dark with passion and anger. Passionate anger? It was hot no matter what it was.

His thumb was out and there was something warm and wet drizzling over my ass. He brought the lube.

I was wrong. I hadn't died before.

I was about to die now. I was going to die impaled on his cock and I shifted on the bed. I wanted this so goddamn much. He slapped my ass again.

"Fuck," I barked out the word. He had big hands and that fucking hurt, but then he massaged the cheek he'd struck and the heat went into my bones.

"Don't like that?" Adam taunted me. Oh, he was definitely taunting.

"Didn't say that—" I regretted my smart mouth almost immediately because he slapped my ass again. This time, the sting was far hotter and I swore. "God..."

"Adam," he corrected with another slap. It was scrambling my brains as he spanked me.

Adam fucking Reed was spanking me.

And what was I doing? Pushing my ass back at him like please sir, may I have some more?

Laughter and tears tangled up in a hysterical mess, but then I became aware of a finger in my ass... wait, no two fingers. Holy shit, he'd distracted me and he was fucking my ass with his fingers. It felt good as he stretched me.

"You don't have to be so careful—" That didn't go over well. He just slapped my ass three times in rapid succession until I was breathless from the heat of it all. His gentle massage as he scissored his fingers inside of me brought real tears to my eyes.

Not tears of pain.

Far from it.

He was adding a third finger.

"This is easier when Lainey is here," Adam said, the words filtered through the wild emotions choking me.

"Yes," I agreed.

"We focus on her." Adam was leaning over me, his hips against my hot cheek while he finger fucked my ass. All three, stretching me and when he teased my prostate, it was my hips that were bucking. "We turn all that aggression on her even as we dance around each other."

"You let me suck you off." It was a plea and an argument.

"I did and I fucking loved it," Adam's declaration threatened to destroy me. I collapsed, almost face first into the bedspread. My arms and legs wouldn't hold me up anymore. "I fucking loved it and I've never looked at a man once in my life and thought...I want to sink my dick into him. I want him to suck me. I want to kiss him until his mouth bruises and he shuts the fuck up."

Jealousy vied with shock as the flip-flopping emotions tore through me. "No?"

"No," Adam said firmly.

"But you do with me?" I didn't want to ask the question, yet I had to.

"Ezra," Adam said, all traces of the rage and exasperation with me just gone.

All at once, he was the man I'd grown up with, the best friend who'd gone to hell and back with me. The man who'd gotten in the way of my father's blows, and who'd put me back together more than once.

Real tears escaped me at the genuine emotion bleeding in his words.

"Yes, I do with you...I love you, asshole. I love your dumb fucking remarks, your crazy antics, your insane decisions, and your jackass temper." His fingers were gone but his words buried themselves in my heart. The feel of his dick against my asshole was right there. "I've never done this before... I'll never do this with anyone that isn't you or Lainey."

Yes. That was how it should be. "We love her."

"Yes, we do," he whispered as he pushed past that ring of muscle and I arched my head up to groan.

There was no patience in Adam, but there was finesse. He rocked into me and it reminded me of how he'd been buried in Lainey's ass and now he was going to be buried in mine. Every thrust took him deeper. He'd slicked himself up and I pushed back, welcoming him.

"I love you," I said in a hoarse voice. "I love you so goddamn much."

"Good," Adam grunted as he sank to the hilt. The rub against my prostate was a tantalizing tease. Fuck, I needed more. Then he ran his fingers through my hair. He wasn't moving, he was just laying there, balls deep in my ass. "This good?"

"Oh yeah," I said, then threw caution to the wind. "Could be better."

"Oh?" He dared me to keep it up and well, who was I, if not consistent?

"Moving would be good..."

His little growl pleased me enormously. Even more when he pulled out and shoved back in. I saw stars.

"Yeah, a little more... fuck me like you mean it." It was my turn to taunt and Adam dragged us both back, pulling me right to the edge of the bed and then he was thrusting into me.

My world narrowed down to the heavy thickness of him filling me with every push and the soft grunts of his breathing.

"You are such an asshole," he muttered, punctuating every syllable with another trust. More precum leaked out of me as he fucked me. I was going to come.

"But I'm your asshole," I told him.

"Yes, you are," he said, possession filling his voice. "This ass is mine. You will give it to no one else. *Ever* again."

That was an easy promise.

"Except my kotyonok," I reminded him, writhing with the heat he ignited. He was gripping my hips so tightly they were going to be bruised. The pound of his cock in my ass was divine. The bark of laughter twisting around his huff of irritation perfection.

We were on the same page.

Excellent.

I beat at the bed as he pushed me right up to the edge. "Right there..." I was begging. "Fuck me, Adam... right there. Fuck you feel so good."

I came against the covers and my chest. But Adam was still pulsing away in me, his orgasm following mine. The heat of him filling me, everything I'd ever wanted and then we were collapsing together.

Filthy. Hot. Sweaty.

"That was almost too quick," I muttered.

"Are you complaining?" The warning there dared me to take it further.

I mean, if he wanted me to, I could. Except... "No," I whispered. "That was perfect."

"Eh," he grunted and I twisted to find him leaning over

me and then his mouth was on mine. A hot bruising kiss he ended with a bite. Pushy bastard. "Not perfect, pretty close. But we have all night to figure it out..."

We had all night to...

Struck mute, I stared up at him as a slow smile crossed his face, even his eyes softened.

"Well, I finally found a way to shut you up that didn't involve you choking on my dick." He winked, then kissed me again before he wrapped his arms around me and just held me close.

I kind of wanted to argue, but he was right. I had nothing to say to that.

"Good boy," Adam soothed and I shuddered all over again. "We need to clean up and then you're going to teach me how to suck your cock the way you like it."

Yep. I could do that.

He laughed again and I grinned. I really wasn't going to argue against any of that.

Ever.

CHAPTER
NINETEEN

LAINEY

The smell of coffee proved too tempting an allure to sleep through. Coupled with the sizzle of bacon from the kitchen area below, and my stomach was awake before the rest of me processed my eyes were open. The combination was a decadent tease for my senses. My body was one long, sensual ache and as I pushed myself up on my elbows, I got my first real look at the loft apartment.

The "bedroom" was upstairs. The absolute lack of walls seemed almost too exposed. Yet, the low railing overlooking the living area below with its warm wooden floors and rich colored furnishings promised a cozier welcome. Then that wall of windows gazing at the park was exquisite.

A king in his castle— No, not a king. Bodhi didn't want to rule over everything and everyone. He just wanted information to identify our enemies and then use his skills to end them before they were a real threat. In his blood, Bodhi was every bit the knight his mother used to weave into her stories.

I had no memories of Isla. I don't think I'd ever met her or

187

if I had, it was when I was far too young to remember. Her influence on Bodhi made me think I would have liked her. Who was I kidding, I would have loved her.

Below, the scent of toast and eggs began to thread through the twin temptations of bacon and coffee. Savoring the ache, I rolled to the edge and slid out. My clothes from the night before were all hung neatly next to an open closet door. Bodhi's clothes were folded over each other in a semi-neat, if disheveled, stack. I claimed the button down shirt and slid it on.

The whole apartment smelled like Bodhi to me. So did the shirt. Leaving it open I rolled up the sleeves before slipping into the bathroom. Once I'd dealt with emptying my bladder and washing my face, I finger combed out my hair. The rough and tumble of bed head seemed to give me large, poofy hair.

The effort to groom it didn't do me any favors. But I was well and truly sated, I kind of liked the look, especially with my puffy lips and the hickeys drawing a heart around my left breast.

I wondered what it would take to mirror that with a tattoo. The desire to see Bodhi *and* have coffee hurried me along. I moved at a languid pace. My cunt was aching and stretched in all the right ways. My ass was a bit sore, not pained but definitely feeling his efforts. Glancing up, I grinned at the hook in the ceiling. It wasn't the only hook present. There were a few and I'd spent half my night suspended over that bed.

A shudder rolled through me. Trapped with my vision muffled and then when he closed off my ears, I'd only been able to savor his scent, his touch, and his taste.

"I want to take all but one away," he whispered against my ear, one hand cupping my cunt when we'd cuddled in bed in the earlier hours after he'd spent himself and purged whatever demons speaking to Hans had provoked. "Strip them all away until you know nothing but my touch. I want you to lose yourself to the only thing you can feel, experience, and know."

He'd traced my earlobe with his tongue as those words sank under the haze of pleasure I floated on.

"Anything you want," I whispered and he'd wrapped me up even tighter. The hand on my cunt flexed, one finger sliding into me like he needed to be a part of me. With his free hand, he spread it over one breast. Maybe I'd get his hand tattooed there instead of the hickeys... all of their hands.

That might take hours though.

"Don't offer me too much, Buttercup. I will take everything."

"I'll offer you what I damn well please, Phillip. You can take anything you want from me. I'm yours." Then lest he think I was being willful or blind, I added, "I know what I'm giving you. I know you'll never hurt me. I trust you."

Trust was a precious commodity in our world. It made for a lonely existence, and it had for me for a long time. Particularly when Adam and Ezra fought so hard to keep me in my bubble. But loving Em, protecting my family, looking after Andrea—they'd all been the gateways to freedom.

Out here, trust was even more valuable.

"I will never betray you," Bodhi promised in a voice soaked with bloody oaths. "I will kill anyone who does."

No wiggle room. Maybe the fact I had zero doubts about the truth in those statements said something terrible about me. I didn't care. "You know, I will do the same for you, right?" Because he was mine to protect too.

The low, heated chuckle he released stroked through me like its own caress. He added a second finger to the first, scissoring against the swollen tissue of my cunt and he began to rub circles against my over-sensitized clit with his palm. One bite to my earlobe as he began to tease my orgasm to life. There was no way I could come again, but I was more than willing to try.

"Yes," he whispered. "I do know, Buttercup."

The ghostly reminders of his touch skated over me as I descended the short steps from the loft. Bodhi shirtless, a pair of gray sweatpants balanced on his hips and giving me a wonderful view of the muscles moving along his back. The look he sent me was molten when he turned to add toast to the plates he was building.

"That's my shirt," he murmured as I strolled right to the breakfast bar. I was very proud that my steps didn't falter.

"If you want it or need it, you can always come and get it." I slid onto one of the leather stools. The cold bracing against my ass. But I was enjoying the partial nudity and there was a relaxed air in this place, away from everything and everyone. We would be back in the thick of it soon, so I was in no hurry to push away the tender cocoon he'd weaved around us.

"True." He turned back to the stove and bit by bit the burners were shut off and then he was adding eggs and crispy bacon to the plates before bringing over a magnificent bowl of fried potatoes with onions and peppers.

"You have many hidden talents," I teased. "I'm not even sure Adam knows how to cook. Ezra barely knows where the kitchen is."

He chuckled before bringing the French press over and pouring a cup for me before pouring his own. "He knows where it is, but I think he's far better at starting the fires than putting them out."

That was true. Cradling the coffee cup in my hands, I pushed up with one foot on the rail around the bottom of the breakfast bar. Bodhi met me halfway with a whisper of a kiss.

"It's a good thing they have us," I murmured.

"Very good thing. You are a boon to everyone." He winked. "Now eat. I burned a lot of calories last night."

"You dirty dog," I teased, sitting back down with care. Yes, my ass and my cunt were still more than a bit tender but in all the best ways. "You just want to see me walking funny."

"Oh, I know you're going to be walking funny." The pure, smug, masculine pride in his smile and his words made me grin. "The rest of the world is going to be there for us very soon. I wanted a little more time with you."

The perfect echo to my earlier thoughts had me saluting him with my coffee mug. "Mr. Cavendish, I am at your disposal for whenever and wherever you would like to escape again."

I needed this kind of time with each of them. It was easy to overlook with so many dangers threatening and even more secrets needing to be unraveled. We couldn't afford to neglect each other, even if it wasn't neglect. We had to be able to ask for what we needed. That Bodhi had?

Tears burned in my eyes as my heart expanded. Milo had, once or twice. Adam had precisely once when he'd finally stopped fighting what could be and embraced what we had. Ezra?

I took a long drink of the coffee. Ezra was a beautiful work in progress, a patchwork quilt of all our damaged parts and the warped tapestry woven by families with too much money at their disposal and far more blood on their hands.

"Thank you for last night," I said and the surprise creasing his smile entertained me. "I needed it too."

"Well, should you ever need or merely want it again..." The invitation dangled there.

"The same goes for you... If you want or need me or it, I'm here. Always."

Our gazes locked and the wordless pulse seemed to bounce from his soul to mine. Poetry existed in these moments. Grinning, I reached for a crispy slice of bacon that I could wash down with my coffee. The world really was waiting for us just outside the door.

"Lainey B?"

"Hmm?" I glanced up.

"Will you go with me to meet my aunt and my grandmother?"

His grandmother. My heart fisted tight.

"It would be my pleasure. Just one request?"

"Name it."

I grinned. "Give me time to change into something that isn't last night's dress or just your shirt?"

His long sigh held amusement and teasing. "If you insist."

"I do."

We were already chuckling.

BREAKFAST PASSED ALMOST TOO SWIFTLY, but I savored the moments. Then it was time to shower and change. The fact Bodhi had clothes for me here—perfectly sized and in my style—told me all I needed to know about how he'd already begun to plan ahead. I checked in with the boys while he took a call.

We'd be back at the penthouse after this meeting. Then it would be time to make our next move. Our meeting with his family kept us in the city and only a couple of blocks over at a lovely little *pied-à-terre* that reminded me a bit of Bodhi's loft that we'd just spent the night in. Having a secure little private getaway in the city was just smart thinking if you didn't live here regularly.

Having it for us to escape to when we shared our living space? Also smart. I was going to have to look into doing that as well. But that was a later problem...

The elevator carried us swiftly up from the garage to the apartment itself. "It's a locked building," Bodhi assured me. "Without the proper code or the invitation, the elevator will lock people out of any residential floor."

That was smart.

Waiting for us were a pair of older women, dressed casually, yet I didn't mistake their easy smiles or assessing looks as anything other than what they were. They wanted my measure and they were both protective of Bodhi. Even more, Bodhi clearly respected them, as well as held them in great affection.

That made me like them even more.

"Sophia, Aunt Eliza, this is Elaine Benedict, but you can call her Lainey if she permits." The introduction carried just a note of warning. One that Sophia seemed to notice immediately even as the wattage of her smile increased.

"Oh, my darling boy," she said, laughing even as she extended her hands to me. "It is a pure delight to meet you, Miss Benedict."

"Lainey," I insisted, accepting her grip and smiling at her. There was just something so classically beautiful about her. Like she wore the air of another time and age settled on her like a crown rather than a weight. "Please. I am very glad to meet you as well."

"Very nice, I know your grandfather," Eliza said as she accepted my handshake. "Leopold always enthuses about you."

I grinned. "Grandfather is proud, but he's also a little biased."

Sophia wrapped an arm around me. "He's very biased,"

she said with a laugh. "But we should always be about the ones we love. Now, you must come and sit with me and let me ply you with some cakes and tea, then ask you all manner of inappropriate questions."

Bodhi cleared his throat.

Chuckling, Sophia gave him the most impudent of looks. "Only if she agrees. Don't tut at me, Bodhi. It's impolite."

"Yes, ma'am." Affection and amusement vied for supremacy in his tone and my heart just squished like I'd been squeezed into the biggest hug. These women were not his mother, but they seemed to love him like they were. I loved that for him.

"You may ask me anything you wish," I offered as we reached the table the women had already set. "But I reserve the right to keep some secrets."

"Oh," Eliza said slowly. "I like her, Bodhi. I like her very much."

"Me too," he said, grinning at me and I winked. It wasn't the pleasurable haze we'd woken up in, but it was warm and wonderful.

CHAPTER
TWENTY

MILO

I climbed the steps from the subway to street level. The colder air was a brisk slap in the face after the warmth from the train. Course, it was also not as smelly up here. Not everyone on that train had showered recently. Still, I liked public transport, particularly if I wanted to flush out any tails.

When I was with Lainey, we drove all over the city. She had a driver. She had a bodyguard—thoughts about that prick were probably better left undisturbed. The fact Karagiani had her in close quarters for so long and hadn't done anything, was something of a miracle.

A flash of movement across the street mirrored my own path. I didn't make a big deal of looking. Not when I could see Jasper clear as day in the reflection in the glass window of a closed store. Not a lot of missing real estate out here, but some of these shops had been closed for a while.

It was another part of King's business plan to gentrify. Drive the residents out and the prices down. Keep retail out until the building owners were practically hemorrhaging money, then sweep in for a save. He would pick up the properties at a steal, and flip them for quite a bit more.

A disgusting process that made solid business sense, but disgusting where human compassion and common decency stood. My phone rang as I cleared another block and I slid it out of my pocket. Jasper's name flashed on the screen with his middle finger.

Snorting at the image, I grinned. Freddie must have pocketed my phone at some point this week. I would have to check the other contact images to see what other surprises he set up. For now, I hit answer on the phone. "Bored?"

"Not particularly. I am freezing my nuts off in this wind. How much further before you show me the top secret new clubhouse?"

I shook my head, chuckling. "It's not a top secret clubhouse, just a little personal renovation project. Future investment and planning."

"Raptor," Jasper said, his tone suddenly sober and serious. "I hate to break this to you, but you don't have enough time to match your girlfriend's bank account or the other boyfriends for that matter. I'd say you need to focus on what you bring to the table and accept your fate as a kept man."

"Fuck you," I told him cheerfully. "One more block, then I'll cross toward you and we'll head east."

His laughter carried over the phone. "Got it." Then he ended the call. One block later, I crossed at the corner and headed down a different street. Fortunately, this block offered something of a shield against the wind slicing down between the building. Which was good, cause my nose was fucking numb as hell.

Jasper fell into step with me. He had a cigarette lit and the familiar trail of bluish, tobacco smoke wreathed him periodically before the breeze would snatch it away. The smoking was a bad habit that he'd never kicked and frankly, I didn't think he wanted to.

We were all a little fucked up. Some of us were a lot fucked up. If he wanted to smoke, he got to smoke. Lighting cigarettes gave him an excuse to check behind us. I paused closer to the building than the street.

"Light one for me?"

He paused, glanced behind us then made a show of patting himself down. Then we huddled to block the breeze while he lit the cigarette. I made a face at the taste but only lipped it.

"We're clear. Pretty sure we lost the babysitters before you took the train halfway around the city."

I chuckled. "There are a lot of different lines. Still trying to learn them all." I turned us down a pathway into the underground garage. The boom gates were both closed and their pathways were marked red, but they weren't actually preventing anyone from walking in. "Sometimes the best way to learn is to just get lost and figure it out."

"Makes sense." Of course, Jasper got it. "Big fucking city though."

Yes, it was. Lainey and the guys occupied the upper echelons. They knew everyone worth knowing and a few more besides. I had a feeling Bodhi had more of a feel for the street as well, but it wasn't his focus. I wanted to know *everything*. Hard to prevent trouble if you didn't cover all the ways it could come at you.

The path down followed a curve. The concrete pavement was discolored by years of vehicles coming and going. By the first turn, the sound from the street behind faded along with the breeze. At the second curve, I turned toward the door that was tucked away there and opened it, letting Jasper inside before we closed it and then waited by the grimy window.

"Ah," Jasper said with a long slow sigh as he extinguished his cigarette then mine. "The good old days of paranoia and keeping one eye firmly over our shoulders."

"You make it sound like we've had new days where we don't." I raised my brows at him but he only shrugged, that faint smirk back on his face.

"Every now and then," Jasper said. "But you know, I don't mind it like I used to."

"You never minded it," I pointed out before heading deeper into the service hallway and taking the stairs up into the building above. The door was locked behind us so even if we had someone following us, they'd have to break the door to get in. That would set off an alarm.

Still, Jasper was right. Paranoia fit like a well-worn jacket and my favorite pair of shoes. At the first floor, I entered the code to unlock the door. It buzzed when it opened. Mickey J turned from where he was standing in the middle of the gutted floor, a cup of coffee in hand. The smell of fresh brewed carried.

"You two are late," Mickey said as we crossed to join him.

"Milo wanted to go fishing on the way here. Sadly, no bites." Jasper rubbed his hands together to warm them before he poured himself a cup. "I thought Liam was going to show up for this one."

"Later," Mickey said, then fixed a look on me. "Where's your head?"

"Where I need it to be." I waited for Jasper to finish then got my own cup. "We have three of his men here. He's going to know someone grabbed them. So whatever details they have are likely to be thin."

"If he's kept anything of his security since making you move in, after you moved out, then he's an idiot," Jasper said. "Of course, I don't mind if he wants to be an idiot. I will happily take a baseball bat to his head and close that chapter."

"I know you would, but Ivy's still on the fence." Not that she didn't hate him, but it was harder for her to make that call where King was concerned.

"She's not on the fence," Mickey said and that dragged my attention and Jasper's. Only instead of curiosity, there was rough agreement in Jasper's expression.

"Agreed," he said and I frowned.

Mickey eyed me briefly then said, "She doesn't want you to have to make this choice or to have to do it. She's trying to work herself up to doing it for you." The compassion in his eyes was no match for the depth of feeling in Mickey's voice.

He loved my little sister. He might be too old for her and maybe once upon a time he made bad choices, but he was also the same man who did penance for those mistakes, who loved her to distraction, and would do everything he could to protect and keep her safe. He was also steady enough in a group of hotheads to keep the peace when they needed it and to tell her no when she did.

"Ivy never has to do that for me," I said, but the rest of the protest died unspoken in the face of the bland looks they were both favoring me with. "But you guys know that."

"So does she," Mickey said, saluting me with his coffee. "Doesn't mean she doesn't want to protect you."

"She's a pain in the ass like that," I muttered and Jasper smirked.

"You love it."

Having my sister back? Yeah. I did. Even if she was with all of my best friends, and I was with hers. Or maybe because of it? Fuck, I didn't care. Considering I wouldn't give Mayhem up without a bloody battle and my corpse on the ground, I could hardly fault Ivy for how stubborn and intractable she'd proven about keeping the guys.

I downed a couple of swallows of coffee before I stripped off my coat. "Do you have a preference on who we start with?"

We'd debated this, the three guys all worked for King. They weren't civilians. They were definitely muscle. He used them for a lot of the dirtier jobs—including watching me. Business was one thing, but these pricks enjoyed hurting people. While I found that behavior rather despicable, it did free me up to deal with them how I saw fit.

"Which one do you like least?" Jasper asked.

"Clive," I answered without missing a beat. That fucker had been on my ass from day one. I'd caught him following me *before* I went to live with King. After, he'd been downright insufferable. "He's been sizing me up for a coffin since day one."

"Well, the first one is usually the hardest to crack." Jasper grinned wide. "It means we get to inflict more damage."

"I like how you think." We saluted each other with our coffee cups and I downed a couple of swallows. After, we all dressed in the plastic coveralls. We were going to be making a mess.

Once ready, Jasper led the way into the room where the three men were secured to hooks buried four feet into pillars around the room. When we were ready for full renovations, all of this would go. For now, it gave us a quiet place to work. With the clocks counting down, I didn't want to waste time.

"Gentlemen," Jasper said as he clapped his glove hands together. "Thank you all for waiting for us. My name is Hawk, I'm going to be your host on this magical interrogation ride. You're probably thinking you can handle the pain. I'm here to tell you, that's okay. Keep telling yourselves that. We'll disabuse you of the notion soon enough."

I didn't laugh, but Jasper was performing like he was the master of ceremonies and this was our three ring circus. Then again, maybe these assholes were very much our monkeys.

"Don't everyone volunteer at once, we've taken the stress out of deciding who goes first for you." He mimed pulling out a card and flashing it at the room before he glanced at it. "Clive... do we have a *Clive* here?"

The man in question gave a little jerk, yanking his death-filled stare off of me to look at Jasper.

"Winner winner, chicken dinner. Good afternoon Clive, I'm Hawk." Jasper strode over to him. "How are you today?"

"Fuck you," was Clive's response.

Jasper made a buzzing sound then swung his fist hard and fast. It caught Clive right in the jaw. He snapped his head too hard and hit the wall behind him, leaving the first stain of blood.

"I'm sorry," Jasper said easily, barely even winded. "You chose the wrong answer. Would you like to try that again?"

"Sometimes," Mickey said in a low voice, his lips barely moving. "I forget just how much he enjoys this part."

Clive spat blood out as he glared at Jasper. He was on his knees, having collapsed there after the first blow. He fought to get up as Jasper waited, humming the song from Jeopardy.

Yeah, Mickey was right. I'd forgotten just how much fun Jasper could have with these interrogations.

"Go to hell," Clive said and Jasper made the buzzing sound again.

This time he slammed his fist so hard into the man's gut that he actually gagged and coughed up bile that Jasper dodged neatly.

"That's two strikes," Jasper informed him conversationally. "Would you like to try one more time? If not, I'm sure you can phone a friend or pass to the next player?"

"Go..." Clive gagged. "Fuck yourself."

Another buzzer sound and Jasper turned away from Clive to look at me. "I swear, manners have really gone downhill."

"They have," I agreed, picking up his bat and tossing it to him. "Once upon a time, a little please and thank you went a long way."

"Still does," Jasper said. "Unfortunately, three strikes and you're out." He pivoted smoothly, swinging the bat. It crashed into Clive's right knee with a sickening crunch. His howl cut off as he gagged again. It was hard to shriek and fight to breathe at the same time.

Definitely sounded like a him problem.

The other two stared at us with varying degrees of disbelief and concern. Probably wise on their part to be *very* concerned. Jasper glanced down at Clive who wasn't quite crying, but he was close.

Kind of depressing how fast he would fold.

Still, the faster we got the info, the faster we could act on it. Probably better to approach this at speed.

Didn't mean I didn't want it to hurt just a bit more.

"Right," Jasper gave a kind of nod, then glanced down at Clive before he looked at the other two. "Which of you guys is going next?"

There was a jagged moment of silence before both men began to sputter.

CHAPTER
TWENTY-ONE

LAINEY

Our car led the small parade of vehicles out toward Brooklyn. All black SUVs. All with increased security, and steel-reinforced doors with ballistic-resistant windows. We were making a statement. A show of unity.

The Vandals were all here. While they couldn't necessarily afford to be absent in total from Braxton Harbor for long, none would let Em or Pretty Boy deal with King alone.

Milo threaded his fingers with mine where he sat next to me. Adam was silent on my right. Ezra had grabbed the front seat and Bodhi drove. It amused me that Adam hadn't even offered up a token resistance to the seating arrangements.

No, we were all growing more comfortable with the rotation of where we sat, though Bodhi almost always drove. A smile flickered through me at the thought.

Control issues. We all had them. Some of us handled it better than others. I didn't think it was possible to love these

203

four more, then they just climbed in the car as though it were the most natural thing in the world.

Maybe it was.

Our new normal.

Bodhi drove and lately, we'd used his cars more than any others. That would adapt over time as we were able to loosen security. The penthouse, though, as lovely as it was, was Bodhi's space and none of us wanted to disrupt it anymore than we already had. I also liked my own and Adam seemed fond of his.

We might need to discuss a pooling of resources or maybe buying a building and redoing the upper floors. That idea had potential. I put a mental bookmark in place for later.

Despite the quiet, plans hummed in the air around us. Em had gotten confirmation of her shows and received two calls from the man who owned the theater in Prague. He was thrilled to hear she would be coming.

Maybe too excited, if Pretty Boy's reaction to the second call had been an indication. The buzz of violence, always present, had grown more audible for a time. But when I locked gazes with him, concerned, Milo had shaken his head.

No, he didn't like the other man's attitude. He didn't care for what seemed to have once been the "normal" in Em's life. The important part, however, was it was no longer the "normal" and Em would not be dealing with any of these people alone.

The Vandals would have her back. So would we. Maybe... just maybe, we would be coming back with Andrea. That part of the nightmare could end while we focused on her recovery.

If I didn't think too hard on what *could* be happening to her right now, it let me breathe. The moment I let my thoughts drift in that direction, the muscles in my back began to tighten and my stomach sank.

We couldn't kill Harper twice, but if I could—I would execute him daily until we had Andrea back with us. There were a number of different ways to kill him. We hadn't really been that creative.

Adam covered my free hand with his and stroked his thumb along the side of my hand. The gentle caress eased my grip, but didn't relax it entirely. As much as I wanted to cover my reactions, I didn't seem entirely capable of it anymore.

Or maybe Adam just knew.

I leaned my head against his shoulder. Without a word, he turned and pressed his lips against the top of my head. Yes, he knew. I flexed my hand around his and he continued to offer his strength.

Milo covered my hand in his with another hand. His support as steady and determined as Adam's, Bodhi's, and Ezra's. We would look after each other and together we would figure this out.

Then as if summoned by the deep breath I took, our fleet of vehicles turned into a driveway that would take us up to the private house King owned. Or at least, the house he was using.

Location was everything, the fact he was here in Brooklyn and not on Long Island had to chafe. It also gave him some distance from the families he'd sought to control for so long.

We were not the first out of the cars. That was the twins. They had been behind us but now they were ahead. The last time we'd all moved on a target, there had been others with us, this time, it was quiet.

Just family.

The two key players were Milo and Em. They'd discussed what they were going to do a few times. The siblings were equally determined to protect each other. Not a doubt existed within me that they were each capable of killing King if it saved the other.

No doubt at all.

At the same time, I wasn't sure either really wanted the burden. Then again, that was why all of *us* were here.

"Ready?" Bodhi asked as the Vandals left their vehicles behind us.

"Absolutely," I told him. I was. This "reckoning," for lack of a better term, had been a long time coming. Adam lifted my hand and kissed it once before he opened his door. Milo squeezed my hand, then nodded toward his side.

It would put the car between me and the house. Adam had already closed his door and opened Ezra's before Ezra could. The brief, albeit sharp, flush of pleasure in Ezra's reaction made me smile wider.

Good things still happened. The tidal waves of darkness threatening our position would not be allowed to drown us. Frankly, I'd always wanted to learn how to surf.

Milo continued to hold onto my hand as we gathered. I slid the purse strap over my shoulder and then eyed the building. It wasn't a bad house. Though it definitely needed touch-ups.

He'd gone ostentatious, but you could see the cracks in the pavement. The paint on the trim was chipped. Even the landscaping showed signs of neglect. The bushes were a little too tall and intruded on the railing along the porch.

The grass was uneven in places, particularly along the longer drive as though the shade from the trees interrupted the growing cycle. It was a huge house, designed to project security, wealth, and entitlement.

Unfortunately, the message was utterly undercut by the myriad of little things that confirmed the illusion was wearing away around the edges. Somehow, I doubted that money was the issue where all of this was concerned.

King had the money.

He just lacked the acumen to make it happen. Perhaps he just failed to bring in the staff who could handle it. Needless to say, he was failing.

We were here to see the wax wings melt and send him plunging back to Earth.

"No security," Ezra commented, his disdainful sniff echoing a dismissive opinion. "How the mighty have fallen."

"Don't get cocky," Adam warned him with a clap against his shoulder. "And stay with Lainey."

With his back to us, Adam didn't catch Ezra rolling his eyes or the way he shot a look at me. Adam's protective instincts were never going to let Ezra or I go first.

"Behave," I mouthed, loving the way his eyes lit up and his smirk. But I still shook my head. He could give Adam shit later. Not now.

Not here.

Huffing out a breath, Ezra winked at me and then focused on the house. Em was out of her car and she stood framed by four of her guys. None of them looked any happier about being here than Milo did.

"Shall we?" I offered, heading for the front doors. We'd given King enough of a show with all of us gathered out front. While his estate wasn't as large as Der Sonne or Waltham Corners or Harrow's Park, it was definitely set back and away from the streets.

The only way to continue to observe us would be with cameras. We had a little surprise for that too. I'd just pressed the doorbell when my phone buzzed.

Fletcher: *You're all clear. I've intercepted his cloud feeds. Happy hunting, Cos.*

Impeccable timing, as always. No one answered the door immediately. Unsurprising. I gave it a solid sixty seconds before I rang it again.

"Well, this is a surprise," King greeted us via the intercom. "Though I thought it was just going to be you and Emersyn, Miss Benedict."

"No you didn't," I countered. "Because you are not stupid. Now, are you coming down to invite us in or should we continue with our other plans?"

One thing about men in power. They didn't like subversive challenges to their control. You'd think they would dislike overt ones more, but no—those gave them a chance to flex and prove something.

Subtle digs, such as the fact he was alone in the house and didn't even have the staff to let us in would sting his pride. The reminder that we didn't have to be here. We didn't need him, he needed us. The salt for the wound.

"Come in," he invited and there was a sound of a buzzer and then the door clicked as it unlocked. Not a servant, but he didn't come out either.

While not a full point, he had taken the first serve and sent it back. Adam was through the door with Ezra moving in his shadow. Bodhi followed, then Milo eased his grip so I could go as well.

Awareness of the Vandals moving with us kept my focus ahead. Kellan fell into step directly behind me. They would watch our backs. The guys had worked it all out in their planning.

The wide foyer faced a grand staircase head on and opened into three other rooms. A walkable mosaic circle decorated the center of the foyer. Everything else was framed around the Venetian marble.

It was too expensive for what was around it. The inlay

made the rest look cheaper, damaged. The design should complement and raise the value of the room around it.

This failed on all levels. The regency table did not match the vintage metal patina plant stand. The gold sheen clashed with the wrought iron of the stair's railings and the fine filigreed work.

If one had decided to cherry pick some pieces from a catalog of different periods and aesthetics, you might have come up with this.

The fact a sitting room was directly off the foyer and boasted Georgian pieces, rather than Regency or wrought-iron didn't promise comfort for decorations or seating.

A line of paintings decorated the walls ascending to the next floor. One of them looked a great deal like Em and I wasn't the only one who noticed. Not that I had time to study it as the man we were here to see descended the steps.

Dressed in a button down shirt, tie, and slacks, he looked like he'd just gotten up from his desk at the office. He'd failed to put on his coat though.

"Emersyn," King said as he reached the last step and focused on her. For the most part, my best friend just folded her arms when King held out a hand to her. "It's good to see you."

"Can't say it's mutual," she fired back. I was very fond of the bluntness. While Em had never been cruel, she'd always gone for the quiet response. The one to mitigate the damage and to disguise how bad things might be.

Not anymore.

"Understood," King said slowly, though there was no mistaking his disappointment or disapproval. He glanced over the Vandals but continued to study all of us until his gaze landed on Milo. "Son."

"Asshole," Milo answered.

Another sigh.

"You know what, Jeff," Doc said as he stepped forward. It cut King off from being able to even approach Emersyn. My initial judgment where he was concerned was a very large question mark.

Doc was much older than Milo *and* Em. He'd known Milo since he was a boy. But the radical age difference wasn't what gave me pause or caution. It was the familiarity with Em when she was a baby and his ties to Milo that were closer than family in some ways.

Some.

Still, he made Em happy. That I could never fault.

"Let's save the bullshit. No one wants to hear it and you really can't sell it anymore." He gestured to the other room. "If you want us to sit somewhere, lead the way."

"Mickey J," King practically tsked as he turned to lead us through to another room. Probably an office or a library. Somewhere he held the power.

Instead of pausing at Em, though he had glanced at her, King came to a stop in front of me.

"Miss Benedict?" He offered his arm. Milo didn't make a sound. None of them did. But if looks could kill, I was pretty sure King would have been dead at least a dozen times over.

"If you insist," I murmured. We had goals for being here. While I couldn't stand the man, I was also not as personally invested as everyone else beyond what he'd done to my best friend and my lovers.

They were very much *my* personal investment.

"I do," King said as my hand came to settle on the crook of his arm. He didn't attempt to touch me in any other way and merely walked through the foyer and into the sitting room, then beyond it to what was ostensibly a library. "Would you care for a drink?"

"Perhaps," I said, considering it. "Why don't I get the drinks for everyone and the rest of you talk?" After all, he wanted to talk to Em and to Milo.

Those were the important ones.

King frowned briefly, but the fact he nearly ran into Bodhi when he turned seemed to give him more pause. Bodhi didn't say a word. He also didn't look away. In fact, King was definitely the one to stop the staring contest first.

"If you insist," King murmured, parroting my earlier comment.

"Of course," I looped my purse strap across my chest so I didn't have to set it down and I turned to the room. "What can I get for you?"

"Milkshakes are probably not on the list, are they?" Freddie's question splintered the frostiness in the air and I grinned at him.

"Unfortunately, no, they aren't. But I can check on beer or soda."

Freddie didn't normally drink, so it was a safe bet he'd go for the soda or nothing at all. "Soda's fine, or water." He cut a look toward King. "I'm not picky."

The man snorted. It didn't take long to get drink orders from everyone. As I took over the bar, Bodhi drifted along with me. He just shook his head when I asked if he wanted anything.

While everyone waited for their drinks, they divided, putting most of them on one side of the room with King on the other. Based on Milo's interrogations, most of King's security had quit. Arguably, some had just disappeared, but you might as well say they quit.

Apparently, the odds weren't in their favor.

Who would have thunk it?

King chose a cognac to drink. I poured a small measure for

myself. Opened wine for Em, though she'd just shrugged. Beers for some of the boys. Water and soda for everyone else.

The only drink I delivered was King's because he hadn't come anywhere near the bar. Since I had both glasses, I gave him the choice of which he would have.

"Thank you," he murmured and I raised my own glass in a quiet salute before I sampled a mouthful. It was sweet, but also spicy. The rich flavor demanded attention. It warmed the belly and spread that heat through the rest of me.

"You're welcome."

I crossed to where Em had taken a seat. None of the guys were really sitting, so I just settled on the arm of her chair. She shot me a quick smile, then we focused on King.

"Who wants to begin?" King asked. It almost sounded like he was offering a concession, but he wasn't the one in control of the room or the situation.

The knowledge of which continued to grow in his wary gaze.

CHAPTER
TWENTY-TWO

ADAM

Who wanted to begin? Condescending prick. Resentment for the years of towing the line to this man burned in me. First, he'd been some anonymous, dark and distant leader of an unorthodox, secret society.

If you were tapped to join, your choices were gone. Extinct. You served at his pleasure. Whether it was killing, stealing, or torture, if the king requested it, you did it.

In his name and under his direction, we inflicted so much damage. What had once just been a club of sorts for the ultra wealthy to sow their wild oats in and do crazy stunts, had become something of a real gang.

We were all soaked in the blood of his choices.

His choices and our own.

"I'll start," I said abruptly. "You've arranged sales with regard to people, particularly children and young adults to Eastern Europe. Who are your contacts?"

King's gaze snapped to me. Shock rippled through his expression before he could suppress it fully.

"While we're on the subject of selling *children*," Doc said, folding his arms and fixing King with a cold look. "Let's discuss the network you use to get them out of the country."

"Paperwork," Kellan Traschel, the current leader of the Vandals added to the list of items we wanted. "You have to do something to remove them or bring in others. I rather doubt it's export *only*." His grimace underscored his disgust.

"While we're on the subject," Lainey said, crossing one leg over the other before taking a sip of her cognac. She couldn't stand the stuff, but you would never know based on her expression. "Let's also discuss the methodology for how you chose who to sell and to keep. I'm assuming that you began by removing possible challenges and threats."

The last wasn't really a question, but I saw her move play out in the seconds after she interjected. We had specific questions, Lainey was going after the big picture stuff.

King took his time in responding. He glanced around the room at each of us. His gaze lingered on Em the longest. I wanted to step into his line of sight, but none of her guys were doing it so I stayed where I was.

Em was fierce all on her own. Didn't mean I had to like her having to fight any battles.

"Is that all?" King asked. The semi-bored note in his voice aggravated me. Worse, I didn't care for the way he zeroed in on Lainey with her last request.

"No," Lainey answered as she pulled a small tin of mints out of her purse. I hadn't seen those in a while. She carried them because her grandfather often did. It was... another charming facet of her personality. "You're a smart man, *most* of the time. Stop asking stupid questions."

I almost snorted aloud at the dry insult in her voice. King

downed the rest of his cognac as though it were a shot and not expensive liquor.

Maybe he needed to fortify his courage. But wrong side of the sheets or not, King was far more suited to the rough streets than the boardrooms and golf courses.

Setting the glass aside, King leaned back in his chair and blew out a breath. "I have a porter in Munich who handles all transactions going from west to east. Conversely there is a courier service available when we need to import product and resources."

The ease with which he discussed trading people made me sick. I understood business and resource management. While solid employees made for good resources, they were not *products*.

"As for the paperwork and the supply chain here, that's on a need to know. You do not need to know."

"Port resources then," I said. "Most likely out of Maryland, New Jersey, and North Carolina. Staying away from New York's ports to distance yourself. He has a list of loyalists in those cities."

Loyalists who seemed to genuinely like him. Or at least they indicated as much when I'd met them previously. This was before I knew who he was.

"You're right," Liam said, snapping his gaze to mine. We'd had to *deal* with some problems in Maryland. It had been a two day trip, most longshoremen were a tight knit group. They didn't welcome strangers or offer up their own.

The moment we'd identified ourselves, however, Liam and I had been treated like we were the king. His people there wanted nothing to do with the open revolt in the other union workers.

King's eyes narrowed. He didn't confirm or deny. Not that he needed to. Anyone not capable of flying out commercial airliner would need other exit strategies. The same to be said for importing.

Shipping containers.

"You worked with Jonathon Warrick," Kestrel said in a tight voice.

"More his mother, Ruth. She was the real brains behind that operation. She also had connections. Jonathon lacked stamina. Not that it matters, I moved up and on. I didn't need their connections. While this whole discussion is far from entertaining, I would have suspected you had more detailed questions for me."

The blunt speculation in his eyes almost made me laugh. Since finding out King was related to Em and Milo, then Ezra, I'd looked for any trace of those three in him. Just one small inkling...

But it wasn't there. Ezra looked more like his mother than his father. A kindness for him. Based on what I'd gathered, Emersyn was the spitting image of her birth mother and you couldn't mistake her and Milo for anything except siblings.

Seven or eight years apart, did nothing to dilute how closely they resembled each other. No, King might have provided some genetic material, but they were nothing like him.

That was a boon for them. All of us really. My feelings where my father stood were complicated. I'd loathed him more than I loved him though. Milo had loved his father, loved and idolized him. That betrayal?

It left a mark.

Em? She had no memories of him. Instead, she got the shit deal with her adopted parents and the disgusting, rat bastard of an uncle. I fought the urge to grind my teeth together. Next to me, Ezra bumped my shoulder.

The light contact helped to settle my temper. There was a

plan in play here. We'd dealt with most of his people and now we would deal with him.

Frankly, I didn't want him waiting when we returned. With all of us going, I didn't want to leave him with the freedom to regroup and entrench himself in our absence. At the same time, we needed the information he had.

"Why didn't you tell us about our brother?" Emersyn's question knocked King's cool facade. His mouth snapped shut, a vein throbbed in his forehead, and the anger that flashed into his eyes held real violence.

He rose from his chair abruptly, and I wasn't the only one stepping forward. Liam and Vaughn were in front of Emersyn and Lainey before the man could take another breath.

"You think I'm going to hurt my own child?" King actually seemed incensed.

"You have. Repeatedly," Doc answered before anyone else could. All that rancor in King focused on him.

"Go to hell, Mickey. Considering the fact you're practically robbing the cradle with her—or is that the point? You got to groom her from—"

The question was never completed. Doc struck King with a blazing right cross. One moment he was still. The next he hit King like a hammer. King wasn't a small man, yet the blow staggered him.

Catching him by his shirt, Doc hauled him forward and slammed his fist into him again. Three blows in rapid succession until blood coated King's teeth and ran freely from his nose.

When he shoved him away, King stumbled back and hit the wall. Yeah, the red marks on his face were gonna bruise. Doc shook his head as he pulled out a bandana and wiped his hands with it.

Not that he had much blood on him, but then I wouldn't want anything of King on me either.

"Circling back to the earlier talking point," Lainey said, popping another mint out of her case to suck on.

She even held it out toward Doc as if he might need a refresher too. An offer he declined with a faint smile.

Snapping it closed, she looked at King. "How did you decide who you would tap? And who you wouldn't? I gather your takeover of the Royals was a far more internal matter thanks to Wallace backing you. That doesn't explain why any of the other families would have gone along with your criminal enterprises, particularly when you weren't cutting them in for any of the profits."

That wasn't a question I'd had before. Yet...

"Does it matter?" King asked.

"I like to be accurate," Lainey told him as if it was the most simple of answers. Through the whole exchange she sat on the arm of Em's chair like she didn't have a care in the world. "What have you got to lose?"

King snorted. "I thought this would be some kind of execution or beating." He pulled out a handkerchief to mop up the blood on his face.

"Plenty of time for that," Ezra said without a trace of irony. "Answer her question."

The blood leaking from King's nose continued its sluggish path. Each time he opened his mouth to speak, he gave us a glimpse of his bloody teeth. It was all rather gruesome.

"The Royals have never been more than an excuse to be wealthy and stupid. To sow your wild oats and to have fun while doing it. Of course there was networking, and as with any group, someone always rises to the top. They set the tone. The rules. It was rather painfully easy for me to take over. Then, I decided who would be tapped for membership."

He glared down at the blood on his handkerchief before returning it to his nose.

"The eldest sons were a good place to start. The past fifteen years hadn't seen the Royals do much more than host a party now and then. Those were too soft, we needed to start younger..."

"Lucky us," I muttered. Because a lot of things were making sense now. Why he'd played it so secretive. Why he hadn't let anyone identify him. His end goals... "What was your endgame?"

That was the one thing that truly eluded me. King manipulated, invested, blackmailed, and killed his way to the top.

"You can exert a lot of power, or you could have—once upon a time. But you'll never take over the Graham fortune. Or the Reeds. Or anyone else's for that matter. Most of that is tied up in family trusts and codicils. So what did you plan to achieve? You wanted the Vandals gone to punish your son."

"Well, none of you could manage that, so it doesn't really matter now. Does it?" He pushed away from the wall and took a couple of swaying steps back to his chair. Sitting abruptly, he looked like someone had cut his strings. "Everyone thinks you have to be in front, leading, to be powerful. There is far more power in the shadows."

"Unless someone cuts you off. What's a puppet master without his dolls?" Lainey sounded almost intrigued. Rising from where she'd been seated she set her empty glass on the bar before she turned to face him again. She linked her fingers together, head tilted as she studied King. "You expected that betrayal... you've expected it for years. You know you have enemies. Most of which were created due to your own actions. You had no one to trust..."

It was like I could hear the moment she solved that

puzzle. The silent 'o' that she didn't release, and the way her head straightened.

"That's why you wanted Milo," Em said slowly. "You wanted to punish him, but then you really wanted him as a son?"

"It was a fool's errand," King said, waving it all off like the fact he could dismiss it would make it not true. "I had a son. A son I was going to raise right. No mother to mess him up or teach him to make stupid choices..."

"But she took him away," Lainey murmured. "Using your resources and your methods. You've been trying to find him, haven't you?"

"If you wanted him found," Milo said abruptly. "You could have saved us all a lot of time and grief by just telling us about him."

"Tell you?" King challenged him. "Your sister can barely look at me. She refuses any kind of relationship because of you. No, I wasn't telling you. At least with..." He mopped at his face again.

The bloody nose seemed to be getting worse. Had Doc broken it when he punched him?

"No, I would not give you the access to deny me another child."

"You're insane," Emersyn said abruptly. She was on her feet and right at Liam's side. The anger practically rolled off of her. "Milo didn't turn me against you. *You* did when you abandoned us. Don't tell me that was different. I was a baby, you didn't want me, and now you do? Why? Because I look like the woman you abandoned? No, it's not about me at all. It's about giving you access to change Milo's mind. You don't give a damn about family. It's always about power."

"Family can be power," King argued and he lurched to his feet only to sit again.

He stared down at the handkerchief then at his legs. The pain on his face wasn't manufactured.

"Family..." He panted out the word, then frowned as he looked at all of us. Blood began to trickle from the corner of his eye. "What is this?"

"It's the end of the road," Lainey told him. "You see, we needed some answers, but we also need you gone. Em and Milo don't deserve the pain of having to be the one who did it. The boys couldn't really decide between them."

She glanced at her watch, then lifted her chin.

"I'm afraid I took matters into my own hands," she continued. "Sorry, Pretty Boy."

"Nothing to be sorry about," he told her and the hint of awe in his expression wasn't lost on me. Yes, she continued to awe me too.

King coughed, the handkerchief to his mouth was soaked in crimson. "How—"

"Cognac?" Lainey reminded him.

"You poured both glasses from the same bottle. I watched you..."

"I poisoned the bottle."

I snapped my head toward her and I wasn't the only one.

"When you finished your drink, I took the antidote." She patted her purse.

The mints.

Holy shit.

"You see, I'm very done with you, Mr. King. You won't hurt anyone I love ever again. I am afraid, however, that the poison is going to be a rough way to die." Not that she sounded remotely apologetic. If anything, it was coldly practical. A fact she offered him so he could get used to it now.

King's shocked stare turned furious and he lurched forward like he had a hope in hell of getting to her. Bodhi closed the distance and got there first. One hand on his throat, he shoved him backward until he hit the wall.

Once he had him pinned to the wall, he stripped the man of his weapons. Twice, King tried to fend him off. On the second attempt, Bodhi slapped him across the face. The crack of the blow echoed in the stunned quiet of the room.

Blood from King's face splattered on the wall. For his part, Bodhi inspected his own hands. Not even a speck of blood. The man really did have his talents.

"No easy ways out," Bodhi informed him.

"Agreed," Lainey said, drifting over to take a seat on a chair of her own. She leaned back with a kind of casual grace and patience. She looked ready to settle in for the day. Head tilting back, she glanced up at Milo. "I won't tell you what to do, but neither you nor Em needs to watch this."

"But you do?" Milo asked, the frank wonder in his voice found its match in me. Just when I thought she couldn't get sexier or more attractive, she proved us wrong.

"Oh yes," she murmured, one corner of her mouth curved upward and she glanced at King. "I've waited a long time to see justice served for you, Pretty Boy. I'm not going anywhere until his cold dead corpse is on the ground and ready for disposal."

The words hung there, suspended in the air, and they held every ounce of the promised malice in her voice.

"We'll have to gut the house, I'm afraid, but I didn't think you were particularly fond of it." She lifted one shoulder and let it drop as if, what could you do?

I suppressed a chuckle because King yanked at his tie. He fought with his shirt, like he could make the air come more easily. The struggle was real.

Milo traced his fingers down Lainey's cheek. "Mayhem..."

"You're welcome," she said, her voice as low and confi-

dential as his own. "I promise you, it was very much my pleasure to deal with him."

I flicked a look to where Emersyn stared at the man who
wanted far too late to be her father. Her grimace at the blood
dripping down his face didn't offer a shred of pity, only
disgust.

"You don't have to stay, Hellspawn," Liam said, not quite
blocking her view. They trusted her to handle it.

"I feel like... maybe I should?" Her hesitance echoed
beneath the words.

"Ivy..." King choked out as he shoved his way forward.
Liam snapped his arm back, his elbow catching King in the
face and it knocked him on his ass.

"You don't have to do anything," Rome told her. "If you
don't want to see this, you don't have to."

A chair shrieked as Freddie dragged it over the wooden
floor and out of his way before he leaned against the back of
the sofa.

"They're right, Boo-Boo, Liam will make sure he's
pushing up daisies... I'd offer to hurry it along but this all feels
dramatic and kind of fancy." Freddie flashed a grin at Lainey.
"Ball Cracker's got style."

"Thank you," she murmured, then switched her attention
to Em. "You really don't have to stay. I promise you, he's a
dead man. The antidote... it's effective, but it has a narrow
window."

She shot King a smug look.

"A very narrow window."

King could barely stand, and seemed to be leaning on the
wall to keep from collapsing. Didn't stop him from glaring at
her. "It's like my body is on fire..."

"I've read that's the way junkies feel when they are going

through detot. I imagine that's how their mother felt before she died... Seemed fitting."

Beautifully, epically, poetic.

"I'm staying," Doc said, then looked at Milo. "Your girl is right, you and Little Bit don't need to see this. But I will make sure he's dead and gone. No more worries about him."

It was the strangest sensation. No more worries about King. I'd cut ties months before, but... for the first time in a long while, I took a deep breath.

My father was gone.

Wallace Graham was gone.

Now King would be gone.

Our lives were our own again.

In the end, Em did go. She and Lainey hugged, then Em left with about half of her guys. Us? We stayed. King kept shooting looks at us when pain didn't crush his expression.

Liam and Ezra watched King a lot like I did. We didn't want to miss a thing. For years, he'd jerked us around. Pulled my strings. Pulled theirs. Made us dance for his amusement.

No, I wanted to soak in this moment. Doc seemed to be of a similar mindset. Milo was harder to read. He sat on the arm of Lainey's chair, one hand braced behind her and his expression impassive.

Bodhi was positioned halfway between Lainey and King. He was also working on his phone, but it would be a mistake to think he wasn't paying attention.

Arms folded, Ezra let out a long sigh and I cut a look at him. "What?"

"Thought this would be more interesting. But he's almost as fucking boring dying as he was at trying to make dinner conversation."

I couldn't tell if he was serious, but then he slid a grin at me and I shook my head. "Don't be a brat."

"Can't help it," Ezra said. "I'm good at it."

"That's the fucking truth," Liam muttered and it was my turn to smile. The simple fact was, it took a while for King to die and he suffered through a lot of it.

When he finally started to beg, I kind of wondered if she would relent. I didn't think so. King had cost all of us and he'd hurt Milo and Emersyn. Then there was the death threat to me and the abuse he heaped on Ezra.

No, I didn't think she would relent. Her mind was made up. Her determination was resolute. Not for the first time in her life, but maybe the first time in our *adult* relationship, I saw the true influence Leopold had been on her.

She was her grandfather's protege and she reflected his values. Particularly one of his favorites—if you wanted a job done, you had to be willing to do it yourself.

The begging and pleading didn't last long either. He was having trouble staying conscious, but the pain? That wasn't abating. Even half out of it, he kept moaning.

A little over seven and a half hours after she poured his cognac, Julius King was dead.

Doc pronounced. Bodhi checked it.

Then we wrapped up the body.

Definitely burning him and making sure there was nothing left but ash.

And maybe some salt.

Yep, ding dong, the king was dead.

I flicked a look toward Lainey and found her watching me with that steadiness that we all needed more than she could possibly know. Or maybe she did.

Didn't care. Loved her and wanted her in my life. Every single part of it.

"What?" A hint of curiosity populated her question and my grin only grew.

"The king is dead," I told her. "Long live the queen."

TWENTY-THREE

LAINEY

PRAGUE

Everything came down to family.

Everything.

Arm in arm, Em and I matched paces as we approached the Charles Bridge. Em let out a happy little sigh the closer we got.

"We're here," she said, her excitement leaking into her voice as she squeezed my arm. We were in warm coats, hats to keep our ears warm, gloves for our hands, and fur-lined boots for our feet. "We're really here."

"You said you never actually saw the city when you were here previously." The minute she'd let that slip, I put a visit to the bridge at the top of the list. We'd arrived in Prague over the past two days, traveling in smaller groupings.

Currently, following not far behind us were Bodhi and

Freddie. They'd both been game when I said I wanted to take Em for coffee and to see the bridge.

"I didn't," she said with a sigh as we paused to cross the Vitava river. "Doing anything touristy was not an option. Not really. Limited schedule, high engagement. I spent most of my not practicing time, sleeping."

"Well, luckily for you, we have time on this trip." The urgency in my blood burned. We had a handful of leads. Leads that the guys were in the process of running down now. Emersyn had to head to the theater today to meet the cast that would be working in and around her show.

But only if we got confirmation that the rest of her crew had arrived. The only people handling her equipment were her people, the ones Liam and the others had vetted. Vaughn would handle all the ties in the rafters and he'd be on one of the catwalks as needed.

No expense spared and no chances taken.

Em pulled her phone out and then turned to tuck her shoulder to mine before she angled the phone to snap a selfie. Our grins matched and then I gave her a kiss on the cheek during another snap.

"C'mon." I tugged her arm lightly. "Let's take a walk across the river. We only have an hour before our first meeting" We didn't make it five whole feet onto the stone bridge before there was an actual bounce to her step.

"This bridge was built in the 1300s," Em said, doing a little dance before linking her arm with mine again. I sipped my coffee. They were still hot which was welcome against the briskness of the wind over the river. "It's older than the U.S. It's older than a few countries now... It's historical and permanent, and I love this bridge."

I chuckled. "I can see that. Should I be glad this isn't tall enough to bungee jump off of?"

Her snort was indelicate and amused. "I like bungee jumping when we get the time. The guys are hilarious about it." She flashed a look over her shoulder.

"That's because you're pretty damn fearless." I wish I could say the same. The sense of urgency, to find Andrea, was like a constant itch between my shoulder blades. We were here, no more delays. Tactically, we'd left our rear guard as clear as possible. Now, we needed to find my sister. Find Pretty Boy's and Bodhi's siblings.

We had names. We had rough locations. We had... we had leads. I hoped the guys turned something up this morning. Hans had also sent word that he would be in Prague directly. So hopefully that meant he also had more leads. For now, we had to stick with the plan.

That plan involved getting Em to the theater and meeting with two of the largest contributors to the fund that brought her to the country. They were patrons of the arts. One, Em said she remembered. The other was new.

It was the new one that I wanted a good look at. I had some familiarity with Valentin Zhukovsky. He was a longtime fan of Em's, and had served as a patron on her previous visits. The theater was owned by him, if I recalled correctly. He had definitely leapt at the chance to sponsor her return visit.

I tossed a glance over my shoulder. Bodhi moved easily, his head on a swivel. When he caught my look, he just nodded. We were fine.

The whole point of this walk, in addition to stretching our legs, was to make sure Em was seen. Hours in the air had left me stiff and a little cranky. Walking to the venue was the fastest way to get noticed.

As much as I wanted to hurry, I kept my steps steady and even. If we rushed, we chanced missing something. Em was putting herself out as bait. I hadn't missed the looks the guys exchanged or how her security precautions in the past had been about keeping her from being stolen.

Dangled like chum...

So many people should have died far sooner. But that was the past. As much as I wished we could go back, we couldn't. Dealing with the present was where we needed to be, especially since tomorrow was not promised.

"You look very fierce," Em murmured as we angled toward the boulevard that would lead to the theater. I'd memorized the route. "I thought you wanted me to be approachable?"

I snorted. "I wanted them to see you. Not come anywhere near you." At the same time, if someone tried to make a move, we were in place to make sure they didn't. We wanted to lure out our targets, but I would not trade Em to get Andrea back.

We would get Andrea back and keep Em, thank you very much.

"Besides, I should have a good frown of disapproval as your chaperone." I made a face at her and she burst out laughing. "You know I'm right," I reminded her. "Granted, I may not be able to do battle axe..."

"Ball Cracker, you don't need to do battle axe." Freddie's cheerful observation pulled fresh laughter out of Em. "Besides, axes are more Jasper's thing."

I didn't ask. At the same time... "That seems oddly fitting," I admitted.

Em winked.

Then we were there. The mile walk seemed suddenly far too short. Though it was early in the day, there was a lot of movement at the theater. Bodhi narrowed the distance between us, falling into step on my right as Freddie took Em's left.

"It's fine," she said. "Those are our people."

That relaxed one worry, but not all of them. Their crew. Their staff. All vetted by them. But we were still in a city we didn't know, dealing with enemies we hadn't fully identified, and far from the resources we were all used to having.

Crossing the street, Em moved ahead with Freddie while I hung back a little with Bodhi.

"It's fine," he said, his tone downright soothing and I grinned at him.

"I know, I just wanted to check if we've heard from Hans yet?"

He shook his head once. There were greetings being called out to Emersyn and she'd paused to chat with some of the techs.

"He'll be here," Bodhi assured me, the lightness of his hand gliding down my back. The touch almost ephemeral and yet it steadied me. "Trust me?"

"Of course," I murmured. Then we were with Em and resumed playing our parts as Emersyn headed inside.

"I won't be here long," she told me, embracing the roles we were playing. Although, in her case, she was just being herself. "But I like to get a feel for the space."

"You've performed here before," I reminded her. Or had I misunderstood?

"I have," she said, stripping off her hat once we were inside and out of the wind. I followed suit. "But... every venue has a different vibe. Almost... a personality of its own. Sometimes that personality changes because of alterations they've made."

She followed a long hallway past several closed doors that had empty nameplates on them. Dressing rooms? Probably.

We had a blueprint for the whole place. I needed to study it more. Her boots clicked along the hall until we reached a wider area where the backstage area bowled outwards to the wings.

The curtains were pulled all the way back and all the lights were on. It was a lovely venue with red velvet chairs and some classic baroque architecture and design. Still, it seemed *wrong* to see all of it and the stage in such stark relief from the too bright lights.

"Other times," Em continued. "I'm the one who has changed. The first time I performed here... I was eleven."

She gave me a tight smile.

"It used to feel a lot bigger. A lot scarier."

"Now?" I studied the seating and then the stage itself. With all the lights on it was easy to see the catwalks and battens where her silks would be suspended.

"Nowhere near as big or scary." The brief moment of wonder in her voice pulled all my attention. Instead of staring at the theater, she looked off to the side where Bodhi and Freddie were speaking. "Lots of things that used to be scary just aren't anymore. I used to think it was because I'd seen worse."

"You survived worse," I reminded her. "But you also have security now." Something she'd never had in all the years I'd known her.

"I do," Emersyn murmured, then refocused on me and her smile grew. "My life is almost perfect."

Before I could respond though, the squeak of the doors on the far side opening echoed through the wide space. Two men strode inside, letting the doors bang closed behind them.

The man on the right was Valentin Zhukovsky. The owner of the theater, and a huge Em fan. He was a big man, a paunch in the front, but a cheerful smile on his ruddy face.

"Emersyn! *Myšáček!*" He spread his arms wide as he strode toward us on swift legs. His companion didn't lag by much, but the tall man with the silver hair that brushed his shoulders and an expensively tailored suit that seemed out of place in the tired old theater.

Too much new money against the declining grace of the old world. Still, I tracked both men as Em crossed the stage to meet Zhukovsky. Bodhi and Freddie moved out onto the stage, staying close.

Zhukovsky was up the three steep steps to the stage and then his huge hands were engulfing Emersyn's. "You look wonderful."

He bussed the air next to each of her cheeks with kisses that never connected.

"It's good to see you too, Valentin. Thank you so much for the invitation."

"You have an open invitation. We sold out the day we announced you were coming. Then when you added two more nights, well..." He kissed his fingers as though he were a chef. "Perfection. I will be right up there in my box. I love to watch you."

The choice of words was a bit unfortunate, even if the man seemed genuinely jovial. His companion hadn't approached, instead he studied me.

Before I could comment, however, Em was turning to me. "Valentin, this is my chaperone, Elaine. She's more company than anything else, but it's her first time in Prague. I want to take her to see some sights and maybe catch them myself this time?"

Elaine. Ugh.

"You need a chaperone?" Zhukovsky frowned, then he shook it off. "We will make arrangements. I would love to show you my city. You were never here long enough before."

"I know, an oversight, and one I'd like to correct while I'm here."

"Done." The man pivoted with more grace than I expected. "Valentin Zhukovsky," he introduced himself and held out a hand to me.

"Elaine," I said, hating my full name. "Hardigan."

Em's eyes widened. But I wasn't taking any chances. The speculation in Zhukovsky's eyes was enough to make me wary. The fact his friend hadn't joined us and continued to stare added to my unease.

Maybe they would recognize me. Maybe not. I'd take my chances there. But avoiding Benedict was probably smarter.

"It is good to meet you, Miss Hardigan. Emersyn is one of my favorites. I want her stay and by extension yours to be as smooth as possible. If you have any questions or concerns, bring them straight to me. I will take care of everything." The lightly accented English seemed to add to his emphasis.

"Thank you, Mr. Zhukovsky, I shall endeavor to do my best." Then I glanced back to his friend. "Is he with you or just..."

"Oh," Zhukovsky said as he released me. "Juraj, stop lurking like some street thug. You're making the ladies uncomfortable."

The man shot Zhukovsky a thin smile that never reached his eyes. As he climbed the steps, he was as reserved as Zhukovsky was boisterous. Frankly, the men seemed polar opposites.

"Juraj Vedriš," Zhukovsky introduced him. "This is Miss Emersyn Sharpe, an exquisitely talented dancer. You will swallow your tongue when you see her perform."

"I look forward to it," the man said easily, though he didn't offer a hand or make any move to get closer. He was holding himself apart. He glanced past me, but whatever he saw there had him jerking his gaze back to us.

Interesting...

Were we making him nervous?

More importantly, *why* were we making him nervous?

"We will make time for tour," Zhukovsky said. "Don't worry, I won't bring Juraj. We will have fun."

Then they were excusing themselves, well Zhukovsky did. His less than chatty friend said nothing as he strode away up the aisle with Zhukovsky following him.

"That was weird," Emersyn murmured.

"Hmm-hmm."

Time to do some research into Juraj Vedriš.

I glanced over to Bodhi who already had his phone out. Good. It could be absolutely nothing. He might just be some street level criminal, but that didn't fit him.

Not at all.

"Okay," I said, taking a deep breath and shaking off that bit of unease. All we could do was remain watchful. "What do you need to do next?"

CHAPTER
TWENTY-FOUR

BODHI

I'd acquired three photos of Zhukovsky and Vedriš during their brief sojourn talking to the ladies. Freddie and I were blending into the background. Ideal for the moment, since neither man had paid any attention to us. No, they barely paid attention to Lainey B.

Except Vedriš had been laser-focused on her until Zhukovsky dragged him into the conversation. The theater owner, however, was all about PPG. What I couldn't tell was how much of that was genuine interest in her skill, pure lust for her beauty, or mercenary desire for acquisition.

"If he keeps looking at her like that, I'm gonna carve his eyes out," Freddie said, his light tone conversational and relaxed. "Take my time with it. Then chop off each finger."

I studied PPG again. She didn't seem upset. If anything, she was more focused on Lainey B at the moment. She'd barely glanced after the men when they left.

"PPG appears to be handling it."

"Because people have been looking at her like meat for

236

most of her life." Freddie's tone didn't raise nor were there any stress markers present. Yet everything about him shifted. "She expects to be used. To be abused."

Head cocked, I narrowed my gaze toward the girls. Lainey B had folded her arms and her smile was genuine. Whatever she was saying to PPG made her laugh. It didn't take Lainey long to notice me staring.

Her eyebrows raised, a silent question. Was I alright? I nodded once. A stir went through me, a shiver that skated over my scalp and down my back to pulse around to my cock and then up again.

Everything about Lainey B was exquisite, from the sharpness of her mind to her unrelenting loyalty to the fierce determination she possessed to protect everyone around her.

Perfection.

"Maybe," I finally said, conceding the point to Freddie. "Maybe she used to expect it. She doesn't anymore. No one will allow any harm to come to her."

We were all on our guard, Lainey B as well and she was well-armed. I'd go over her weapons again later. Make sure she had everything she needed. If someone tried to make off with the women, they were going to be in for a world of pain.

If Lainey let any of them survive long enough for us to get there.

Amusement speared me at the thought.

"You look way too happy about something," Freddie observed. "Want to share with the class?"

"Not really." I cut him a look. "You need to talk though."

Instead of responding, Freddie frowned and looked back out at the stage. More crew had begun to arrive. O'Connell and his twin had arrived with Vaughn. My phone buzzed with a message from Adam. He and Ezra were almost ready for the meeting with the local Bratva.

The Dovzhenko family had provided introductions and arranged a meeting with potential allies. We'd take all we could get in the city. Adam and Ezra would have backup from a pair of Vandals.

I sent back an acknowledgement then checked the tracking app. Everyone was popping on the screen.

Adam.

Ezra.

Milo.

Me.

Lainey B.

Each one of us demarcated by a different color. If for any reason the apps lost connection with a tracker, a warning message would go out. We'd gone over the program a few times and tweaked the responsiveness.

It was solid.

Didn't mean I wouldn't check even with Lainey right there.

"I'll be fine," Freddie said after a marked, and a far too long hesitation. "I should probably—"

"We're going for a walk," I told him. "Go tell PPG bye." Then, taking my own advice, I crossed to where Lainey was talking to PPG and the twins, who'd arrived with coffee in hand.

Sliding an arm around Lainey's middle, I pressed my lips to her ear. "Stepping out to talk to Freddie. Might be a bit. Stay with them until I come back?"

She relaxed into me and tilted her head back so she could meet my gaze. Fresh worry filled those eyes and I smiled.

"Nothing to worry about." The conversation was for Freddie. Something was up with him.

"Okay," Lainey murmured. "Don't disappear on me."

"I'll do my best," I promised.

"All I'm asking," she quipped easily, the callback made me grin.

I gave her a gentle squeeze then dropped a kiss on her lips before I swung my attention to O'Connell. "Keep one eye on her."

"Not a problem," Liam said with a salute. Freddie had already spoken to Emersyn and retreated. He flicked a look toward Freddie then to me. I met his gaze easily. They were Freddie's people, but this wasn't a conversation I would invite anyone else to unless Freddie wanted to ask them himself.

Leaving Lainey with them, I headed toward the wings where Freddie waited. We could have used the way Zhukovsky and Vedriš exited. Those doors were closer.

Close wasn't our destination. I followed him past the technicians and crew working to bring in equipment, costumes, and more. This wasn't a small setup and PPG wouldn't be using anything that hadn't come in with their people, been vetted, and double checked.

When we reached the back doors, they were all standing wide, letting in the cooler air. The sun shining down decried the chillier temps from before the sun was up. Spring was arriving in the Czech Republic, but it wasn't that warm yet.

I followed Freddie as he went around the clusters of crew. We were leaving the theater entirely and heading toward the river. I scanned the area as we walked. The last thing we needed to do was get sloppy and pick up a tail or borrow trouble.

We had enough issues.

The breeze shifted over the river. Fried meats, garlic, and onions joined the fresher air.

"Goddamn," Freddie said as he took a deep breath. "I wasn't hungry before."

"We'll find something." I nodded toward the shops a block away. "Probably cafes down there. We can scout lunch for the ladies."

"Boo-Boo shouldn't eat in public." The swiftness of the response betrayed another layer of Freddie's agitation.

"We can pick stuff up. You know what she likes, right?"

"Maybe." The non-committal, almost sullen, intonation was not Freddie. I slanted a look at him. His tone wasn't an invitation. So, I wouldn't push the issue.

I'd just have to let him talk to me.

The selection of meals varied. Bread dumplings. Ghoulash. Potato soup. Fried potato pancakes. Dishes I could identify. Some I couldn't. The combination of scents were enticing.

At the fourth restaurant, Freddie paused to read the outdoor menu. I tracked other movement on the street, but nothing stood out as problematic.

"I suppose being able to read Czech would be helpful," Freddie said with a long sigh.

"Or you can read the English translation on the other side of the door." There were two menus posted. He made a face and then crossed over to the second menu. The delaying tactic only worked for so long.

We headed for another shop. Three shops later, we paused for coffee. I paid for both of us while Freddie paced the space, studying what was on the shelves. The restlessness radiating off of him seemed to set off tremors in the air.

Ten more minutes.

I'd let him take ten more minutes.

He ended up cracking at the six minute mark while we stood outside of a bakery window where we had an excellent view of the bread being kneaded and other treats being prepared. There was something hypnotic about their work.

"Bodhi... How the hell do you fix something if it's broken beyond repair?"

"You don't," I told him. "If you think something or someone is that broken, you can't—restore it to a state where it has never been harmed. You have to incorporate the pieces you can and strengthen the bonds with new things."

"What if you don't have enough pieces?"

"Kintsugi," I said, then took a sip of the coffee. Clearly, he was talking about himself. But I also didn't think he was being kind about himself. Broken? Yes. We were all broken. Beyond repair? Compared to what? Still, those were arguments to be made *after* I identified the issues.

"Gesundheit?" Freddie gaped at me and I grinned.

"It's a traditional repair method in Japan. You take broken pottery, a bowl, a dish... some vessel that has been damaged. You glue the pieces back together with lacquer, while painting the seams with gold or silver powder. The dish is not restored to what it once was. But it becomes something new, something beautiful for its imperfections."

"Kintsugi." He repeated the word as though he needed to turn it over and test the syllables. "Think that works on people?"

"Yes."

"Okay, don't run me over with your explanations there." He downed more of his coffee and turned away from the bakery window. I fell into step with him before he'd made it three strides. "I don't think it will work for me."

"Why?"

"Because there are too many pieces. Too much is broken. I don't even know what I should look like, much less know how to put it back together."

"You should look like you."

"Helpful," he said in a tone that declared my comment

was anything but. The belligerence in his voice was frustration and not targeted at me. "If I ask you a question, can you just give me a straight answer?"

He paused, pivoting to face me. His nostrils were flared, his pupils slightly dilated, and his breathing coming in swift pants. A sheen of sweat dotted his forehead.

"Yes."

The shortness of my answer seemed to stump him for a moment. He looked at me, then down, then at the surrounding shops, then back the way we'd come before he blew out another harsh breath.

"I hate this."

"Take your time," I told him. Something was tearing him up. I didn't know if it was the situation or having to discuss it.

"You know some of Boo-Boo's story." The words came out a hushed whisper, his voice dropping to something confidential. "What her uncle did. How her past dance partner treated her. The doctors at the facility. The abuse she took?"

"Yes." I was very clear on it though no one had given me specifics, it hadn't been that hard to put together. I'd rather enjoyed helping them get into Sharpe's little fortress.

"She should hate men," Freddie said. "Hate all of us and never let anyone touch her again. She would be within her rights."

Then as if he couldn't stomach standing still anymore, he set off walking. Agitation detailed in every single step.

"But she doesn't—and everything they took from her, she's fought to take back. She..." He downed the rest of his coffee, then tossed the cup into a trash can before he folded his arms. The need to self-soothe and protect was right there. "She's let the others push her, especially when she hits a roadblock and they—we do everything we can to make it easier for her."

"But she doesn't want easier." PPG didn't seem the type. She was more of a throw herself right into it and fight. It was something she and Lainey shared. Probably what drew them together in the first place.

"No, she wants to feel what she feels. To touch us when she wants and for us to be able to touch her without any of those memories coming back to her. She's winning... Fuck she's incredible."

He scrubbed a hand over his face. The distress rolling off of him made my teeth itch. I wanted to kill whatever was bothering him, eliminate the threat, so he didn't have to think about it anymore.

"I want to be able to let her touch me," Freddie admitted. "But I can't... Sometimes, if it's just my hand or she's just leaning against my shoulder. That's fine. But when the clothes come off...I can't stand the feeling of her hands on me, cause then I see them and I don't *want* that."

See them.

Information began to slot into place and I spared Freddie a long look. He stared at the ground, hands opening and closing. More than once he reached for his pocket. The knife he usually carried. A lot of weapons had to be stored before we came here or replaced by items found here.

"How long?" I wasn't going to ask for details. If he wanted to give me those and names. I'd take care of it, for now, I'd listen and see what I could do.

"It was how I grew up until I was seven. Kiddie porn. I was in a lot of them. All I ever knew about it was a lot of pain and strange people touching me. Eventually... I got away. But..."

He raised his hand and held it out in front of him. It trembled violently.

"Boo-Boo has let me do whatever I want to her. I can

almost touch her and not hear those people or feel those memories... but if she puts her hands on me, it all crashes in and I can't figure out how to make it stop."

"You want it to stop." Not a question. "You want to put that part of your life back together without the cracks or the breaks."

"Yes." One ragged syllable.

"Does she know?"

Eyes closing, Freddie seemed to deflate. "Yes. When she told me her truth in Pinetree, I'd told her mine... I needed her to know she wasn't alone. Hardest thing I ever did, and I'd do it a thousand times over if it would help her."

"So, she isn't upset that she can't really touch you yet." Again, it wasn't a question. I'd seen PPG with Freddie. She adored him. She was also very protective. Of all the people in the world, she would understand.

"You'd think that would make it better," Freddie said. "But it doesn't. I feel like I'm letting her down. She's so damn brave and I can't—"

"Don't count yourself out," I said, finishing my own coffee. Then pointing to a pub down the street. We needed a real drink. "I mean it, don't. Wanting something and having it —they aren't the same. You love her. You want to be everything for her."

"Yes." He spread his hands. "I'm not scared of her. I know she isn't those people."

"You know that, here," I told him, pausing to tap the side of my head. "Your cerebral cortex knows. It understands. It's got the reasoning and logic skills to know that she would never hurt you and that she is not those people."

"Then why—"

"Because your amygdala is all about your survival. It has one goal, one primary driving force. Survive. Sometimes, survival means rejecting all touch, no matter what. Or rejecting all contact. Sometimes it can mean do nothing. Lay still and quiet, wait it out, and soon it will be over. If you don't fight, you'll survive."

Freddie paled. Yes, I understood the problem very well.

"Then I'm always going to be like this? Even if I really want to be like her? To push my boundaries?"

"No," I said. "Not at all. You just have to find a new way to fight that instinct. Your amygdala learned everything it knows from trauma. It's kept you alive. That's reinforced what it knows..."

"But?" The sharp demand accompanied his stopping on the sidewalk to face me again. "Bodhi, there has to be something. Don't say therapy. I tried... I really did. I hate talking to people I don't know and that crap we did at Pine-tree was only fun when you were terrifying the group leader."

I grinned. "Fair. No, I think you and PPG need to make it a game. Find a contact that you can take from her. Reward yourself when you get to feel her. Train your amygdala that her touch is welcome."

"That sounds stupid easy."

"Unfortunately, it won't be," I admitted. "We are a product of our experiences. The darker, and more traumatic ones leave scars so deep down they become a part of us. Then when we look in the mirror, we want to see what was there before, but that person is gone. We can only ever be the product of our experiences."

"Kintsugi," Freddie said abruptly.

"Exactly."

He scowled and I rested a hand on his shoulder, a light touch. Though he stilled at the contact, his physical reactions did not betray new stress.

"Talk to PPG. Make it a game for the two of you. She'll want to help."

"She shouldn't..." He didn't finish the sentence, and I let him go before I pulled open the door to the pub. "She really shouldn't," he murmured. "Everyone else is so much better for her."

"Word to the wise, my friend," I told him as I waved him inside. "Don't argue with your lady. They have very creative ways to prove you wrong."

His soft bark of laughter was exactly what I wanted. "She is stubborn."

"This is a good thing. You both survived. Now you both need to thrive."

I ordered the beers and then moved with Freddie to the back of the pub. I checked my phone for tracking data after I took a seat. Lainey was still at the theater.

Across the table, Freddie studied the icy cold bottle the bartender had served. I'd watched him open both and declined the glasses.

"You think I can really do this?" Freddie asked and I met his gaze evenly.

"Do you love her more than yourself?"

"Yes." No hesitation. No reconsideration.

"Then you have your answer."

It wouldn't be easy. But then, nothing worth having ever really was.

"I really want to believe you," Freddie admitted. "I am so scared of fucking up. Sometimes, it gets so hard and then I think, I'll do a hit or two and that will make it okay. One or two can't hurt and then I remember that I'm an addict, and there is no such thing as just one or two."

Silence draped the table at the end of his statement and he tipped his bottle up and took a long drink.

"Thanks," he said eventually.

"Always," I told him before taking another drink of my own.

This wasn't an overnight problem nor was it an overnight fix. But I had faith in both of them.

"Would you like me to tell you a story and distract you?" It was the one thing I could do.

"Fuck yes," Freddie said, damn near sagging then he shot me an almost chagrinned look. "I mean... Please?"

"You asked me once why I kept going into the facilities and I told you I was looking for someone."

I leaned back in the seat, aware of where everyone in the room was and how close they might be. At the same time, my attention was on Freddie.

"The person I was looking for... my brother."

My. Brother.

I'd been looking for one and as it turned out, I'd found two. But I'd save the mushier part of that for later, when Freddie was feeling better.

"Holy shit. I didn't know you had a brother..."

"Not many do. You see, my mother..." This was how I could help Freddie. He opened a vein to talk to me. I would do the same. I'd meet trust with trust. Teach his amygdala to take that leap...

Eventually.

TWENTY-FIVE

LAINEY

Our second day in Prague dawned before the sun came up. Adam and Ezra were leaving—again—to continue dancing the dance with local crime families and other power brokers for the region.

"I can come with, if you want," I said around a yawn as Adam dropped a kiss on my head.

His soft chuckle wrapped around me as he stroked a hand over my hair. "Keeping you in our back pocket like a secret weapon. I don't want them to know how dangerous you are unless we have to."

It was the indulgence in his eyes that had me reaching out to snag his hand. "Be safe?" I flicked a look to where Ezra stood by the door. "Please?"

"Well," Ezra said, smirk firmly in place. "Since you said please, Kotyonok."

Adam rolled his eyes, then glanced past me to where Milo had been sprawled. "You with Lainey today or is that Bodhi again?"

"Me," Milo said. "You two check in, regularly."

"I'd be happy to oblige," Ezra quipped. "But you forgot to say please."

I snorted, but that just made his smirk grow. "He's incorrigible." It came out far more of a groan than a scold.

"He is," Adam said. "But we'll check in. I expect to hear from you if anything comes up. Liam told me you had watchers yesterday."

The Vandals were all in hyper aware mode. Not that I blamed them. Em was the one we were hanging out in front of us. She was both bait and a distraction. Neither were terms I wanted to apply to her.

"I know, but they kept their distance. Could be people working for Zhukovsky. He's got a large investment in the show and maybe he wants to make sure it goes alright."

Heavy emphasis on the maybe.

"Be careful." Adam stroked a finger down the center of my face to the tip of my nose. The warmth in his eyes wrapped me up into a tight embrace. "Stay armed."

"Promise." I caught his hand and squeezed it. One last, light brush of his lips to mine and then he stood. Ezra pushed off from the doorframe to cross over to the bed. "Behave," I murmured to him when he cupped my face and kissed me.

"But I like being bad," he protested with a grin.

"You're good at it," I teased, then cupped his cheek. "While we're here, just—be less bad. Please."

With all the drama he was capable of, he clutched at his heart. "You had to say the magic word."

Behind me, Milo chuckled. "You're terrible."

"The absolute worst," Ezra agreed before he focused on me again. "And yes, I'll be mostly not bad."

"Hmm... why don't I believe you?"

"Because you are brilliant as well as beautiful," Ezra said. "And you know me too well."

"I've got him," Adam reminded me and the flash of delight in Ezra's eyes gave him away. He grinned at me, then winked. Too soon, they were out the door and it was just me and Milo.

I twisted to glance at him before I scooted back to lay down. He wrapped his arms around me and rolled me over so I was pressed against his chest. Tucking my nose against his neck, I smiled.

He stroked his hand against my back, rubbing a slow circle. "Going back to sleep?"

Another yawn worked its way free. Tracing my fingers over the ivy inked into his skin, I considered my response. "Tired?"

"Some," he admitted, cupping a hand over my shoulder. "You and Ivy didn't stop all day yesterday, and you were both at the theater until late."

"Wanted to go over everything." It was fascinating. "I think it's genuinely the first time I got to see everything she does or has to review *before* they set up, then after setup begins. She also wanted to test the load on the silks and we had to wait for Vaughn. The crew wouldn't set up until he was there."

Em's irritation when the crew informed her that they weren't *allowed* to set up until Vaughn got there had also been entertaining. Still, I couldn't blame anyone for being overprotective where she was concerned.

There had been accidents in the past. Whether because of sabotage or carelessness, she'd nearly been hurt before. No one wanted to take any chances.

"How are you doing?" I tilted my head back so I could study him. From this angle, the bristles along his jaw and cheeks gave him a roguish look. It didn't make him any less pretty though.

"I'm fine," he murmured, the husky note in his voice a reflection of his own tiredness. "Worried about all of you."

"All of us?" I pushed up a little so I could meet his gaze. The heat of his skin scorched next to mine. I would never be cold when Milo was there. "What about you, Pretty Boy?"

"Me?" A smile tipped his lips.

"Yes, you. Why aren't you worried about you?" I could probably answer the question myself, but I wanted to know what was going on inside his head.

He ran his hand down my arm. "I have the most beautiful woman in the world so in love with me, she takes my name."

Amusement sparked in his eyes and I raised my brows. "Em told you?"

"Bodhi." He circled my wrist with his hand and then lifted me almost bodily until I draped him like his favorite blanket.

The smug response made me laugh. "I didn't realize he'd heard." I probably should have. Of course, he had. Very little escaped Bodhi's notice.

"Hmm," Milo hummed a little, as he ran his hand along my back to the hem of my t-shirt. He lifted it easily and then clasped his palm against my ass. "I think he didn't want me to miss being claimed."

Shifting, I straddled his waist and tilted my head. "We didn't want me to be Lainey Benedict here. On the fly, I said 'Elaine Hardigan'." Scraping my teeth over my lower lip, I studied the smile softening his mouth. "You don't mind, do you?"

"Why would I mind?" Pretty Boy settled his hands on my hips. "We can make you Lainey Hardigan anytime you want."

It was my turn to straighten a little and to raise my brows. "Are you proposing?"

"No," he said slowly. "Before you think I'm rejecting you... I'm respecting the fact that we're not just a couple. If it were only you and me? I'd have put a ring on that finger the day you killed King."

Possessiveness swarmed through his voice.

"You... have taken my breath away since the moment you strutted out of that car in the warehouse and told me to have a little more shut the fuck up while you spoke."

I had to bite back my own smile. "Not the exact wording."

"Eh," he said with a shrug, running his fingers along the hem of my panties beneath the shirt. "The sentiment was the same, Mayhem. You walked in, in charge, and ready to go to battle."

"I mean..."

He chuckled. "Don't apologize. You were gorgeous. Filled my head with all kinds of inappropriate thoughts." The fact his cock was growing steadily stiffer where I straddled him served to illustrate the point.

"Then you locked me in your room."

"Well, you were being stubborn. I had to keep you safe."

"Locking someone up isn't necessarily considered keeping them safe, it's generally called kidnapping."

"Potayto," he teased. "Potahto. As I recall, you got even by stripping off that towel and letting me see every inch of this gorgeous body." His little groan at the end tickled me. Then he gave a little bump with his hips.

"One must always wage battle with the weapons at hand." I dropped my hands to the hem of the shirt I was wearing... oh it was one of Adam's. I didn't even know when I grabbed it. For now, I tugged it up and off to toss behind me.

Pretty Boy's smile grew and my nipples went taut as he adored me with his eyes. He dipped his fingers beneath the band of my panties and then there was a rip.

Pausing, I glanced down to see where he'd just torn the seam right out of the side.

"Really?" The dry tone was exactly the right one to take with him because his smile only grew more wicked.

"Yeah, if you're going to remind me about how this body wasn't for me. There were no panties in that particular interaction."

A burst of laughter, so indelicate I snorted in the middle of it, escaped me. Pretty Boy's chuckle rumbled out of him, but it didn't slow him from tearing out the seam on the other side and then I lifted my ass a little so he could tug the now useless scraps off.

"You're going to make me have to buy lingerie while we're here."

"I'll happily go with you and let you try on everything in the dressing room. You know, so we can make sure it fits right." He wagged his eyebrows playfully.

"Oh, see and here I thought you wanted to figure out how easily they ripped off."

A real gleam came into his eyes. "Oh, there's a thought. The easier to tear, the better. We might have to buy several pairs to figure out the best ones."

Head tilting back, I laughed. "I'd offer to just not wear any, but some outfits do require them."

"I don't mind tearing them off you, Mayhem. Make me work for it. Besides... I love those sets you have where everything matches."

He ran his thumb along the outside of my thigh. At this angle, he could see my cunt quite clearly, and there was something heady about him watching me while we just lounged like this.

I wanted to rock against his dick, but that might break the mood we'd woven. I was loath to interrupt this closeness.

"Pretty Boy?"

"Hmm?"

"When we first got together... you had no idea we were going to end up in a relationship like this."

"Don't worry, Mayhem. You're not losing me." Those four words offered a kind of comfort. A reminder that we were sticking this out.

"That's not what worries me." It wasn't. "You've never broken your word to me. You listened, you supported, and even when you were disappointed... You didn't abandon me."

"One, the only disappointment I ever felt was in the idea that Ezra was being cruel to you." Sobriety marked every word. Sitting up abruptly, Milo slipped an arm around me to keep me close and in his lap. "I'm serious, Mayhem. Did I plan on sharing you with three other guys? No. Not something that was on my radar. That said, they *love* you. They would *die* for you. Hard to say no to that kind of commitment."

"But Ezra worried you."

"Still does, but not for those reasons. He's a bit too reckless. He needs to take better care of himself for you and for Adam. But right now, he's also giving Adam something to do with the side of him that wants to control everything."

Milo was not wrong. "I like them together," I murmured. "They fit."

"They fit you, too." He brushed his nose against mine gently. "Just like Bodhi fits you."

"Like you fit me," I murmured before pressing a kiss to one corner of his mouth. "I love you, Pretty Boy. I couldn't do this without you."

"Yes you could." He stroked his thumb in circles against my hip. "You could do anything. Loving us? Allowing us in your life? That's a gift. I can't say we don't all complicate things for you… because we do. But I will always be grateful that you're letting me love you too."

A kiss to the other corner of his mouth, then he captured my lips. The kiss was a slow, devastating connection as he fisted my hair. Liquid heat poured through my system. Need that grew with every stroke of his tongue.

I ran my hands down his chest and then to the boxer briefs he wore. His cock damn near leapt when I stroked him through the fabric. I couldn't rip the clothing off him, but I could free his dick up.

He groaned in between licks, then nipped my lower lip when I wrapped my hand around him. When I angled upward and then slid down on him. The stretch was a glorious burn.

I had some slickness, not quite enough and I didn't care. I wanted to feel every inch of him. I craved the intimacy. His hiss as I took him to the hilt made me smile and then I kissed him again.

With one hand on my hip and the other on my nape, Pretty Boy urged me to move. I tilted my head back as he kissed a path down my throat to my breasts.

We rocked together, the slow grind of every deep thrust teased me. When he locked his lips around one of my nipples, it was like being struck by lightning. Then his fingers were between us and he massaged my clit.

My hips bucked of their own accord as pleasure shot through me. I continued to ride, but I added a twist to my hips. The pressure from both of us was enough to make me want to just come, but I fought my orgasm.

I wanted us to come together. Or at least, closer…

"Fuck," I blew out a breath as he pinched my clit between his thumb and forefinger, thrust upward and sucked against my nipple. The combination of actions all at once, shredded my control and I came in a rush.

He slowed his motions, petting me through it as I spasmed around him and then I was flat on my back, staring up at him dazedly as he pressed my legs to his shoulders.

"That was one," he told me and then began to thrust deeper as he teased my clit again.

"Oh... Pretty Boy..."

I stared up at him. Two of us could play that game.

He grinned and I thrust my hips up to meet his. He had so much control like this.

It was fantastic.

"You're going to come again," he murmured. "And again. I want you a mess on this bed and I want to feel you pulsing around my dick for the rest of the day."

I fisted the covers as he increased the pace. Where the first part of the coupling had been slow and deliberate, this was fast, frenetic, and I couldn't catch my breath as he shoved me over the edge.

I was still shaking when he pulled out, flipped me over and then thrust into me again. Lips next to my ear, he chuckled. The dark, delicious sound teased me as did the depth of his thrusts. At this angle, he could go much deeper.

A third orgasm caught me unawares and slammed me right into a fourth. I couldn't catch my breath or my mind as heat and pleasure obliterated my thoughts. Eventually, the hot pulse of his release filled me and we collapsed together.

One kiss to the shell of my ear. Then another just behind it.

"I love you too, Mayhem."

CHAPTER
TWENTY-SIX

MILO

I checked the address against the GPS on my phone. I couldn't speak Czech and I didn't try. The translation apps made navigating at least doable. Three days in Prague and our leads were thin.

Too thin.

In addition to not even getting a whiff of interest beyond the security Zhukovsky put on the theater and Ivy, Bodhi's "friend" had failed to show up.

"He'll be here," Bodhi had said over breakfast a few hours earlier. The confidence wasn't feigned. Until Hans showed up, we were still flying blind.

Then we got a call from—of all people—Margareta Waldemar. Well, Mayhem got a call from her. It had come in late the night before, not even five minutes after we arrived at the apartment we were renting. I didn't want to focus on how closely the woman had to be watching us.

Half of me wanted to ignore the information, but the rest of me understood it wasn't an option. Adam and Ezra had finally secured a meeting with the leader of a local Russian group.

At some point, we might have to pretend to be buyers to break into the rings. Cracking the cone of silence around the underground rings was proving even more difficult than I'd imagined.

"This is it," Lainey said as she threaded her arm through mine and leaned against me. She'd chosen thicker pants to combat the wind and a silk blouse that hugged her curves. Not that I got to appreciate it as much as I'd like.

The jacket she wore offered her more protection, it also provided camouflage for her weapons. The shop across the street was, of all things, a print shop of some kind. At least, that was what it looked like.

Phone in one gloved hand, Lainey rubbed the edge against her chin as she studied the storefront. "Should we get coffee and drift back?"

I scanned the street. It wasn't the busiest street we'd walked down and there were a number of other businesses. Sadly, there was nothing resembling a coffee or tea shop.

"No," I finally answered her question. "There's nothing out here to give us cover for why we're lingering." Speaking of which, we couldn't keep standing here. It didn't matter that I had my phone out as a partial cover for why we weren't just continuing.

That wouldn't provide enough of a distraction for long.

"Then Plan B," Lainey said, tilting her head back to glance up at me.

"Which is?" I didn't tighten my grip on her or make sure she stayed with me. Sunglasses hid her eyes from me, but I could read the rest of her body language. The *waiting* was taking its toll.

"Walking inside and talking to her."

Yeah. I had a feeling that would be it. "We don't know what's waiting for us in there."

"We don't, but I'm willing to find out. Do we go? Or do you want to call the guys and wait for them to join us?" Not an unreasonable suggestion.

"You're indulging me."

"Whenever I can," she said easily. "But Margareta would not have called with this woman's name and her former profession of being a 'chaperone' without some cause. She knows why we're here or at least she suspects."

Yeah, that was the feeling I got too.

"Split the difference," I decided. Phone in hand, I sent a message to the group chat with the guys. I gave them our location and plan.

Second message went to Jasper. He and Kellan were here. They might be closer. Either way, backup was backup.

"Messages sent." I stuffed my phone into my pocket. I wanted nothing in my hands. "If I pull the plug, retreat. Understood?"

Her lips pursed, but she seemed to be struggling to suppress another smile. "Understood."

Chuckling, I checked for where the gun was secured. Weapons in the Czech Republic were not as easily obtained as they were at home. The guys all knew a guy. Bodhi had made arrangements for all of us.

Still, I'd rather not be caught carrying, especially since they'd covered my conviction up so I could get a visa to enter the country in the first place.

"Do you mind if I take the lead on talking to them?" Lainey asked as we crossed the street.

"You speak far more languages than I do. But I didn't think Czech was one."

"It's not, but the sign there indicates they also speak

German." I followed her gesture to where the German flag appeared on a small sign in the window. I couldn't read it either, but I trusted her.

"All yours then. Just let me know if I need to punch someone."

That earned me a swift smile and a chuckle as she reached for the door. I got to it before she did and opened it for her. The bell overhead jingled, announcing our arrival. Not that anyone would be able to hear it over the racket inside the shop. The air was hotter than outside. Warm, humid, and it smelled of dust, paper, and something kind of burnt.

Everywhere I looked, there were stacks of paper, some printed, some not. The machine near the front was running and it was printing off large sheets with three or four pages per sheet.

Lainey made her way through the center of the shop toward an archway made out of more paper and boxes. Everywhere you looked there were boxes, not all of them stacked neatly. The precarious nature threatened bodily harm if they were bumped.

A woman appeared through the archway, a stack of hard covers in hand. She nearly ran into Lainey because her attention was elsewhere. Fortunately, her gaze snapped up at the last second. Stopping in her tracks, she let out a shriek.

Eyes wide and sweat decorating her brow, the woman stumbled back a step and Lainey caught her arm to keep her from falling. She said something in German. The rapid-fire speech sounded lovely from her, not that I could follow it.

Fuck, Ezra was right. She really was brilliant *and* beautiful. Her mind was sexy as hell. I was going to sign up for one of those language courses. While Lainey spoke to her, the woman shot me a look then her attention went back to Lainey again.

She answered in German, her speech not quite as rapid-fire. So, not a native speaker. She spoke enough to get by. I scanned the front of the shop. Then glanced past the woman toward the back.

"Is she here alone?" The question in English, just loud enough to make sure she could hear me, was a test.

Did our erstwhile target speak a third language as well?

"She is being evasive," Lainey said. "I startled her and she has a large order. Do you want to go check the back?"

"Stay away from the windows?" Compromise offered.

"I can do that," she said with a smile. Compromise accepted. I cut around the woman who suddenly let out a shrill amount of words.

Yeah, she didn't want me going to search. Too bad. The back of the shop was worse than the front. There were literally boxes upon boxes. Books and magazines spilled over from large, unbalanced stacks. I'd never seen so much paper.

It was hotter back here than it had been out front. More equipment rumbled and hummed as it ran. The sound of paper crinkling and rolling carried. It was loud, too damn loud.

I was just about to head back up front when I spotted a photo on a desk. Stalking over to it, I tugged the photo off the pinboard. Pivoting, I headed back to the front of the shop. I bypassed the women to head to the door. It didn't take me any time to secure it, then close the blinds and flip the light off to indicate it was closed.

A burst of excited, and aggravated, chatter burst out of the woman. She'd put down the covers she was carrying and gesticulated wildly.

Lainey never turned away from her. Good girl. Don't give her your back. When the woman started forward, Lainey stepped back into her path. I crossed to them and the woman shut up abruptly, though she glared daggers at me.

Saying nothing, I held the photo out to Lainey. She glanced at it. The stiffness in her posture seemed to harden even further as though she were becoming stone.

The woman spit something out in German. Lainey took the photo from me and turned it around to show the woman. As abruptly as she'd begun her new tirade, she shut up again. Her pallor gave her away.

I didn't need to speak her language to read her physical reactions. Lainey's next question was phrased so carefully, I could almost taste the anger vibrating between the words.

The photo was of Andrea. She was with another girl. The fact the photo was *here* confirmed some of our worst fears. It was also a solid lead.

"The door is locked?" Lainey asked over her shoulder.

"Yep."

Our host tried to bolt and I caught her before she could make it three steps. She whirled and tried to hit me, but Lainey blocked her fist and wrenched her arm down and around.

"Then we're going to have a chat with Katerina. Could you let the boys know?"

Armlock firmly in place, Lainey marched the woman into the back. I scanned the front again. The printer was still generating a stack of pages so I left it to that.

When I followed them into the back room, I found Lainey directing Katerina into her desk chair. The woman argued, then snagged something off her desk to use as a weapon. She never touched Lainey. In a move that I had to admire, she disarmed her, then smacked her across the face with the—what the hell was that? It looked like a heavy ruler.

Katerina let out a cry, clutching at her face as she staggered back into the desk. Lainey pointed the oversized two by four shaped ruler at the chair. This time, the woman obeyed.

It didn't take me long to find tape. It wasn't duct, but packing tape. Still, it would do. I secured her arms to the chair arms and her feet to the base. The woman kept protesting, but then she tried to spit on me.

Yeah, I'd be fighting too but the language barrier was getting old.

"You got this?" I could easily inflict the pain to get to the answers, but I didn't have the language. Lainey could communicate.

"I do." She glanced down at the photograph again. It was like a ripple of force passed over her as she studied it, then her expression went fierce and her eyes flat.

I messaged the guys while she spoke to Katerina. Adam wanted to see the photo, so I snapped a picture of it and sent it to him. While I did that, Lainey went through the woman's desk and found a scissors, a file, another two-by-four shaped ruler, a rotary cutter and a pair of pliers

Katerina paled again when Lainey returned to her. Pliers in hand. Whatever she said in a rush did not make Lainey happy.

Lainey asked her one more question.

Apparently, she got the wrong answer... again.

She pulled one of the woman's fingernails off. Yeah, that would fucking hurt. Katerina's screams agreed with me.

It took Lainey an hour.

And most of her fingernails, but Katerina finally admitted something while sobbing. The words came out far more rapidly, but Lainey was wholly focused on her.

When she finally went quiet again, Lainey turned away from her and paced three steps. Her brow drew together tight, and her eyes pinched.

"Mayhem." I kept my tone even and quiet. I didn't want to surprise her.

The torment in her hazel eyes gutted me. "She's alive."

"That's good."

I was waiting for the but.

"But there are auctions coming up and she's fresh, and new. Perfect for the right clientele."

My upper lip curled as I stared at the pale sobbing woman in the chair. "How is she a part of this?"

"A chaperone. Exactly what Margareta said she was. She goes to Germany regularly for her shop, so she brings back girls when they need a ride. She's also 'safer' for them because she seems so friendly."

Disgust filtered through me.

Katerina snapped something out and Lainey whirled. In one smooth movement, she struck her across the forehead. The blow cracked audibly. The second came out meatier. Then Katerina sagged as blood spattered the paper beyond her.

It was a wild burst of rage, directly focused on the shop owner. Lainey's arm lowered, the two-by-four dangling from her fingers. I closed the distance, checked Katerina's pulse.

Dead.

My phone buzzed. I let it go unanswered for a moment as I took the heavy strip of wood from Lainey. She closed her eyes and when she reached for me, I dragged her close and just held her. Dropping the wood to the side, I pulled out my phone.

Bodhi was here.

I eyed the dead woman and then the shop.

Good, we were gonna need help with the body cleanup.

CHAPTER
TWENTY-SEVEN

LAINEY

For what felt like the hundredth time, I checked my watch. Bodhi and Milo took care of the shop, while we made some payments to deal with the CCTV. Fletcher couldn't be here, but Vienna had a number of connections. So did Bodhi.

We used all of them.

Three hours after clearing the scene at the print shop, we were back at the apartment. Bodhi had poured me a drink but I didn't want the alcohol. I couldn't sit still.

It was like someone had dropped me into a bell and then struck the side of it. Everything under my skin vibrated. The trembling kept translating to my hands unless I kept moving.

So rather than sit there and stare at the photo of Andrea, I paced. The photo itself was in a plastic bag on the table. Face up.

Each time I made a pass, I looked at her beautiful face and the gong rang again. Every single time.

"Mayhem," Pretty Boy tried. He'd stopped asking me to sit

down. But he had made me change. It was a compromise. They wanted my bloodied clothes and I wanted to be ready to leave as soon as Adam and Ezra were back.

"How much longer?" I asked, glancing at my watch, though it hadn't changed in the twenty seconds since I last looked at it.

"They're close," Bodhi answered. He stood with his hands braced on the back of the sofa. Since arriving to help us with the body, he'd been steady as hell. I'd killed before. Katerina was not my first.

When I poisoned King and slit Wallace Graham's throat, it had been thought out ahead of time. Planned. Well, to be fair the slitting of Graham's throat had been a bit more of an impulse for how we would kill him. Killing him had been at the top of the list since I learned what he'd done to Ezra.

However, those impulses had been tempered by planning and foreknowledge. When we went to the print shop today, I'd been more curious than anything. So far, every avenue we'd taken to find Andrea found us at an impasse.

What could a print shop possibly have to do with anything? The woman had sputtered a bunch of half-formed lies when she found us inside. The fact that her gaze kept sliding off and she went from defensive to belligerent back to defensive told me a lot.

Grandfather once stressed that finding the truth meant listening to more than just the content of what was being said. Observe *how* it was being spoken. How direct were the speaker's actions. Did they make eye contact?

Beyond the physical cues, there were also the nonverbal, verbal adjacent cues found in tone and word choice. Liars tended to use far more hyperbole. They cursed more, used distracting word choices, and hedge words.

Nothing was ever their fault. A dozen different explanations. Conversely, when that didn't work, go on the offense. Attack the interrogator. The strangest part of it all... Liars tended to use far longer, more convoluted sentences than people telling you the truth.

Katerina had checked off every single box. Evasive. Abusive. Pleading. When she finally gave me the name of a school, it had been more in terror and pain than anything else.

The realization that I'd pulled out all of her nails without hesitation began to sink in. When I would have retreated, taken a breath, she'd taunted that I was probably too late anyway. There was a huge auction coming and little virgin westerners were very popular.

Rage spilled into my veins. Without an ounce of cool contemplation or remorse, I'd swung the wooden brace I'd been holding. Not once, but twice.

The first time had been a reaction. The second? Pure action. Both had come from the frenzy of pure fury. Selling people in the first place was disgusting. The fact she'd actually participated in getting my sister here just—

No, Katerina needed to die. We'd wrapped the body in shrink wrap from one of her many machines. A crew would come to deal with the scene, while another took care of the body. It had all gone surprisingly smooth.

On some level, it should likely trouble me that we could make people disappear like this. Not only could we, we had been. One by one, we scratched off from the list of who had wronged us.

Harper.

Karagiani.

Wallace.

King.

Katerina.

There were more. There would *be* more. As unsettled as I was following the interaction, I wouldn't hesitate to line the streets with bodies if we had to. I wasn't leaving without Andrea.

Bodhi's phone vibrated, as did Milo's. Mine was on the table, so maybe it did as well. Less than a minute later, the front door to our rental opened. Adam was the first one through.

Pivoting, I went straight to him. He opened his arms and wrapped me up tight. "Lainey," he murmured, the name a hug and chastisement in one. The trembling increased, even as I fisted the back of his jacket. He squeezed me to him, lifting me right off the floor as he moved us back into the apartment.

Ezra closed the door and followed. Half of me was aware of him. The worry rolled off him in waves. It rippled through the room, colliding with the concern coming off Milo and Bodhi.

"I've got you," Adam said, his arm around my middle a steel band. I squeezed him tighter. Tucking my face against his neck, I let him do the carrying right now. "Where's the photo?"

"Table," I murmured even as Pretty Boy echoed the same word in a much clearer tone. Not letting me go, Adam moved toward the table. When he sat down and settled me in his lap, I finally lifted my head.

The shaking was worse. But Bodhi was already holding the photo out so Adam could see it. His harsh exhale echoed the one that ripped through me at the shop.

It felt like centuries since the last time we'd seen her. I drank in the image, studying the way her hair was styled, the light cosmetics on her face, and the absolutely wrong shade of lipstick she loved to wear.

I'd told her once that shade of pink was too much. She'd laughed and said she wore it because she liked it. My heart crushed as if someone were balling it up like paper to discard.

The pink was just a little too bright. A little too pastel. A little too... pink. Yet, Andrea liked it. I wanted to trace over the lines with my fingers, but I couldn't look away from it.

"She looks older," Adam said, the hushed observation adding to the unsettled feelings in my soul. "Am I imagining that?"

"No," I said with a sigh, forcing my gaze up and off of her. "You're not. It feels like forever since we saw her. Too long."

Since we saw her.

Since we spoke to her.

Since I'd *hugged* her.

Adam pressed his lips to my temple. The firm grip of his hands coupled with the way he balanced me on his lap and didn't press me to do more or think anything else—helped.

It helped tremendously. I could pass this burden off to any of them. Adam had been trying to shoulder it for me, for years. Ezra always wanted to make things easier. Pretty Boy and Bodhi? All I had to do was ask.

Neither would just take it from me. It had taken Adam and Ezra time to learn that I needed to handle things my way. Right now? I wanted to be reckless and out of control. I wanted to storm the dance school, interrogate every single person there, and find our sister.

Could we do that? Could we do it safely? If we tipped our hand too early, they could disappear with her. Our leads could dry up. Anything could go wrong really.

Anything.

Ezra sat on the sofa next to us, settling one hand on my knee as if to remind me he was there. I summoned a smile for him. Bit by bit, it wasn't so impossible right now. Everyone was here.

"Brief us," Bodhi said gently. "From the top."

I'd told Pretty Boy and Bodhi a good chunk already while I texted Fletcher with the name. He promised to get back to me as soon as possible.

"She's a Czech citizen, the print shop is a family business. It's struggling." That had been sprinkled throughout her babbled explanations. She kept changing her story, repeatedly. "She took on too many projects over the past few years, failed to meet her deadlines and then had to refund deposits and more."

Hemorrhaging money.

Licking my lips, I shifted against Adam and he lifted me to resettle me in his lap with my back to his chest. Ezra put his hand back on my knee and I leaned my head to Adam's shoulder. Lifting my gaze, I glanced from Bodhi to Pretty Boy and then back.

"The financial loss apparently crippled her." Not that I gave a damn. "So, she went back to work she's done on and off over the years..."

I touched my tongue to my teeth. I was so angry. She discussed going to other countries, like Germany, and picking up girls of all ages, and nationalities. Her licenses and business let her bypass a lot of border checks.

The girls never protested. They never complained. That was the argument she tried to make, justifying her participation. Her excuse.

Bitch.

I cleared my throat and Bodhi shifted, he crossed back to the bar and returned with water. I still hadn't knocked back the whiskey, but it was waiting for me. If I couldn't get the trembling under control, I'd do it.

Everything being equal, however, I didn't want anything to compromise my judgment or my reactions. I took a long drink of water. It helped.

It helped a lot.

"Anyway, she picked up Andrea and this other girl. She didn't have a name for either of them. So either she didn't want to know, or she was lying. Her job is to pick them up, bring them into Prague, then deliver them to a school."

"A school?" Adam repeated, testing the word as if examining it for veracity, "She picks up girls from other countries and brings them to a school. No questions asked?"

"I wondered if she was just playing dumb or didn't want to know. Desperate times." Probably far too generous on my part. "Then she screamed something about us being too late. There was a huge sale coming, an auction, and she'd fetch a lot of money."

Adam's fingers dug into my hip. "The name of the school?"

"Radoslav-Tanzakademie," I said, before translating the German. "Radoslav Dance Academy." The name wasn't easily found in the local information directories. "I sent the information to Fletcher." Guilt assailed me. "I should have checked before I finished with her."

As much as I hated to admit it, she'd pushed me too far. The impulse to strike her had been right there and I hadn't fought it.

Now she wasn't available for further questioning.

"It's a name," Adam said. "If it's attached to anything real, Fletcher will find it. We can also do a little looking of our own."

I twisted to look at him. "How?"

"The Mikhailovskaya head has agreed to take a meeting." Ezra said, drawing my attention. "We just got the all clear from his people when you sent the message. It will be dinner tonight, we need to go formal and bring a gift."

Chewing on my lower lip, I considered him and then glanced at Bodhi and Milo before returning to Ezra. "How long do we have?"

Bodhi nodded once. "And how do you want to play it?"

Just like that, the shaking left me as we tackled planning. We were closer. Not close enough, but closer.

We weren't stopping until we found her.

CHAPTER
TWENTY-EIGHT

EZRA

The apartment Bodhi arranged for us boasted some decent amenities. It was too small in my opinion, but living on top of each other while we were in Prague wasn't a problem.

Especially not when Adam kept proving to me he could be a cuddler. I didn't want to examine that too closely, but I'd woken up more than once, curled onto my side, with him wrapped around me.

I fucking loved it.

I reworked the tie on my tux. The black tie affair was not my idea. The *Avtorityet* for the Mikhailovskaya organization extended the invitation on behalf of the *Sovietnik*. The *pakhan* would not be there.

That was fine. I didn't want to pay homage to anyone. I merely wanted to secure some support for us on the ground. Speaking fluent Russian got me a lot further than I expected.

"You're thinking too hard," Adam informed me as he stepped out of the bathroom shirtless. He already had his dress pants on or I would be reconsidering the knot for this tie.

I shifted a glance to the clock on the wall.

"Don't even think about it," Adam informed me.

"Killjoy."

"Yes, that's me, the slayer of all things fun for Ezra." He smirked as he tossed the hand towel he'd been drying his face with back into the bathroom then shut off the light.

"I mean... not the worst thing I've ever called you." I caught him shaking his head via the mirror as I tied the black silk one more time.

"You're butchering that." The dry advice had me rolling my eyes, but Adam was pulling on his own silk shirt.

Before I could respond, a light knock on the door pulled my attention. Bodhi and Milo knocked a lot harder than that. "Come on in, Kotyonok."

Adam pivoted, drawn by that invisible tether that connected us to Lainey. An awareness of her that we always had to maintain and when she was there, that was where we focused.

The door opened to reveal her in a stunning green dress. The deep emerald shade added something almost elusive to her. I twisted around to get a good look at the dress.

It was a simple sheath with a halter top. Everything about the way the silk moved with her had me wanting to stroke my hands over her. A pair of green heels peeked out from under the dress as she moved.

Fuck me, she didn't even have a hint of panties on under there.

She coughed lightly and I jerked my gaze up to find her watching me with amused eyes.

"You look gorgeous," I told her. She'd styled her hair up and pinned. It emphasized the column of her throat that the halter encircled like a collar. Blood pulsed to my dick.

They were both beautiful. It wasn't fair. I was gonna spend this whole evening with a damn hard-on.

"You do look beautiful," Adam murmured as he closed the distance and brushed the corner of her mouth with a kiss. It was a gentle touch, possessive but not proprietary. "You sure you're up for this tonight?"

Not an unfair question considering the news she found today. I swore, she was so damn strong it made me ache. But the sadness in her eyes and the way she'd clung to Adam left a gaping wound in my soul.

Finding news about Andrea and learning she was alive was very much a double-edged sword. She was alive. But was she safe? They were planning on selling her. Could we get there in time?

If we didn't?

We were going to be burning our way through Eastern Europe until we found her.

"I'll be fine," Lainey said, cupping Adam's cheek with her palm. "I have a knife on the inside of my thigh and I'll have my baton and a taser in my purse."

All weapons she'd need to close the distance with to use. Then again, if Lainey needed weapons at all it would be because someone closed in around us already.

After she set her clutch down on the nightstand, she came to me and brushed my fingers aside from the tie. "Let me," she said and I trailed my fingers down her bare shoulders, just for the excuse to touch her while she began knotting the tie in short, direct motions.

"Thank you," I told her and when she was done, I dipped my head to kiss her. The gleam of her lipstick said it was a gloss, but I didn't want to smudge it.

Well, that was a bit of a lie, I'd love to smudge it. Especially if I had her mouth wrapped around my cock. Or anywhere else really.

"Later," she said, as though she could read the lust in my eyes. Fuck, maybe she could. It wasn't like I could hide it anymore.

"I'll keep that in mind."

When she picked up my jacket, I let her hold it while I slid my arms into it. The gun I wore under it was hidden well. As tailored suits went, it wasn't the best. But we'd had to get them on short notice, so I wouldn't complain.

I tracked Lainey as she drifted toward Adam. He just held out his tie to her. There was a stillness to Lainey, a hesitation of action. Like everything she needed to do and say was on hold, bubbling under the surface and just waiting to explode out of her.

If I had to guess, she was keeping herself under rigid control. I hated it though. I preferred it when Lainey could let herself just *be*. Fuck, who was I kidding, I liked it when we could all just be who we were.

This wasn't one of those times. We were trapped by the world we inhabited. There were rules we couldn't break, and lines we should never stretch. Yet, we'd done all of that. Tonight was about shoring up a potential ally, but it was also about taking another step in the direction to find Andrea.

One was far more important than the other. And as much as I wanted to find their sister, I was also a selfish bastard. I didn't want to lose either one of them to do it.

Lainey smoothed down Adam's shirt after she finished the tie. Then she reached for his shoulder holster and helped him slip it on.

"You don't have to go," Adam told her quietly. "Ezra and I

can handle the meeting. We can take Bodhi with us, you and Milo stay here while we deal with this."

"I'll be fine," she assured him. "Unless you really don't want me there, then let's go ahead and fight about that so I can win and we can go."

I snorted a laugh at the bland, easy delivery.

"What?" Lainey said, glancing at me over her shoulder. "Do you think I won't win?"

Adam settled his hands on her bare shoulders and she faced him once more. The closeness between them seemed to blur away all the hard edges. They belonged in that bubble of closeness. Their mutual grief and terror bonding them further.

"Of course you'll win," Adam said without an ounce of irony or argument. "But you shouldn't have to do this if it's going to upset you any more than you already are. You did the hard part. You got us a lead and you dealt with a problem."

Dealt with a problem. She dealt with it all right. She ended the shopkeeper. The woman would disappear and become just another mystery. I might experience a twinge of guilt if she hadn't been involved. That said, she participated in trafficking and stealing girls.

She could die in a hole, buried alive for all I cared. As it was, Lainey ended it quickly for her. Maybe too quick, but again, the printer wasn't the important one.

"I admit," Lainey said as she leaned into Adam and stretched a hand out behind her. I wrapped my hand around hers and closed in against her back. Then Adam and I were wrapped around her. "I want nothing to do with some techni-cally challenging meal where we have to make nice with criminals."

I opened my mouth to correct that, then just let it go. She wasn't wrong. They were criminals. Not that we were much better. Not a point to argue on. "You don't have to," I assured her, dropping my head so I could press a kiss to the bare skin below the collar of her halter. "You don't have to do a damn thing."

"Ezra's right," Adam agreed with me, but I doubted he thought she'd take him up on it any more than I did. "If you want or need to sit this out, we'll take care of it."

Lainey lifted her head and leaned back against me, and I looped a hand around her waist. "Can I tell you how much I like that this is a discussion and not an order?"

"Orders never really worked on you," Adam told her without a hint of apology.

"Never stopped you from barking them out." The smile in her words belied the accusation.

"No, because I will always choose your safety first. Always."

Adam had one hand on my shoulder and the other cupping her chin. His gaze bored into hers and I drank in the sight of them together.

"As much as I want to lock you away and keep the rest of the world from ever touching you again," Adam told her in a silky soft tone that wrapped around us like an embrace. It was Adam at his most dangerous.

Indulgent and sweet, wrapped up in the most deliciously dark promises that he meant every single word. Goddamn the man made me hard.

"But?" Lainey prompted him, her smile almost as indulgent as his.

"But—that's not what you need from me. From any of us. You're more than our equal, Lainey. It won't ever stop me from wanting to keep you safe or protecting you every chance I get."

"It won't stop any of us," I added. "Just like it won't stop you from protecting us."

I almost said *trying* to protect us. But Lainey *had* protected us. My kotyonok was ever fierce with her teeth and her claws.

"That's the way it should be," she said and Adam lifted his gaze to meet mine. I read the worry there. The worry he wasn't sharing with her. The worry *for* her as much as about her.

"It is the way it should be," I said, turning the words over even as I spoke them. Adam's look of reprimand made me grin. That wasn't what he wanted from me right now. "It is though," I told him as much as her. "When we're together, we can look out for each other. Fuck knows, Kotyonok is much prettier than any of us. They're going to be trying to steal her when they see her tonight."

Adam's lips flattened and I had to swallow back a little bit of glee at the retribution-filled promise in his eyes. "You're not making this case for her."

"I don't have to make it for her. She's already made it. And again, we'll be right there. How much you wanna bet anyone who gets too frisky will disappear five seconds after Bodhi notices?"

For a brief moment, Adam opened his mouth then snapped it shut. A vicious gleam entered his eyes. "He really does have a way of dealing with interlopers."

"Exactly," I said, then to my delight Lainey laughed as she leaned back against me. The earlier smile had been more than welcome, but her laugh? That was a gift.

"You two are terrible."

"The worst," I agreed. "But like us, Bodhi wants you safe and he has far fewer lines that need to be crossed before he takes action."

"True," she said in the same breath as Adam. "However, I

suggest we keep it as business-focused as we can tonight. I'll play arm candy."

I snorted. "Not that you aren't stunning, Kotyonok. But you are so much more."

"I love you too," she said, tilting her head back and then winking at me.

"Every once in a while, you remind me why I didn't drown you when we were kids," Adam informed me and I just smirked.

"That and I can suck a dick like a god." Since I had literally done that between finishing my shower and starting his, Adam really couldn't disagree.

He shook his head then focused on Lainey. "Remind me to put him in a timeout later."

Yeah. Timeout my ass. That sent a wonderful shudder through me. I wouldn't be opposed. "Fine, let's go, the sooner we get this fucking dinner over, the sooner we get back here. I'm in the mood for Lainey to suck my cock and Adam to watch. He can *enjoy* all the things I do to you, Kotyonok."

"That *you* do to her?" Adam challenged.

"Oh yes, that *I* do to her. You already got your dick wet today."

"Asshole," he muttered and I grinned. Lainey's soft laughter circled around us. The distraction wasn't much, but I'd grab every single bit of one I could with both hands.

"Keep laughing," Adam murmured next to my ear. "I bet I can make her come more times than you can."

Liquid heat spilled into my blood. "Challenge accepted."

"Come along boys," Lainey said, still chuckling. She claimed her clutch and headed for the door. I wasn't the only one groaning because that silk sheath flowed with her steps as though caressing her.

I had no idea if I'd even survive the dinner, but what a way to go...

LAINEY

A car was waiting for us when we came down. The driver—Kellan Traschel—was a familiar face. The Vandal slipped out of the driver's seat and opened the back door for us. He was dressed in a black suit and had the look of a professional chauffeur.

"Miss," he murmured in polite greeting, ignoring Milo's snort of amusement as the others waited for me to get in first.

"Thank you." The back of the vehicle was quite spacious. I didn't take any of the edge seats. Instead I chose the middle seat facing forward. Ezra climbed in next and he dropped into the seat right behind the driver. Adam took the seat on my right with Bodhi going across from him and then Milo next to me on the left.

"You have the address?" Milo asked after Kellan climbed into the driver's seat.

"Yep. Already scouted the area and Jas is there keeping watch with Rome."

"Efficient," I said even as Milo threaded his fingers with mine.

"Not taking any chances," he said by way of explanation, but I waved it off. I didn't need them to tell me about mitigating risks. We were in an unfamiliar city, meeting with unfamiliar people with a measure of influence.

We needed allies here. If we couldn't find them and we had to do this on our own... Well, there were people we could hire to bring in if necessary.

So, no chances needed to be taken beyond what we were already doing. The drive from our apartment to the home of the evening's host, Dimitri Solohub, took just a little under thirty minutes. I wasn't sure how much of that was the roundabout route that Kellan took or the fact it was further out.

I could let my mind wander while we were in the vehicle. I needed to focus when we were inside. The house turned out to be a luxury villa in the Troja district. It occupied a hill with a pair of other villas flanking it. Close, but not immediately on top of it.

"All three homes are under the control of the Mikhailovskaya as far as we can tell. Doc called his friends. Alphabet did some looking and they reached out to some people they know in the region. Most won't have anything to do with the Mikhailovskaya because it's not good business."

"Good to know," Bodhi said. "Any warnings?"

"Just the standard," Kellan replied as he pulled up the drive and then reached out to choose a button on the call box. No challenge was offered, just a buzz and an accented voice saying something in Russian.

"He said come up," Ezra translated. No one said anything more until Kellan's window was closed and we were moving once again. "It took us three days to get someone to even consider an introduction, now we're invited to dinner."

He rubbed at his jaw. The playful flirt from earlier was absent and replaced by a far more troubled man.

"And we're here..." I let that trail off, waiting him out. Despite the assurances earlier that they wished I would stay behind where it was "safe," we were all here.

Ezra and Adam would have fought a lot harder if they suspected a trap.

"We're here," Ezra agreed. "I just don't know what we might be walking into." Then he glanced at Bodhi. "I don't think it's a physical trap, but it feels more like they got an idea of who we were and that opened the door."

"Which could be a problem all by itself," I murmured. Adam settled his hand on my thigh.

"Whatever it is," he said. "We'll deal with it."

Then we pulled up in front of the house. Before he got out, Kellan turned his head so he could glance back at us. "Hit the panic button if we need to crash in and get you out. Jasper and Rome are watching, I won't be far. Hopefully they'll just let me stay. If they won't—not a problem."

"We got this," Milo said and he patted the pocket of his jacket. "Let's not keep our hosts waiting."

Despite the familiarity of formal attire and a luxurious location for our dinner "party" or whatever they called it here, unease settled in my bones. I liked when events were a little more predictable.

Especially when we weren't sure if we were dealing with potential friends or new enemies. Allies didn't have to be friendly, but they did need to be trustworthy.

The cooler air sent shivers rippling over my skin. I had a wrap but it wasn't as warm against the breezes here as it had been next to the apartment building. I took a good look around, letting the scenery appear to capture my interest as I scanned who was here with us.

So far, I hadn't seen any guards standing out. Didn't mean they weren't here. If anything, they were more than likely watching us from several locations. Jasper and Rome were out there too, but I hadn't expected to see them and I didn't.

Security you could see were there to intimidate. Security you couldn't? Well, they were there to do a job and it increased the likelihood that they would get you first. Ezra offered me his arm and I threaded mine through his.

I could almost read the regret in Kellan's stoic expression as the guys fell in around us. He couldn't go inside. Sympathy welled up in me. I would not want to be the one left behind.

With Ezra leading the way, we headed for the front of the villa. It was elegant and had a touch of French countryside chic to it. The driveway did not let us out immediately in front of the villa's doors.

Instead, we had to follow a cobbled walkway to stone steps and then up a flight to a patio balcony where the double-wide doors with their etched glass awaited.

Secure, but with the appearance of openness. I rather like the effect. Ezra moved slowly up the steps as I climbed with him. The doors opened just as we reached them to reveal a silver-haired man in a tailcoat, bow tie, and gloves.

Maybe we should have brought calling cards. The man swept us with a look, before he focused on Ezra and myself.

"Mr. Graham, Miss Benedict, please, you're expected."

We were expected. The tension in Ezra's arm seemed to stiffen the muscle under my fingers. Once inside, the butler offered to take Ezra's coat and my wrap.

A part of me wanted to resist, but then we could leave without the coats. The uneasiness that settled in while we were in the car surged through me once more.

"Mr. Cavendish," the butler said as he took Bodhi's jacket. "Mr. Reed." His accent was distinctly British, not Czech. He would be right at home in Downton Abbey. "Mr. Hardigan."

Milo eyed him but let him have his coat. The butler passed off the jackets to a pair of footmen.

"Please, if you'll follow me."

He turned on his heel and led us deeper into the ornate home. The wood grains in the floor gleamed, freshly polished. Even the floors that looked like marble were wood. They were exquisite.

The first sitting room was clearly where guests might wait to be introduced. We bypassed it entirely as the butler led us to a much larger room beyond with a fireplace, bookshelves, sofas, and billiards tables.

Two of them.

Unexpected but not unwelcome.

"If you don't mind waiting in here, I will get you drinks and Mr. Solohub will be with you directly, along with his guest. He had to take a call and wanted to express his deepest regrets for having to make you wait."

"That'll be fine..." I said, then raised my brows.

"Andrews, miss," the butler introduced himself. "Would you care for a glass of wine?"

No, but probably a good idea to make a show of it. "Yes, please. Wine would be lovely."

"Whiskey," Adam said easily.

"Water," Bodhi answered.

"Same," Ezra followed suit.

"Make that three," Milo added.

I had to hide a smile as the butler excused himself.

Ezra glanced at the guys. "You can drink, you know."

"They are," Milo said. "I don't want anything right now."

Which was fair. I didn't really want any alcohol either. In

fact, I'd rather just get the meeting over and done with. The social niceties demanded a lot.

"Relax," Adam ordered Ezra, because that always went well, before he began to move around the room. I understood the need to inspect the space. What clues could we glean from the architecture, the art, and the decorations.

I didn't follow him, but I did study the layout of the room, the Georgian furniture scattered amongst the Queen Anne, and far more modern pieces. It was—eclectic. Likely put together more for comfort than the aesthetic.

Andrews didn't keep us waiting long. He returned with the drinks and there was a second glass of wine on his tray.

Before I could ask about the wine, the sound of heels striking in a two-beat rhythm echoed from down the hall. Each step, two-beats, growing gradually louder, the closer they came. Bodhi moved to stand right next to me.

Wine in hand, I composed myself. Perhaps it was our host's wife or...

"Are you fucking kidding me?" Ezra muttered under his breath.

Shock stapled itself to me.

"Mrs. Waldemar," Andrews said as Margareta Waldemar sauntered—and yes, she was absolutely sauntering—into the room in her gold filigree dress, looking like she'd just stepped out of the opera. "May I present our guests for the evening..."

Andrews introduced us all by name, not that she needed such formality. Still, we all played our parts, even Margareta. Then Andrews gave her the wine.

"Thank you, Andrews," she told him in her cultured voice, the barest hint of an accent present. "Do go take care of whatever it is, Mr. Solohub requires. I'll be just fine with our guests."

"Ma'am." Andrews all but clicked his heels together, nodded his head, and then strode out again.

"Mrs. Waldemar," Adam said in a chilly tone. "What an unexpected surprise."

"Well, if you'd expected me, dear boy," she told him with a smile. "It wouldn't be a surprise, now would it?"

"No," Milo said, his tone damn near as guarded as Adam's. Ezra didn't say anything but the stiffness in his posture and his arm betrayed every inch of his unhappiness with this whole situation.

The only one not responding at all was Bodhi. He merely stared at her. She glanced at each of us before finally bringing her cool gaze to rest on me. The amused smile on her lips flickered, then dimmed before she sighed.

"I suppose it would have been a great deal to just assume you would be pleased with my presence."

"I am neither pleased nor displeased." Not every occasion called for blunt honesty. This one did. "I am, however, in possession of a great many questions."

"Then come and sit with me, darling girl, and we'll talk. Also that dress is absolutely beautiful on you."

"Thank you." I ignored the hand she held out to me. "I'm also fine with standing. I haven't decided whether I'm staying for the rest of this or not."

Margareta sighed for real and it lacked any of the teasing hints of affect. There was real regret in her eyes. It was the first genuine sign of regret I could recall tracking from her. Normally, she played it much closer to the vest, not betraying any emotion.

So why would she have...

"Oh."

It hit me and our gazes locked all at once.

Her smile grew a little sadder. "You really are gifted."

288

Brushing aside the praise, I studied her. "Who knows?"

I could almost feel the question Ezra wasn't asking. Adam's fierce frown came into view as he and Milo joined the four of us and we stood in a semi-circle in front of Mrs. Waldemar.

"Not as many as you might think. I learned a long time ago that ingrained misogyny and chivalry aren't too far apart."

"Son of a bitch," Adam muttered. I didn't glance at him. He had to have guessed, just like I did.

"It's not just being the power behind the throne, you are the throne. Everyone else is the window dressing."

Margareta raised her wine glass. "People see what they want to see. In a bratva, they want powerful men with dark scowls and mysterious motives. As for me? I'm merely a hostess. A wealthy widow. A philanthropist."

I tossed back the glass of wine like it was the whiskey that Adam had ordered.

"If you were curious, yes, the Mikhailskaya was once my husband's—well, part of it was. I've grown it considerably since he died. The men who report to me are good, honorable, and they do good work."

"But you are still the pakhan," I said, testing the term.

"Or I can just be Margareta. You and I could be friends, Lainey."

"Why?" Bodhi asked, the question landing into the silence with a crack like a gunshot.

"For a great many reasons, Mr. Cavendish, not all of which you've earned the right to know or even ask me. Rather than play this game of two steps forward and one step back, let's address directly the reason you were invited here tonight."

My heart fisted in my chest.

"Andrea?"

THIRTY

ADAM

Margareta Waldemar. At this point, I wasn't entirely certain if I should be impressed or infuriated. The woman turned up everywhere. Since discovering her connection to King—he killed her son—and how it related to her interest in the rest of us, I'd been wary.

Having her popping up everywhere in Manhattan and Long Island had been one thing. She had connections and ties there. She'd been entrenching herself. Carving out a space of her own amidst the elite. For the most part, she seemed to be on our side.

For the most part.

Her appearance here? This hot on the heels of her showing up at the funerals? Not something we could just overlook. There was so much more to Margareta Waldemar than we'd already uncovered.

Maybe too much more.

"Andrea?" Lainey's soft exhalation of our sister's name had me shifting closer, ready to intercede between her and

Waldemar. Bodhi put himself a half-step in front of her and Ezra locked his free hand to Lainey's.

I'd never fault his protective instincts, even when he was committed to winding me up. Like me, Milo moved a little closer too. We weren't just closing in around Lainey, but erecting the barrier to Waldemar.

"What do you know about Andrea?" Lainey's question snapped me back into the room.

"Not as much as I would have liked," Margareta admitted. Her snowy white hair was styled in a to her shoulder bob, with a part on the side that gave it a razor-sharp effect.

The dichotomy of edginess blended almost too neatly with her aura of power and authority. The charm and charisma this woman possessed made her infinitely more dangerous than even I originally suspected.

It was so easy to overlook her as the major threat in the room. But that was exactly what she was...

"Be more explicit," Bodhi said abruptly. "If you don't mind, Mrs. Waldemar. I think Lainey would appreciate the directness and I know I would."

Agreed. Though I said nothing. I watched for the trap. There had to be one. Why else was she here? Leopold had put her on notice back in New York. We hadn't informed anyone other than a select few of our destination.

Now, here she was.

"I didn't know that her father had made arrangements to sell her," Margareta said, this time she took a sip of her own wine and then crossed the room to take a seat in a wing-backed Queen Anne chair. The eclectic mixture of old world and new suddenly made more sense.

It had shades of her home in Queens. A place where she seemed as comfortable baking in the kitchen as she was ordering an assassination. Since I'd seen her do both at the same time, it didn't surprise me like it once had.

"Harper Reed was a detestable man," Margareta continued with nary a flicker of apology to me. Not that I needed one. I wholeheartedly agreed with her. My father had been a complete bastard. "I did not suspect that even he would have done this. The girl is a child..."

"We were all children once," Bodhi commented. While I was aware he was just drawing her out, his cavalier tone irked me.

"Yes, some of us are still children," Margareta said, meeting Bodhi's gaze with a kind of equanimity that I could envy. Bodhi wore murder face, whether she was aware of it or not.

A perfectly pleasant mask that promised he could turn on a dime. I'd seen what he'd done to my father. I didn't envy Margareta's chances should she truly aggravate him.

Ezra was right about one thing. Cavendish might be insane, but he was on our side and I'd take that every damn day of the week.

"Mrs. Waldemar," Lainey said abruptly, moving toward her. I didn't like it and neither did anyone else but she crossed over to where the woman sat and took a seat of her own.

"Margareta, dear," the older woman said. She focused on Lainey with utter kindness. That made me even more uneasy than her velvet glove of steel that she delivered her threats in.

"Mrs. Waldemar, I am perfectly capable of all the verbal jousting you might want to play. I am, however, not in the mood for any of it at the moment. It might not be politic or even especially kind, but if you know something about my sister—please tell me and don't waste my time with more games." It was the most direct, and gentle, no bullshit ultimatum I'd ever heard.

"There are a dozen different avenues in and out of Prague. Trafficking is a dirty business, but it's also a lucrative one. Western girls are not usually found here as often. The custom is to prefer girls from disenfranchised areas of the world. Or girls from an ethnic background." Distaste filled her expression. "They want women who can disappear and no one will look for them."

"Yet, this is a place that Harper, King, and others used to remove 'problems.'" The counterargument was solid. "Harper told me himself that he sold her. I spoke to a woman who participated in getting Andrea from Germany to Prague. She indicated there was an auction coming up." Lainey laid it out for her, clear facts. As much as she tried to keep her emotions in check, she couldn't quite mask the anger and sadness twining together in her voice.

"There are many organizations, some fledgling, and others, that do business in and around Prague. At one time, it wasn't about what you were willing to do but what you were allowed to do." She shook her head. "But power—power that is spread out amongst so many becomes dilute. There is no central figure who wields enough influence of Prague to close off some of those avenues. Like rats, they always come back and bring more detritus with them."

"So you know who has her?" It was as direct a question as you were likely to get.

"We have a few likely suspects, yes." She went from being open about everything to seemingly guarded. Lainey shifted to glance at us then back to Margareta.

"Do any of those suspects have dance academies?"

For a moment, I forgot to even breathe. A flicker of recognition in her eyes gave Margareta away. She knew.

She could tell us right now.

Like a rubber band being stretched too tight, I worried I

might snap. As it was, I forced myself to be still and not drag the woman out of her chair and shake her until all the answers spilled out of her.

Footsteps in the hallway had Milo shifting. I moved closer to Lainey while Bodhi and Milo arranged themselves to put whoever joined us next right in their crosshairs.

Margareta glanced toward the doorway as a dark haired man with a brutally blunt square jaw entered. Like the rest of us, he was also dressed in a tux. Formal dining all the way around.

"Dimitri darling," Margareta said, holding out a hand to him. The man in question swept the whole room with one cool look. There was no mistaking the assessment in them or the very real threat in the way he moved.

Fine suit aside, this man was a pure predator. What fascinated me was how he fixed on Milo first, almost bypassing Bodhi but then their gazes clashed.

Yes, please note you are not the only psychopath here, sir.

The random thought bordered on slightly hysterical. Still, as fierce as Dimitri Solohub appeared with the scar bisecting his left eye and digging deeper into his cheek, I'd put my money on Bodhi.

Every.

Single.

Time.

Dimitri accepted Margareta's hand and bent to press a kiss to her knuckles. He murmured something, but it was Russian or maybe Czech. Either way, it wasn't a language I spoke.

As he straightened, he turned those cool eyes on Lainey. I half-expected some smarmy comment, but the man merely inclined his head. "Dimitri Solohub, Miss Benedict."

"Mr. Solohub," Lainey replied. "Thank you for inviting us this evening."

Margareta's eyes narrowed but her lips twitched. Amusement filtered through me. The invitation was clearly from Margareta. Lainey was just tweaking her. Still, I enjoyed it.

"It is my great honor. Margareta is a dear friend."

"Family," she reminded him almost primly and he snapped his heels together with a light bow of his head.

"Of course," he said, acquiescing like a good soldier. Then he glanced at Lainey once more before focusing on Margareta. "Did you want to go through to dinner or..."

"Somehow, I don't think a meal is really in the cards tonight." Margareta finished her wine, then rose. Lainey followed her to her feet. "If you'll call a car, Dimitri, we're going to need a few men as well."

"I'll make arrangements immediately. Destination?" He already had his phone in hand.

"Vedriš Dance Academy." That wasn't the same name Lainey got from Katerina. Maybe that was why we hadn't been able to identify it.

"Juraj Vedriš?" Lainey questioned, not bothering to contain her reaction. She was *angry*.

"You've met him?" The snap in Margareta's voice hadn't been there earlier.

"Yes, just a couple of days ago."

"Then you can give us a description, because that man has proven quite difficult to pin." She transferred her attention to Dimitri. "I want him alive. He has questions to answer."

"You have my word," Dimitri said as he pressed numbers on the phone before retreating a few steps.

"You won't ride with us, will you?" Margareta was focusing on Lainey again.

"No, we have our own car and a driver."

The older woman nodded. "Do you have a change of clothes?"

"No," Lainey said.

"Pick one of your gentlemen to escort you and come with me. We will get you changed. I'd rather you could move more easily than in those heels."

I was already moving, and waved Ezra back. I had a few questions for Margareta. She moved briskly, not glancing back to see if we followed. Lainey was right behind her, and I trailed Lainey by two steps.

At the top of the stairs, Margareta turned to a room and pushed open the doors. "This is a guest room. I keep new clothes for any guests we have that might need them. Multiple sizes."

She strode in ahead of us and pulled open a walk-in closet then three drawers on the dresser.

"These should all do. As for shoes..." She glanced down at Lainey's feet. "I have a pair of boots that will fit you."

Not waiting for our response, she retreated from the room.

"Margareta," Lainey said before she could vanish fully. The woman in question paused in the open doors and met Lainey's gaze evenly. "Thank you."

Whatever she'd expected from Lainey it wasn't that. "You're very welcome. While this isn't the time or the place. I would very much enjoy getting to know you and hopefully teaching you that you can trust me."

"Definitely not the time," Lainey said. "But I'm more than willing to consider it later—after Andrea is home."

Very safe, with new bodyguards and whoever took her carved up into a thousand pieces and buried. Not that I thought we needed to state that aloud.

"I'd like that," Margareta said and then she turned to go.

I glanced at Lainey. "Are you fine to change? I'll be in the hall."

She shot me a look then flicked a glance to the retreating Margareta. I nodded once. Yes, I wanted to talk to her.

"I'll be fine."

I pulled the doors closed as I stepped into the hallway. Margareta hadn't gone far, she stood a half-dozen steps away, clearly waiting.

"I thought you might want a word," she said. "Though we should probably not take too long."

"We won't," I said, sliding my hands into my pockets. It was rude, but I kept experiencing the urge to throttle her until she told us everything. Better to curb that for the moment. "I just wanted to know how much of all of this has been about Lainey since the beginning?"

"More than you suspect, less than you fear." While that vague answer was as clear as mud, at least she wasn't denying it. "Adam, you and I had a deal. As far as I'm concerned, that deal is done. Paid in full. No debts owed."

Good cause I had no intentions of paying anything more.

"This conversation will have to wait until Lainey and I have time to truly talk."

"Fine," I said. "But I want to make something clear. That woman means the world to me. There is nothing I won't do, nothing any of us won't do, to protect her. Occasionally, I like you, Margareta."

"But you love her," she said, a smile tipping her lips. "That's as it should be, Adam. Now if you'll excuse me... I am going to change. Hopefully in a few hours, I will see your sister returned to both of you."

Fuck.

My stomach bottomed out at the idea. Hot and cold

flashed over my skin. The only way the past few weeks had been at all tolerable was because of Lainey and Ezra. Milo and Bodhi had done their part, but not knowing where Andrea was and not being able to protect her had been killing me slowly.

The doors to the guest room opened and revealed Lainey in a black turtleneck tucked into dark colored combat pants.

"She'll be back in a minute," I told her.

"Did you get what you needed from her?" Curiosity hovered in her eyes.

"For now," I said.

If Margareta proved more problematic, well, we could deal with that too. No more enemies.

Clear the board.

CHAPTER
THIRTY-ONE

LAINEY

By the time we descended the stairs once more, the others appeared ready to depart. I still couldn't quite fathom Margareta Waldemar. She was definitely a puzzle wrapped in an enigma. Yet, she seemed genuine and that bothered me more than I cared to admit.

The boots she'd brought to me were knee high and added to the combat vibe of my appearance. I caught the faint smile on Bodhi's lips when he gave me a once over. The same from Milo. Ezra flicked a look from me to Adam then back again before he seemed to relax.

Oddly, the men now all seemed like they were over-dressed or really sexy spies. As focused on Andrea as I was, that thought still made me smile. I hadn't bothered to bring the dress back down with me. I'd secured my weapons from the clutch in one of the many pockets on the pants.

"Dimitri?" Margareta asked as she reached the last step. Like me, she wore black combat pants, a turtleneck, and boots. The unrelieved black added to her icier appearance.

Maybe it was the way she'd pulled her bob back and secured it at her nape. The pull of her hair gave her a harsher appearance. In that moment, not only could I picture her giving an order to kill someone, I also could see her pulling the trigger herself.

"The men are ready," Dimitri said. "Do you wish us to go in and secure the location—"

"No," I said, cutting him off and glancing at Margareta. "We don't know for sure if she is there. But if she is and she sees a bunch of armed men bursting in... there are just too many ways that can go wrong."

Head canted to the side, Margareta seemed to consider my words. "How would you prefer to do this?"

With the ball being served back to me, I turned to Bodhi. He and Milo were a lot more familiar with these kinds of operations. So were Adam and Ezra for that matter. I'd seen the plan they all put together with the Vandals to deal with Bradley Sharpe—may he rot in hell forever.

"We need to see the facility," Bodhi said. "Layout. Ingress. Egress. I would also like to know how many are inside."

"But it's late," Milo said, checking his watch. "Evening. Would the—" He hesitated and gave me a gentle look. "Would the *students* still be there?"

Students wasn't the word he'd intended to use. But I didn't want to look too closely at whatever the correct word would have been. I just—didn't.

"The academy is also an *internátní škola*—" Dimitri frowned. "Internat." I'd already begun that translation when he switched from Czech to German.

"It's a boarding school," I told Pretty Boy. "That means they might be living there."

Andrea could be there.

Right now.

"I am sending plans for the location," Dimitri said. "I will have my men close off access around the facility. We won't let anyone leave and do our best to minimize violence."

Minimize it, but that didn't mean eliminate it entirely. It had to do. I took a deep breath. It *would* do.

"Acceptable?" Margareta directed the question to me and I nodded.

"Thank you."

"Then let us depart."

Bodhi held out a hand and I narrowed the distance to take it and then we were heading out. They fell in around me, keeping Margareta and Dimitri at a distance. Kellan was waiting for us just outside with the car.

He swept a look over each of us as he opened the back door. "Jas and Rome will follow. Liam and Vaughn are going to meet us there, Doc is holding back with Freddie and Em."

But he would be available if we needed him.

"Ivy listening?" Milo asked as I climbed into the back.

"So far," Kellan said with a wry smile. "Let's see how fast we can wrap this up so she doesn't decide to go rogue with Freddie." He didn't sound terribly concerned. Em wouldn't make a move without the guys being good with it.

Not when she would worry more about being a distraction. No, she would do her best to keep from scaring anyone. Restlessness invaded my veins, a wild kind of buzz that both muffled the world and made it seem too loud all at the same time.

Milo put a hand on my right knee, the gentle touch drew my attention to the fact my foot was bouncing. I stopped, dragging a deep breath to fill my lungs.

"We're going to find her," Milo said, the sincerity in his voice insisted that I believe him. It was all I wanted to do.

302

His skin felt like fire under my palm when I set my hand on his. "I hope so."

It was the best I could do and when my gaze snagged on Adam's, I saw the same worry reflected back at me.

"Milo is right," Adam said. "We're going to find her. She's going to be fine. And we're going to gut anyone who has laid a single finger on her."

"For starters," Bodhi tacked on to the end.

"And we'll make sure it hurts," Ezra added.

"For a long time," Kellan chimed in from the front.

The ease with which they circled the party line made me smile. "I'm down for that."

For all of that.

The ride from the villa to wherever the school was located took us from one side of Prague to the other. I knew very little about Prague despite the research I'd done on the flight over. Maybe, someday, I could come back and be an actual tourist.

I could take Andrea on a proper European tour. England, France, Belgium, Germany, Italy, and so much more. We would find her and she would be up for this trip someday.

She had to be.

Milo turned his hand over and threaded his fingers with mine. The cold inside of me seemed to continue to spread until ice sheathed the hum, and put a very firm wall between me and the rest of the world.

My heart seemed to race and beat too fast at the same time. I couldn't quite regulate my breathing. When Ezra pressed his leg against mine, I tried to absorb the comfort they were all offering.

"I'll be fine when we get there." The wild energy invading everything made calming myself down almost impossible. That said, I would not be the reason this got screwed up.

"Yes you will," Bodhi said. "Inside, you're with me or Milo. Does she know Ezra?"

"Yes," Ezra said. "I've known her since she was a baby."

"Okay, then we'll put you with Liam. Milo or I will be with Adam. We'll sort the Vandals out after that."

Three teams.

Three teams, each team with someone that Andrea knew.

I blew out a breath. "That's smart."

"Thank you," he said easily.

"He's modest too," Milo added.

Ezra let out a hysterical little snort and even Adam snickered. Laughter swam up from under all the noise and I had to bite my lip as I started to chuckle. The sound cracked some of the ice surrounding me, bringing the world closer.

The tectonic shift helped. Closing my eyes, I drank in their nearness and focused on my breathing. With every inhale, I pulled in calm and exhaled my stress.

My system wasn't really listening to me. Despite it seeming to take a century, we were finally there. The slowing of the vehicle had me sitting forward. Milo's hand tightened on mine.

"I'll go with Adam," Milo said. "You take care of Mayhem." He locked gazes with Bodhi. The two seemed to be in a wordless conversation but they also resolved it swiftly.

"Done."

Milo looked at me. "Mayhem..."

"I'll stay with Bodhi," I told him. "I promise."

"Thank you."

Then the car stopped and Kellan glanced over his shoulder. "We're gathering here..."

By here, he meant not far from the drive leading to the school. It was cold, dark, and there weren't a lot of streetlights.

The area seemed to be trapped in time where old cobblestone roads intersected with freshly paved areas. There were buildings that dated back to the previous century, but just a half a block up, was a corner store and it looked far more modern.

"This area is being gentrified, more or less," Margareta said. She'd arrived right behind us and slipped out to join me as I studied our surroundings. "The academy is located on five acres above. I believe it has more land attached, but I'm waiting for more information from my people."

"How many ways in?"

The Vandals had arrived and they were talking strategy with Bodhi and Milo. Adam was within arm's reach. Ezra split the difference, partially with the guys but also closer to Adam and me in case we needed him. I didn't think I could love these men more.

"Three," Margareta said and she held her phone over for me to see the screen. A map appeared with the local area highlighted.

The school was in the center. There were routes stretching away from it in three different directions. The fourth butted up against the river.

The red ticks were where her people were setting up, including where we were standing right now. The roads—driveways—leaving the property were all direct. At least according to the map.

"If they have a boat—that could be a problem."

"I have people watching the river. Dimitri has a good group here," Margareta assured me. "We will find your sister, Lainey."

Like the guys before, she sounded so confident, I wanted to believe her.

Bodhi appeared next to me. "We're going," he told me.

"You and I are going over land. They're giving us a fifteen minute head start."

"Coat," Margareta said briskly as she stripped off the jacket she was wearing. "Are you armed?"

I had my baton, my taser, and my knife. "I have enough and I have Bodhi."

She glanced from me to him. "I won't ask if you're armed."

"Thanks," he said. "I appreciate the confidence. Let's go, Buttercup."

The use of that nickname in front of everyone made me splutter even as I tugged the coat on. "Right behind you, Trouble."

"Next to me," he said, cupping my elbow. He set the pace, but he didn't lengthen his stride. I wasn't having to take two steps for each one he did. The dark around us seemed to close in as we left the puddle of light around the cars.

I didn't glance back. I knew they were there. That was enough for me. The cold air was almost abrasive to my lungs, but I found myself craving it.

Between the walking and the cold, the shaking in my system eased. "What's our job?"

I'd heard portions of it, and I should have paid closer attention. It had grown more difficult because we were so close. Impatience had never been such a battle for me before.

"Our job is to find Andrea. I have a rough idea of the layout for the school. Multiple training and class rooms on the first and second floor. Third floor and then in the back are the dorms. Or at least, what looks like dorms."

I licked my lips.

"We have no idea how many are in there, what the security situation is going to be. I will handle any on the ground security guards. You will watch my back."

"What about electronic surveillance?"

"One thing at a time, Buttercup. One thing at a time."

The darkness enveloped us as Bodhi led us off the driveway and onto the lawn. If not for the half-moon above, I wouldn't be able to see anything.

It wasn't long before the building loomed ahead. "Trouble?"

"We're going to find her," he said. "Keep that a fixed point in your head. We're going to find her."

CHAPTER
THIRTY-TWO

LAINEY

As we approached, the building loomed larger and larger. Outdoor lighting was definitely at a premium because it was sketchy at best. I kind of wished I'd gotten to see what the building looked like in daylight or even a photograph of it.

The Gothic-appearing architecture just added to the creep factor. I half-expected there to be some eerie soundtrack playing.

"Breathe," Bodhi said, half-exhaling the word next to my ear. We'd paused and he'd gone to a crouch, bringing me with him. I tried to scan the darkness, looking for any potential threats. "Lainey B."

The command in his voice was impossible to ignore so I turned my attention to him.

"Tell me the truth, can you do this?"

"It's a little late if I can't," I admitted.

"I can get you back to the others," he said. "I need you to

308

be okay with going in. I need you to be aware of your surroundings and not panicking."

The adrenaline dump had my nerves singing again. "Bodhi, I need to be there for her. I can do this." I took a deeper breath, the vise around my chest easing. "I know I can do this."

He ghosted his fingers down the side of my face. "Then stay with me, watch my back, and let me clear the obstacles on our way."

"I'm going to kill anyone who tries to hurt you." It came out far more matter-of-fact than the match striking against my temper would suggest. But I needed the fire of that to combat the icy chill in my soul.

He paused, as though considering it, then nodded slowly. "Very well, I will allow that."

I could practically taste his smile. Trusting his instincts, I leaned forward and pressed my lips to his. It was a fierce kiss, a promise and an oath. It wasn't about passion or desire, though they were both present. This was claiming and faith.

"Hmm... I give you shoes, I get a declaration. I give you permission and I get a kiss."

"You give me gems and I get orgasms."

His soft chuckle brushed right over me. "Hmm, that's going to demand a repeat performance."

"Whenever you're ready, Trouble."

Silence wrapped around us, then he slipped his phone from his pocket. I braced for the screen light to blind me, but it didn't come on.

"We're going in now," he said softly, then hit send.

A voice clip.

Phone back in pocket, he slipped a knife from its sheath. I stuck my hand in my pocket and pulled out the baton. It was the weapon I was the most comfortable with. It was also good in close quarters.

"Moving now." Bodhi didn't look back for me or offer me a hand. He trusted me to follow him.

He was just another shadow in the darkness, visible against the faint light outlining the two sconces near the main door. Or at least what I thought was the main door.

No sign of security to warn us off. Even when I searched for them, I didn't see cameras. That did not mean they weren't there. We wanted the strike to be surgical, quick and efficient. When I left this place, I wanted it to be with my arm around Andrea.

At the door, Bodhi reached for the handle and tested it. Locked.

"Keep watch," he said over his shoulder and then he was kneeling. As curious as I was to watch him work, I planted myself against the edge of the alcove so I could scan the darkness.

The seconds ticked toward a minute and then there was a distinct sound of tumblers releasing.

"Eyes," he warned and I raised a hand to shield my eyes when he turned the handle and pushed the door in. It gave the faintest of squeaks like maintenance on the hinges had been an afterthought.

Lights were on inside, but they were low, night burning lights, tucked up against the ceiling and in little vents along the walls that led up the stairs.

It illuminated a path, but it wasn't blinding. Bodhi held one hand up to me as he eased inside. I swore, he moved more quietly than a cat. He scanned the left, then the right. With a nod, he curled his fingers to beckon me inside.

I pushed the door too, but I didn't close it. We left it for the others. Bodhi headed for the stairs and I followed him up.

First floor were classrooms and practice rooms.

Second floor, more of the same. The stairs took us right to a juncture in the center that let you look down below. The fat square opening took up a lot of space. But it also didn't have the next flight of stairs to take us up higher.

Like the first floor, this one was illuminated with dim track lighting. The pools of light were intermittent, probably because this wasn't a residential floor. Made sense.

If anything made sense in this insane world.

The stairs were tucked at the end of the hall, these doubling back on each other to get us to the next floor. Bodhi turned to glance at me just as the click of a door touched my ears.

"Down," Bodhi said and I dropped. The knife he'd been holding flew through the air and slammed into someone. There was a grunt.

A single grunt, but Bodhi was on him, hand wrapped around his throat and dragging him into a room that he'd probably exited.

It wasn't a class room or practice room at all. It was an office. The man gurgled, but Bodhi didn't let him make another sound. Then he was dead. I scanned the wall of monitors.

There were a dozen different kids on those monitors. Most of them were in rooms. They had cameras on them in their bedrooms. Cameras with night vision that let them see clearly.

I kind of wished the bastard was alive so we could—

Andrea.

"She's here," I whispered, fastening my gaze on my sister where she curled on her side. Hugging her pillow with a white knuckled grip that translated even over the grainy footage

311

There were numbers at the bottom of the screens. Room numbers maybe. Andrea's was 314. That was upstairs.

Bodhi stripped the guard of his weapons, then pulled his knife out so he could wipe it off on him. I scanned the other kids on the screens and blinked before taking a step closer to it.

The angle of the jaw.

The cheekbones.

The—

He looked like Bodhi. We needed to get all of these kids. If Bodhi's sibling—Levi—was here, then there was a good chance we might have also found the third King child, Theo. It was hard to tell on the screens.

We'd be better off doing it in person. When I pulled away to look at Bodhi, he was checking the computer. "All of the security feeds through here. But there aren't any cameras outside."

Disgust curled through me and Bodhi's stony expression reflected my feelings.

"They won't be in there any longer than absolutely necessary."

He scooped up keys off the desk and nodded once. "Stay with me."

"Never losing me," I promised and that earned me a flash of a grin. On the third floor, the lighting didn't change, but the doors did.

The locks were all located on the exterior. They weren't securing their rooms from the inside. No, they were locked from the outside. When I found Juraj Vedriš, I was going to make sure they gutted him slowly.

The first door across from the stairwell was 302. 314 would be at the other end of the hallway. As desperate as I was to rush straight for her, I made myself wait. I let Bodhi lead.

There were eighteen rooms up here. All tiny little dorm rooms, each barricaded by a locked door to keep their prisoners inside. As impatience fountained through me again, I stuck with Bodhi. When we reached a room that didn't have an exterior lock, he motioned me back.

The knife was in his hand, tucked and hidden against his arm. He tested the door knob and then pushed the door inward. The smell hit me first. The faint odor of too much cleaning product, maybe some mildew, and soap.

So much soap.

It was a communal shower.

There were thin curtains hanging as a suggestion of privacy, but that was it. Just a suggestion. Gritting my teeth, I checked the hallway behind us as Bodhi moved again and then we were at 314.

One by one, he tried the keys from the ring he'd taken from the guard's office. The fifth one slipped into the lock easily, then the tumblers as the deadbolt released echoed in the silence of the hall.

"Let me," I said before Bodhi opened the door. She was in there alone and Bodhi might scare her if she woke up to him looming out of the dark with a knife in his hand.

That image sent a shiver right through me. Not the time, I reminded myself. Absolutely not the time.

He nodded and turned the handle to push the door inward. I slipped inside. The room was so tiny. There was barely room for the single bed, an old night stand with a drawer at the top and a shelf at the bottom. No other furniture decorated the room.

My entrance hadn't woken her. Pocketing the baton, I

tried to cross the wooden floor to her quietly but it creaked and groaned with every step.

Andrea let out a sudden shriek as she jerked awake.

"No, no, no," I chanted, closing the distance. "It's me, sweetheart. It's Lainey."

Panting like she'd just run a marathon, Andrea stared at me wide eyed. The pillow had left a red mark on her cheek. No, that was a bruise.

Someone had hit her in the face hard enough to leave a bruise.

"Lainey?" The half-broken, half-disbelieving whisper refocused all my attention.

"It's me, sweetheart. Adam's here too. We're getting you the hell out of here."

Then she was lunging forward, crashing into me with a hug that knocked me on my ass. Shouting came from the hallway, someone slamming their fist against a door.

Tears burned in my eyes as I glanced at Bodhi. "I'll deal with them..."

"No," Andrea said abruptly, pulling back. "That's Levi. He's my friend. Kostya is here and Theo. They aren't the guards or the man who runs the school."

"I won't hurt them," Bodhi said. "But they heard you scream and—"

There was another slam in the hallway, it sounded like someone was throwing themselves bodily at the door.

"Go," I told him. "I'm going to get Andrea dressed so we can go."

More shouting came from outside. It seemed a thousand miles away, but that could have something to do with the shutter barricading the single slit window. When the distinctive pop-pop of gunfire reached me, I pulled Andrea to the floor.

"Is someone shooting?"

Her eyes were wide and the whites were wild. A teenage boy was suddenly filling the doorway.

"Get away from her," he ordered as he charged to where we were. He never made it, Bodhi hauled him backwards and Andrea waved her arms.

"Levi no, this is my sister," she told him, tears coating every word and it made my heart jerk painfully in my chest.

"Let me go," Levi argued with Bodhi who had him in an armlock he couldn't break.

"I will when you calm down."

He had pressed against the wall, one hand flat against his shoulder blades to keep him there.

"I heard her scream," Levi argued. "After what happened—"

"They startled me," Andrea said as I pulled her to her feet. "But I told you they would find me."

She sniffled and Levi seemed to calm down. "You're okay though?" He studied Andrea like he was looking for signs of injury.

"Yes," she said. "Now get out, I gotta put clothes on." The familiarity and the order made me snort.

Bodhi eased up and then backed off a step as he let go of Levi. The teen pivoted to face him and the light from the hallway cast across his face just like it was Bodhi's.

Yeah, there was no mistaking the resemblance.

If I saw it, Bodhi had to, though his expression didn't shift. He studied the kid in front of him with narrowed eyes.

"Let's go, kid," Bodhi said in a gruff voice darkening with emotion. I doubted anyone else would hear it but finding Levi was messing with him. "We're gonna let the others out. Help me do a head count."

It didn't take long to find Andrea's meager clothing. The

thin tops and pants were not meant for colder temps outside. She also didn't have a coat. Had they taken all of her clothes from her too?

A pair of ballet slippers fell out of the cabinet where she stacked her clothes as she rooted around and finally came out with a pair of low boots.

"Are we really going home?" Andrea asked me and I dragged my attention from the room back to her.

"Yes," I said, nodding. "We're going home."

The sound of multiple male voices in the hallway drifted inside. There was more thumping.

"We can take the guys with us, right?" Andrea said and I didn't have a direct answer for that one. Levi for sure. Maybe Theo if he was here. But the others?

We'd need to find their families.

"One thing at a time," I told her and then I was back at the door and opening it now that she was dressed.

"Lainey..." Adam called my name and I turned to find him striding down the hall. I stepped out of the room and beckoned to Andrea. She didn't even make it across the threshold before Adam swallowed her up in a hug.

The tears burning in my eyes made the whole thing waver. We found her.

We *found* her.

THIRTY-THREE

BODHI

Counting the guard I took out on our way in, we found a total of four men on the grounds. They were all low-level men, hired more for brawn than brains. The people who ran the school, including Juraj Vedriš, were nowhere to be found.

A sweep of the offices showed they'd left in a hurry. Papers were scattered, computers were broken, and files had been shredded.

Someone warned Juraj Vedriš we were coming. I couldn't even get that angry about it. Too many people were involved the moment Margareta Waldemar and her people involved themselves.

The operation wasn't shut down. I could only imagine they hadn't taken the kids with them because they lacked the time to get them all into vehicles without threats of bodily harm.

Despite the locks on the doors, the kids didn't seem

afraid. Uneasy? Yes. Unsettled? Definitely. They were more worried about us, though, than their captors.

Levi—Levente Cassidine Noble—matched the picture Hans had sent through. He'd finally arrived in Prague an hour earlier with many apologies. He'd been tracking down more physical data on the boys.

As it turned out, we'd found them on our own. But there was a lot to do. Margareta Waldemar had brought in more people. Lainey had Andrea wrapped up in a blanket and parked inside a car where she was still speaking to her.

In addition to Andrea, there were five boys and three girls in residence. The girls were silent as ghosts, they barely made eye contact, and didn't respond to English.

Adam hovered near Lainey and Andrea both, but he was letting the girls talk. A lot had changed in Andrea's world. Ezra was inside with the Vandals, tearing the place apart for any information they could find.

Levi had been standing with his arms folded and a mutinous expression on his face while he watched Andrea. He clearly wanted to go over there but he didn't. The other boys were all beginning to isolate themselves from each other.

Abruptly, Levi left that grouping and headed toward me. I spared him a look and took a sip of coffee. The only thing it had going for it was that it was hot.

"Are they really her family?" It came out more a hostile demand than a question. "Like her *actual* family?"

"Yes," I told him. "Adam is her brother. Lainey is her sister."

He blew out a breath, deflating a little. "So they'll take her back to the States."

"That's the plan." I studied him. "What about you?"

Frowning, Levi twisted to face me. "What about me?"

"Where do you want to go?"

Levi snorted. "Nowhere. Pretty much where I've been my whole life." He waved his hand back at the building that seemed even uglier with the floodlights that someone had set up. "This place...just the latest in a long line of places that take me and eventually don't want me. I'll skip the next one."

I couldn't blame him. Yet, I wanted to know more. More about what happened to him. Who...

I would need to make another list.

At the same time, I couldn't stop staring at him. Years of looking. Years of searching. Years of wondering whether he really existed. Now I could reach out and touch him.

"You could take a picture, it might last longer." The sarcasm fit, but the hostility and the damage shouldn't. Finally, he shifted and glanced behind him before looking at me again. "Why are you staring at me?"

"Debating how to tell you something." No point in lying.

"If you're about to tell me I've been sold or something—"

"No," I said, cutting off that train of thought before he could pick up any speed. "You said you have nowhere to go. That's not true."

"Unlike Andi over there, I don't have any family."

"Also not true."

He scowled at me. "You know something I don't?"

"I know a great many things that you don't. I will tell you if you let me finish." I could see elements of me in him. The belligerence. The need to challenge authority. To push back.

My mother—*our* mother loved to rebel. Apparently, she gave it to both of us.

"Look, I get you're trying to you know comfort me or something. I'm not a little kid. I figured out how the world works a very long time ago. My mother dumped me on

319

someone to pay a debt. Sold me for service. I just had to grow up to be useful."

Cold rage spread out from my center. The lies. The lies told to everyone. Him. Mother. Me. "Your mother's name was Isla."

Levi blinked. "What?"

"Her name was Isla Cavendish. You were born in New York, in the United States. She was the wife of a powerful man, but unsuited to the pressures of his cut throat world. The first time she exhibited signs of distress and mental exhaustion, he had her packed away to a facility where he didn't have to see or acknowledge her."

This time, Levi did not interrupt. He stared at me, and I could read the thoughts running through his head like he had a banner scrolling. *This is bullshit. This has to be bullshit.*

"Isla loved many things, mysteries. Stories. Adventures. She loved to build adventures and to tackle the bad guys and save the good guys. Some of it was painfully simple, yet the answers to some of life's most complicated issues can often be found in the simplest of games."

An ache opened under the bruise on my heart. One that was always there. Probably always would be.

"She was moved from a couple of facilities. She got pregnant once, or so she said. The baby was lost. She was never sure about the story. I confirmed it—eventually—that the first time she was pregnant in one of the facilities, she miscarried when she was about four and a half months along."

It had been in the records the doctor had kept.

"Did her husband go to see her or something?" Levi asked, a fierce frown tightening his brows. "Facility sounds like a mental hospital or something."

"No, to my knowledge, he hasn't seen her since the day he

had her committed." Soon, that bill would be coming due. "He didn't want to be bothered. He paid generously to make sure she was looked after. But only one or two people ever really visited. As time went on, people forgot she was there. They stopped asking about her."

"So you're saying that someone raped her..."

"I don't know the answer to that. She never called it rape. All I know is, she got pregnant a second time. She was determined to keep this baby. She didn't want them to take it away again. She did everything she could to hide the pregnancy from her doctors and her caretakers..."

"Kind of hard to do after a while." Levi raked a hand through his dark hair.

I took another long drink of the terrible coffee. It kept me grounded to this place, the here and the now. It helped keep some of my rage at bay.

"Eventually they found out, right?"

"Yes. The baby was taken. Though everyone tried to say she was never pregnant. The records were erased. Her caretakers were reassigned or retired, they disappeared, one by one. Until the only thing left was a memory..." A memory and a letter she'd left with Lainey's grandfather.

"So how do you know that she's really my mother?" Levi stared at me and as hard as he tried to disguise it, there was a rawness to him. A hunger for the knowledge. The world had given him a lot to be angry about. Too much, really.

"Because I was one of the people who knew. Isla Cavendish was my mother." I let those words sit for a moment, the shock rippling through his expression erased the scowl for the first time since we met. "She'd told me she was pregnant. I knew it. I saw her as often as I could. My father moved her many times, tried to put her farther and farther away. He wanted me to forget her, like he had, like so many others had..."

"That means..." Levi blew out a breath.

"I'm your brother. I've been looking for you for the past fifteen years. I knew you were out there. I didn't know if you were a girl or a boy. But I knew you existed."

"Holy shit," Levi said, then scrubbed his hands over his face as he backed off a couple of steps. Truth could cure a lot of things. Didn't always make the process pleasant. "How can you be sure I'm him if you didn't even know if the baby was a boy or a girl?"

"Because you have her eyes." Eyes I hadn't seen in a very long time. "I thought I'd forgotten them. Little pieces slipped away, here and there, over the years. But when you charged out of your room—the look in your eyes. The determination. The fire. That's Isla."

"Is she...you keep talking about her in the past."

"She died." I suppose there were easier ways to say that. "She died and she left a letter with a family friend. It took a while for me to figure out what it was and who had it. But in the letter she detailed everything—and asked me to find you. One last quest."

"And—the husband isn't my father?"

"No," I said, then shrugged. "As far as I know. We can certainly do a paternity test. The idea he lied all these years is plausible. Either way, we'll figure it out."

Levi paced away and then back. His hands opened and closed. I'd just dumped a lot onto him. Maybe I should have waited.

"So what happens now?" He stared over to where Lainey was cradling Andrea now. We needed to get them all out of here. It was cold, ugly, and the gothic horror show of this so-called school made me want to raze it to the ground.

"You come home with me."

"Just like that?" He spun to look at me.

"You're my brother." I was finally talking to my brother and I didn't know what to do with the tremulous emotion that kept trying to inflate in my chest. Anger kept it in check, but at the same time...

I'd found him.

"So, yes," I continued. "Just like that, you come home with me."

"You make it sound easy. I don't even know where my passport is."

"Doesn't matter." There were ways to deal with paperwork. "I'll get you there. You'll have a home, family, unfortunately school. But we can get you caught up. Do all the normal things." Whatever the hell normal was.

"Whatever that means," he echoed my own thoughts on it. When he looked toward Andrea once more, I took a chance and put a hand on his shoulder.

"Her sister lives with me," I said. "You'll still be able to see Andrea."

One squeeze and then I turned to walk away. Better to give him time to process that. For all that we were brothers in blood, we were strangers. It would take time.

It would take all of them time.

Even as I walked I caught sight of Milo talking to Theo. He wasn't alone, Doc was there with him. I must have missed when Doc arrived on the scene. Made sense to have him here though.

"Hey," Ezra said as he jogged up. "We're doing another head count."

"Why?" I studied him.

"Cause we're short a kid. I keep getting four boys, and four girls."

I frowned, then scanned the area. Levi was where I'd left him. He watched me, though he looked away when I glanced at him. I counted.

Four boys.

With Andrea, four girls. The other three were huddled together in another car with a woman who worked for Margareta Waldemar.

"Dark haired boy, maybe 5'8," I said. "Hundred and fifty pounds, maybe. Definitely in the ganglier stage. Darker skin, more olive in complexion. No scars or significant marks that I can think of."

I'd let all of those kids out.

There was definitely one missing.

"Fuck," Ezra said. "We need to get out of here. Get Andrea back to the apartment. I'm assuming Theo over there and your brother…"

I nodded. "I'm going to do another sweep. Just make sure he didn't go inside to hide in a familiar place."

"I'll be here," Ezra said.

I didn't even make it to the first stairs to go up to the second floor before Levi caught up with me. "What are we doing?"

"One of the boys is missing. The one who was in 309."

"That's Kostya," Levi said and he turned to go back to the door and stare out at the vast number of moving parts and vehicles out front. "Are you sure he's missing?"

"Yes," I said. "I'm going to sweep the building. See if he came in to hide."

"So no one grabs him and sells him onward or worse, turns him over to the government." From the way Levi said it, the latter was far worse than the former.

"Precisely. Do you know any spots he liked to hide in?"

"I can think of a couple." Then he locked eyes with me. "What are you going to do if we find him?"

"Make sure he gets home."

Levi stared for a long moment, searching my face for the truth. Whatever he saw must have settled him, because he started up the stairs and took them two at a time.

"There's a place on the fourth floor near the roof access..."

THIRTY-FOUR

LAINEY

I n the kitchen, I wrapped my hands around the huge mug of coffee that Ezra had made for me. I hadn't even realized there was an espresso machine in the place. It made sense, I supposed. Exhaustion draped me like a cloak, but there was elation amidst it all.

Andrea was with us. Doc had checked her out briefly at the site, but he advised a more thorough exam at home. I planned on that too. I'd broached a couple of uncomfortable topics with her. As much as she told me about the school, about the other kids, she was circumspect on so much else.

The only saving grace I received at all was the fact she hadn't been raped. She promised. It had taken coaxing to convince her to leave and come to the apartment we'd rented. The guys were all on edge, they needed us out of the open. *I* needed us out of the open.

When Andrea realized two of her friends were coming with us, she relented. Margareta took charge of the rest of the children. I would call her later. She told me we were going to identify them, and see if we could get them back to their families.

"And if they don't have families?" Levi did, but no one had known about his family before Bodhi found him.

"Then we will find them new families." The absolutism in Margareta's voice convinced me more than the words themselves. "Go on. Take your sister back. Get some rest. We'll talk tomorrow." She turned to go then.

"Margareta..."

She paused and glanced back at me.

"Thank you. Thank you for—" I motioned to the school then just spread my hands. "Thank you for everything." We would never have located Andrea so quickly but for Margareta's intervention.

"Get some rest, darling girl. We'll talk tomorrow." Her smile was gentle, but firm.

The drive back had been almost as exhausting as the rest of the day. Theo rode up front with Kellan. He'd refused to get in the back with Levi and Andrea. Despite everything, he was holding himself aloof from Pretty Boy.

It irked me, but Milo shook his head once at my questioning glance. Levi had taken the news from Bodhi with a kind of curious calmness. Theo was just angry. Frankly, all things being equal, who could blame them? Once back at the apartment, I stayed with Andrea while she showered, then helped her into my clothes.

After I tucked her in, I kept staring at her and she'd given me a plaintive look. "Lainey, I'm tired."

"I know sweetheart and I promise to get over this need to keep my eyes on you soon, but I'm going to sit here for a few more minutes until you sleep. Okay?"

She groaned, but then reached for my hand and squeezed it tight. "I missed you too," she whispered. "I missed you guys and Mom and Dad and everything."

I pressed a kiss to her head and just stayed there holding her hand until she was asleep.

Adam ducked into a shower while I came down. Unsurprisingly, he'd been in the hall listening. When I slipped out of her room, he'd wrapped me up in a tight hug and I had to blink back my own tears.

We still had to tell her about Harper and Melissa. I just didn't have it in me tonight. That brought me down here with the coffee and the standoff in the living room.

Theo had his arms folded, his expression mutinous and the hard line of his jaw did not belong on a teenager. Or maybe it did. He was in that awkward stage, lanky and a little awkward, like his body was too big for him.

Where Levi *looked* like Bodhi—the resemblance was clearer in actual light—Theo and Milo looked nothing alike. Theo looked like King though and even if we hadn't had his identification courtesy of Hans...

"You should get some sleep," Ezra said in a low voice, while running his knuckles up and down my arm. "It's going to be dawn soon."

Was it? "That explains why I'm so tired." Leaning my head against his shoulder, I hugged the coffee to me. As weary as I was, I didn't think I'd sleep if I laid down.

Too many loose threads. Far too many. Em's show opened tonight too. I wouldn't miss it.

Across the room, Levi frowned as he glanced toward Ezra and me.

"Look, I don't care who you are," Theo snapped suddenly, charging forward until he was chest to chest with Milo. "You can say you're a fucking royal ass prince, and I still wouldn't care. I don't have a family. I don't *want* a family. You can get fucked if you think I'm just gonna buy your bullshit and go back with you."

Hostility wreathed the room around them. Theo was tall, but he lacked Milo's bulk. Pretty Boy's face must have given Theo confidence though, because he was all wild challenge and asking to have his ass handed to him.

"Theo," Levi said into the charged silence. "Let it go. You don't have to like him—but so far, they've done everything they said they would."

"What? They rousted us and dragged us to some rental apartment in the city? That doesn't mean much." But he backed off from Milo. For his part, Pretty Boy hadn't said a word. Instead, he studied Theo and the kid shifted under his scrutiny.

"Actually," Bodhi said into the quiet. "The only promises we made were you would be able to still see Andrea and we would figure it out."

Theo turned that contemptuous look toward Bodhi and I sighed.

"Kid," Ezra said, wrapping an arm around my shoulders. "I cornered the market on shitty tempers and letting my mouth write checks the rest of me wasn't ready to pay. Shut up while you're ahead. No one says you have to like us or the situation. No one says you have to trust us yet, give Milo time, he's probably one of the most trustworthy guys I know. But stop being a dick to just be a dick."

Blinking, Theo jerked his head to look at us. I had a feeling he'd forgotten that Ezra and I were here.

"Who the fuck are you?" The demand almost made me laugh.

"A bigger dick than you are with a lot more practice. So

zip it. Take the win, get a shower and go to bed. We can argue more about this later today."

"That was almost mature," I murmured.

"Keep it up, Kotyonok," he half-growled under his breath.

"Promises, promises." I hid the words behind my coffee and took another sip. As it was, I leaned on Ezra and soaked up his nearness.

The standoff lasted another thirty seconds and Theo backed down. Again. The kid was a fighter. Like his siblings, he was fierce and ready to fight for what he believed in.

Now, we just had to teach him he wasn't alone anymore.

"Fine," Theo said. "Where is my room?"

"Upstairs," Milo said evenly. "Second door on the right. It shares a bathroom with the fourth door on the right. That's Levi's room."

"Great." Theo spun on a heel and stalked up the stairs. I was kind of impressed that he didn't stomp his feet. Then a door slammed. Well, so much for that.

Milo dropped his chin and shook his head. His long sigh spoke to how exhausted all of us were.

"Theo's... Theo doesn't mean anything." Levi offered. "It's just, he's had a harder time than some. Kostya was his best friend."

Kostya. The missing kid.

"We haven't stopped looking for him," Bodhi said.

"What about when we leave to go back to the States? That's what you're planning, right?" The demand lacked Theo's animosity. Levi just sounded worried.

"We can keep people on it," I said. "We will keep people on it." Margareta had her people looking. "If we find him, you three will be the first to know."

Levi cut a look to me and Ezra again, his frown tightening

and then he nodded slowly before he glanced at Bodhi. "I'm going to sleep now..."

It wasn't definitive and despite the fact he didn't seem to be asking, there was a hesitation and question in the air after the statement.

"Get some rest," Bodhi told him. "We have time. We don't have to solve everything tonight." Once Levi was upstairs and we were alone, Milo sat abruptly like someone cut his strings.

Ezra kissed the top of my head as I began to pull away. Pretty Boy needed me. I crossed the room to where he was and he dragged me into his lap. I even shared my coffee.

Bodhi brushed his knuckles down my cheek and Adam eventually descended the stairs. The five of us should probably go get some sleep. But none of us moved.

We'd found all of them. But there was still such a long road ahead of them—ahead of us.

~

SLEEP PROVED ELUSIVE, by lunchtime, I'd given up and went down to order food. When the kids woke up, I had a number of different offerings and food for us as well.

"I'm going to the theater," I said after I finished a croissant sandwich that tasted far better than it had any right to. I flicked a look toward Andrea who frowned at me. "I'd prefer it if you stayed here, and got some more rest."

"But Em is performing?" She looked crestfallen.

"Tonight and tomorrow. If you're feeling up for it tomorrow, I'll totally sneak you in." The Vandals had all said if we wanted to leave with the kids, they'd support it. But Em was here and doing this show because of us.

"Promise?" Andrea perked up.

"Yes," I said, easily enough. "But take it easy today. Indulge me for a bit more?"

Her long huffed sigh made me smile. "Fine." She elongated that word, but a smile hovered around the corners of her mouth. It didn't quite touch her eyes, but I had other reasons for keeping her here.

Bodhi caught me while I was changing. "You're not going alone."

"I'm not," I told him. "Even if you just dropped me off, I wouldn't be there alone. The Vandals are there."

"That's fine. They can all keep an eye on PPG. I want one of us there with you."

Putting on an earring, I turned to face him. I'd gone for something nice but also comfortable. I wouldn't be in the audience. I'd be backstage with Em. Still, appearances had to be kept.

"You and Milo should both stay here. Your brothers are..."

"Difficult. They'll be fine. That logic says Adam should also stay and while I trust Ezra's heart to be in the right place, I worry about his skills."

Ezra's heart.

The heart damage was still an issue too.

I met Bodhi's firm stare and smiled. "I would love it if you went with me."

"I'll give Milo the option. He may not want to deal with his brother. But if he wants to stay. I'll go."

"I'll enjoy whomever's company is with me." I could hardly fault them for being overprotective. Margareta hadn't called with any news on Juraj Vedriš and he was one of the sponsoring hosts.

Another reason I wanted to be there with Em.

"Thank you for indulging me," Bodhi said, cupping my face and I tilted my head back to meet his gaze. The gentle stroke of his thumbs soothed some of the worry invading my whole being.

"Any time I can," I promised. "Any time I can."

As it turned out, Milo wanted to stay with Theo even though the kid was making a point of ignoring him. I really couldn't fathom what was going on in his head.

"Besides, if I go, I would want him to see Ivy perform. I don't think he's ready for that." Translation, Milo wasn't ready for Theo to give Em that attitude.

"Well, you could always put the boys in charge of him. I'm sure they'd handle that attitude." I was only partially joking, but Milo chuckled.

"Something to keep in our back pockets." He kissed me. "Be safe tonight, please."

I didn't scold him for worrying. I was armed. I would be surrounded by allies and I would also be doing my part to look after Em. Adam pulled me in for a hug.

With his lips pressed to my ear, he said, "Andrea's still holding a lot back, isn't she?"

"Yes, we need to give her time." When he leaned back a little, I smiled and rubbed my hand against the center of his chest. "She's off center. We need to let her get her balance back. But we won't let her flounder."

He nodded, dropped a kiss on my lips and then released me to Ezra who just wrapped me up from behind. "I'll look after them all," he whispered against my ear. "Be responsible and adult-like."

I grinned. "Don't pull anything."

"Ha." He bit my earlobe, just enough to leave a sting. "Come back in one piece, please. No bruises."

"Do my best." One more kiss and then Bodhi and I were at the door. I didn't miss the gawping look Andrea wore as she stared at all of us or the narrow-eyed speculation on the boys' faces.

Right. Not a conversation I was going to have right now.

Maybe not ever.

"They will have an interesting evening," Bodhi said as he pressed the button for the elevator. I bit back a smile, but when I got his grin, my own escaped.

Our gazes locked and we both said, "Not it."

Then laughed. Definitely *not* it.

THIRTY-FIVE

LAINEY

The last time I'd been in this theater, it had been filled with workmen and crew. The lights had been up and the seats emptied. It had—potential. Tonight? This evening? It was electric.

Em answered her dressing room door at the first knock. "You're here!" Excitement filled her eyes and she threw her arms around me. I hugged her tight and let her pull me inside. "Girl time, Bodhi."

"Have fun, PPG. I'll be out here," Bodhi said with a faint smile before the door closed.

Leaning back against it, she stared at me with wide eyes. Her cosmetics were done and there was enough glitter and shimmer highlighting her eyes and along her hairline to make her sparkle in the air.

"Well?" she asked, stripping off the robe. Beneath it she wore a body suit that hugged her frame. The suit was sheer across her torso and arms, with the only filled in areas covering her breasts and her groin. It was black and silver.

"How are they? Andrea first, then the boys. Milo's been... less than direct about answering my questions."

"Andrea will be fine," I told her, setting my purse down on a side table before going to the small fridge and pulling out a couple of waters. "She's still in some shock that we found her and I don't doubt a bit of denial. But we'll get her home and look after her."

Em accepted the water bottle, then turned to put it down. Her outfit was backless and the phoenix tattoo across her back was stunning in its wild reds, oranges, and golds. It actually looked like living fire.

"I love that tattoo," I murmured before taking a drink of the water. I'd only gotten to see it a couple of times, but the work was really exquisite.

She flashed me a smile. "Vaughn did it. I love it too. If you ever decide you want one..." She dangled it out there. But I wasn't sure I was a tattoo girl.

Em had a few. The one on her abdomen that told her head up and wings out. A circle of birds flying around one thigh. The phoenix on her back. She had a Vandals tat too, but you couldn't see that in her outfit.

"Maybe," I told her. "As for the boys—Levi seems to be more open to the idea of a big brother and family than Theo is. But they're both—very guarded I suppose is the best description. Who can really blame them?"

Chewing her lower lip, Em retrieved her bottle of water and opened it. "Milo isn't sure Theo is ready to meet me."

"Well, to be fair, I don't think Pretty Boy is ready for Theo to meet you. If he cops an attitude with you, he's probably going to get punched." From more than one direction.

"Look, when Milo and I met, we were not... well, let's just say I was the belligerent one then." Her smile was almost wistful. "I gave him a really hard time. So maybe..."

"Maybe you understand where Theo is coming from?"

She shrugged. "Maybe? I don't know. I do know Milo did not deserve quite as much of the shit that I gave him."

"That doesn't mean he didn't deserve some of it." I pointed my water bottle at her and she grinned.

"True. But Theo—Theo is different. We had no idea he existed." Em went silent, looking at her water bottle before blowing out a breath. "I didn't know Milo or the Vandals existed. At first... knowing they knew about me and I had no idea about them. It hurt."

"Em..."

She shook her head, a small smile in place. "It's okay now. I mean, I got over it. I forgave them for the secret because I understood it. But there's a loneliness there... that I had this possible family out in the world who knew all about me. I had no idea. Theo doesn't know that much about us. He has to learn to trust us, like I had to learn to trust them."

Maybe Em would be the best one for him.

"We'll figure it out," I told her. "None of you are in this alone. Not you. Not Pretty Boy. Not Theo. We will make the time. The important thing is they're *safe*. If it takes ten days, ten weeks, or ten years, we'll get there."

"Have I mentioned how much I love having you for a real sister now?" Emersyn said. "Even if it means having sex with my brother, which you absolutely do not do. You have a very chaste relationship."

I snorted and she laughed. "*Anyway...* you ready for tonight?"

"I think so. Valentin came to see me an hour ago." She turned to check her appearance in the mirror.

Sitting forward, I frowned.

"Don't get upset," she said over her shoulder. "Yes, he

came to see me. He was alone and he wanted to thank me again for coming to do the show."

Alone. Juraj Vedriš hadn't been with him. He would turn up. Sooner or later.

"You look mad," Em said, pivoting to face me again. She had a pair of thin slippers that she wore until she was ready to go on stage. "I wasn't alone. Liam and Rome were right there. In fact, Rome is right next door." She leaned over and tapped the wall in a quick tattoo of knocks, that was answered immediately.

"They're only letting me be alone in here because you were coming. They've got eyes everywhere."

"Have I mentioned how much I like them all? They are *almost* good enough for you." The droll tone was the right one to take. Her grin was magnetic. "Now, stop worrying about me. I can't wait to see you perform tonight. It's going to be amazing."

"You didn't have to come," she reminded me and I just rolled my eyes. "I know, I would have come too. But I did have to say it."

We both stuck our tongues out at each other and then laughed. Rising, I crossed over to where she was standing and hooked my arm through hers. "Always going to be here for you," I reminded her.

"Same," Em promised and we leaned our heads together. Standing there in silence, I drank in the calm and Em seemed to be doing the same. "Okay," she said with an exhale. "Time to go to work."

❧

Going to work involved finishing the last touches on her cosmetics, then snagging her robe to head along the backstage to where she'd climb up to where she would be starting her show.

The hum from the crowd was electric. The crew, familiar from a long time of working together, greeted Em with easy smiles and salutes as I followed her along the back behind the curtains.

Rome was with us. Ahead, Vaughn waited at the foot of the ladder she would use to climb up to the catwalks. I tilted my head back to check the height. It never failed to amaze me how comfortable she was up there.

"I'm going to be stage left," I promised. "I want to be able to see everything."

Em squeezed my hands, then she was climbing the ladder with Rome right behind her and Vaughn lifted his chin to me. "Bodhi is with Freddie, they went to get drinks from the green room." He pointed back the way we'd come.

"We're good for me to just get into place though?"

"We should be," Vaughn said. "I'll let them know where you are."

"Thank you." I gave him a little wave and then made my way around to the side stage area. Crew with a headset on turned to me as I approached. "I'm just going to be over here, out of the way."

"You're fine, Miss Benedict. We can set up a chair if you'd like it."

I waved him off. "No need to worry about me."

The hum from the audience had grown louder. There was music playing from the speakers, but it was too low to make out. Across the visible stage, crew moved swiftly but stayed well-away from the curtains.

Head tilted back, I studied the darkened area above. I could barely make out the catwalks, but I could see where the silks were suspended and ready to be lowered.

A shiver went through me. The next crew guy sauntered past and I did a double-take. Jasper grinned, then handed me a fresh water bottle. "Enjoy the show, she's doing something new tonight."

Chuckling, I saluted him with the water. Not even three minutes after he walked away, did I catch sight of Kellan on the far side of the stage. He just gave me a measured look and a nod.

The Vandals were everywhere. I didn't make the mistake of thinking they weren't keeping an eye on me too. I appreciated them for it. Still, I slung my purse crosswise over my chest. I'd left my jacket in the dressing room.

My baton was in easy reach and I had a knife in my boot. The layers of security made me feel better, especially because Em was the one—

The lights flashed once.

Twice.

Three times.

The din of conversation from out front diminished. The lights backstage shifted, everything on the side stages dropped into shadow and I put my water bottle onto the chair next to me.

The music through the speakers increased with just the faintest crackling to betray the age of the equipment itself. As the volume turned up, the crowd grew even quieter.

A hush of movement next to me had me turning to find Bodhi sliding into place behind me. He wrapped his arms around my middle and I leaned back against his chest. We didn't need words.

Anticipation threaded through me. I found myself holding my breath. Watching Em perform was always something of a revelation.

The house lights went down. The stage lights shut off.

The whisper of the curtains opening drifted past me. I noticed it more for the breeze than the actual movement. My eyes hadn't adjusted fully, not yet.

Pressing two fingers to my lips, I went utterly still as the music cut off abruptly.

Darkness.

Silence.

The sense of the audience shifting, leaning forward. I had my eyes glued upward, she was going to—

The music rose suddenly, a spotlight kicked on, and Em tumbled from the ceiling in what looked like a rolling free fall that she caught herself neatly, breaking all rules of gravity.

Applause welcomed her and I couldn't stop smiling. It was the Carnival overture by Dvořák. Her twist and dance in the air to the Czech composer's work made her truly seem like a fairy.

My smile grew as I watched her. The distance softened everything about her. You didn't see the way her muscles shifted as she caught the silks, twined them around her to climb and dance on the air itself.

No, all you saw was the ethereal beauty with her absolute gift. It was amazing. As the Carnival played onward, I found myself swaying to it. Almost exactly as Em was, only she was making the silk begin to rotate — ballroom dancing in the air.

The audience applauded and I would have joined them except gunfire exploded through the dark, a spray of bullets striking the catwalks above and sparking like deadly fireflies where they hit. Screams erupted from the audience and the spotlight cut off.

Had Em been hit?

Bodhi's arm around my middle tightened and he pulled me farther back into the backstage. Three steps back and suddenly even the back stage area's blue lights cut off. Chaos descended with the blanket of darkness as the flash of gunfire sliced through the dark.

Someone slammed into us and only Bodhi's arm around my middle kept me from being knocked down. One moment he was there, the next I was behind him and there was a pained grunt.

What the hell?

As abruptly as the lights had cut off earlier, they flashed to life again—brighter. Too bright, like someone turned up all the power. Tears flooded my eyes even as I tried to squint away from the intensity.

Even with my vision blurred, I could see Bodhi grappling with not just one, but two men. There were more men charging toward us.

Men in balaclavas waving weapons. More gunshots sounded from the audience. Fighting spilled out onto the stage. I wanted to look for Em, but as it was, I couldn't take my gaze off the fighters making their way toward Bodhi.

Taser out, I shocked the guy before he could close the distance behind him and I kept my finger on the voltage until he dropped. The lights slammed off. Then back on.

Once my target dropped, I started forward only to pause as the hard muzzle of a gun pressed against my spine and a hand clamped down on the nape of my neck.

Bodhi's gaze cut to me and I looked at him even as more men swarmed him.

"Come with me," Juraj Vedriš ordered. "Or I will kill everyone here and I'll start with him."

THIRTY-SIX

LAINEY

His grip on my neck bit into the flesh painfully. Dread scraped through me as I fought to steady my breathing. The sounds of sporadic gunfire added to the pandemonium. I was still staring at Bodhi as he vanished into a swarm of balaclava-wearing assailants. The need to rush to him burned in my veins, but Vedriš' grip was far too tight.

Darkness plunged down again and Vedriš yanked me backwards. I was torn between digging my heels in and fighting or cooperating, for now, until a better opportunity presented itself. As it was, I couldn't see where we were going.

Blue lights came on then cut off abruptly. At this point, whatever they'd done to the light board was just adding to the confusion.

"Keep moving," Vedriš ordered. I wasn't entirely sure

what was more painful, the gun pressed against my spine or the way his fingernails dug into my neck. Still, I continued to move obediently.

While I didn't quite drag my feet, I also didn't hurry. It was dark and I didn't plan on disappearing out into Prague somewhere. I also didn't want Vedriš shooting anyone. If we could get to a little more private area—

"Faster," he hissed the command and pain from his grip digging into my neck had me gritting my teeth. Now he was dragging me backward. I tried to track where we were going as the lights flashed on, then off, then on. The strobing effect just added to the horror movie flavor of it all.

We were backing down a narrow little hall that I hadn't seen, it cut away at an angle. A door swung open behind us and I wanted to turn, but Vedriš didn't give me the opportunity.

Then we were on a set of stairs. He didn't make any pretense of dragging me down them. The lights down here were steadier and I barely got my head up in time to see the door to the theater close with a kind of ominous finality.

My stomach dropped.

Fantastic.

"I don't know what your specific plan is Mr. Vedriš, but you should know—it's not going to end the way you think."

"Arrogant American bitch," he muttered, hauling me around at the base of the stairs. If not for his grip, I probably would have gone sprawling. As it was, I was off balance, but it didn't seem to bother him at all.

Using my neck like a handhold, he yanked me to my feet and then marched me down the stone tunnel. He moved swiftly and I was half-running to keep to his pace. The route curved and continued away.

Tunnels. Catacombs beneath the city? Or just the theater?

Even as I tried to map it, I suddenly understood how they got in. The arrival of so many men invading the theater from the back as well as the audience made sense. The Vandals had everything else covered, but they didn't know about these.

This was going too fast. How long before we were too far away from the theater? "Mr. Vedriš, name calling really isn't going to do you any favors either."

He hauled me back against him, the sting of his nails cutting into my skin abrasive. Lips next to my ear, he growled, "Shut. Up. You have caused me enough problems."

The heavy stench of onions and garlic threatened to smother me. "You need a new chef." The last comment really aggravated him and he shoved me forward, releasing me abruptly. Probably hoping to slam me into a wall, but I caught myself with my hands and spun around to face him.

It put me eye to eye with his gun. Not ideal, but we were also not moving farther away anymore. I lifted my gaze to focus on the man behind the gun. LED lights seemed to run along the ceiling and the floor level, illuminating the way. The light was faint, but it didn't need to be bright to let us see.

Did they use this often? Was this how they hauled people in and out without others being aware? A problem to solve another day. I studied the man with his silver hair, neatly brushed until the ends seemed to feather against his shoulders. He was dressed in a fine suit, though the tie was pulled loose and his shirt disheveled. Sweat dotted his face and there were heavy shadows beneath his eyes.

"You don't look well."

"You stupid little bitch with your stupid little comments as though the whole world is here to serve you."

"Not the whole world," I said easily enough. There was a musty smell down here, dampness and dust. "Just the morons who can't elevate themselves above it or are smart enough to avoid it."

It was a kind of arrogant attitude I'd heard from my mother more than once. There were our people and then everyone else. As disgusting as the sentiment was, baiting Vedriš with it had his mouth compressing into a hard line and his eyes narrowing.

His hand also shook.

Just the slightest bit.

Drug abuse?

Alcohol?

Stress?

So many potential causes.

"Are you blind to the gun I have on you?" Spittle flew from his lips. He really was a mess. "Walk."

"No. You have it right in my face, that's a CZ 75? I've only seen pictures of them." I focused on his face again. "If you were going to use it, you'd have already shot me. You had the drop on me from the moment you walked up in the theater. But you didn't—you threatened everyone else to get me to go with you. That means you need me. For something."

His expression transformed from fury to consternation and back to fury again. "I could just kill you right here."

I spread my hands. We were alone, in this tunnel, and far enough away Em and the others would be safe. "Then do it."

Daring him was a gamble. A huge one. But one I was willing to bet on since I didn't think he could afford to kill me. People like him didn't threaten—they just did.

I gave it to a count of sixty in my head and then I "crossed my arms" and leaned back against the wall. The race of my pulse thundered in my ears. He'd just ceded some of the power in this interaction, gun or no gun.

"So, as I was saying earlier, you want something from me. Let's hear it and see if I'm willing to deal or not."

The longer I delayed him the sooner Bodhi would find me. I had no doubt that he would. Bodhi seemed more aware of me than I was of myself. He'd seen Vedriš taking me.

I really wanted this man caught, dropped in a hole, and bury him forever.

Vedriš took two steps forward until the gun was right in my face again. It took some discipline to maintain my bland expression. The closer he got the more obvious his trembling was.

"You've cost me a small fortune."

"Hmm. Let me see, how do I feel about that?" I mused, canting my head and looking past him to the way we'd come. I couldn't really see that far, the turns in the tunnel just made it a blind curve. Taking my attention off him was a risk, but he shifted a step then glanced back to see what had my attention.

I unzipped the side pocket of my purse.

"Hmm, not remotely troubled by that at all. In fact, I'm sorry I haven't cost you everything. I do like to be thorough." I pulled his eyes back to me.

"You're not funny," he snapped. His accent grew more pronounced with his agitation. The rather suave, bland Eastern European turned almost distinctly German for a moment.

Interesting.

"I never said I was." I could brush the cool metal of my baton with my thumb. It would take a moment to pull out, so I'd have to choose that moment carefully. Raising my free hand, I snapped my fingers. "Can we get on with this? I have plans."

"You took the children."

"Yes, I did. Never going to apologize for it. Just because you're a sick perverted creep who makes his income on peddling flesh and kids, doesn't mean you're owed anything but maybe a .50 cal to the groin."

"You took the children. Three of them are already under contract. One is worth several million. I want her back."

"Let me see, how do I put this?" Free hand up, I ticked off the words to engage his attention. "Too. Fucking. Bad."

He shifted his grip ever so slightly and jerked the gun back like he was going to swing it at me. Yeah, that would hurt if he connected, but I closed my hand around the baton.

"You had no right to take her. To take any of them."

"Actually, that's where you're wrong. I had every right. She's my sister. I'll die before I let you anywhere near her again."

He barked out an unfriendly laugh. "You are going to die," he said, scorn salting every word. "Americans always mess everything up. You shouldn't have taken what belongs to me. Now call and have her brought here."

"Nope." He could shoot me. I hadn't stuttered when I said I'd die before I let him have Andrea. Period.

He charged forward, waving that gun. Pointed at me.

Away.

At me.

Away.

At me.

Away—I yanked out the baton, snapped it to full length and struck his wrist with all the force I could muster. He let out a roar of pain, the gun went off. A bullet slammed into the stone, ricocheted and then hit the stone closer to both of us and sending out shards of dust and rock. It also sent the gun skittering down the tunnel.

Win.

He reared back with his fist, but I jabbed forward, driving the baton into the soft flesh below his arm. He grunted, grappling with it. But I had the leverage and I shifted my stance to use his weight and when he jerked, I rolled him around me and ran him into the wall.

The grunt he let out wasn't pained enough for me. Swinging my baton, I slammed it against his lower back, right over a kidney. But he was faster than I expected, and his fist caught my cheekbone.

Pain exploded through my face and I staggered, slipping on the smooth stone. I was fighting for my balance when Vedriš dove to the side and grabbed his gun. I had nowhere to go.

A gunshot ripped through the tunnel. The loud report echoing against the stone and threatening to deafen me. Skidding onto my knee, I braced for more pain, but nothing happened. Lifting my chin, I stared at Vedriš who looked stunned himself.

A dark stain spread over his shoulder. The hand that had been holding the gun had already released it as his arm just hung there. The click of heels on the stone made me look.

Margareta Waldemar stepped out of the shadows, coming from ahead of us, like some kind of silver-crowned avenging angel. She held a gun with the kind of familiarity that served as a testament to her shooting Vedriš.

"Thank you," I said, trying to catch my breath. The trembling in my hands told me the adrenaline rioting through my system was going to lead to a hell of a crash.

She didn't say a word to me as she continued her approach. When she was next to me, she held out her free hand. I accepted it and let her help me to my feet.

"You're welcome," she said, her accent more pronounced than I'd ever heard it. But her attention wasn't on me, it was on Vedriš. She shook her head slowly. "Jürgen."

The name was different, but the disappointment in her voice made my heart hurt. "You know him?" It came out a little jerkier than I meant, but it was clear.

"Mama," Vedriš said, wheezing a laugh that held no humor.

Mama.

I blinked. Wait... "You said he died."

"I thought he died," Margareta said and the profoundness of her disturbance echoed beneath each word. "You had them tell me that. You played dead so I wouldn't look for you."

The anger grew with every additional syllable.

"You would not approve. You and Papa. He never listened, you didn't say anything when he threw me away. So why should I care if you knew I was alive or not?"

"Because I am your mother and I would have protected you."

"Clearly," Vedriš said on a harsh exhale. "That's why I'm bleeding right now." Despite the blood soaking his clothes, he was still moving toward the gun.

"You're bleeding right now because you were about to kill my granddaughter."

Granddaughter.

My head spun. What?

Vedriš laughed. It was an ugly, harsh sound. "Did you adopt another child?"

"No," she said. "This is Elaine Benedict—the daughter of Melissa Benedict."

The man sobered.

"Andrea is her daughter..."

"Her second daughter. The child she had with Harper Reed."

He snapped his gaze to me.

"Wait...I was told my father's name was Yuri Leistung."

"Yuri—it's a name he chose for himself when he was a boy and he wanted to pretend he was someone else. Leistung was my mother's family name before she married my father." Margareta focused on him again. While her gun never wavered, she didn't close the distance. "I knew Lainey was your child from the moment I first saw her. But I had no idea what she knew...or how it worked out."

"So—she is Melissa's bastard," Vedris or Leistung or whatever his name was said. "I have no need for a bastard child. Especially not one as weak as a woman."

"You steal children?" Margareta ignored his statement and switched the topic. "You peddle in the flesh of children?"

"Papa did worse. What do you care? You think I don't know about your pet Dimitri or how you have kept a hand on Papa's empire?" He coughed, putting his free hand up to his bloody shoulder. It was a cover, he eased to the right more. "Why should I care how you judge me? Your jewels and furs and art collection—someone's soul paid for it."

"Answer my question, Jürgen? Are you a flesh peddler? Do you deal in the misery of children?" Ice cold anger crackled between the words.

"I am a wealthy man with needs and clients. They are no one. Pets. Disposable. Replaceable." He coughed, gripping his wounded shoulder as he tried to stand. "Even the little cunt there. She would bring a decent price, might even be worth the trouble she's caused me."

Margareta stared at him.

"Disappointed, Mama?"

She tilted her head, her expression solemn. "I've already mourned you."

"Wha—"

She shot him and the boom of sound shocked the shit out of me.

A second shot.

Finally a third.

She shot him twice in the chest. The third shot went between his eyes.

I stared at his body and then I looked at Margareta. She'd lowered the gun, but she hadn't put it away.

Running feet echoed down the tunnel resolving into Bodhi as he skidded around the corner. Blood marred his face and his hands and soaked into his shirt. But I'd never seen a more beautiful sight. His gaze went to me and then past me to where Jürgen or whatever his name was lay dead and bleeding in the empty tunnel.

Freddie was just there and Liam. Kellan also appeared from the other direction. Had they followed Margareta? Maybe it should have surprised me, but Dimitri strolled up to join us.

"I'm going to check his pulse," Bodhi said, putting a hand on my arm as he stepped between me and Margareta. He swept me from head to toe, and his eyes narrowed when he looked at my face.

"I'm alright," I promised him, even if the shaking was already beginning to hit.

He nodded once, then went to the body. Two fingers on a pulse point.

The quiet was unnerving. We were all waiting for the verdict.

"Dead," he said, standing. "Pity, I'd rather have skinned him."

"That's a new one," Freddie said. "Takes a while, doesn't it?"

"Yes," Bodhi commented, his gaze fixing on me. "A long

while."

"Dimitri."

"Madam?"

"Take care of the body. Burn it. Bury it with the garbage."

He nodded once and held out his hand. "Gun?"

She passed it to him. "Thank you."

"My pleasure." He nodded to me and then whistled. More men appeared, some from the direction of the theater and more from where Margareta had come from. The empty silence of the tunnel hummed with sound. They moved swiftly to take custody of the body.

Almost too fast. I watched the body disappear. My father? Or at least the biological contributor, died on the same day I discovered him. I was having a hard time feeling bad about that. What had my mother said about him?

He's a terrible man. Stay away.

When Bodhi held out a hand to me, I clasped his and then he carefully took the baton that I still held in a death grip. My fingers and palm were numb from holding it so tightly.

The shaking hit in earnest then and Bodhi stripped off his jacket and wrapped it around me before he pulled me close. Eyes closed, I held on and just breathed him in. The copper scent mixed with his sweat and the faintest hint of the after-shave he'd used earlier.

The world faded away as I fought the reaction. Then the two-beat click of heels on stone hit me and I lifted my head.

"Margareta..."

The woman was walking away. Not toward the theater, but back the way she'd arrived from. Had she told the others about the tunnels? I had so many questions.

She paused and turned back to look at me. Elegant from her styled updo to her beautiful gauzy lavender dress. "You need time, Lainey. Time to recover from the shock and to look after your sister."

"But…"

"I'm not going away, but I am going to give you time."

"You knew I was your grandchild?" It wasn't my only question but it was one of the loudest.

"Yes. When I saw you at that first charity event. You arrived with your grandfather, a powerful, poised young woman with a gambler's eyes and the soul of a warrior. I knew exactly who you were, but I didn't know what you knew. It took time to learn that no one knew who your father was."

She gave a sad smile.

"No one will now and that is as it should be." She took a breath and straightened. "I was going to watch the show tonight. I've heard wonderful things about Mrs. O'Connell, but I think I will retire for the evening."

"Thank you," I said. It seemed so damn weak for what she'd just done. She'd killed her son for me.

To save me.

She was my grandmother…

"I will always protect my family," she said. "How did Mr. Cavendish put it? I will always protect you and what is yours." Another sad smile that twisted my heart. "I'll send word when we're both back in New York. Maybe we can have lunch."

"I'd like that."

"So would I." Then she turned and bypassed Kellan and Freddie, before disappearing with Dimitri and his men, leaving me wrapped up in Bodhi with the Vandals around. Eventually, they peeled off one at a time to go back into the theater.

"You really alright?" Bodhi asked me, his arms keeping me firmly grounded.

"No," I whispered. "But I will be."

We'd won.

Despite the enormous cost of it all, we'd won. My face hurt and so did my heart, but I had my grandfather, my sister, my lovers, their families and now... I had a new grandmother.

No, I wasn't alright, but I definitely would be.

We. Won.

EPILOGUE

LAINEY

ONE MONTH LATER...

The spring sun cast a warm glow on the gardens. They were coming back to life after what felt like too long of a winter. The financial news was up on my laptop screen so I could listen while I caught up on emails.

Since returning from Prague, we'd been as busy or busier than when we left in the first place. Adam had officially taken over at Reed, and Hamilton was out. We'd almost been willing to throw Hamilton a bone until he tried to sue for custody of Andrea.

It was a bad choice on his part. We'd removed him from Reed, shut down his access to most of the accounts and evicted him from the penthouse in Manhattan and the summer estate in Rhode Island.

Hamilton relocated to California fairly swiftly when Adam told him he had three days to get out of Manhattan and to never come back. If he did... well, we'd leave him destitute. Jason had been promoted and worked with Adam to tear apart the books and dig into every legal and, in some cases, illegal projects Reed had on tap.

When given the option, Ezra decided he'd rather work at Benedict with me or Reed with Adam. He wanted nothing to do with his father's company. Since discovering how much of the Graham fortune came from criminal activity, Ezra wanted to take it all apart.

With that in mind, Collin Cavendish was lending us his expertise to go through the entire company with a fine tooth comb. Ezra had given him the power to hire, fire, and tear it apart. The internal panic of the board had given us several targets to investigate.

In addition to cleaning house at Reed and Graham, we'd begun to break down all of King's various holdings. So much was buried inside a series of shell companies, we might not find it all. What we could find? We tore it apart and used the money to donate to various causes—including Pretty Boy's new project.

He was building a community center and safe space for homeless kids in the city. The minute he described his plans for the building he'd worked to acquire, I'd written the first check to invest. Adam and Bodhi had been right behind me. Ezra promised more funds as soon as he had the sanitized ones.

It was entertaining how close Ezra and Milo had grown over the past few months since Pretty Boy followed me to Manhattan. Ezra also volunteered to help at the soon to be renovated community center and Milo put him to work stripping paint. The sheer volume of Ezra's complaints had tickled me.

One of the last on our list to be dealt with was Phillip

Cavendish, III. I'd gone with Bodhi the morning we'd dotted the last "i" and crossed the last "t." We had the shares and the votes to remove him from Cavendish et. al.

His bank accounts had been closed since they were nearly all corporate-based. His personal accounts we'd drained and left him with the bare minimum of an allowance, the exact amount he'd been willing to pay for Isla Cavendish's "commitment."

Predictably, the older man had not taken it well. His breakdown had been witnessed by several members of the family and the staff. When he had to be sedated by paramedics and a doctor recommended a psych hold, Bodhi had signed the papers.

Phillip Cavendish, III would spend the rest of his life as Isla had. Locked away, and unlike her, he would be truly forgotten. Bodhi said he might go visit him every year or so to remind him of everything he lost.

Granted, it wasn't the vengeance Bodhi had once desired or so he told me. But it was justice he could live with and when we consulted Levi on it, he'd been stunned but also agreed.

Levi and Bodhi were taking the time to get to know each other. We'd set up a room for him at Der Sonne. Andrea also had her own space, Grandfather had informed me of it as soon as I got her back to Manhattan. She had regular appointments with a psychologist and she'd been thrilled to get back to her horses. We brought in a trainer for Levi, who wasn't sure about what to do with the animals.

Andrea also asked about dance classes. While she'd never been that interested before, she'd developed a passion for it. I was hardly going to tell her no. Fifteen days after we returned to Manhattan, a judge signed the official papers appointing Adam and me as her legal guardians.

Grandfather volunteered, but he'd already had to raise one grandchild. I preferred that he got to just be a real grandfather for her. They were getting to know each other and he went out to the stables regularly when she was there.

Healing was going to take all of the kids time. Theo, Milo's brother, had asked a week earlier to go to Braxton Harbor. The friction between Theo and Milo hadn't eased. Milo hadn't wanted to send him away, but he also didn't want to force him to stay where he didn't want to be.

Andrea had been angry at Theo's request and they'd had a huge blow-up the night before he left. It was also the first time she'd truly cried since we found her. For now, Theo would stay with the Vandals. Maybe Em could get through to him. Maybe he just needed time.

Or maybe it was as Milo suspected that Doc was the stabilizing influence. He'd actually come back with us and the kids on our return to the States. His medical knowledge came in handy when it came to explaining to the kids every step of their physical exams and more.

Thankfully, despite all the wild gunfire in the theater that night, the worst of the injuries had been a wrenched ankle and a couple of flesh wounds. Em was perfectly fine and the boys had hauled her up and out of the line of fire as soon as it started.

She was going to take a break from the tour for a few weeks to get Theo settled, then go back out. I promised to show up for her first night as much for her as for me. A knock on the door had me glancing up with my coffee cup in hand.

"Yes?"

"Brunch is ready, Miss Benedict, and everyone has begun to gather."

"Thank you," I said and shut down the laptop and finished the last couple of swallows before I left my room to go downstairs. Currently, we divided our time between Manhattan and Der Sonne.

Andrea needed stability. The first week we were back, Grandfather resumed Sunday brunches. We hadn't done these since my grandmother's declining mental faculties made it unbearable for him.

Bodhi was at the foot of the stairs when I reached them. I feathered my fingers along his cheek. The bruises had gradually faded. There was just a hint of a scar along his hairline where he'd taken a blow.

"Heads up—Levi and Andrea are quarreling about something."

I glanced toward the solarium where brunch would be laid out. "Oh?"

"I don't know what, neither is saying, but they are glaring at each other. A lot."

Rising on my tip toes, I kissed him lightly. "They'll figure it out."

"They better," Adam grumbled as he joined us. "He keeps scowling at her like that and I'm going to—"

Bodhi cut him a look and Adam sighed.

"I might punch him if he deserves it." The amendment was not what he'd planned on saying.

"Every guy who looks at your sister deserves it," Ezra said, slinging an arm around Adam's shoulders even as he winked at me. "That was our rule for Lainey."

"Oh don't start." I took Bodhi's hand and descended the last step. "They'll be fine. They're still adjusting and we just need to keep everything as normal as possible. That also means letting them have their disagreements."

"Are you sure I can't punch him?" Adam sounded so irritated it almost made me laugh.

"If I think he needs it," Bodhi offered. "I'll consider it."

"Well, that's better than telling you 'no,'" Ezra teased and Adam gave him a not so gentle shove. They mock punched at each other—at least until Grandfather cleared his throat.

I hid my smile as I let go of Bodhi's hand and greeted my grandfather with a kiss to his cheek. He gave me a fond look. Milo was already at the table and he pulled out the chair next to him. It put me to my grandfather's right and Bodhi had the seat directly across from me, on Grandfather's left. The guys were spread out with Andrea seated between Milo and Adam across from Levi who was sandwiched between Bodhi and Ezra.

Clearly there was a lot of scowling going on. The doorbell rang and Grandfather nodded. "Our last guest is here... excellent. I do prefer promptness."

I hadn't taken a seat yet so I turned as Margareta Waldemar walked in. She was dressed in an impeccable morning suit, but managed to appear casual despite the formality.

We'd spoken twice since that night in Prague. Today was the first time I'd seen her since then. Despite her declaration in the tunnels that she'd already mourned him, I suspected her son's death for a "second" time, particularly at her own hands, had left her with more to deal with.

"Margareta," I greeted her as I crossed to take her hands. She brushed the air next to each of my cheeks with a light kiss before she squeezed my hands. "Welcome to Der Sonne."

"Thank you," she said, glancing from me to Grandfather then back again. "Leopold invited me. He was rather insistent that this was a tradition I shouldn't ignore."

"He was right." I offered her my arm. "Sunday brunch is always fun."

Or it used to be.

I walked her to the other side of the table. It had a place

setting and everything. It had been my grandmother's spot. No one sat there and when I gave my grandfather a questioning look, he nodded.

After she was seated I returned to my chair. Once I took my seat, the guys all took theirs. Then my grandfather lifted his orange juice flute and we all picked up our own. "Thank you," he said, his tone warm and his gaze sweeping over all of us. "Thank you for helping us to rekindle a tradition that we've not had in too long. Sunday brunches... it's important to make time for family. To enjoy and to not play politics. To engage with each other, and to make plans for the future."

"I'll drink to that," Adam said and we all toasted before taking a sip. Even Margareta looked pleased.

Once Grandfather took his seat again, he motioned for service to begin and then focused on me. "So darling girl, which one of these boys are you actually going to marry?"

Silence greeted his request and I met his gaze. Pure devilment danced in his eyes. "You just want to start trouble," I murmured and his grin warmed my heart.

We still had so much to do. So much healing to do for the kids, for Ezra, for our families. We had relationships to repair, or in this case build, as with the new siblings and my new grandmother.

So much to do.

But, now, also had the time to do it.

The Bay Ridge Royals still existed. The connections and investments were there. Rather than let it languish or worse be taken over by someone with the kind of aspirations King had, I'd stepped into the role.

With the support of my guys, we were going to make changes. Big ones. Some day, Andrea would be a Bay Ridge Royal, a legacy, and it would be a safer, more controlled environment. It would be what it once was...

"Hey," Milo said, turning to study me. "You look very fierce."

I grinned. "Just savoring our victory and planning for all the mayhem…"

That made his grin grow and he dropped a kiss on my lips. Levi and Andrea didn't stare every single time now, but Andrea did make a groaning sound.

"Can we please dial back on the PDAs? It's so gross that Lainey kisses all of you."

Grandfather cleared his throat, but it was Margareta who laughed as she said, "Give them some grace, little one. They have fought hard to be where they are and we're family. We shouldn't have to hide anything from family."

Andrea's disgruntled expression suggested she was definitely not on board but under Margareta's firm yet kind look, she let out a sigh. "Fine." She cast me a plaintive look and I laughed.

"We'll talk," I promised her. "Now eat and tell us about this new class you had me take you to this week."

We'd been investigating dance schools and the minute I brought it up, her expression brightened. She immediately launched into what she loved about the class and kept all of us entertained.

Der Sonne was alive again with family. Our family.

Tomorrow?

We'd conquer it when it got here.

AFTERWORD

Hey, welcome to the end of the Bay Ridge Royals saga. I hope you enjoyed reading it as much as I did writing it. If you need a minute to grab a drink, stretch, and then come back—go for it. I'll be right here, waiting.

Back?

Fantastic, I want to tell you a story. It's going to take a minute. Way back at the beginning of 2021, I was in the process of releasing Frankie still. I think we were on book six or seven (honestly I don't remember) but we were also coming up on the release of Savage Vandal.

Also, in 2021, I herniated a disc in my spine in February of that year (yes right before Savage Vandal came out). This left me laid up hard for months, but I figured out ways to keep writing. In the meanwhile, I had this fun conversation with Steph—and for those of you who know Steph, you know how much I adore her.

She had a funny request. She said, "I would love it if you would write a Dark Archie and Frankie." Frankie is the FMC of the Untouchable series. Archie is one of her MMCs.

I said, we have a dark Archie and Frankie in their parents,

his dad and her mom had a very unhealthy relationship. A dark mirror if you will. But no, Steph wanted something more...

From that conversation Lainey and Adam were born. There were even a couple of chapters written and a blurb. Tally was there and Ezra. It opened the day of Melissa's wedding to Harper. It a bit bully, very enemies to lovers, dark, and extremely M/F.

record scratch

Yes, you read that right, it was initially M/F. Then Adam popped up in Vandals and so did Lainey. I mean, that's okay, my worlds re tied together. I planned this whole M/F Bay Ridge Royals series with the second book focused on Ezra and his "arranged marriage" and then a third book focusing on another of the families, etc etc etc.

Yeah, that didn't happen. Why?

One word answer:

Steph.

The chaotic energy from Ezra made her adore him and she was like, you know, they could be MFM. That would be really fun and all that angst.

Then Milo and Lainey connected and Steph said, "Three is a great number. I love the number three."

If you are wondering how did Bodhi show up? I direct you to the moment he shows up at the Clubhouse, sees Lainey and greets her enthusiastically.

Yeah, Steph was like, "it'll be so perfect!"

That's right my darlings, from an M/F series to an RH with characters I had no idea how to make sure they worked together. If you recall the scene where Adam goes off and says Lainey was always meant to be his? She was.

She still is. But she's not only his.

She's Milo's Mayhem. She helped him heal. She's Ezra's

Kotyonok. She helped him rediscover what he really wants out of life. She's Bodhi's Lainey B, the girl who kept his secret and became the woman who could be his partner.

Yes, she's still Adam's Lainey. The girl he's protected her whole life.

This whole series has been dedicated to Steph because she asked for it. She asked. She so rarely asks me for anything. Yet, from the moment she got to read the first few pages and came back all shouty caps, to just recently when she read the end and she cried happy tears (and yes shouty caps too), I have never been so happy to tackle such a challenging project.

Thankfully, Lainey B was more than up for the task.

xoxo

Heather

P.S. You're very welcome Steph. I love you too.

Reader group:
facebook.com/groups/heatherspack
Spoiler group:
facebook.com/groups/teammadatheather

BENEDICT FAMILY

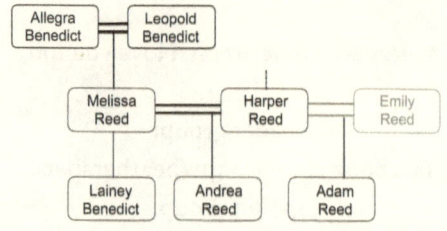

Hardigan Family

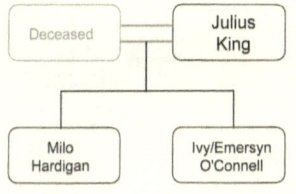

REED FAMILY

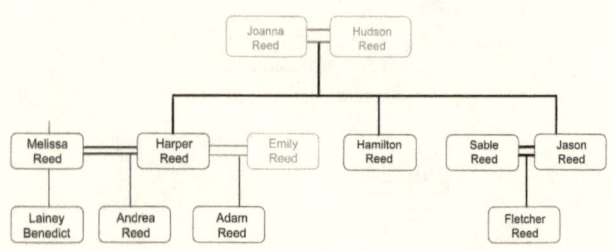

GRAHAM FAMILY

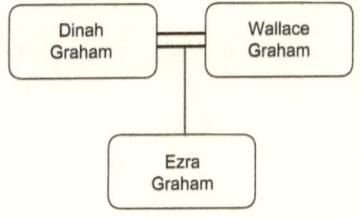

CAVENDISH FAMILY

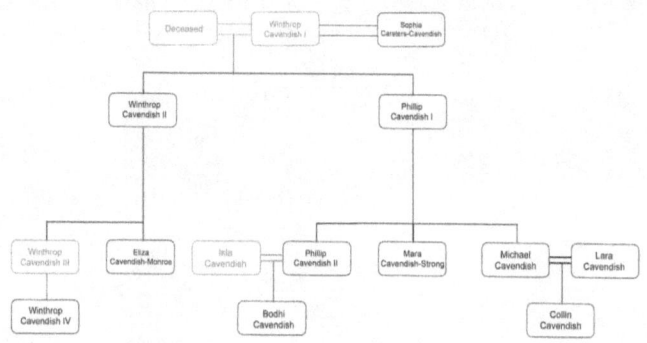

MARLOWE FAMILY

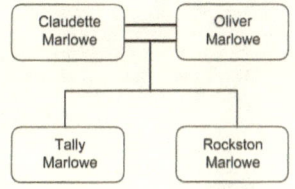

About Heather Long

I *love* books. Not just a little bit, but a lot. Books were my best friends when I was growing up. Books didn't care if I was new to a town or to a class. They were always there, my trustiest of companions. Until they turned on me and said I had to write them.

I can tell you that my own personal happily ever after included writing books. I've always said that an HEA is a work in progress. It's true in my marriage, my friendships, and in my career. I am constantly nurturing my muse as we dive into new tales, new tropes, new characters and more.

After seventeen years in Texas, we relocated to the Pacific Northwest in search of seasons, new experiences, and new geography. I can't wait to discover what life (and my muse) have in store for me.

Maybe writing was always my destiny and romance my fate. After all, my grandmother wasn't a fan of picture books and used to read me her Harlequin Romance novels.

Follow Heather & Sign up for her newsletter:
www.heatherlong.nct
TikTok

Also by Heather Long

82nd Street Vandals

Savage Vandal

Vicious Rebel

Ruthless Traitor

Dirty Devil

Shamelessly Loyal (Novella)

Brutal Fighter

Dangerous Renegade

Merciless Spy

Reckless Thief

Fierce Dancer

Bay Ridge Royals

Shamelessly Loyal (Novella)

Battle Lines

Deceptive Truce

Wicked Surrender

Violent Chaos

Desperate Victory

Blue Ivy Prep

Problem Child

Mad Boys

Party Crashers

Money Shot

Bravo Team Wolf

When Danger Bites

Bitten Under Fire

Cardinal Sins

Kill Song

First Chorus

High Note

Last Word

Chance Monroe

Earth Witches Aren't Easy

Plan Witch from Out of Town

Bad Witch Rising

Fevered Hearts

Marshal of Hel Dorado

Brave are the Lonely

Micah & Mrs. Miller

A Fistful of Dreams

Raising Kane

Wanted: Fevered or Alive

Wild and Fevered

The Quick & The Fevered

A Man Called Wyatt

Heart of the Nebula

Queenmaker

Deal Breaker

Throne Taker

Lone Star Leathernecks

Semper Fi Cowboy

As You Were, Cowboy

Shackled Souls

Succubus Chained

Succubus Unchained

Succubus Blessed

Shackled Souls (Omnibus)

STANDALONES

Kiss of Fate (w/Blake Blessing)

Taste of Karma (w/Blake Blessing)

I'll Be Home... (w/Tate James)

Switchboard Duet

Talk to Me

Don't Let Go

Untouchable

Rules and Roses

Changes and Chocolates

Keys and Kisses

Whispers and Wishes

Hangovers and Holidays

Brazen and Breathless

Trials and Tiaras

Graduation and Gifts

Defiance and Dedication

Songs and Sweethearts

Legacy and Lovers

Farewells and Forever

Hellos and Happily Ever Afters

Wolves of Willow Bend

Wolf at Law

Wolf Bite

Caged Wolf

Wolf Claim

Wolf Next Door

Rogue Wolf

Bayou Wolf

Untamed Wolf

Wolf with Benefits

River Wolf

Single Wicked Wolf

Desert Wolf

Snow Wolf

Wolf on Board

Holly Jolly Wolf

Shadow Wolf

His Moonstruck Wolf

Thunder Wolf

Ghost Wolf

Outlaw Wolves

Wolf Unleashed

www.ingramcontent.com/pod-product-compliance
Lightning Source LLC
Chambersburg PA
CBHW030552020726
47494CB00005B/1585